Hidden Doorways

Liah S. Thorley

Published by Kara Fox Publishing. Copyright © 2016.

Liah S. Thorley

The right of Liah S. Thorley to be identified as the author of this work has been asserted by her in accordance with the Copyright, Designs and Patents Act 1988.

The story contained in this book is a work of Fiction. The majority of names and characters are the product of the author's imagination. For those characters that are based on actual historical figures, their personalities and any conversations undertaken by them are purely fictional. Whilst historical accuracy has been attempted the story is in no way intended to be a complete and true reference to the real historical events experienced by the characters. For all other characters and any resemblance to actual perosns, living or dead, is entirely coincidental.

All rights reserved. No part of this publication may be reproduced, stored in a retrieval system, or transmitted in any form or by an means, electronic, electrostatic, magnetic tape, mechanical, photocopying, recording or otherwise, without the written permission of the publishers: Kara Fox Publishing, Abingdon, Oxon.

ISBN-13: 978-1535286152

For my parents, Michael and Gloria for their continual love, support, encouragement and inspiration.

&

For all those men and women who gave service in WWI whichever side they were on. With special thanks to my Great Grandfathers who each served in their own way.

John Benjamin Craythorne — Royal Navy/Marines 1887–1909 & Coast Guard 1909–1919 to retirement.

Ernest Harrison — Reserved Occupation

Ernest Hudson — Army. King's Own Yorkshire Light Infantry Honourable discharge. Wounded in action; amputee and gassed.

Arthur Simpson Thorley — Army. Argyle and Southerland Highlanders 2nd & 6th. Killed at Amiens 25 August 1918 after four years at the Western Front.

Hidden Doorways

CATHERINE

Hertfordshire – 28th August, 1646

A blank page can be a daunting thing, especially when the words one is about to write may endanger the lives of others. Perhaps I should not begin at all. Yet the quill itches in my hand as though being drawn to the ink, and I find the need to record the events of my life overwhelming. In so doing, I can only pray for the safe keeping of those who have shown me great kindness, and for the child whose weight grows heavier in my belly with each passing day.

It is a glorious afternoon. The day is bright outside and the room in which I must sit is filled with light and warmth. But there are happenings out there, beyond these walls, that sour the air and strike fear into the best of us. Despite all I have experienced in my twenty-three years of life, I never envisioned that I should face England in the midst of the Civil War, and yet here I am. You may wonder at my lack of foresight on this account and I cannot blame you for it, for surely someone who lived through the events of the last twenty years would have expected such a thing. But there is the rub, dear journal. I did not grow up here. As queer as it may sound, I cannot say for certain from which century I truly hail; I can only say that it was not this. Time, you see, has played games with me, sweeping me here and there and all against my will. I have no understanding of the manner of these actions and never a warning as to where or when I shall go next, only a continual feeling of inevitability that one day I shall be moved on once more.

Perhaps this sounds bizarre or bemusing right now and my

story is a peculiar one, 'tis true. But I shall tell it to you, and I promise it will all make sense. I have learned to keep my eyes, ears and mind open over the years. All I ask is that you do the same.

Oxford, 1491

It was the first of the month and the year still held the promise of a good summer. By eleven o'clock the sun was glowing high in the sky. As I approached the heavy doors of St Mary Magdalen's, the sweet scent of damp grass drifted on the breeze and a blackbird serenaded me from the tree by the church wall. Nervous and alone, I paused in the doorway clutching a posy of pink roses. A single thorn remained and stabbed at my palm. As I stepped though the porch into the peaceful cool of the church, a small blue butterfly hovered in the doorway as though about to follow me in, but it changed its mind and fluttered away. I took a deep breath and walked down the aisle towards Daniel More. At that moment my life seemed to be of little consequence to the world, and it never occurred to me that things might not stay as we planned.

When I first met Daniel I had been a mere fourteen years old and he a little over a year more. He was a student at Balliol College. One morning my father sent me on an errand there: one of the masters had ordered a new travelling cloak and I was to deliver it. I had walked past the building many times and looked out at it from my father's bedroom window most days, but until then I had never set foot inside. With their closed doors and grand stone facades, the colleges were something of a mystery to the town's children. And the men who walked their halls did nought to dispel their unfavourable image, stalking about in their rich clothes, conversing in Latin or Greek and frowning down at the locals. Understandably I was nervous when the door creaked back. The only woman to set foot inside, I fancied. But as I walked across the quad the sun was shining brightly and the elegant architecture seemed not at all frightening.

The porter gave me directions, and I set off down a long corridor. In a room towards the end I could hear voices speaking Latin. My curiosity got the better of me, and I stopped outside the door and pressed my ear to the wood. Thanks to my excellent tutor, Father Thomas, I was able to follow the debate with little effort. So I set the cloak down on the floor and settled into eavesdropping, wishing I could join in..

Suddenly I felt a sharp tap upon my shoulder. I screamed in surprise and whirled round to see a tall man squinting down at me. My heart leapt up to my throat so fast that I jumped back and hit my elbow on the door. It swung open it to reveal a spiky, hard-nosed figure, robed in black, heading towards me. In the classroom behind him I could see several young men sitting on benches and all staring in my direction. Most were leaning forward to observe the commotion, but one was sitting back with his hands resting upon his belly. He had a handsome face beneath a thatch of russet hair and pale eyes that glinted in the sunlight streaming in through the window. For a moment I was distracted. He caught my glance and smiled.

"What do you think you are doing?" The petulant master lowered his face to my level. His features were long, as though stretched upwards by his queerly arched eyebrows. I was trapped between the two men and acutely aware of the brand new cloak now gathering dust on the floor. The one with the anomalous eyebrows sneered at me.

"Well?"

"Delivering Master Crambourne's new cloak, sir," I gulped.

"And that required listening at Master Fallows' door?" said the other.

I shuddered as the first man raised one of his eyebrows even further towards his receding hairline.

"Listening at my door? Well, Master Collins, can you think of anything that would interest a young *girl* in my classroom?"

"Not a thing, Master Fallows."

"Sorry, sir, I had not meant to listen. I... was simply interested."

The men exchanged an amused glance. I could feel the eyes of the russet-haired boy upon me and my cheeks began to burn, not from my situation, but from the heat that rushed through me under his gaze.

"*You* speak *Latin,* do you, child?" smirked Master Fallows.

"Yes, sir." I stammered.

"Well now, impertinent *and* educated. What will become of women next, will they all speak out of turn and begin to educate us?" He laughed at his own jest.

The handsome boy winked at me and the gesture gave me courage enough to speak. I bobbed a short but polite curtsey, looked straight into Master Fallows' narrow green eyes and said,

"One day, sir, we just might."

I have no notion to this day where such an idea came from. It was contrary to everything I knew. But somehow, deep inside me, I knew I was telling a truth.

Master Fallows almost staggered backwards. I saw my champion behind him attempt to stifle a guffaw and I struggled to hide my grin. The other students, like the masters, were staring at me open-mouthed, and for a moment I thought I would be sent for a whipping. But Master Fallows just wafted his hand as though I were a bad smell and said,

"I suggest, young lady, that you learn to hold your tongue before it gets you sent to the stocks. Now, Master Collins, would you be so kind as to relieve her of her delivery so that the scholars may continue with their *education?*" He stressed 'education' with every element of sarcasm he could muster.

Conceding, I bowed my head and sheepishly dusted off the cloak. As I was led away I risked one last glance at the handsome boy and found he was still looking my way. There was a desire in his eyes that he would not get the chance to act upon until several years later.

By the time Daniel and I met again, I was seventeen and running my father's business. My loving parents, William and Hannah Harris, who had taken me in from the streets at six years old, had left me alone in the world once more. Hannah died from the sweating sickness when I was nine, and my dear papa was taken by consumption a little after my seventeenth birthday. His passing left me despondent. He had been my world, raising me better than any real father could, teaching me his trade and allowing me the indulgence of a superior education, something most out of the ordinary for a female. Perhaps he gave me too much freedom to think and speak for myself, but I cannot regret any of it, not even now. Upon his death William's home, guild rights and tailor's business passed to me. This rare state of independence for a woman should have been a blessing beneath the pain of his loss. But I am ashamed to admit that I wasted it with the follies of a silly young girl. I allowed myself to be persuaded into bed by a pair of strong arms and the sweet whisperings of a handsome man.

Daniel was an apprentice at Trimble and Blake's, a highly reputable law firm in Oxford town. When he came to order a new tunic I knew him at once as the boy from the classroom, and he knew me. His smile was flirtatious, with just the same amount of brazen cheek as I recalled. He was taller and his countenance even more confident. Instantly I was his and I did not hesitate to step out with him when he asked. I was by no means the only girl with whom Daniel had formed an attachment, or smuggled into his rooms, though I was perhaps the most naive. By the time I turned eighteen I was with-child.

Father Thomas intervened on my behalf. His blue eyes were like glass – I could always read his mood – and when I confessed my predicament I could see at once how disappointed he was. Yet, in his never-failing compassion, he never voiced those feelings. Instead he summoned Daniel to a meeting and persuaded him to marry me.

It is curious when we compare our expectations of a situation with what actually transpires, and my marriage to Daniel most certainly did not follow the presumed path. Perhaps I had hoped that we would grow to love each other, or perhaps I simply thought we would get by and manage. What is certain is that when we wed I believed we would settle into a faithful life together. That we had been forced into the situation did not give me any cause for concern. As I said my vows that June morning, neither of us could have imagined the truth.

To begin with there was great passion. Daniel was as loving and kind as I had imagined, and I tried to be a good and obedient wife. But I was sick throughout my pregnancy. That I felt fat and uncomfortable was all quite natural, yet the nausea was un-abating. I lost weight rather than gained it. I began to look gaunt and pale and I found my spirit and my work began to suffer from my weakened state. They say a woman's temper runs high like a fever when she is with-child and I was the perfect example of such. As time went along an insane fear possessed me.

I noticed my husband began to pay less attention to me. I would see how he smiled and flirted with other women. I had not been jealous of his ways before we wed, yet there it was, burning beneath my skin. Each time a pretty girl passed us by I watched how she would look at my husband, how she would always catch his dazzling eyes and how he would always, so very gentlemanly, bow and doff his hat. I tried to hold my tongue, but free as it had always been, I could not.

"Has it not occurred to you that I might feel rejected by your flirtations?" I sobbed one evening as my husband left the room to retire early to bed, rather than sit up with me.

I recall the exhausted look upon his face as he turned and replied, "Mistress More, you show me great disrespect on a daily basis by standing alone in that shop, pinning tunics upon *other* men."

"I am a tailor! Tis the nature of my work." I was astounded at his assertion.

"Work, oh, yes. And how can you be a good mother when you conduct yourself in a man's world?"

"How ridiculous! Many women work in such professions. You knew my way of life before you bedded me."

There was a pause. I knew he could turn the argument against me. The fire spat a cinder onto the hearth. Daniel twisted his lips into a sneer.

"Other women are not so quick to snap at their husbands," he growled.

"Who?"

"Mistress Blake would not dream of making such accusations."

"Or of protesting against those made to her," I yelled. Mistress Blake was the unassuming wife of his employer.

"Quite right. And you should take her example and refrain from impolitic discussions with men to whom you are not married."

I was livid.

"Tell me husband, what *do* you accuse me of?"

"I know not what you do whilst alone with other men."

"I am not alone, Master More. Bessie is always here." Bessie was our housekeeper and had lived under the same roof with me since my mother's death. She was, at that very moment, asleep in her room, not ten feet from where Daniel was standing.

"The company of a servant is hardly chaperone."

At this I stood, so quickly that the air rushed around me and blew out the candle at my side. My head became light and I swayed back.

"She is an honest woman!" I cried.

"Perhaps she is..."

Outside, some students wassailed their way back from The Catherine Wheel to the gate of Balliol. Daniel turned to look through the window. "But it is the manner of your conversation to which I refer."

"My conversation? Confess your meaning, husband!" I was crying bitterly now.

His shoulders sank and he rested his forehead against the glass. I slumped back onto my chair in a sweat. When he turned to look at me, he found me pale and shivering.

"Nothing, I meant nothing, I simply cannot comprehend why you behave so. Why you cannot be like other women," he sighed, his temper quelled. "I am tired and so are you. I'm going to bed."

As his footsteps sounded on the stairs I closed my eyes, the fight gone.

As time went on and my pregnancy progressed I began to feel certain that the child's arrival would be the answer to all, that one look at our babe's face and my husband's heart would melt. The day a woman first feels her child move inside her is the most magical moment she can ever experience, and when those movements were enough for Daniel to rest his hand upon my belly and feel them too, the look on his face gave me great hope.

"Quick, quick, place your hand here." I urged. Daniel had just come to bed, though I had been resting for a while. Sleep has never been a faithful friend to me and I had been watching a spider crawl across the ceiling, criss-crossing from one corner to the other, for quite some time. A foot or an elbow aimed a second swift jab at my infant's prison wall. "Quick! Before it stops."

Daniel groaned.

"Here," I said again, taking his drooping hand and pressing it gently against my growing belly. The child obeyed her mother and seemed to turn on her head. Daniel sat upright as though a broomstick had been shoved up his spine. He stared first at my belly and then at me.

"I feel it! My good lord, I feel it!"

He was shaking his head, his eyes wide like a small child at his first fair. Our babe kicked again as though she knew he was there. I could not help myself, I began to cry and when I looked up at my husband, I found tears in his eyes too. He kissed me with such great tenderness, and in that moment I was certain that his wandering eye would soon rest firmly upon his wife, and once the child was born my heart could finally be still.

Sadly, moments like this remained rare. Increasing bitterness spread between us like a contagious fever. Daniel began to blame the sickness of my pregnancy on my work. He told me I was doing too much and wearing myself out, so I took on an apprentice to ease the burden. I sat for hours doing less and less until I thought I would run mad for lack of occupation, but nothing prevented the accusations. I am by no means innocent in all of our troubles, and I take responsibility for my part, but I cannot blame myself entirely. I must skip ahead here, dear journal, for this was not a happy time in my life, and for once I should like to forget a vast deal of it. There is one day, however, that I must take you to, for I believe it was the moment that changed it all. Forgive my hand, for I tremble as I write.

One damp October afternoon I was sitting in the shop, stitching the hem of a lady's gown. The smell of the street was seeping in through the gap beneath the door and the sun was sending grey daggers of light through the workshop. I set down the dress and rubbed my tired eyes. Without warning, panic struck me so hard that I leaped from my seat and ran. I bolted from the shop as best as my round belly allowed, crossed the street and through the doors of St Mary Magdalen's.

Father Thomas was kneeling before the altar, his pale hair gleaming like a halo in the streaming sunlight. Crossing myself, I watched him pray. When he slipped his rosary into his pocket I walked towards him and sank down upon a nearby bench.

He turned to me with a start.

"Catherine, are you unwell?"

"Shall I be a good mother?" I muttered.

He stayed there for a moment and stared. Then his eyes crinkled around the edges as his mouth slipped into a sympathetic smile. The smell of incense drifted up from his cassock as he rose and came to sit by me.

"I mean to say, I do not seem to be managing as a wife. If I cannot make myself good and obedient to my husband, how can I be a good mother to this child?" I rested my hand on my belly. The priest slid his cold fingers over mine.

"My dear girl, I have known you since you were six years old and had the honour of being your teacher from not long thereafter. You were a bright and studious child and you have grown into a clever and strong woman who has born life's trials better than most. You have many virtues, though patience is perhaps not your best. If you can find patience and trust in God to guide you, he will show you the way."

The pain that had been scraping at my back since dawn took a tighter hold. I cried out.

"What is it?" he asked urgently as my hands clenched around his.

"It cannot be, it is not time."

I doubled over in agony.

"The child?" His fingers were turning white in my grasp but I could not release them.

"It is too soon, weeks too soon," I gasped.

Father Thomas waited patiently until the pain eased. Once my composure was regained he tried to assist me to stand. I managed only a few steps before I collapsed onto all fours. He called for help as I attempted to breathe.

The floor was hard and cold and the pain pierced my knees leaving bruises that would mark me for weeks. But I did not notice then, nor care. No one had told me how it would be. I had never attended a birth. I knew not what the gruesome puddle was that flooded from me, all streaked with blood and staining the stone beneath. I gripped at my belly as it contracted around my poor child and shoved her towards the world before her time. It was apparent I could not be moved.

Father Thomas never left my side, holding my hand through my screams until the midwife came. By the time she had been fetched I was propped against the bench, my legs spread wide and the babe crowning. I think then Father Thomas was grateful to be relieved of his duty, for he was shaking and his face ashen as he got to his feet. The midwife looked at him with a thin-lipped expression that could only be taken as the worst kind of acknowledgment.

It is strange what one can recall from such an event. The same birdsong I had heard at my wedding was bleeding through the window openings, and the bell in the tower creaked with the strength of the north wind. The St Christopher pendant I had worn all my life seemed to weigh heavy at my neck. I tugged it outside my gown, but when Father Thomas offered to remove it I refused to permit him.

Women began to congregate. Not so many as was usual to attend a birth, but there were faces all around me just the same. Once they were there the priest hurried off to fetch my husband.

By the grace of God alone, I did not perish along with my child. I cannot tell you how long it took, for it felt like only a moment and yet an eternity. I recall how the sun moved from one side of the church to the other, crossing my face and warming my skin, then leaving me to grow cold. The pain furred my head and racked my body with screams that could not have been mine. There may have been times when I was not conscious at all, yet I felt every second of that agony.

My daughter left me before she left my body, for she never drew a single breath. I lay there, my legs as white as milk, streaked scarlet with my own blood, and my heart barely beating in my chest. They lifted her up and severed her from me. I wanted so desperately to hold her, to gaze at her face just once. My only glimpse of my stillborn child was of the blue-tinged arm that hung from the swaddling as she was carried away. I had to beg them even to tell me the sex. I named her Anne.

My poor girl. How is one supposed to bear the loss of a

child? I know not and I do not think I shall ever understand. She had not even a chance to open her eyes and take in the world around her. How is that right? Losing her is a pain I shall feel like a knife in my chest each day that I wake and breathe. Now another child stirs within me, and the joy of that feeling brings with it the stark fear that such a thing could happen again.

Forgive the stains upon the page, dear journal. I could not prevent my tears.

Father Thomas wept by the altar as the women cleaned me and made me decent. Once I was fit to be seen it was the Father who lifted me and placed me in my husband's arms. It is perhaps fortunate that I fainted the moment the fresh air hit my face, and I knew nothing of the hours that followed.

MICHAEL

Oxford – 13th May, 2012

The kettle was boiling with increasing urgency, sending a spiral of hot steam up the window and coating it with condensation. Michael put down his slice of toast and flicked off the switch. He leant forward, wiped the window with the tea towel and sighed. Upstairs the ageing floorboards creaked. He looked up in surprise. He had not expected his wife to rise so early. But then the toilet flushed and the footsteps made their way back across the landing. Michael ran his hands over his face and rested his elbows on the worktop. Three years to the day and it felt like only yesterday. A knife-sharp pain twisted in his gut as he fought back tears.

"You OK, Dad?"

Michael turned to face his son. Paul's sock-covered ankles were showing beneath his grey school trousers. *Must remind Imogen to buy some new ones,* he thought, *he grows so damned fast.* He put his arms around the boy and hugged him tightly.

"Ouch, I can't breathe... Dad!" Paul gasped, patting him on the back.

"Sorry," Michael said, releasing his son. "Just be good and don't be late home today, will you?"

Paul picked up his dad's toast and took a bite.

"She doesn't blame you," he offered.

Ignoring the toast theft, Michael looked at his son's ocean-blue eyes and ruffled his dark hair.

"I know, son. But I do." There was a pause as he watched Paul munch on the toast. "She would be nine today," he added.

"*Is*, Dad, she *is* nine today." Paul poured hot water from the kettle into his dad's coffee mug. "You always say she's still out there somewhere, and I believe you."

Michael forced a smile. "I just wish I knew where," he replied.

Paul took a swig of the coffee and looked up at him.

"You *will* find her. Mum thinks so."

"Thanks, son."

Something dropped through the letterbox in the hall. It ought to be birthday cards for Catherine, but it wouldn't be. Michael wondered if any of her friends even thought of her now.

Paul seemed to read his mind.

"I saw Millie and her mum the other day. She's having a birthday party on Saturday. She said she wished she could share it with Cat, just like before…" His words petered out.

Michael recalled the streamers, frilly dresses, *High School Musical* playing on the MP3 player and the birthday cake iced in bright Barbie pink. He thought of his younger child's pretty little face beaming up at him as she and her best friend blew out the candles. That had been her fifth birthday. Her sixth he had tried to block out.

Paul glanced at the ceiling.

"Is Mum taking a sicky again?"

Michael took a deep breath. "Too many anniversaries today."

"*You're* going to school, though."

"I know, but your Mum has to deal with things in her own way. Let her be."

There was a knock on the front door. Paul swallowed the last bite of toast and grabbed his book bag from the kitchen table.

"See you tonight, Dad."

"See you..." he called as Paul vanished down the hall, the front door slamming shut and sending a vibration through the walls and rattling the crystal vase on the hall table, "...later."

Michael sighed again and shook his head. It was going to be a very long day. Perhaps it would be better if Imogen went to work; the kids would surely distract her. *Perhaps I should stay home with her,* he thought, but he knew she wouldn't move all day and he needed distracting, even if she didn't. He dropped another slice of bread into the toaster and peered out of the window to the bottom of the garden. The outhouse stood dark and louring behind the blossom-covered apple tree. He checked his watch: 8:15. Not enough time.

The toast popped up. Taking it out, he buttered it, picked up his briefcase and made his way to the front door. As he passed his study he glanced in. There were papers everywhere, sketches, calculations, books left open and the photograph of Catherine. Next to the frame stood the brass Eiffel Tower paperweight she had insisted on bringing back for him when Imogen took her to Paris, six months before she disappeared. Upstairs his wife stirred. He considered popping up and saying goodbye. He put a foot on the first step but Imogen saved him the time.

"Try to have a good day," she called.

"You too, love," he yelled back with a forced smile.

CATHERINE

Oxford, 1492

It was morning when I woke but there he was, Father Thomas, still sitting by my bedside, turning his rosary through his fingers and murmuring a quiet prayer, just as he had when I was sick with scarlet fever as a child. Daniel was there too, standing in the doorway watching me. He looked as though he had been trampled by a bolting horse, his face paler than mine and his eyes shadowed with dark rings. I beckoned him. Agony and relief clouded his face as he came and seated himself at the foot of my bed. I lifted my hand and he took it. Beneath me the bed-strings creaked and gave a little, sending a pain into my back. Ignoring the discomfort I turned to my old friend, forcing the question from my lips.

"Is she with Our Lady?"

My daughter never lived beyond my womb and had not the right to a Christian burial, but Father Thomas replied in kindness.

"She was born in God's house, take comfort from that. She was blessed by the very nature of her birth."

"Then she is not damned?" I whispered gladly.

"I do not believe so," he smiled.

"And how is it that I still live?"

Father Thomas closed his eyes and shook his head.

"Sometimes it is God's way, Catherine. Your daughter was not meant to survive but your own journey is not yet done, that is all."

Oh, how right he was. My journey was barely begun.

"Thank you, Father," Daniel said, as the priest stood to leave. "You have been most attentive, as always."

My husband was as God-fearing as the next man, but there was something in his tone as he spoke to my old friend that I did not care for. But it was not until several weeks later, when I was almost well enough to return to work, that I found the nerve to ask him what he had meant.

The aromas of cooking drifted in from the kitchen and Bessie could be heard humming brightly to herself as she clattered about. My stomach growled in anticipation of supper. I was sitting by the fire stitching toggles to a tunic. I stretched and yawned. The door to the shop swung open sending a cold gust of air rushing through the room. The fire swayed in the grate with a hiss. I heard my husband's voice.

"Good evening, John, still here?"

"'Fraid so, sir. There is a lot to be done."

John was a good worker and nimble-fingered, and I intended to retain his services.

"Mistress More will be back to normal in another week or so, I dare say."

"Oh, that is excellent, sir. I have been very worried. It is never easy when… I mean to say… the loss of a child never leaves them."

"Aye, well," Daniel sighed. "I am sure we shall be blessed with more children soon enough and then she will forget."

What he said was a lie, for the physician had told us it was unlikely I should ever bear another child, and how could one ever forget? How glad I am now that the physician was wrong.

"Good night, then, sir."

Another cold draught blasted through the house and I was forced to shift my feet further away from the swaying fire. My husband entered the room, removed his hat and took his seat. The wood groaned as he leaned heavily back.

"I am feeling much better today," I offered when he failed to enquire. By then my weakness was far more in my heart than my body. Daniel picked at a loose thread upon his sleeve.

"Here, let me mend that," I offered.

"It does not need you to mend it."

I raised my eyes to meet his. In the kitchen, Bessie continued to hum.

"The physician said I do very well," I tried again.

"Yes, I am sure you do," he replied flatly.

"He is a reputable man, Master More. I see no reason to doubt him."

"Nor I."

"Well then, why speak of him in such a tone?" It was warm and stuffy in the room and a string of sweat beaded at the line of Daniel's hair.

"I cannot tell you." He looked directly at my face for the first time since entering the room.

"Husband, please. You must…"

"I *must* tell you nothing." His voice was raised and sharp. I flinched.

"Please," I begged, "if my health is at risk, I should like to know it."

"Not your *health*, Mistress More, your *reputation*."

I was all astonishment.

"Reputation? I insist you explain your meaning, sir."

Daniel stood and began to pace back and forth, his hands clasping and unclasping like the claws of an angry cat.

"Your level of conversation with your patrons far exceeds that expected of a woman. And the closeness of your relationship with Father Thomas is unhealthy. There have been… accusations…"

"Have you lost your mind? You cannot possibly imagine there is anything improper in my friendship with Father Thomas." The effort of keeping my voice steady was making my face burn. "Why, he treats me as though I were his own daughter!"

I was on my feet. I stood before my husband and blocked his path across the room. He raised a hand and for a moment I thought he might strike me. Then his face turned ashen and he lowered his arm. It took every ounce of my resolve to remain calm. "You cannot believe that he and I…"

"No, Catherine, I do not, and neither would anyone else who knows him. He is a good man. It is only your mind that can sink so low."

I closed my eyes in relief.

"Then I *beseech* you, tell me your meaning."

My husband growled.

"It was Father Thomas who educated you. The physician believes that… a woman's mind is not capable of such knowledge. Such strength of mind in a woman can do nought but imbalance the humours. Your mind has taken the strength of your body, Catherine."

I stared blankly. His voice grew colder, more distant.

"And you cannot think the physician did not realise you were with-child before our marriage? You allowed your feminine lust to control you and entice me. You went to my bed as freely as a common whore.…"

"That is as much your sin as mine." I was so furious I could have struck him over the head with the fire iron. Instead, I gripped the back of the chair.

"How can I even be certain the child was mine? If you are as free with your body as with your mind, you could have been with a dozen men."

"You know that isn't true!"

"The physician believes you poisoned our child with your impurities."

"What?" I breathed, sinking back into the chair.

"And I blame your father and Father Thomas for moulding you that way."

Bessie was at the kitchen door, spoon in hand and eyes wide. For once in my life I could not find another word to say. I stood there with my mouth gaping open and stared at my husband.

Daniel said, "Thank you, Bessie, all is well. Return to the kitchen."

"You truly believe that Anne's death was the fault of my education?" I croaked at last.

"I do not know what to think. But as you said yourself, he is a reputable physician and there has been something wrong in you since the moment your pregnancy began."

There was nothing more I could say then, for the guilt I felt was too unbearable to admit.

When William and Hannah took me in at six years old they found me wandering the streets, orphaned or abandoned. But however hard I tried, I had never been able to recall my life before the day they found me. That is, until that last morning in fourteen hundred and ninety-one. With the chilly November sun slicing across the street like a sword, the first glimmer of my early life presented itself. But what I recalled was so out of context, so far from everything I knew, it terrified me.

After our fight the previous evening, Daniel and I had remained in silence. When he entered my room in the morning and reached out a hand to me, I was too distressed to take it. Guilt burned in my gut like an open sore, for spurning his apology, but also for my failings as a wife and mother. I could not even bring myself to look at him. He sat for a while, watching me as I feigned sleep. I wanted to reach out to him, truly I did, and yet I could not bring myself to do it. I lay there, eyes closed, feeling his presence and praying I could make everything go back to the way it had been in the beginning.

When he eventually gave up and left me alone I let my tears flow, and as I did so I saw an image of myself as a child, sitting in the graveyard at St Mary Magdalen's and pulling weeds from the edges of an ancient grave. My childish fingers trailed a weatherworn date on the stone: 1884. How could that be? My stomach clenched and I sprang from my bed, tugged on my gown without fastening myself in, grabbed my hood and ran down stairs. Bessie called out to me as I bolted past and I almost knocked poor John from his feet as he came through the shop door.

I searched the churchyard frantically, but each stone bore a date from our own time. I began to doubt my mind, thinking I must be mistaken and the date I had seen was in fact 1384. Yet deep inside I knew what I had seen and it was from a memory, not a dream. I stopped at my dear father's grave and caught my breath. As I did so, something flickered in the corner of my eye. Slowly I turned around.

The woman who stood by the church door was a mere

shadow. She seemed to be wearing a dense fabric over her legs that hugged her body indecently. Her hair flowed in wild dark waves about her head as the blustering wind wafted it over her face. I tried to make out her features, but I could not. I called out to her but she did not respond.

I tried again. "May I be of assistance?"

This time her lips parted and her authoritative voice called out, "Come away from the graves, Catherine, it's nearly six. Daddy will be waiting."

I began to shiver and my heart thumped so hard I thought it might burst through my bodice, or choke me trying. I rose and made my way over to her, twisting the St Christopher pendant at my throat nervously. A butterfly dusted its wings so close to my face that I was forced to close my eyes. When I opened them I had the most curious notion that I was a child again. The woman seemed so familiar, so warm. The scent of strawberries and the feel of her soft hair flooded my memory. I reached out to her but she turned and walked away. She strode around the side of the church and for some reason I followed. She had vanished. I rubbed my eyes but the path was still empty. I cannot say if I stood there long, but as I tried to make sense of it all my head became light.

There was a loud noise. Scraping, like a heavy door over uneven stone. I grasped for the church wall but my hands failed to find it. Bright lights danced around me, almost blinding my vision, and for a moment I felt I was sitting in a dark, cold room. A tall figure stood watching me from the shadows. Then suddenly I was sprawled on the ground. A mighty clattering of hooves thundered towards my head. I rolled over in the dirt and screamed as a horse reared over me.

London, 1906

Clouds above my head hung low, holding the summer heat down over the crowded street, and the air had a bite that caught in the back of my throat. I had never seen so many people hurrying about. On hands and knees I scrambled to the side of the road and into the gutter. The rearing horse crashed down and a man leapt from the front of the great carriage it was pulling and onto the street beside me. I stared. The carriage had two levels and there were people both inside and on the top, all staggering about and straining to see what had caused such an abrupt end to their journey.

The world was spinning like a carousel. I pulled myself onto the kerb and put my head in my hands. People began to gather about me as though I were a circus freak. I could not catch my breath but the nauseating dizziness was abating. A piercing whistle-blast came from close by.

"Are you all right, miss?" I lowered my hands to see a man in a dark tunic peer down at me. His screwed up his nose as though I were a foul smell.

"I swear she just appeared from nowhere," a man was saying frantically to the crowd. "Did you see her? I'm sure I did not."

Everyone looked and sounded so peculiar and for the life of me I could not make out where I was. I had the queer sensation that I was watching it all from behind some distant window.

"Quite right, driver, one second the road was clear and the next she was in front of us," a woman said in a calming tone.

I looked towards her as she stepped down from the footplate of the carriage. She wore an elegant powder-blue gown trimmed with lace that tapered from a high neckline to a waist as tiny and pinched as a wasp's. I had never seen anything like it. Beside her was another woman, somewhat smaller in stature and a few years younger, but almost identical in feature. She had removed her hat to reveal shiny blond curls and was dusting herself down. Mesmerised, I felt as though everything else around me was vanishing into a fog; all I could see or hear were these two women.

I opened my mouth to speak, but my throat was dry and I began to cough. Someone in the surrounding crowd thrust a pewter flask at me, but when I took a grateful swig I near choked. The contents heated my throat and burned in my chest.

"That ought to cure you," the man laughed, offering me a hand up. "There now, miss," he said as I got to my feet, "you seem fine. Would you like a cigarette?"

Since I had no notion what that was and could not form the words to ask, I politely declined with a shake of my head.

"Where is she? Was she hurt?" The elegant woman was glancing about, squinting and shading her eyes as the sun broke through the clouds.

"Who, madam?" replied the driver.

"That girl you almost hit. Heaven help us!"

Her companion was attempting to re-attach her hat to her head. The woman turned to her and adjusted it so it was straight.

"Really, Lettie, you must use more pins, a good gust of wind will have it off again in an instant."

I patted my own head to ensure that my hood was still in situ, but it was gone completely. The woman caught sight of me and began to move my way but was stopped by the man in uniform. He said something to her that I could not catch. She forced a smile at him. As they conversed, her companion's eyes scanned me from head to toe, her expression growing increasingly astonished. My heart was still pounding and I was yet unable to make sense of anything. I wanted to run but knew not where. The woman's head tilted to one side like a curious dog. She looked down at her slender fingers encased in neat white gloves before coming over and offering me her hand. I felt the compulsion to wipe my own hand on my gown before taking it.

"Good day," she said in a lightly clipped voice. "You are not hurt?"

I shook my head.

"Well, that's good," She frowned. "Are you quite sure? You look terribly pale." Her eyes rested on the right side of my face. "You seem to have got some dirt from the road on you. Do you have a handkerchief? I think I have one in my purse."

She popped open the silver clasp of a pretty pouch and began to dig about inside it. The purse was not large yet it contained a wide variety of items. She handed me a small wallet, a flat silver case with initials engraved on the lid and a delicate little scent bottle. Finally she extracted a perfect square of pure white embroidered fabric.

I did not wish to spoil it and tried to offer it back, but she said, "Please, I have others."

I looked at her gratefully and began to wipe my face.

"What's your name, dear?" The woman in the blue gown came to join us. As she smiled the coolness of her ice-blue eyes softened.

I tried to think but nothing would come. My heart skipped a beat. I found that not only did I have no notion of how I came to be there, but could not recall from whence I came. The women glanced at each other.

"I... am... Catherine," I murmured hesitantly at last, with some relief. That much, at least, I knew.

"Are you quite sure? You don't seem entirely convinced," the elder woman said gently.

"Yes, yes, I am certain." I replied, praying they would not ask anything more.

"Well, then, Catherine, I am Miss Rosaline Winston and this is my sister Mrs Leticia James. We are very pleased to meet you."

Rosaline offered me a firm handshake without hesitation. I took her hand and bowed over it. A flicker of surprise ran over her features.

"And I you," I stuttered.

"Will you be all right? You do look rather shaken."

Rosaline's eyes skimmed over my gown. She raised a puzzled eyebrow at her sister. I looked down and noticed a rip to my left sleeve and substantial tear to the hem.

"Please allow us to get you a carriage home. Is there someone to take care of you?" My head grew giddy and clammy panic swept through me. As I swooned her steady hand grasped my arm.

"Oh dear, I think perhaps we should take her to Papa," Lettie's smile had faded into concern.

"Yes, I think you're right," Rosaline replied, and turned back to me. "Papa is a doctor. He can take a look at you and make sure everything's all right." She threaded my arm though hers without awaiting my response.

"I… thank you," was all I could manage.

The next thing I knew, I was being ushered up the step into a great black hansom cab. I had never ridden in anything so grand before. It swayed about and bounced us around, shaking our bones over every lump and bump the street offered. I gripped the window ledge until my fingers were white, and prayed I would remember my way home before the afternoon was gone.

I began to notice the buildings, vast structures of stone with endless panels of glass windows. Clusters of bright billboards hung from the facades. We swung wide around an octagonal monument that was stuck in the centre of a junction like the axis of a giant wheel of streets. On the top perched a bronze boy balancing on one leg with his wings spread wide and his bow drawn, ready to fire at some unsuspecting passers-by. I had never seen anything like it. We turned along one of the spokes. Crowds of people rushed in all directions. Noise thundered in my head. Dazzling colour pressed against my eyes. It was all too much. I closed my eyes and tried to remember how I came to be in such a place, or at the very least, awake in this outlandish dream.

The Winston family home was an elegant grey town house on the west side of Russell Square. It seemed upright and sturdy, like a soldier standing at attention. The rooms were bright and the furniture of such an elegant quality that I could only imagine these people must be royalty. The upstairs drawing room afforded a pretty prospect. Opposite the rosy bricks of the Hotel Russell dominated the south side; all its comings and goings gave that otherwise unremarkable square a buzz of life. The doorman in his braided green jacket was always ready to open the door, doffing his tall hat to the graceful women and the high-collared men that glided in and out. I recall how much I stared at him on that first day, barely able to tear my bewildered eyes away. His constancy was soothing somehow.

This all seems so very long ago now, yet 'tis, in actuality, a mere four years past, in real time.

My distraction was broken when a young girl scuttled into the room with a tray. She dropped a curtsey and set it down on the table in front of us. Leticia got up and moved a pretty bouquet of flowers to the sideboard as the girl carefully set out the fine china cups and saucers. I stared at them in wonder.

"Thank you Sissy, you may go."

The girl bobbed again and scurried out, leaving Rosaline to pour out the hot brown liquid and offer me a delicate slice of cake.

"What is it?" I asked, sniffing at the cup she had just handed me.

"It's lemon sponge, I hope you like it," she said, presuming I meant the cake atop the fancy silver platter she was holding.

"Thank you, yes." I replied, without the slightest idea what lemon sponge was, either.

"I'm sorry Papa isn't home, I'm sure he cannot be much longer," Leticia added, extracting the flat silver case from her purse and popping it open to reveal a layer of thin white sticks. "Markham said he went to visit a patient at three and it is now a quarter after five." She took out one of the tiny sticks and tapped the end against the case.

"Don't, Lettie, you know Papa thinks they're bad for you."

Lettie parted her lips to protest but resigned and put it back.

Later I learned these were cigarettes, the same things I had been offered by the stranger after the accident. I shall never understand the concept of smoking; it seems such a strange habit.

Rosaline bit into the cake delicately and I decided to follow her lead. As I took a tentative nibble a flood of memory overwhelmed me. The texture of the cake was light and fluffy and as the sharp tang of lemon bit through the sweet sponge, the drawing room blurred into a bright, flower-filled garden. The cushioned chair I was sitting on seemed to become a vivid red and green blanket, spread out over fresh scented grass.

"Catherine, may I ask where it is that you live?"

Shaking and dizzy, I blinked myself back into the room and

considered how on earth I was to answer such a question.

"The shock must have been greater than we thought," said Leticia in alarm. "Have a sip of tea – that will make you feel better."

"I… really…" My sentence was never finished, for there was a rattle downstairs and a moment or two later Dr Winston entered the room. Both women rose to their feet, so I moved to do the same. But as I did so my jittering hand let my tea cup clatter to the floor and my knees cracked the corner of the coffee table, sending the tray spinning over the side and the cake sailing through the air, landing topside down at his feet. I gave a cry and fell to my knees apologetically, attempting to clear up my mess. Leticia rang for the maid and Rosaline helped me back to my seat.

"My dear, do sit down. My father is an excellent doctor. Please permit him to examine you. You are in shock, I think."

I made an attempt to regulate my breathing as Rosaline explained the accident.

"I am fine, truly," I gasped, as Dr Winston put a cool, soothing hand on my forehead.

"You feel a little feverish," he said, setting down his bag. For a brief moment that thought eased my heart. I was sick and this was all some kind of delirium. The doctor flipped the latches of his case. Inside were all manner of terrifying instruments. Instinctively I tried to move away but my legs were too weak to stand and my head spinning too fast. He took out a flat metal stick and asked me to open my mouth. Unable to think, I did as I was asked. He pressed the stick down onto my tongue. I gulped dryly and coughed. Turning my face to the light he then peered into my eyes and bid me follow his moving finger with my gaze.

"A little concussion is all. A good night's sleep should set you right," he concluded.

"You *do* have somewhere to go, do you not?" asked Rosaline cautiously.

I took a long deep breath and with my eyes firmly fixed on my dusty gown admitted, "I'm afraid I do not know. I think I have forgot. Is it really possible to lose such knowledge? Do you think I have been hexed?"

I raised my eyes to the physician nervously. He flashed a quick glance of concern at his daughters.

"My dear child," he said gently, "you had a bump on the head. Such trauma can do peculiar things to the mind."

Rosaline seated herself next to me again and laid her hand on my ragged sleeve. A time-piece on the sideboard ticked loudly, long black fingers clunking over its face with each sound. I had never seen such an elaborate clock I was certain, and yet in the back of my mind the image of another such instrument stirred. Its sound echoed through my head and I felt myself sink back into the chair.

There was much discussion over the next few minutes as to what to do with me. From my apparel they assumed that I was both poor and eccentric. I just sat there and let them talk. As their voices washed over me like the hum of a flowing river, I searched my mind. Some things were there, but for the most part it was like attempting to see the bottom of the dish through a thick soup; glimpses were clear when I scraped over them with the spoon but concealed again in an instant.

That was when it struck me that I could understand these people with ease and yet their language was so very different from that to which I was used. I was overwhelmed with the familiarity of everything around me and yet 'twas all so foreign, and as I answered their questions I realised I was speaking just as they were, with barely faltering ease.

"Would you be happy with that arrangement? Catherine?"

I looked at Leticia's smiling face.

"Would you be happy to stay here for a little while and allow Papa to treat you, at least until we can establish where your family are?"

"The workings of the mind are of great interest to me," he offered. "I would very much like to help you, and you would be a great study for me."

"You're very kind."

Unable to decide if I had somehow been taken in by royalty or trapped in the fevered imaginings of some strange sickness, I heard myself accept. What else could I do? I prayed for God to keep me safe.

The maid was called and a bath was run. I recall staring at the tub of steaming water and considering whether it was really a good thing to get in it. But Leticia had thought I would enjoy cleaning myself up and, looking back upon it, likely scrub off the grime, for I must have appeared, and smelled, quite appalling to them. So I slipped out of my dress and stepped over the tin side. Oh, how blissful a hot bath can be! Sinking into the warm water I began to believe I would survive whatever this wild situation was.

By the time I was finished, Leticia had gone home. Rosaline showed me to the guest room. It was right next to the drawing room, at the front of the house. The beauty of it took my breath. The walls were coated in a shimmering paper that sang with bluebirds and pink flowers. A washstand was placed opposite my bed, a wardrobe of burred walnut towered up at its side and a smoothly curved dressing table stood under the window. As she set my supper tray down and offered me a glass of brandy to aid my sleep, I felt the kindness of a lasting friendship creep upon me. After she had gone I crawled onto the bed, more exhausted than ever in my life before. I closed my eyes and allowed the soft feather mattress to mould itself around me.

MICHAEL

Oxford — 22nd October, 2017

The first day of half term had proved extremely productive. The sun was beginning to sink and the light in the outhouse was not the brightest. A bird landed on the roof and began to scratch about. Michael set down his notes and rolled his shoulders. He would have to call it a day. He didn't want to, but he knew he needed his mind to be as sharp as possible if he were going to start testing the machine again. His stomach complained at the lack of food. Remembering he hadn't stopped for lunch, he wondered what would be for supper. Paul was going to play rugby with some pals and wouldn't be home before nine, so it would only be him and Imogen at the table.

There was a call from the house.

"Michael, phone for you."

His wife's voice was warm and kind yet there was an authoritative quality to it that could freeze any of her pupils to their seats if she so intended. He got up and opened the door.

"Who is it?" he called back, as he slid the padlock through the hook on the outhouse door and clamped it shut.

"Sounded like Raymond."

Michael stopped by the back door and stared at his wife. Her dark wavy hair was pinned up into a ponytail, showing off the silver streak that ran back from her hairline like a shooting star. She smiled and opened a cupboard door to extract a saucepan.

"What on earth does *he* want?"

"Don't know. Shepherd's pie all right?"

"Eh? Oh, yes, lovely."

Michael's mind raced as he made his way down the hall to the study. The handset of the phone lay on top of an open newspaper. The telephone was an antique, abandoned by the previous owners of the house, left sitting on the circa 1975, grisly brown-and-orange living-room carpet. He had rather liked it – the phone, not the carpet. *That* had been ripped up in 2008, about a minute after they were handed the keys.

He picked up the chunk of black Bakelite and held it to his ear.

"Hello?"

"Michael old chap, how's things? Wife sounded jolly."

Michael sank down in his soft leather chair and began to fiddle with the Eiffel Tower paperweight on his desk.

"She's good, thanks."

"And Paul? I hear he's doing brilliantly at school. Getting him ready for Oxford?"

"That's up to him, I suppose."

"Come on, Michael, I'm sure you don't resent us enough to send him to *the other place*." The man laughed at his own joke.

Michael moved the receiver away from his ear and closed his eyes until the laugh stopped.

"What do you want, Ray?"

There was a chilly pause.

"Don't be like that."

"Hard not to be."

Another pause.

Michael put the paperweight down and let his eyes wander

over the bookshelves that surrounded him. The failing light from the window streaked across the room and caught the jacket of a single book. The gold lettering glinted like fire. 'H G Wells,' it said, *'The Time Machine'*. Michael almost laughed at the irony.

"You know the position we were in. All that press coverage. Damned reporters never know when to stop. Governing body under pressure to act and all that."

"Too many posh schools threatening to send their best to the opposition?"

Michael felt slightly hypocritical for the comment; both he and Ray had attended 'posh schools', but it was true. He heard Raymond draw a breath.

"Something like that." His old friend cleared his throat. "Look, there's a position coming up at the end of the year. One of the Physics lecturers is abandoning us for Harvard, family in Boston or some such."

Michael waited patiently for Ray to get to the point so he could decline.

"So the thing of it is… we think enough time has passed now since… well, all that kerfuffle, and we thought you might be interested in taking up your old post. Can't give you head of department mind, but we can pop you back into the faculty."

Michael tilted his head back and opened his mouth to speak, but Ray continued.

"You don't have to answer right now. Big decision." His voice quietened. "Look, you were the best the university had, we would love to have you back, never wanted to get rid in the first place myself. You know that."

"Thanks for the offer, but…"

"Please, Michael." Raymond's voice softened further. "Just say you'll think about it."

"The kerfuffle," Michael sighed, "may have died down, but my daughter is still missing and *I'm* still responsible."

"You don't know that for certain."

"Yes, I do."

Ray swallowed loudly.

"Even so… Catherine wouldn't want you to just give up your life, would she?"

Michael screwed up his eyes as a painful twist of guilt shot through his heart.

"All right, I'll think about it. But don't hold your breath."

"Thanks, old chap. Let us know before the start of Hilary. Oxford needs you," Ray added with a bright chirp, then rang off before Michael had chance to change his mind.

Michael placed the handset back in its cradle and picked up the photograph of his daughter. It had been taken three weeks before her sixth birthday, three weeks before he had sent her back in time with his stupid experiments. She beamed up at him from behind the glass, her sea-blue eyes shining in the sunshine that warmed her face. She was sitting on the swing that still remained in the back garden, and hugging her favourite teddy bear, Albert. Albert was upstairs in her room now all alone, resting on her pillow with his worn coffee coloured ears, threadbare paws and his chocolate brown eyes staring up at the ceiling, waiting for her to come home.

Her room was untouched, exactly as it had been when she left it that last morning. Imogen dusted it each week and hoovered around the toys abandoned on the floor. Catherine would be fourteen now, and her room would look very different if she were still here. There would be posters on the wall, no doubt of some dreadful boy band with pretty faces and scruffy hair. But she was not here to hug Albert and she was not here to put the toys away and pin the posters up. He wondered where she could be and whether tomorrow he and his machine stood a chance of bringing her home.

After Catherine vanished and the university dismissed Michael, he had packed up his office at Balliol and brought all his notes and sketches home, to the outhouse. He had not worked for months afterwards. His nerves had been shot and even Imogen was unable to rally him. Eventually he'd taken a position in the local comprehensive, teaching A level physics to spotty-faced teenagers, most of whom barely showed more than a passing interest in the subject. But there was the odd one who made it worthwhile.

When the time came for Paul to go off to school as planned, neither of them had been able to part with him. So their son had been enrolled nearby at Magdalen College School, as a day boy. Ray was right, Paul was doing well. Catherine of course would have gone to Headington, where Imogen taught French. Michael found himself imagining her as she would be now, but then had to stop himself before anticipation got the better of him and he hoped too much that he would find her.

CATHERINE

London, *1906*

I blinked my eyes open to the sound of a ringing bell. I was about to ask Daniel what was happening when the previous day's events came at me like an iron fist. Daniel was not there though the memory of him was as clear then as if I had never forgotten. I looked around the room and pinched myself to check I was not dreaming. But I was not. I was in a stranger's house and far from home. With a prayer, I breathed slowly to abate the rising panic and considered what Father Thomas would tell me to do. I resolved to keep a calm head whilst I tried to make sense of things.

There was a vaguely familiar scent coming from the nightstand next to the bed. A cup of tea had been set there and I marvelled that I had not woken when it was brought in. Somewhere a bell was still ringing. I slipped from the bed, took a shawl from the chair by the window, wrapped it about my shoulders and crept out onto the landing. The frantic jingling was from a bell over the front door. At the bottom of the stairs a rotund woman was searching for something.

"All right, all right, I hear you," said the woman shaking her head as she peered into a cupboard.

"Ada, what's going on?" Rosaline emerged from room to the side.

Ada turned over a vase that had been resting on the top of the cupboard. A key clunked out into the palm of her plump hand.

"I see." Rosaline said with a tone of amusement.

The door finally swung back to reveal a tall gentleman with a generous amount of dark hair, both upon his face and his head. He removed his hat and bowed.

"Good morning, Miss Winston, are you well?"

I stepped back into the shadows.

"Your father is in his study, I presume?"

"Indeed, Dr. Campbell. Though be prepared to find him a little excitable this morning. We have a rather curious houseguest…"

Behind me a door clicked open. Startled, I spun around to see a young man with golden hair. I could not help but notice his clearly slept-in shirt was open to his waist, revealing a smooth and lightly tanned chest. There was also a faint smell of alcohol about him, mingled with something sweet and not altogether unpleasant. I almost fell backwards over the banister. The only man I had ever seen in such a state of undress was my husband. The man yawned and stretched with his eyes closed.

"Sorry, Sissy, didn't mean to startle you. What time is it?"

I could do nothing but stare. The man opened his vivid blue eyes.

"Forgive me, dear lady, please do forgive me." He was trying not to laugh. "I had no idea we had guests." His gaze danced over my semi-covered cleavage. Rather than feel shame at this blatant voyeurism, I found all my fears and confusion vanished and I too began to laugh. And once begun neither of us could stop. It took several minutes to regain our composure.

When I had almost managed it, I offered, "It is I who should apologise, sir, I should never have been standing here without purpose."

"Not at all, I can assure you. Well, I think we can forgo a formal introduction," he grinned flirtatiously. "Arthur Winston at your service." A single dimple pinched in his right cheek and made my heart flutter.

"Catherine More," I said a little breathlessly. Arthur stepped back and bowed with comical exaggeration.

"Then, Miss More," he glanced down at his naked chest and crumpled trousers, "it is a great pleasure to meet you."

"The pleasure is mine," I said, steadying myself. "Though, sir, I am not a maid, I am married." This said perhaps more as a reminder to me than a warning to him, for I do not mind admitting, I was rather attracted to Arthur in the beginning.

From the study below came the solid footsteps of a confident woman.

"Arthur?" Her voice had the ring of a mother checking her unruly child. I pulled my shawl over my breasts and tried not to blush.

"Good morning, Rosaline," Arthur replied. "I hope I didn't wake you last night?"

Rosaline looked up and caught sight of me. "Oh, Catherine, my apologies, I was not aware you were up yet. I trust Sissy brought your tea?"

I gave a nod.

"And please don't put the key in the vase;" she added to Arthur with exasperation, "you will chip it."

"Then it ought to be kept elsewhere," he said with a wink in my direction. I suppressed a smirk. "Why didn't you tell me we have a houseguest?" Arthur began to button up his shirt.

"I see you've met my younger brother, Catherine. I hope you were not too shocked by his appearance, we were not aware he was to return home last night." The latter part of the sentence was aimed at Arthur.

"Ah, good point you have there, my dear sibling. I *had* meant to telegraph you. It must have slipped my mind."

"I should return to my room to dress," I offered.

"Arthur has been staying with friends in Hertfordshire for the summer," Rosaline said to me. Then with a threatening glare towards her brother, "Can we presume your company for the remainder of the holidays? He's reading History at Oxford," she added as an aside to me.

Oxford. A pang of guilt twisted in my heart. I should have been desperate to return to my husband, and yet I found I was rather pleased with my surroundings and was not ready to abandon them as I had Daniel.

Arthur flashed his dimpled grin again and flung his arms wide.

"I'm all yours for the next, oh, eight days."

Rosaline laughed and shook her head.

"I suppose that will have to do." She turned to me. "I should take care around my brother, dear. He can be rather *too* charming."

I smiled more coyly and Arthur laughed.

"I'm rather afraid Mrs More is already taken."

Rosaline clapped in delight. "You've remembered?"

"I…a little." Tears began to well in my eyes.

Rosaline beamed. "That is wonderful."

Despite my resistance, I began to cry. Rosaline was quickly up the stairs and at my side. She wrapped an arm about my shoulders and led me back to my room. Arthur was watching with a raised eyebrow.

"I'll explain in a moment, Arty," she said as she opened the door to my bedchamber. "Perhaps if you wash and dress, Mrs More, you will feel a little more like yourself. I'll fetch something for you to wear from my wardrobe. You can't possibly put on your own gown." She paused, then added hastily, "It was rather... torn in the accident."

I closed my eyes and prayed that when I opened them again I would know my past fully and had made sense of my present.

An hour later, having been jammed into the hard bones of a corset for the first time in my life and wearing an ill-fitting day-dress of Rosaline's, I was taken to Dr Winston's study. He was sitting behind a large polished desk and Dr Campbell was standing by his side.

"Take a seat, Mrs More. Make yourself comfortable."

I should have laughed at the irony had I not been so utterly terrified. Comfort is not something I could associate with my restrictive attire, for I could barely move or breathe. I lowered myself onto the chair opposite. The doctor took in my pale complexion and rang for some tea. He peered at me over a pair of pince-nez then softened his fat cheeks into a smile that puffed out his thick white sideburns like furry pouches.

"This must be very distressing for you, but there's no need to worry."

I nodded.

Before me was an impeccably neat desk. A leather-bound book was closed and perfectly aligned with the edge. In the centre lay a large fold of papers. I marvelled at the type-faced print, for printing was only in its infancy, or at least it was where I had come from. Next to it stood a silver frame. Rosaline was quietly standing by the window. She followed my gaze.

"It's a photograph of my mother. Would you like to see?" She lifted it from its resting place and handed it to me. I was grateful for the distraction. The imprint was of a woman very like Rosaline, the same thick fair hair framing her delicate features. Unsure what a photograph was, I ran my fingers over the smooth sepia surface, trying to feel the marks of the artist.

"She died three years ago."

"Oh, I am so sorry. It is hard when one loses a parent." I handed the photograph back. "She was very pretty."

"Thank you, yes, she was."

Dr Winston leant forward, "Mrs More…" At his side Dr Campbell had begun to scribble in a small leather notebook.

"Do call me Catherine, please," I said, exhausted by the formalities.

"Very well, Catherine, you speak as though you understand the loss of a parent. Can you explain this?"

I appraised the question and the implications of my answer. Not only had I lost the parents whom had accepted me as their own, but also those who abandoned me in the first place. I could recall one pair perfectly but knew nothing of the other. How was I to explain anything without giving them cause to think me mad or bewitched? I also feared they would send me away if they believed my memory was returned, and where would I go?

"Catherine, are you all right?" Rosaline gave me an encouraging smile.

"I… yes. My father passed away not two years since. I cannot recall my mother." I blanched as I compromised with two half-truths. It was not so much a lie as an omission of facts.

"Very good, Mrs… Catherine." Dr Winston was talking to

me from the depths of a large leather chair, its high back and sides cocooning him like an upright cradle. I tried to focus on what he was saying.

At that moment the door swung open with a soft whoosh. Sissy entered and placed a tea tray on top of the folded papers. The doctor raised an eyebrow at her.

"Not on the newspaper."

"Beg pardon, sir," she said, lifting the tray and allowing the paper to be extracted.

As it was removed I tilted my head so that I could make out some of the print. 'Alfred Dreyfus exonerated,' I read. Then I froze, forcing my eyes back to the top of the page. In glaring black lettering was a date: Friday, 13 July 1906.

I was certain I must be delirious. But as I felt the pinch of my undergarments and the fullness of my skirt, so different from what I had been wearing yesterday, alarm bells rang in my head. I thought of the decor in my bedchamber and Arthur's casual greeting. I looked at the suit Dr Campbell was wearing, and the loose-fitting legs of his trousers. My eyes shifted around the room frantically. The lantern on the desk that had space for a flame but no candle. The walls lined with books taunted me: gold and black lettering glittered in the sunlight. H G Wells, Sigmund Freud, Copernicus, Newton… the names ran through my head with dizzying speed, pushing on long-lost doorways in my mind. Finally a most outlandish suspicion was formed; I had somehow shifted from one period in time to another.

The tray not only bore the tea things but a plate of cut bread.

"Would you like a sandwich?" Rosaline offered. "Cheese or Egg?"

To hide my panic I grabbed one and stuffed it into my mouth.

"What else can you tell us, Catherine?" Dr Winston asked, once we had all had a good sip of tea. (Leticia was right, tea really is soothing.) "Do you recall how you came to be in the middle of the street at Piccadilly yesterday?"

In all honesty I could not have answered that question had my life depended upon it. I shook my head and gulped down the last bite of my sandwich.

"Hmm, I see. And what is the last thing you recall before the accident?"

I have a nervous habit of turning my St Christopher pendant betwixt my fingers, but my high-collared dress denied me access, so I began picking at the skin on the side of my thumb.

"Visiting my father's grave." *Pray don't ask me the date.*

The doctor's brow creased. He drew a slow breath through his nose.

"Where is he buried?"

"St Mary Magdalen's."

"I'm not familiar with that church, where is it?"

"By the north gates, sir, next to Balliol."

"In Oxford?" interjected Rosaline. Dr Winston scratched his silvery head.

"Yes," I replied with increased caution.

"Hmmm... and this was when?"

I looked down at my thumb; I had made it bleed.

"Yesterday morning."

Dr Campbell unclasped his hands from behind his back and stroked his copious beard.

"Can you recall what time that was?"

"I cannot be sure." I glanced at the ornate time-piece on

the mantle, the hands twitching rhythmically across its elegantly painted face. "We have not the luxury of a clock at home," I offered, "but early, before breakfast."

"I see... and you cannot recall your journey to London?" That was the first time I had heard reference to the city we were in. I almost choked on my tea. Why the displacement of some sixty miles took me so much by surprise, when I had already contemplated the removal of some four hundred and fifteen years, I cannot say. I shook my head.

"The train takes less than two hours. Even if she walked from Paddington to Piccadilly there's time to spare," Dr Campbell surmised. *What on God's earth is a train?* I restrained myself from voicing the question.

Rosaline observed my expression and said,

"I think Catherine has had enough for today, Papa."

"Of course, my dear. We shall continue tomorrow and see if we can extract some of those hidden memories." A kind smile spread across his lips and I noticed that beneath his heavy sideburns was the same one-sided dimple as Arthur bore. To my own astonishment, I felt utterly at ease.

MICHAEL

Oxford – 22nd October 2017

Michael woke with the sunrise. Butterflies had fluttered in his stomach all night, periodically waking him. Imogen stirred as he slid his feet out from under the covers and into his slippers. He walked over to the window and looked down at the outhouse. Inside were two decades of study and work. Eight years ago he had made a breakthrough at the expense of his daughter. For several years he had abandoned it all, unable to face his own failure. Recently, however, he had turned back to his life's work – but this time it was not about progress, but about finding Catherine and bringing her home. He just had to find the right time portal and he could bring her back to the present. He rushed his shower, grabbed a cup of coffee and a slice of toast and made his way down the garden.

Thirty minutes later, shuffling his notes around for the umpteenth time, Michael said a prayer. He hadn't prayed in years, not since he'd been a small child, not even after Catherine had gone missing; he didn't even believe in God. Yet today he felt the need.

"Please help me find the right combination and give me courage. Bring her back to me, please, bring her home," he muttered under his breath, and then hurriedly added, "Amen." He was about to uncover the machine when there was a tap on the door.

"Dad? You in there already?"

"Come in," he called. The door whined open and his strapping six-foot son strode in. At sixteen, Paul was the same height as his father already, and was in danger of growing even taller. He had turned into a handsome lad with the soft features of his mother highlighted with Michael's olive skin and blue-green eyes. Paul ran a hand through his shaggy fringe.

"Please let me help, Dad. I really wish you wouldn't do this all alone."

Michael looked at his son's broadening shoulders.

"Don't you have homework to do? You've mocks coming up before Christmas."

Paul grunted and shrugged. "On top of it, Dad, don't stress."

"Even so, I can't have you here. I can't risk anything happening to you."

"It's different now. I'm not a little kid any more, and…"

"I still don't know how she made it work. Whatever she did was a fluke and I can't find the right calculations to replicate the ruined circuit board."

"You're so much closer, if you let me help you then maybe…"

"No, Paul. I just…No."

"Who's going to look out for you?"

"I said no!"

For a moment Paul looked hurt, but then he shrugged again.

"All right, but if you change your mind I'll be in my room."

Once Paul was safely in the house, Michael pulled off the dustsheet to reveal the cabinet. It was the same one that had once stood in the corner of his lab at the university. The best way to make sure something goes unnoticed is to place it in open view, which is exactly what it had been until the incident. At first glance it was just a regular cabinet, a large, grey metal, utilitarian cupboard, but behind the doors was an intricate network of microchips and fuses. No one but his technician, Oliver Brown, had ever even asked what it was for.

Michael turned on the power. He wished he didn't have to switch it off at all but it ate electricity faster than a rabbit munching a carrot, and his home generator couldn't maintain it for more than a few hours. One by one each connection light flickered from red to green as the machine fired up. From under his desk he slid out the re-locator pad and pushed it into the centre of the room. This was new and untested, but he couldn't risk himself or anyone else being dragged off through time again without a secure way of getting back. It was meant to concentrate the vortex into one place and hold it there. Michael hoped it worked rather than trusted it would. He put the replacement recall disk around his neck just in case and held his breath.

Facing the machine, Michael could see the tiny glowing particles of energy begin to encircle the re-locator pad, bouncing around the room and crackling wildly. He was forced to duck as a whirr of darkness swirled over his head and gravitated towards the disk. For a moment the whole room seemed to vibrate; the glass in the windows rattled and the floor shuddered. Even he was unnerved by the violence of the electricity that fizzed in the air. To Catherine it might have felt as though she were caught in a tornado or been struck by lightning. *Jesus, she must have been terrified,* he thought, as a loud crack of light bounced past his head and zoomed in on the pad. Michael forced himself to watch despite the urge to shield his eyes.

Then everything went calm. The wormhole that had formed in the centre of the room settled and for a brief, wonderful moment, a ghostly female form hovered there right in front him.

"Kitty Cat?" he whispered, confused. The woman looked familiar, yet how could she be his little girl?

There was a fizzle and a loud crack.

Michael sank to his knees and sobbed as smoke spiralled up

from the cabinet in the same place as it had that first time it blew. All that work, and now he would have to begin again.

CATHERINE

London, 1906

My next session with the doctor began in very much in the same fashion. I asked Rosaline to accompany me when I sat before her father. My friend pulled in a chair from the breakfast room and perched at my side. As Dr Winston began his questions I stared at the inkwell upon his desk, the neat glass bottle filled with deep blue ink and the pen tipped with a pewter nib. I wanted to reach out and examine it.

"Perhaps we should go right back to the beginning, Catherine." I looked up and nodded. "Good. Close your eyes, my dear."

I glanced at Rosaline. She must have seen the panic on my face for she took my hand in hers. I did as I was asked.

"Now, I want you to breathe slowly and listen to my voice, only my voice." His tone had softened so much I had to strain to hear him. I drew in a long deep breath. "Good, now imagine yourself going back in time." For an instant my eyes flickered open, for I feared he had found me out, but Rosaline squeezed my fingers and he continued.

"Imagine your life in reverse, go back from today, past yesterday, past the accident. Go back to when your parents were alive, back through your childhood to your first ever memory."

Images began to flicker through my mind. I saw my father in his sickbed, his brow grey and slick with sweat. I saw dear Hannah the day the priests told her I could stay with them, standing in the kitchen, flour covering her hands and smudged on her flushed cheeks as tears streaked through the grainy dust. I saw Father Thomas sitting at my bedside when I was ill with scarlet fever, holding my hand and telling me Bible stories. Finally I reached that day, the one that began it all.

"Tell me what you see, Catherine."

For a moment I couldn't speak. Swirling lights of violet and green flashed in my head and a nauseating twist churned my stomach, then I was there, with my back to a wall, sitting in the filth of the street like an urchin. In my mind I saw the street that became familiar to me as I grew up. Ramshackle houses jammed together, homes squeezed in between others like an afterthought and the rotten stench of streets ankle-deep in manure. Someone opened a window opposite and tipped out a bowl, its contents splattering the cobbles below, and behind me I heard the toll of bells.

"Catherine?"

I screwed my eyes tighter shut.

"There's church bells."

"What are they ringing for?"

"The time. It's six o'clock. Where's my daddy?" I pressed my fingers to my lips for I had no notion what I meant. It was as though I were a small child again, living it all over.

"That's good, Catherine. How old are you?"

"Six. Today's my birthday."

"Very good, and can you tell me where you are?"

"It stinks, there's mouldy food and a dirty horrid boy is shovelling horse pooh into a barrow. I want to go home." I sounded so unlike myself and yet I knew that was how it had been.

"Everything's all right, Catherine. First tell me what else you can see."

"There's a man. He looks funny." I laughed involuntarily.

"Why does he look funny?"

"He's wearing woolly tights and he has knobbly knees that stick out like apples."

"That does sound odd, Catherine. What else?"

"He's topped by a tall felt hat and bottomed by pointed leather boots like from a story book, and he's wearing a skirt!" I laughed again. There was a brief silence as Dr Winston pondered my description.

"What is he doing?"

"Standing with one hand scratching under his hat, looking at me."

"Does he say anything?"

"Yes, but I can't understand him. He talks funny, like from that play."

"Which play?"

"The one mummy took us to last summer in the park, with the fairy queen and that donkey-man called Bottom." I giggled again.

I could hear the doctor scribbling away in his notebook.

"Are you at the theatre?"

"No, silly. I'm in Oxford... but it looks all wrong."

"What's wrong with it?"

"I don't know. There's houses where there weren't any yesterday, lots of houses that look like they're falling down, and they're all dirty white like they need a wash and there's this big building with narrow slit windows like a castle. I'm frightened." For no reason I began to cry. I felt Rosaline's hand gently stroking my arm.

"It's all right, dear," she hushed.

"What happens now?" the doctor pressed on.

"A woman is running from a shop at the end of the row. She's coming towards us.

Her cap is slipping about on her head and her dress is dragging in the dirt. I spin around so I can make everything go back to normal like Dorothy and Toto, but it won't work. The lady bends down to talk to me. She takes my hand and she feels all warm and soft. She wants to take me home."

"Do you go with them?" I nodded. "Do you know them?" I nodded again.

"Not before, but now they want to be my new mummy and daddy."

"Where do they take you?"

"Home," I said, suddenly feeling more myself again. My childish world began to fade into the distance as I continued. "They took me home. They were both so kind to me. Hannah spoke so much more slowly than William, I could understand her even at first when I could not follow anyone else.

"'You can wait with me whilst Master Harris tries to find your folks if you like. You'll be safe with Hannah, I promise,' she told me. I wondered whether she was Hannah or if she had meant someone else I was to meet. I knew I should not go but there was something good in her manner that made me feel safe. I placed my fingers in hers and allowed her to lead me away. I must have been shivering for she paused and rubbed her hands up and down my arms. 'Poor little mite,' she said.

"She took me inside the shop. There was a large table upon which sat a measuring stick and a pair of sharp scissors that glinted in the fading light. Tall shelves piled high with fabrics covered every wall."

That vision had frightened me as a child, yet now I find I miss that room greatly.

"Hannah opened a door and led me through a large living room into the kitchen. On the stove at the back something was bubbling in a large pot that smelled like rotting vegetables. Hannah took a trencher from a shelf and placed it on a table before me. She gestured at a chair.

"'Take a seat, child. I can at least feed you whilst we wait.' She fussed over the pot on the stove, spooned a ladle of thick pottage into the trencher and broke off a chunk from a large fresh loaf for me. I did as I was told. I grabbed the bread and chewed hard on it. The grain was rough and it felt like lead as it sank into my stomach. I was ravenous yet all I could imagine eating was a big slice of pink cake.

"With the stove burning an open flame and the lack of windows in the dim kitchen, the air was so heavy and stifling it made me drowsy. I watched a candle dancing its light over the table, making a bright ring of white encircle the bread as I tried to prevent my eyelids from drooping. I must have been unsuccessful for the next thing I remember was waking under a course blanket on a sagging, itchy mattress."

My head was beginning to throb.

"May I stop now, please?"

"Of course, Catherine. Just bring yourself forward through your life, that's right, now picture yourself as you are today. Picture this room and yourself in it. Good. Open your eyes."

When I did so the room seemed bright and alive compared to the dull vision in my head, but I could remember it all as if it was yesterday. Dr Winston took off his pince-nez and rubbed his eyes.

"Who were they?"

"My parents, William and Hannah. They found me living on the streets when I was six years old. They were desperate for children of their own and Hannah saw me as a gift from God when the priests allowed me to stay with them."

"Why was that up to the church?" he asked with mild caution. "You were from a Christian orphanage perhaps?"

"No. That is just how it was. I cannot tell you more than that. They applied to the church to keep me and Father Thomas, our family priest, gave them permission. I had nowhere else to go, sir, and they were good people."

"I don't doubt it, my dear… It just seems a little… never mind. We shall continue tomorrow."

MICHAEL

Oxford – 4th April, 2019

The bell sounded and the exodus began.

"Chapter thirty-two, read and digested for Thursday, please," he called after the deserters. There were a few acknowledging grunts. It took only a matter of seconds before he was alone in the classroom. Michael scanned the empty desks for debris, picked up a discarded crisp wrapper from one and paused to read some rather interesting graffiti on another, then, retrieving his briefcase, he headed for the door. As he pushed down the handle he glanced back. There were moments when he wondered if he'd done the right thing in declining the University's offer to return, but as he read his own calculations typed on the big screen he smiled to himself. At three thirty he could go home, mark a few papers and run up tomorrow's lesson plan before dinner and still find time to slip down to the outhouse for an hour or so whilst Imogen watched her soaps. It would have been a constant worry, trying to keep his work quiet from the department. Here they didn't care what hobbies he had in his free time.

He made his way down the characterless corridor and pushed open the door to the staff room. A billow of coffee-related steam engulfed him as he stepped inside. He wafted his hand in front of his face and blinked.

"How's it going with the A-Phys class?" asked Jon Clarkson (History).

Michael sat down and cracked open a sport-size bottle of Evian.

"Not bad. The course work seems to be going all right; I guess we won't really know until the exams are done and the results come in," he replied.

"Well, the mocks were looking good. I reckon we could jump up the league table a few places this year," chipped in Ryan Hardy (Maths). Michael's eyes glazed a little as he thought of his daughter. *Catherine would be taking her exams this year,* he mused; *I hope she had a decent education, wherever she ended up.*

"Just to divert the subject-matter slightly, I set C2 a research assignment last week. Had 'em doing a little genealogy. Got them to write out their family trees back three generations; dates, occupations, photos et cetera. Sent them off to interview their grandparents," said Jon.

"Really?" Ryan sounded uninterested.

"They got well into it, turned up a few juicy skeletons too," Jon continued, "this one kid…"

Michael put his fingertips to his lips as a thought hit him.

"You all right, Mike?"

Michael hated his name being abbreviated but he had long since ceased to correct his colleague.

"Brilliant, thanks," he said with genuine enthusiasm. He couldn't believe he hadn't thought of it before. He'd used up so much energy trying fix his damn machine to bring Catherine back to the present that it hadn't occurred to him to look for her in the past. He shook his head and a grin slid into place on his face.

"Well, don't know what I said, but I'm glad it made you happy," Jon said with surprise. Michael knew his colleagues saw him as rather a geeky, lacklustre creature, weighed down with the burdens of his past, but he didn't mind. The less they knew about his experiments with time travel, the better.

"History, Jon, history is marvellous."

"Not angling for my job, are you?" Jon jested.

"Nope. But I think a bit of extracurricular research might just be the ticket."

"Ticket to what?" Ryan asked.

"Filling in a little missing link."

"And again, for what?"

"I just found a new hobby, that's all."

Ryan and Jon glanced at each other and shrugged. Michael stood, adjusted his belt then headed for the door.

"Too many years spent in dusty labs at the uni, that one," he heard Ryan say as he left the room. Michael smiled to himself and strode down the corridor to his next lesson with a little extra bounce in his step.

At three fifty Michael chained up his bike at the corner of St Aldates and Queen Street and headed for the public library. He'd never been there before; he'd always had access to the Bodleian and university records when he had been at the university. Since he lost that access he had found he hadn't needed their services anyway. Anything he wanted he obtained from the collection in his own study or ordered from Blackwell's. But not this; this he couldn't get from the latest edition of the *New Scientist*, this called for outside assistance.

He made his way to the reception desk and waited patiently for the young woman behind the counter to stop tapping at her keyboard and notice him. When she eventually did break her concentration, she blinked up through the thick brown-rimmed spectacles that seemed to run parallel to her even thicker black eyebrows.

"Oh sorry," she said, "didn't see you there."

Clearly, thought Michael. *Probably chatting to some boyfriend online.*

"Where would I begin if I wanted to research a family member?" he asked, attempting not to sound too enthusiastic.

"Well that would depend on how infamous they are." She snorted at her own joke. Michael smiled patiently.

"Have you tried any of the websites?"

He had been so eager to check out the library for information, he hadn't even stopped to consider the Internet.

When he looked blank the librarian said, "Well, that's the best place to start. Ancestry dot com is a good one. You have to pay but they give you access to all sorts of useful records. Of course you're welcome to look through our archives as well," she added. "I assume you know the person's name and rough date of birth?"

Michael considered the answer to that question very carefully.

"Well, yes and no."

He fidgeted his feet and looked down at his hands. It wasn't going to be easy.

"I see," said the woman. "Well, there are a lot of local records here. There's the electoral role, baptism records, or newspapers. They were local, I assume." This wasn't a question, just a flat statement.

"Erm... I believe so. I think I'll start with newspapers, please. How far back do they go?"

"Current local rags, as far as they were first printed, nationals to 1800. Anything more specialist or earlier than that and you'll have to apply to the Bodleian."

"Right," he said. At least it was a start. He looked around for the direction board.

"This floor, right at the back to the left, past the periodicals. There's quite a lot on our microfiche database if you want to start there," she offered.

"Thanks."

Michael's eyes were beginning to sting with tiredness and he knew it must be getting late. He closed the December 28th 1905 edition of the *Oxford Times* and looked at his watch; half past five. He ought to be getting home. He could check out that Ancestry site after dinner.

"Where have you been? It's gone six." Imogen called from the kitchen as he opened the front door.

"Sorry, love. I went to the library."

"Library?" she said, popping her head through the kitchen door.

Should I tell her? he wondered, not wanting to upset her. But he couldn't lie.

"Just a little research," he replied hoping she wouldn't press him.

"What kind of research?" Her voice was only mildly curious.

Michael hung his jacket on the row of hooks by the front door and followed Imogen into the kitchen.

"Oh, hi, Paul," he said as he entered the steam-filled room. For the second time that day he wafted his hand in front of his face and tried not to cough. "I'll just crack the back door for a minute." The Cajun spice caught in his throat as the steak sizzled in the pan. Imogen and Paul seemed immune, but it got him every time. "How's the study going?" Paul's A level exams were coming up fast.

"All right. Mum says you've been at the library."

Obviously he wasn't going to get out of an explanation.

"Yeah, I… I was inspired to do a little family research."

"Oh?" Imogen said, lifting the frying pan off the hob and flicking off the switch to the chip pan at the same time. Michael admired her dexterity.

"Now, don't get upset…"

"Oh?" Her tone more enquiring, she turned to face him. Her brown eyes had gone from warm chocolate to cold earth.

"It occurred to me that there might be evidence of Catherine in history somewhere. If I can just pinpoint her position then I would have a better shot at…"

He didn't finish. Imogen had gone back to serving up dinner, rather too hastily. She had her back to him. Her hair had been cut short a few months ago and since then the grey streak at the front seemed to have sprawled out over the rest of her head, smattering the darkness with silver like a meteor shower. She kept saying she was going to dye it, but he thought it rather fetching.

"Im, please look at me."

She plopped the frying pan into the soapy water in the sink heavily so that it fizzed in the water, sending even more steam soaring into the air.

"I want her back too," she said, turning around, "but I just can't face it the way you can." There were tears in her eyes. His wife could never talk about their daughter without crying.

"It's just my way. I have to try."

Paul got up from his seat at the breakfast bar and headed for the dining room. Michael wrapped his arms around his wife and held her tight. She rested her head in the crook of his neck.

"I know," she said into his shirt.

Half an hour later Paul followed his father back into the kitchen. Uncharacteristically, he had offered to help with the washing up. Michael tipped out the greasy pan water and turned on the taps to run fresh.

As he squeezed a glob of Fairy Liquid into the bowl, Paul said, "Did you try Googling her?"

"Catherine? Yes, but I drew a blank. Well, unless you count all those who couldn't be her. Have you any idea how many Catherine Alexanders there have been in the world?"

"I can imagine," replied Paul. "Look, I'd like to help."

Michael smiled gratefully. Paul was not following in his father's footsteps, though Michael suspected that was his fault. Paul's interest in Physics had dwindled more and more each time he had refused his assistance. History was a good choice, though, and he was proud of him either way.

"That would be nice," he said, and was pleased to see the smile of relief that spread over his son's face. "But only when your exams are over."

"Cheers, Dad," Paul said, dropping the tea towel on the worktop. "Better go finish my classics coursework, it's due in tomorrow."

Michael shook his head and went back to the washing up.

CATHERINE

London, 1906

During the first week of my stay with the Winstons each morning began the same. I was interviewed by the doctor, recalling bits of my life, telling him and Rosaline about my parents, our business and of my husband and our ill-matched marriage. I had thus far, however, refrained from telling them of Anne. That memory was yet too painful to repeat. Whilst they were clearly concerned by some of my stories they did not seem to be suspicious of my omission of dates, and I was careful over those details that did not correlate with their modern world. That is, until the day before Arthur was due to return to Oxford.

I was in the drawing room, peering through the patterned holes of the drapes and considering how I was going to forge a new life for myself. In front of the Hotel Russell were a woman and a little girl. The woman was instructing a porter on how to arrange her trunks onto the back of the hansom cab. She had already had him load and unload them once. Judging by the amount of boxes and trunks I presumed that they were either returning from or embarking upon a long journey. The little girl was standing with her arms wrapped tightly around a mauled teddy bear, looking terribly bored. Her mother said something to her and she shook her head in response, lowering her eyes to the ground. The door behind me opened with a cool draught. I looked around just as Arthur spoke.

"Here again, Catherine? Really, I haven't the faintest notion what you find so interesting to look at through that window." He flopped onto the couch and tilted his head at me with that now familiar smile.

"People," I said, looking right into his beautiful eyes, "I find them fascinating."

"Quite right too, intriguing creatures." He shuffled closer and joined me at the window, lifting the lace curtain.

"They will see us." I said urgently.

"Nonsense, they're bound to be too wrapped up in their own business to notice us, and what if they do? They will only shrug and ignore us, you can count on it."

I smiled. "Well, maybe you are right."

"Absolutely. So whom are we watching?"

"The carriage collecting the woman and child," I said attempting to point surreptitiously.

"Ah, yes, interesting case," he said with a knowing nod, "the husband has run away with the governess and she has been forced to divorce him and emigrate to America for the shame of it all."

I looked at him for a moment then laughed.

"Really Arthur, you are incorrigible!" I said. "I almost would have believed you if I did not know that there is no such a place as America! And what on earth is a 'divorce'?"

And there was my downfall.

"Now who's making jokes? As if I could believe you have never heard of America or the concept of marital breakdown. My dear, you are not so far without memory."

"And you continue to tease me, sir!" I said laughing rather less assuredly.

Arthur stopped for a moment and his expression became serious.

"You really don't remember, do you?"

Now I was growing frightened. Tears began to sting my eyes.

"Oh, Catherine, you are serious! You really have no recollection of such things."

"I am afraid I have not. Do show me. I long to recall everything," I said, trying to sound calm. I had already found it most shocking that these good people were not required to attend church and I was further astonished now, as Arthur explained how this modern 'Church of England' would allow a marriage as miserable as mine to be dissolved legally and without consequence.

"It isn't easy and it's very expensive but very possible."

"How incredible," I said, woefully wishing I had been brought up in another century than one from which I had come. "And America?"

He adjusted the fabric of his trouser legs and rose.

"Here, come into father's study." He held out a hand to assist me. "Good Lord, Catherine, you're shaking," he said with increased gentleness. I bowed my head. "Forgive me, I didn't mean to cause you alarm."

"I'm fine, really. Please, do show me."

"Are you sure? Perhaps a cup of tea would be more in order."

"Please," I said again with a little too much urgency.

"Very well." Arthur opened the study door and ushered me inside. Having spent several hours in that room by then I was quite familiar with it, and yet as I looked around I realised I had been so absorbed in my own memories that I had not truly seen it before.

"Come over to the globe and I'll show you."

Globe? I had no notion what he was referring to. I glanced about desperately. He went over to a large patterned ball and began to spin slowly it around in its wooden frame. I had seen it before, several times, but it had not occurred to me that it had any geographical significance, just some strange ornament. As it whirled around another image crept into my head; a black window dancing with moving pictures, another globe just like this one, glittering blue and green in the centre. I shoved the memory away. As I joined him he caught the globe with the tip of his forefinger and stopped it turning.

"This is the Americas; north here," he said, pointing a wide scattered portion at the top, "that is Canada and that is the United States." I could not make my mind absorb his words. "And this is South America, mostly Spanish but some of it is ours, like Guyana, here," he said pointing at a small country at the top of a large cone shape. "There are still some Dutch areas, and French of course. Mother's family were plantation owners in Barbados at some point, right here." His finger moved to a smattering of tiny islands.

With the tight constraints of the undergarments restricting my breath, my head began to spin faster than the globe had been. I grasped for the St Christopher at my neck and prayed that I might understand what was happening to me.

"Are you all right? You've gone very pale." He caught me just as my knees gave way and lowered me into his father's chair.

"But how can it be? Everyone knows the world is flat!" My stutter was barely audible, but it was coherent enough for him to latch on to.

"Where on earth were you educated, the middle ages?" he said, staggered at my sincerity.

I lay my head on the cool wood of the desk in the hope the room would stop moving.

"Forgive me, Catherine," Arthur said, holding back his

outrage as he watched me, "but you did just say you believe the world to be flat?" He placed his hand on my forehead to feel for fever, but there was nought but the clammy chill of fear. "My dear, you really do think that, don't you?"

His question was rhetorical; he could see the truth of the matter on my face. He went over to the cabinet in the centre of the bookcase and dropped down the hatch. Inside was a large decanter of single malt. He removed two crystal cut glasses from the shelf and poured us each a hefty measure. I sat up and gratefully took a good gulp, then coughed as the heat of the alcohol stung the back of my throat. Arthur grinned as my eyes watered.

"Sorry, I should have warned you. Good stuff though, hey?"

He brought a large map of the world to the table and spread it out before me.

"My education was excellent," I volunteered nervously. "My father taught me reading, writing and arithmetic as part of my apprenticeship and Father Thomas taught me French, the Classics and the Trivium. He is a most learned man, though perhaps geography is not his strong point."

"Clearly not." Arthur lent against the edge of the table and looked down at me kindly. "The Trivium?"

"Grammar, Rhetoric and Logic," I said, unsure why an Oxford man was asking such a thing. He's a good man" I went on. "Father Thomas would never have deceived me knowingly. Why, he was a forward thinker; he did not even hesitate to educate a woman when I asked."

"Women may not be permitted at the University, but there cannot still be people who believe women should have no education at all," he said, his curiosity mounting.

I closed my eyes.

"Where I am from there are."

"My dear, I simply..." Something changed in his expression, not disbelief but caution. "Tell me, if you had to ask for an education, how did that come about?"

I took another swig of whisky.

"I contracted scarlet fever when I was nine. I was very sick for a while and Father Thomas came every day to see me. He was so kind and so worried. As I recovered a little I begged him tell me Bible stories. After a while I wanted to be able to read them for myself. At first he laughed and said it was hardly necessary. But he could see how keen I was. When I asked again he said it would take a lot of study and dedication but when I persisted he agreed."

"If your father had already taught you to read, then why could you not...?"

"My father taught me English, not Latin." When Arthur said nothing, I continued, "By the time I was twelve I was competent at both Latin and Greek and fluent in French."

"Gracious Catherine, you speak four languages?" I nodded. "But, tell me, why did you need Latin to read the scriptures?"

I sipped at the whisky again and shook my head.

"Catherine..." he sounded especially careful now. "Can you recall where exactly it is that you live? What street, for example?"

Praying I was not about to dig myself a deeper hole I said, "My husband and I live in the tailor's shop on the corner of Horsemonger Street and the North Gate, just opposite Balliol College."

"Horsemonger Street?" My companion furrowed his forehead and narrowed his eyes.

"Do you not know it? The cluster of houses at the back of St Michael's and the Bocardo?"

I was grasping at straws now. I knew it was unlikely the city looked just as it had when I had last seen it, but I could never have dreamed that the gates and the prison would be gone entirely. It was the look in his eyes that showed me the reality. I had not just dug the hole but I was burying myself in it too. There seemed to be no escaping it now. The magnitude of what I was about to confess tore at my stomach like a knife. I would be sent to the lunatic asylum, I was certain.

Arthur chose his words carefully.

"I believe you mean Broad Street, my dear, Balliol is on Broad Street. There are no tailors at the back of St Michael's, I can assure you. The North Gate is long gone and I have no idea of anything by the name of Bocardo. Perhaps you are confused and this isn't Oxford you recall, or maybe you have history lessons mixed in with your memory."

Suddenly he sighed with relief and me with him; there, an explanation I could cling too. "Yes, that must be it; either that or you've been transported through time in Mr Wells' Time Machine."

I breathed slowly before throwing caution to the wind and daring to ask the question.

"There is such a thing? A machine that can transport someone through time?"

My voice was shaking and my knees were knocking together beneath the table.

Arthur stopped and stared. "Only in the fanciful imagination of a writer."

He stood up and walked around the table to the bookcase. He turned a small key in the lock and pulled open one of the glass panels. "Here, perhaps you should read it. Father and I loved it. Made me wish I were clever enough to invent such a thing myself.

Would it not be wonderful to observe the past as it happened?"

Something marched through my mind like a thunderous army. It was a dream from my childhood. In it there was a book-lined study. Through the window I could see a grassy bank bordered by bright summer flowers, and young men and women congregated, all donning short black cloaks tied about their shoulders. In the room, in a case, was a book just like the one Arthur was holding; only it was tattered and ancient, as though it had been read a thousand times over. That copy was kept behind a glass panel, too, and something told me I was not allowed to touch it. On the desk were drawings and pages covered in numbers, pinned down by a queer brass object that looked like an arrowhead.

The thought of that object brought on other memories: standing beneath a great tower just like the arrow, people speaking French, and something called Physics, what was that? I just could not quite reach the recollection.

"Did you remember something else? Catherine?"

I realised Arthur was talking to me. I looked at him, still with the book in his hand and a dimpled smile on his lips.

"A recurring dream I have had since I was a very little girl. A room like this one, and that book too, only it was very old. But I doubt it means anything."

"Well, this book was only published in '95, so when you were a child it would have been new. You must be remembering a different book."

"No, I am certain of it, this book, exactly, when I was no more than five years old. In my dream I can see the gold lettering on the spine just as clearly as I look at it now."

"Really. I think you are mistaken."

"I can assure you, sir, that is most assuredly the right book and it was kept behind glass to keep it safe."

My companion thought for a moment, his gaze drifting to the window. I followed his view. Reflected, the brightness of the morning sun matched the fairness of his hair and made it glint like gold. There was a small draught whistling in through the window frame and it made me shiver. The movement broke his thought.

"You are a great puzzle, Mrs Catherine More, and I'm exceedingly intrigued." He took off his jacket and draped it about my shoulders. At that moment the front door rattled and Rosaline and her father could be heard in the entrance hall.

"Do read the book," he said, helping me to my feet and opening the door.

Later that afternoon, Rosaline and I were in the parlour. She had taken it upon herself to teach me to play the pianoforte; rather unsuccessfully, I'm afraid to say. Arthur knocked on the door and entered without awaiting an invitation.

"Sister, I've been thinking. Catherine and I had a conversation this morning of which I am sure you've been informed…"

"Of course, Arty. Are you quite all right?" Rosaline interrupted, somewhat alarmed at her brother's curious expression. I stared at the pair of them, afraid of what he was about to say next.

"Fine, thank you for asking," he said hurriedly. "Now, I have been considering this conversation carefully, and I've come to the conclusion that Catherine's past needs further investigation."

Rosaline was watching him now as blankly as I.

"I propose that the two of you accompany me back to Oxford tomorrow. I'm sure we can find you rooms at the Clarendon."

Rosaline blinked.

"What on earth has got into you? How can I leave Father at such short notice? Besides, whatever frightened Catherine away from her home may still be present there. She may not be ready to return."

Arthur flashed her a grin.

"My dear, I believe Catherine would find a trip to Oxford beneficial. She need not visit her husband but she should reacquaint herself with the surroundings of her hometown. There is a mystery afoot and I intend to be the one to solve it."

"You've been reading too many Sherlock Holmes stories…"

Rosaline was about to dismiss his idea when I interjected, "I think Arthur is right."

I needed to go and see for myself how much had changed, and perhaps say goodbye to my past. I needed to see for myself that my house and husband were truly gone.

"Well, I suppose we could go for a couple of days," she acquiesced.

"Of course you can," he said triumphantly. "Then it's settled. "I shall go to the post office and telegraph the Clarendon at once. We can take the twelve o'clock train tomorrow."

The following morning, as we waited for the carriage, I was growing increasingly uneasy. Rosaline was sitting calmly on the hall seat before me. Arthur was still upstairs dressing and I was pacing about the floor, just as I had been in my room for half the night. The black and white marble tiles clicked beneath the soles of my shoes with each anxious step. Rosaline patted her hand on the gold brocade cushion at her side.

"Please take a seat, Catherine, you will exhaust yourself before we even set out."

She spoke in the same manner as she usually spoke to Leticia and Arthur. I took a deep breath and placed myself (stiffly, for I was still adapting to the tight constrains of an Edwardian lady's undergarments) next to her. My friend had her hair tightly pinned into a roll under a small blue hat that brought out the lightness of her eyes. Everything about her was immaculate. It mattered not how well Sissy helped me tie up my hair, it always managed to come loose. I felt for unruly strands around my head and looked down at my second-hand clothes. They were good clothes and yet despite my having adjusted them to my own measurements, the gown still managed to betray that it was made for someone else. I lifted the heavy skirt enough to reveal my feet and stared down at my flat leather shoes, one of only two pairs I owned.

"We can buy new ones in Oxford if you like," Rosaline offered.

Horrified that she might have thought I had been hinting for such a thing, I dropped the hem back over my toes.

"Thank you, but I'm sure they will do." I said not quite able to raise my eyes to meet hers.

"Forgive me," she said, looking mortified that I should have felt her charity so keenly.

"There is nothing to forgive, but you have been so generous already and I fear I shall never be able to repay you."

"You may be a new friend, Catherine, but you are still a friend, and you are in need of temporary assistance. If I cannot give you that, then what kind of a friend would I be?"

I could not argue with her, nor was I in a position to.

The sight of the railway station near stopped my heart. Before me was a large open space filled with people. There was a huge concourse that culminated in a set of long grey platforms that ran out under a great glass canopy. Wrought iron columns stood at regular intervals, holding up a glittering roof of iron and glass that arched above them like a massive fan-vaulted cathedral. Along these platforms were great monsters of engineering. Huge chunks of metal stood, puffing out grey steam that curled up from their snorting chimneys. These long slender creatures trailed off into the distance like caterpillars. Doors hung open from their bellies and people were clambering in and out. Luggage was being loaded and trunks lifted into the goods cars at the end. A woman scurried by, impatiently dragging a small boy by the hand. I stared after her as she pushed past the guard, practically threw the boy through a swinging door and vanished in after him. A great loud whistle screeched and I staggered backwards. Rosaline tightened her hold of my arm.

"You have never ridden a train before?"

"I cannot tell," I said helplessly. There was more than one memory banging at the inside of my skull, but one in particular was hammering hard: Another great station, grander and wider, slender tubes of metal, speeding countryside and soft comfortable seats, men in uniform checking little red books. None of it made sense.

"You are remembering something, I can tell. What is it, Catherine?" asked Arthur with a cunning smile of encouragement.

"Gracious, look at the time." Rosaline grabbed my hand as though I were a child and began to bustle along the platform.

Grateful for the diversion I glanced at Arthur. With each new thing he learned about me I could see increasing curiosity in his eyes as he began to form his conclusions. Catching me looking he grinned. As he took my hand to assist me aboard I felt a twinge of anxiety rush through me. Could he truly have found me out?

MICHAEL

Oxford – 25th November, 2020

The newspaper cutting in Michael's hand was faded and yellow. Too many hours had been spent trawling through records for evidence of his daughter. Each lead had proved fruitless and each hint had led them on a wild goose chase. Imogen had begged him to slow down and in the end he had to agree. Catherine simply did not exist outside her own time. The only proof she had ever been in the world at all was her birth certificate and that report. He didn't need to read, he knew what it said word for word.

Girl of six goes missing from university lab

Yesterday evening the daughter of eminent physicist Prof Michael Alexander vanished from his laboratory at Oxford University. She had been dropped off at the Banbury Road building by her mother and left in the care of a trusted technician, Oliver Brown, to await her father. The professor was in a tutorial in his adjacent office. Brown left Catherine alone while he took some paperwork to a student in another lab. The door to the computer room where Catherine was apparently 'sitting quietly' had been closed and the windows locked from the inside. 'It's a complete mystery, I was only gone two minutes,' said the technician in a statement to our reporter. Mr Brown is not under any suspicion.

Catherine was celebrating her birthday and was due to attend the theatre with her father. While waiting it is thought she may have unwittingly tampered with a radical experiment. The university has denied all knowledge that the professor was working on anything that might have endangered Catherine and have refused to comment on the nature of the experiment. There has of course been much speculation surrounding the disappearance; some sources have even gone so far as to suggest the professor was building a time machine and that little Catherine is now lost somewhere in the past.

Michael's thoughts flashed back.

A loud hum and a crack of electricity sizzles across the hall. His heart almost stops. He abandons his student and runs. Everything around him is white noise. Fuzzed images of doors and walls blur in his head. He turns the door handle. Jammed – blasts of black and violet light forcing it back like a freight train. His hands rub over his eyes. Disbelief. A wormhole swirls. His shoulder rams against wood, again and again. He didn't remember doing it till after, when he felt the pain.

Latch breaks, door swings open. Smoke, liquefied metal, dark indigo light, air spinning and crackling like a dozen catherine wheels. He can't breathe. Oliver, the technician, face white like paper, staring at the Time Console. Michael is on his knees.

Everything stops.

Catherine is gone.

Like petrified wood he sits.

Oliver turns to him.

"I'm sorry. I should never have left her here." He is crying. "How did she know the combination?" The words echo around the room, bouncing from the walls and beating against his ears.

Why did I use her date of birth?

Someone calls her name. He turns toward the door but no one is there. The voice calls again and he realises it is coming from him. His heart beats so hard he thinks it will explode.

Oliver is shaking him now. Large hands grip his shoulders tight. Michael looks up into the young man's eyes.

"Professor... Professor... What do we do?"

Michael gasps as though oxygen has rushed into his lungs for the first time. The air begins to clear around them and with it his mind focuses.

"We call the police and report her missing."

"And that?" the technician glances over at the machine, "I don't think we should just leave it there."

The lights on the console are a dying red, flickering on and off.

Then there is nothing.

Suddenly Michael is on his feet again, prising open the front panel, only to release the stench of burned-out wires and smouldering plastics. The circuits are nothing more than a mangled glob. He presses every key, turns every dial but nothing will awaken it. Slowly he pulls open the drawer at the bottom of the cabinet, all the time whispering, "Let it be gone."

Yet when he sees the St Christopher pendant is missing, the horror makes his head reel.

Michael rubbed his hands over his face and put down the tattered page of newsprint. It had amused him when he decided to use the patron saint of travellers to disguise the tiny homing device, but once he realised Catherine was gone and he couldn't get her back, he wished he had used something else, a man's watch perhaps, something she might not have bothered to look at.

Michael and Oliver had attempted to drag the cabinet out of the lab that night, but it was too cumbersome:

"Don't breathe a word of this to anyone. If the press find out I'll be crucified, and I can't get her back if I'm locked in a prison cell," he had begged.

"I won't, I promise," Oliver had spluttered, but Michael knew he had, because he had since apologised profusely for breaking his confidence. And once they had reported Catherine's disappearance the police had searched the house, his office and especially the lab. They had confiscated the machine. But when they found it was broken and no one knew what it was for or how to fix it, they'd delivered it back, weeks later, to the Alexanders' home. He had seen the way the police had looked at him, though, how they eyed him suspiciously, but Michael didn't care; all he cared about was finding his little girl. He just wished he knew how. The machine, the Time Console as he had always called it, hadn't been finished. Even he hadn't known how to make it work properly, yet. Aside from unlocking the cabinet door, Catherine had unwittingly set the machine in motion. If only there had been CCTV in the lab, he could have watched what she had done and replicated it.

Michael put the article back in his desk drawer and closed it. There had been many reports for weeks afterwards, but that one, from the front page of the *Telegraph*, was the only one he had forced himself to read. He kept it now, away from Imogen's sight, as a constant reminder of what he had done. All other traces of Catherine were upstairs in her room. She had not even occupied that for very long. They had only moved into the house the year before she disappeared. And now he had drawn a blank. Paul had helped when he could, but now his work load at university was getting heavier and Michael was left alone again. For a moment he'd considered giving up altogether, but then he had opened the drawer to put his reading glasses away and seen the cutting. *I must simply be looking in the wrong places, he thought, I'll have to think of something else.*

CATHERINE

Oxford, 1906

I was astounded at the difference in my city. The enclosing wall half removed, the North Gate and Bocardo demolished, The Catherine Wheel gone and The Bell with it. There were so many new colleges, shops and homes that it quite took my breath.

Arthur deposited us in front of the Clarendon Hotel then went off to settle back in his rooms at Christ Church. As the porter lifted Rosaline's trunk onto a great brass trolley a wave of tiredness washed over me and I needed a moment alone to still my heart.

"Would you mind if I rested a while before venturing out?"

Rosaline's eyes flickered over my nervous hands and ashen face.

"Of course, dear, just come to my room when you're ready."

My chamber door clicked behind me and I was as solitary as is possible in a hotel bristling with guests. Below, the chatter of people going about their business droned through the floor and from the room to my left came the muffled tones of Rosaline speaking to a maid. I heard a cupboard door creak open and the clunk of a hanger as it met with a rail. I began to look around at my extravagant surroundings. Everything was so perfectly set in its place that I feared to even rumple the bedding.

The day was dim and I went to turn on the lamp. I reached for the cord and flicked the switch, then stared. My heart thumped in my chest and I was forced to sink onto the bed. Beneath the shade a perfect ball of glass burned with the light of a small sun. I had never seen such a thing, and yet I had turned it on as though I had done so a thousand times before. Rosaline had had to show me how to work the gas lights at 52 Russell Square, but with this lamp there had not even been a hesitation. I was still staring at it when there was a rap at my door. I almost leapt from my skin at the sound. Without taking my eyes from the light I called for the maid to enter.

A slender girl of about my own age swept into the room with a breezy smile. Her uniform seemed a little too large and her dark hair was coming unpinned beneath her cap. In another life that could have been me.

"Miss Winston sent these for you, miss," she said, opening the wardrobe doors. As she folded a shawl and laid it upon the shelf she caught my expression. "Is there something wrong, miss?"

"Forgive me, no, not at all. I... well..." I stuttered, "I mean to say, I have never seen a lamp such as this."

She nodded with a knowing raise of her eyebrows.

"My Ma's just the same, miss, she thinks the electricity gives off vapours, but I was talking to a professor at the university and he says it doesn't. There's no smell and it's so much brighter than gas."

"Electricity...." I mused.

"It's safe, miss, I promise."

She closed the cupboard door and dropped a curtsey.

"Is there anything else?"

"No, thank you," I said, wishing I dared ask her to explain this 'electricity'.

When she was gone I ventured to open a window. The day was warm and heavy from the brewing clouds over the spires. As the frame eased back the muggy air hit my chest like the heat from a furnace. I leaned out onto Cornmarket Street and took in the vision of a modern city. This street was familiar to me, so very familiar, but not in the way I had expected. There were buildings I knew and should not. The feeling disturbed me, rattling at the doorway to the memories from those first six years of my life, but the lock would not give. My heart fluttered and I looked along the street cautiously, searching for something that I could recognise from my time.

The cluttered buildings with their heavy timbering and dark mullioned windows were all but gone. A carriage rattled past, sending a shudder up through the hotel and into my bones. My head was growing light when, to my great relief, I saw St Mary Magdalene's to the far north of the street, still standing like a reliable old friend. Suddenly my heart ached for the confidence of dear Father Thomas. I had missed him greatly, and, I am ashamed to say, more so than my husband.

Directly across the way, a couple emerged from the dark front doors of the Roebuck Inn opposite. The woman held out a gloved hand and felt the first drops of rain fall. She stepped back under the canopy whilst her husband wrestled with a large black umbrella. I rested my elbows on the windowsill and leaned out so that the rain tapped against my forehead and cooled my skin. As I continued to survey the street, one particular building caught my attention. Its bowed timber frame drew my eyes towards it. The upper storey overhung the lower precariously, giving the impression it was about to fall flat upon its face. The windows were irregular and randomly positioned. It looked tired and in need of painting, yet just the same, I wanted to run right over and go inside. 'Trimble and Blake, Solicitors of Law' still stood. A swinging board hung from a rail over the door. I squinted to read it. 'Zacharias and Co.' I knew not what that was, but rain or not I had to find out.

I found Rosaline seated at a writing desk in her room, pen in hand, scribbling away in a neat leather-bound book.

"Oh, forgive me, I did not mean to interrupt," I said, turning to go.

"Not at all," she replied, setting down the pen and blotting the page, "I was merely taking the opportunity to write in my journal whilst we wait for Arthur, but if you are ready I would much rather take tea and scones."

"That would be very nice, but… there is somewhere I would very much like to visit. Would you mind terribly if we went there first?"

Rosaline tilted her head at me in the same way Leticia had done when we first met.

"My dear, are you quite sure you are up to this today? We have barely arrived and besides, it's raining." She looked at me thoughtfully for a minute. "Come, let's go down to the lobby and order some tea."

"All right." As I replied I caught sight of my reflection and almost wept. It was not the ill-fitting clothes or the tired shadows around my eyes that hurt; it was the sight of me, in that room, in my city, yet so far from home. Until that moment I do not believe I had completely accepted the verity of my situation.

"Oh, my dear, I did not mean to upset you." Rosaline rose to her feet and came to stand behind me, looking into the mirror at us both. "We shall go on your visit."

"I did not mean to…"

"I know," she said laying her hand upon my shoulder, "but perhaps we should. We can have cakes when we come back."

"Thank you," I said. The thought of food, for which I could not pay, suddenly made me consider my lack of home and finances with growing fear. I decided at that moment that I could no longer prevail upon the Winston family without earning my keep. I would venture to seek employment the moment we returned to London.

It looked so out of place, standing there all alone with its Tudor façade. Every building around it looked modern in comparison, save for the tower of St Michael's, and that had been already some two centuries old when I had last seen it. As we reached the front doors I stopped and looked up at the arched wooden windows, the building opposite reflected there, as clear as in water. They had been shuttered portholes in my day, tightly closed in winter and blowing with fresh warm air in summer. Staring out from the large bay window on the ground floor was a life-size mannequin dressed in a great shining coat and galoshes.

"This shop is familiar to you?" Rosaline asked, intrigued.

"Well, in a manner of speaking, yes. But when I was last here it was a legal establishment, that is to say, it was the solicitor's office where my husband…"

"I see," she said, her eyebrows flattened into a frown. "I think you must be confused, my dear, Zacharias has been here for years."

Increasingly afraid my friends would believe me to be nothing more than a fanciful liar, or worse, a lunatic, I said, "I cannot explain, but that is how I remember it."

Rosaline gave a pensive nod.

The inside of the shop was nothing at all as I had known it. The desks where my husband and Master Blake once sat were replaced by a counter with a cash register upon it and a small bell to ring for assistance. There were displays of clothes that boasted to be waterproof and a glass cabinet containing floppy hats and small silver whistles. And yet for a brief moment I thought that I could smell the scent of my husband and hear the scratching of his quill.

"I'm sorry, Catherine," my friend offered when I turned to go.

"It's not your fault that everything is different."

"I meant that I am sorry this visit has not turned out as you hoped."

"Thank you, but I do not think I am disappointed."

And that was the truth. Guilt might have strangled the words as they left my throat, but I could not deny it. I felt free. Free from the unhappiness of my marriage and free from the oppression of my old life. The pain, the constant reminders, the weight of the darkness that surrounds me when I remember those I have lost will never leave me, but I cannot deny how much easier it is being so far away.

That evening we dined at Boul's. The restaurant was a blur of people, diners chatting over the clatter of cutlery, waiting maids buzzing from one table to another like flies, and inviting smells of cooking wafting around us, making it feel warm and welcoming. As we waited for our dessert to arrive I began to feel at home, as though this time, 1906, was where I was meant to be.

Then Arthur spoiled my mood by turning the conversation back towards my situation.

"So, Mrs More, how well does this city fare? Has your mind been recovered by the sights?"

Rosaline explained about Trimble and Blake's and Arthur sat back in his chair with his arms folded, listening with great interest. There was a mischievous look in his eyes that I could not quite make out.

When she had done he responded, "I did a quick bit of research before I came to meet you tonight. The Bocardo, it was a prison?"

"Yes, right there on the North Gate, next to St Michael's."

"Torn down in seventeen seventy-one," he said with a flourish.

I closed my eyes and prayed for guidance.

"Well, you said it yourself, Arty, Catherine must be confusing memories with something she has read in a history book." Rosaline removed her hands from the table to allow the waitress to set down her trifle.

"And Broad Street was once called Horsemonger," he continued.

"Gracious, Catherine, your memory may be faded in places but it is sharp as a needle in others," Rosaline said.

Arthur did not look as convinced by this as his sister. His eyes were beginning to twinkle brightly.

"I think it's more than that, my dear. Catherine, tell me, who was the last King of England?"

"What has that got to do with anything?" Rosaline asked, baffled.

"Indulge me, please," he replied

I offered a hopeful response based on my perusal of the morning's newspaper.

"Edward."

"Not the current monarch, who was on the throne before?"

he said.

Rosaline opened her mouth to protest, but Arthur silenced her with a rising of his hand. I shifted uncomfortably in my seat.

"I… I am afraid I cannot recall."

"You know she is having trouble with her memory," Rosaline said with a sigh.

Arthur stuck his spoon in his spotted dick and took an oversized mouthful, forcing him to cover his mouth with his napkin whilst he attempted to chew it all. Rosaline and I laughed.

"Forgive me, Catherine, I don't mean to press you," he said, when he had recovered, "I'm simply testing out a theory. I want to know exactly what you know and at what point in history your memory ceases."

I felt the swish of Rosaline's leg pass my skirt and connect with her brother's shin. He flinched. "I mean, perhaps your memory is confused, stuck as it were, in the past."

Unsure at this point whether he meant this in earnest, thought me a liar or whether he actually knew my secret, I decided that, at the risk of being sent to an asylum, I was going to have to tell them the truth.

"The last king I know is Henry."

"Which Henry?" Rosaline asked, unable to stop herself.

"Tudor," I replied flatly.

"Seventh or Eighth?" Arthur set down his spoon and leaned his elbows on the table, his chin resting on his clasped hands.

"Elbows, Arthur," Rosaline said half-heartedly. He tilted his head in her direction and fluttered his long blond eyelashes like an innocent child.

"There were eight?" I asked, exhausted.

"Henry the Seventh, then," he said.

Now I frowned and gave up all pretence.

"Henry Tudor's son shares your name. He is Arthur, not Henry."

"That really does narrow things down." Arthur took a contemplative breath. "If Arthur Tudor is still alive, then your memory is sitting somewhere around the turn of the sixteenth century." He smiled kindly but his eyes glinted with excitement. "Catherine, what year did you think it was on the day of the accident?"

I swallowed my last mouthful of trifle and let the brandy sponge warm my chest for a moment.

"The year of Our Lord, 1492." I closed my eyes and prayed that when I opened them I would have thought of a way to explain myself.

"1492," said Arthur triumphantly as he flopped back in his chair, "Of course it was. Pre Columbus, only just, but still. I should have guessed." His voice was growing louder.

"Really, Arthur, this is insane."

"I think not, sister. Let me have my theory and work on it for a day or two." He turned back to me. "I don't think there is anything remotely insane about any of this, just a wonderful mystery. Oh, Philip is going to love you," he added, shaking his head with a sideways smile.

"Oh, no, you don't," Rosaline protested, rather too quickly.

"What is a Columbus and who is Philip?" I asked, beginning to contract Arthur's enthusiasm.

"Columbus is the man who discovered the Americas," Arthur replied simultaneously with Rosaline's, "Someone you are not going to meet."

"Oh," was all I could manage.

"Spoil sport," said Arthur with a childlike pout.

He then asked if I would like a 'post fifteen hundred' history lesson. I agreed and thus we began.

The next few days were filled with learning, and not only for me. Arthur, too, grew enthused by all the knowledge of my home he could glean from me. Of all the things we discussed, however, the moment that settled his opinion and my fate was when I translated a passage of medieval French from an ancient Bible we found in the Bodleian. The astonishment on his face told me I had gone too far.

On the last morning of our stay I was at my toilet. As I reached for the towel to dry my face I overheard a heated discussion coming from Rosaline's room. I could not help myself. I crept up to the partition wall and pressed my ear against the silkiness of the pale green wallpaper.

"The notion is incredible, Arthur, how can you even entertain such ideas? Your mind has become pickled with all that whisky you drink."

"Dearest, I may like a good single malt or three but I have never been one for excess…"

"Ha!"

"Fine, so perhaps I have, but that has nothing to do with this…"

"And you spend too much time with the likes of…"

"Oh, that'll be right, point your finger at my friends now. I know why you dislike him so much. It was all harmless and you know it."

"Really?" That was the first time I had heard Rosaline actually raise her voice at anyone. I cringed and pressed my fingers to my lips.

"Forget about everything else and think about the situation for a moment. Catherine has either been trapped in a bubble away from the world with nothing but a Latin dictionary and an ancient French Bible to keep her company, or she has somehow been removed from one time to another," continued Arthur a little more calmly.

"Such things are just not possible."

I found I was holding my breath.

"I know it sounds incredible, but there *is* no other conclusion. Her hand is flawless when she writes with an untipped quill, yet she scratches at the page and ink splashes everywhere if I let her use a pen. Her knowledge of the fifteenth century is unaccountable, she can tell me every detail right down to what fabrics they wore and how they were stitched together, yet she knows nothing of Shakespeare."

"Yes, she does," interjected Rosaline, "the first time Papa took her back to her childhood, she recalled seeing *A Midsummer Night's Dream*."

"Really? Hmm. We didn't look at that one." This revelation did not deter him for long. "Nor had she any knowledge of Charles Dickens, Da Vinci, Michelangelo or Isaac Newton. She was horrified at Cromwell, practically distraught with Henry the Eighth and she cried so hard when she heard what happened to Thomas More you would have thought he had been family. And the clothes she wore on the day of the accident 'looked as though she had just walked off the stage from a production of *Romeo and Juliet*', those were your very words."

As he drew a breath my stomach flipped over. The clothes I wore. How could I have never thought of that? For one terrified moment I wished I were back in my father's shop so that I might go to the linen chest in my bedchamber and pull it out. The dress I had been found in on the streets that day when I was six years old. Hannah had kept it for she could not make out the fabric. It was vivid pink and trimmed with fine ribbon and dotted with tiny flowers. It shone in the sunlight like silk but was finer than any fabric that we had ever seen before or since. The top layer was so fine you could see your fingers through it.

"There is evidence enough, however improbable." Arthur was saying.

"It's true, I cannot deny you that." Rosaline gave an exasperated sigh. I could hear her fingers tapping on the writing desk.

"And in Piccadilly you said 'she just appeared out of nowhere'."

I glanced at my reflection in the mirror and flinched at the site of my blanched face. *This it is,* I thought. I had to join them.

When I entered, Rosaline was seated at the writing desk and Arthur half way across the room where he had been pacing back and forth.

"Catherine!" Rosaline said, with the guilty look of a child caught in the larder.

"Forgive me for interrupting. But there is something I need to explain."

Arthur sat down on his sister's bed and gawped like a fish as I spoke. Even though only moments before, he had been proposing that very idea to his sister, hearing the account of my journey from my own lips left him dumb.

"Well…" Rosaline gasped when I was done, "you are a phenomenon. And you have no idea how you do this… time travel?"

"None at all. Do you think it will happen again?" I asked, considering Daniel with a twinge of guilt.

"I'm afraid if *you* don't know how it happened, then I have not the slightest idea." Arthur was grinning now, and so excited that he was practically bouncing up and down. "But there *are* people here who can help us," he said eyeing his sister carefully.

"Oh, no, Arthur, I already told you not involve poor Catherine with any of your eccentric friends, especially not Philip. I don't care what you say, I am not letting *him* anywhere near her." The thin purse of Rosaline's lips and the chill in her glare made me shiver.

"Philip Boden-Howard," she said, turning to me, "is one of the more bohemian romantics in this place. He behaves as though he is a cross between Lord Byron and Sir Isaac Newton, and if you think my brother is a charmer, then you have never met Philip. He is an utter cad who uses women more ill than Casanova. Really, dear, you will do better to stay away."

"All those comparisons, my sweet, he will be flattered. He may have an artistic temperament, but he is a brilliant mathematician. If it is possible to mix artistry with science, then Philip is the finest example."

"Nevertheless, he is a boy with too much privilege." She looked at me. "His father is Lord Rupert Boden-Howard, twelfth Earl of Hatherley."

I blinked at her, unsure whether to be impressed or afraid. Turning back to her brother she continued her tirade. "He has a wild temperament, he's unpredictable and he does as he pleases. I forbid you to bring him within a hundred yards of Mrs More. She has enough to contend with, without the likes of him attempting to corrupt her."

"Not cricket, my dear, not cricket." Arthur folded his arms and pouted. Rosaline's glower melted and flickered into an unwilling smile.

"You can sulk at me all you like, but the answer is still no."

I was dumbfounded. The pair of them would have been wonderful entertainment had I not been so utterly confused.

"Very well. He isn't due back until tomorrow anyway," he conceded, "but I should like to put the case to him nonetheless, as a hypothetical study of course." His tone dripped with sarcasm. "Will that suit?" he added.

"Oh, I suspect it must," his sister replied.

"What say you, Catherine? Would you mind awfully if I use your case for an experimental study?"

"I... er." I stuttered, "of course, if you wish."

"Capital!" he said with a satisfied grin.

After our return I fell into an exceptionally comfortable life. Dr Winston had a heart as large as Dr Campbell's beard. He was more than happy to allow me to reside with them on a permanent basis, on the condition that he might continue to study my early memory loss. Though he never showed it, I must have been a great disappointment as a subject, for I am afraid the best of my recovery was already done. Over and over again I recalled events which were already clear in my mind, but the only things before my sixth birthday were the same snatched-at snippets I had already glimpsed. Dr Winston was an optimistic man, however, and we continued despite my lack of progress. He was a man generous with his affections too, for I soon came to feel as though I were his favourite niece.

I also managed to make myself useful. I advertised and began to take in sewing work to earn my keep, mending jobs at first, tightening loose seams, adjusting off-the-peg gowns and fixing tears and snags. But after a while I started to make up dresses from scratch again. The gowns were easy enough to work out, for there were ready-cut patterns, though I was astounded by my initial encounter with a sewing machine. I was reluctant when Rosaline first showed me hers, but once I had threaded the needle and attached the foot, the excitement tingled down my arms, through my fingers and into the fabric. My work load could be double that of my former business, with no need for the assistance of anything but Mr Singer's machine.

    I also resolved to continue my historical studies, something which I am very grateful I had the foresight to do. Everything seemed to be running along as smooth as silk. That is, until Christmas.

MICHAEL

Oxford — 26th March, 2021

The front door slammed shut and sent a shudder through the floor and up the legs of his desk. Michael set down his book and glanced at the carriage clock on the mantel; ten minutes past eight.

"Anything wrong, love?" he called. "I thought your class didn't finish 'til nine."

"You're gonna love me!" Paul burst into the room with a beam across his face so wide Michael thought he must have won the lottery. "Mum taken up another night school course?"

"Embroidery," he replied.

"Really, wow! She made anything decent?" Paul threw an envelope onto his father's desk, flopped onto the couch opposite and lay back with his hands behind his head, wearing a self-satisfied smile.

"Not yet, it's only her second week. What on earth?"

"Open it, then."

"What is it?" Michael picked up the envelope and looked at his son with dubious amusement.

"Just open it and tell me what you think."

Michael flipped it over. It was unmarked and unsealed. There was something fairly thick and a little weighty inside. He lifted the flap and tipped the contents onto his hand. The photograph bounced off his palm and landed face down on this desk. His hand began to shake. Paul sat up and watched him eagerly.

"Tell me it's not her." said Paul with defiance.

Slowly Michael turned it over. The sepia group that looked back at him were a jovial bunch. It seemed odd for a photograph of its time, when the sitters were usually poker-faced and characterless, but these people were laughing. The two women were seated. One, a blond in her late twenties, was an elegant creature in a light-coloured Edwardian dress with immaculate hair and a smooth, cool face, every feature of which she shared with the angelic man standing behind her. The other couple were not so alike. He was tall and dark with unkempt hair and a scarf thrown wildly about his neck, dramatically handsome and worryingly charismatic, but it was the girl sitting in front of him that drew Michael's eye.

"She..." Michael couldn't get the words out.

"Looks exactly like Mum," Paul finished for him.

"My God, Paul, where did you find it?" Michael's voice cracked as he spoke. She was unmistakable. Her thick dark hair was pinned loose enough to show its natural wave, her cheekbones were high and neatly cut in her heart-shaped face, and her bright eyes were light in colour. No one could look that much like another human being and not be a relation. He flipped the card over but the only name was that of the photographer's studio; Gillman & Soame, 101 High Street, Oxford.

"She could just be an ancestor, your great-great-grandmother, perhaps," he offered, but the idea that it was Catherine romanced him with too much hope to allow the notion to pass by. "Or a distant aunt," he added, desperate for Paul to give him reassurance.

"And it just might be her," his son obliged. "Donovan asked a couple of us to help shift his bookcase..."

"Donovan?"

"Professor Donovan. There was a damp patch on the wall in his office and they needed to re-plaster it, so anyway, we were shifting the bookcase and lying on the floor behind it was that photo. It must have been there years. I didn't really look at it at first, but then I saw her. It's got to be Catherine, Dad. She just has to be."

Michael extracted a magnifying glass from his desk and peered more closely.

He stared at the pretty young woman for some minutes. Eventually he set down the glass and looked up at Paul.

"I don't know if the studios still exist. I only found the photo this afternoon and I came straight here from a lecture so I didn't have time to check. But it's worth a try."

"She looks happy," said Michael, not sure whether to laugh or cry. "If she is happy, do we have the right to bring her home?" This question had not occurred to Michael before, or if so, he had suppressed it. But now that he had seen the image of this blithe young woman, the thought stung him like an aggravated wasp.

"Let's find out for sure who the woman is first, then we might be able to find out what sort of a life she had."

Michael wasn't certain he wanted to know.

"What if I sent her to something terrible? Or maybe she had a good and full life? What if the life I can offer her is not as good?" Michael's questions tumbled over each other like rocks. Paul laid a hand on his father's arm. "Good God, Paul, her life has already been lived, years ago, are we selfish in wanting her back?"

"Let's just find her first," Paul soothed.

CATHERINE

London, 1906

Rosaline and I had passed a pleasant afternoon with Leticia in town, stopping in Mrs Henderson's for a buttered scone on the way home. From the confines of the Tea Shop we watched heavy grey clouds gather, and when the clock on the mantel chimed four we decided we had better make the two-block dash to Russell Square before they ripped apart. Sadly we were not fast enough and were consequently drenched right through. This caused rather a commotion of servants and towels when we arrived home, which in turn caused a letter which had been left sitting on the hall cupboard to flutter off and fall down the back of it, and thus become quite forgot. It was only on Thursday, when Sissy moved the cupboard to mop behind it, that the letter was discovered.

I was about to leave Rosaline to read it when she said, "Catherine, wait. It's addressed to us both."

Astonished, I asked who it was from.

Rosaline cleared her throat and began to read.

> *My Dearest Ladies,*
>
> *Over the past few weeks I have had ample opportunity to discuss Mrs More's unusual situation with my learned friend Philip Boden-Howard. As you are aware, PB-H is a rather brilliant student of Mathematics here at Christ Church. What you may not know is that his interests also expand into theoretical physics.*

> *Whilst he has, as yet, been unable to find an answer to Mrs More's apparent shift through time, he is fascinated by her case and would very much like to meet her and so I have invited him home for Christmas.*
>
> *Now sister, I know Philip is not your favourite person, but trust me when I say he will be the perfect gentleman. Do forgive the short notice. We shall be home the morning of Friday week.*
>
> *Your loving brother and friend,*
>
> *Arthur*

"It's post-marked *last* Thursday." Rosaline handed me the letter with an exasperated sigh. "That means they shall be here tomorrow."

"Why did he not write to Dr Winston for permission?" I asked, a little bewildered. After all, Rosaline had made such a point of my *not* meeting Philip that I thought him quite the monster.

"Father never minds house guests, and much to my continual dismay, he rather likes Philip."

"Ah," I said, suddenly finding it all rather amusing. Rosaline rolled her eyes and gave in to a smile.

Friday began with a fluster when the doorbell rang a little before eight thirty.

"Good Lord, they can't possibly be here yet," Dr Winston grumbled through a mouthful of poached egg.

"I doubt it. It must be someone for you, Papa; no one ever comes this early unless it is an emergency." Rosaline replied.

A moment later there was a clatter in the hall and a cry. We all rushed out to find Markham in a crumpled heap at the bottom of the stairs and Sissy apologising profusely.

"What the devil is going on?" asked Dr Winston as he bent down to attend to the injured butler.

"Sorry, sir. I didn't mean to leave the mop there," the maid sobbed.

"Just get to the kitchen, girl," Dr Winston muttered. Rosaline opened the door as her father ran a hand over Markham's ankle.

"Good morning," breezed Leticia with a bright smile, sweeping into the hallway cradling a squalling baby, closely followed by her rather exhausted-looking husband, Ernest. Rosaline cringed as the child threw his little bald head further back against his oblivious mother's arm and wailed even louder. "Oh, dear, Sissy been at it again?" Leticia added, taking in the commotion.

"I really don't know why you keep that girl," said Ernest.

Rosaline looked just about ready to throttle someone.

"You know why, Ernie, Papa rescued her from the workhouse when she was eleven and he's determined to make a good servant out of her, no matter how long it takes," his wife replied with a shake of her head.

Dr Winston, choosing to ignore both these comments and the screaming child, said, "No harm done, Markham, just take a little rest."

"It feels fine now, sir, I shall be all right."

"Very well, but if it starts to bother you get Sissy to take over and ask Ada to make up a cold compress."

"You don't mind if we leave the perambulator by the front

step, do you?" Ernest asked, taking off his hat and handing it to Rosaline. "It's such a tedious job to bring it inside."

Rosaline shook her head. "Of course. Just make sure it's not in anyone's way," but Ernest was already stepping past poor Markham and heading up the stairs.

"Would you like to hold the baby?" asked Leticia, thrusting the child at me. I had never held an infant before. The moment he was in my arms, my body ached to keep him there. Never have I missed my own child as much as I did in that first moment I held Leticia's eldest son.

"You're very early, dear," Rosaline commented politely, as we all followed Ernest towards the drawing room.

"My husband thought it might be fun to be here when the boys arrive." Leticia fluttered her eyelashes innocently.

"I thought they might fancy a little trip to the club." Ernest winced at his son's piercing wails. "Good lungs, that boy."

We had barely sat down when the doorbell rang again. Feeling obliged to answer it myself I got up, the fussing baby still in my arms, and went downstairs. I could hear Ada in the kitchen, yelling at Sissy, with Markham trying to appease her and Sissy protesting it was not her fault that the baker's boy was late.

I opened the door to Dr Campbell, who said observantly, "I hope I didn't catch you at a bad time."

"Not at all, do come in, we're all upstairs," I replied with an apologetic smile.

Despite the polite reserve between Rosaline and Dr Campbell, I had noticed her heightened colour whenever she set eyes upon him. On this day Simon Campbell's appearance in the drawing room resulted in her father adding him to the guest list for dinner the next evening. If Rosaline wasn't flustered enough at this point, Ernest supplemented her anguish by nudging the doctor in the ribs, nodding in her direction and saying loudly, "Getting your feet under the table nicely, hey, Campbell?"

"Ada will be most put out, Papa, all the orders have gone in for groceries," my poor friend hissed at her father. But I observed she was also suppressing a smile beneath the scarlet glow of her cheeks.

"Nonsense, where's your Christmas spirit, girl?" he replied with a pat on her hand. Dr Campbell shyly looked down at his feet and adjusted his shirt cuffs.

There was no time for any further discussion, for the front door bell rang once more. Everyone rose their feet and Leticia, I noticed, dusted down her dress and patted the back of her hair. In the hall Markham unlatched the door and Arthur's voice rang out cheerfully.

"Greetings of the season to you, Markham. Well, I hope? You remember my friend Boden-Howard, of course."

Anticipation of the meeting was beginning to make my stomach flutter. I tried to breathe slowly as footsteps drew close. But when the door finally opened, I found I could not breathe at all. Philip's glittering chocolate eyes glanced around the room with unfaltering confidence. His dark hair was ruffled in a most disorganised manner, his sideburns were trimmed to highlight his cheekbones perfectly, and his face looked as though it *had* been clean-shaven – the previous day. He smiled and the room seemed to brighten with the vibrancy of him. Arthur was, by all accounts, an extremely attractive man, but Philip Boden-Howard eclipsed him entirely.

Leticia gave a pretty little curtsey and Sissy, who had entered the room with the tea things, giggled and almost dropped a cup when she laid eyes on the new guest. Only Rosaline seemed immune to Philip's staggeringly good looks. She glared at him with her hands clasped firmly behind her back.

"Well, what a reception for an old friend," he said, breaking the silence. For a second his eyes rested upon me and the child in my arms. I squirmed. No man could be that attractive and have a good heart to go with it.

"Of course, old chap, do come in, you're always welcome." Dr Winston grasped Philip's hand and gave it a hearty shake.

Philip grinned with casual ease. As he patted the older man on the back one could have assumed it was his own father he was greeting. I thought of my husband and how easily all had befriended him, how I had fallen for the warmth of his smile and the glint in his pretty eyes. I was determined not to let such a thing happen again, ever.

"I have the pleasure of introducing to you Mrs More," Arthur turned to me with a sly smile.

"Good day, Mrs More, the pleasure is mine," Philip said with a polite nod in my direction. Suddenly I felt angry at his lack of attention. For once in my life I was at a total loss for words. Rocking the crimson-faced baby in my arms a little too vigorously, I stared at Philip.

Arthur took one look at his nephew's quivering bottom lip and said, "May I?"

For a second I didn't move, then Arthur extended his arms and I realised he meant to take the child.

"Oh, of course,' said I, praying my face was not flushing. Arthur scooped up Ernest Junior, swung him high above his head, and instantly the boy was giggling. Feeling the emptiness in my arms and the sting of regret that I had been unable to calm the child myself, I tried to smile.

"How's my favourite nephew?" Arthur inquired as the baby gurgled cheerfully. "Good as gold as always."

I watched Arthur in astonishment, for I had not imagined

such a side to him. I had never seen a man behave in such a maternal fashion before. Disappointment added sharply to my feelings, in the knowledge that I should never have the chance to be a mother again. Oh, how glad I am now, that I was wrong!

"He's your only nephew, old chap." Philip laughed at his soft-hearted friend and made a silly face at little Ernest, then looked up at Leticia. With apparently no sense of impropriety he added, "Very handsome, he looks just like his mother."

Leticia blushed and Ernest edged a little closer to his wife's side.

"You're just in time for morning tea," Rosaline interrupted.

"Ah, excellent," both men exclaimed together.

Several cucumber sandwiches later, the welcome party began to disperse, finally leaving Arthur, Rosaline and myself alone with Philip. The guest blinked his long eyelashes, sat back into his chair, ran a hand through his unbrushed hair and gave what I can only describe as the most contagious grin I have ever seen. I pursed my lips into a polite smile.

"I cannot tell you what a pleasure it is to make your acquaintance."

Rosaline eyed him suspiciously.

"Do you mind if I ask you some questions about your travels? I should like to know more about the events on the day you arrived here. I'd like to try to establish a cause or pattern to your experiences."

"Already, Philip?" Rosaline complained. "You've only just arrived.

"I don't mind," I offered, wanting to get the discussion over with so that I might avoid further conversations later.

"Excellent!" He extracted a pocket notebook and began to scribble away as he asked me a series of rapid questions.

What path had I walked that last day in fourteen ninety-two? How many steps had I taken to get there? How fast was I running? What had I eaten for supper the evening before? I was beginning to feel as though I were in session with Dr Winston, only conducted in a far less friendly fashion.

"I understand you cannot recall anything before your sixth birthday?"

I glanced at Rosaline, for no one outside her father's study would have known that. She winced.

"Forgive me, Catherine. Arty asked me how your treatment was going. I didn't think it would do any harm to tell him a few things."

"Nothing to forgive. I was just a little surprised, is all," I said truthfully.

Rosaline relaxed her shoulders and gave me a grateful smile.

Turning to Philip, I continued, "Dr Winston has been teaching me a technique to help me recover that lost time." I raised my eyes to meet his and found an intensity in his gaze that made my heart flutter. Quickly I lowered my eyes again and said, "I imagine my mind as a great house, filled with corridors and many rooms. Each time I go there I open new doors in the hope I can unlock that elusive part of my life."

He twisted the chain of his gold fob watch through his fingers.

"And you have not succeeded?"

I shook my head. "Each time I reach that door, it is locked and I cannot find the key. There have been only a few fleeting images that may belong to my early life, brought on by seeing something or going somewhere familiar, but I cannot be sure of anything. They are more like faded dreams than memories."

His eyes wandered over my face pensively. I began to turn my St Christopher pendant between my fingers. He had many more questions. Was there anything unusual about the weather? What could I hear? Did I recognise the woman I saw in the graveyard? I told him how light-headed I had become and how the lights had flashed about my head. It did not occur to me then, however, for I did not recall it until much later; that there had also been the queer vision of the man in the darkened room. Perhaps if I had remembered… ah, but there is little point considering anything now but what has actually transpired.

As he concluded his interview, Philip Boden-Howard clasped his hands together on the flat belly of his impeccably tailored waistcoat and drew a breath.

"Catherine." His words came slowly. "Are you quite certain that you have never been in contact with any kind of apparatus that could have engineered your initial transportation?"

Rosaline was shaking her head in disbelief. I considered the notion.

"I have no recollection of any such thing."

He sighed.

"Thank you, Mrs More, you have been most enlightening." Then his eyes lit up. "Now, would you all care for a nice stroll? It's a lovely crisp day out there; it seems a damn shame to miss the fresh air whilst we have it."

He was right, too. The sky was clear and the ground shimmered with a light coating of frost. Rosaline scowled at Arthur as Philip took my arm and threaded it through his, but Arthur neither did nor said anything to intervene. My instinct was to pull away, but I felt obliged to be polite. Philip's conversation was gentlemanly enough, but when he made enquiries regarding my family, a sudden chill of guilt scuttled up my spine as I thought of my husband. Philip stopped, assuming I was cold, removed his overcoat and draped it around my shoulders. As he did so, I felt a crackle of electricity when his gloved hand brushed against the back of my neck. Neither of us admitted to noticing, but I know he felt it too.

Dinner on the Saturday was entertaining yet uneventful. Philip flirted openly with every woman present, even Sissy. Rosaline raised her disapproving eyebrows more than once and I noted the look of horror that crossed her face when he leaned a little too close to Leticia and asked her how she liked her dessert. Later, as Rosaline sank back onto the chaise lounge in the parlour, I asked her why she minded so, when Ernest did not seem to. Rosaline looked over at me coolly and rested her head against the back of her chair.

"Ernest never notices anything." She lowered her voice and glanced over at where the gentleman were gathered by the fire. "But there was a time… when Philip and my sister paid each other a good deal of attention."

"Oh! Leticia was in love with him?" I asked, irritated at the tinge of jealousy that bit into my stomach.

"She never owned it, but…" Rosaline closed her eyes for a moment as though unsure how much to explain.

"When was this?" I asked carefully.

"1904, the summer before he and Arthur went to Oxford. They were at Eton together; they've been pals since they were boys. Lettie always showed a partiality towards Philip, even though she's two years older. That summer Philip's family invited us to their country home. We were only there a fortnight, but he gave us all cause to believe he had intentions towards her."

"He was so young," I found myself interrupting defensively. Considering I myself was married at a similar age, it was hardly a valid case for argument. Rosaline's lips thinned.

"Old enough to know better," she replied. "When we left they spoke privately and we all assumed they had come to an understanding." Rosaline rose and poured herself a glass of sherry from the sideboard cabinet. "Would you like one?"

"Thank you, yes."

"It was only after a month or two, when he had not written, that I asked her about it." She handed me the drink and sat back down. "Lettie defended him and said there had been no suggestion of a proposal, but I cannot imagine that she had not expected it to come. I heard her crying at night more than once. When she met Ernest a few months later, she seemed to improve. By the following Easter they were married. There was not even a flicker of regret from Philip; he simply sent a telegram congratulating them."

"Perhaps her love was not so strong as you thought," I mused.

"She and Mr James seem happy enough and now they have little Ernest... well, I suppose no harm came of it all in the end. But it's only a matter of time before Philip truly injures the feelings of some other poor unsuspecting woman. Or worse, gets them into trouble."

I wondered what Rosaline would think of me if I confessed my own sins. From that moment my distrust of Philip Boden-Howard was settled. He was no more than a wealthier version of Daniel.

MICHAEL

Oxford – 27th March, 2021

Placing his finger underneath the number, Michael removed the telephone receiver from its cradle and dialled. His hand was shaking so much he didn't turn the dial far enough and the number didn't connect. 'Bloody antique chic', he muttered, cutting off the call and beginning to re-dial. This time the numbers all clicked into place and the line began to ring. Paul was sitting on the couch where he had been the evening before, only now he was perched on the edge of the cushion, eagerly awaiting the response on the other end of the line. He had been as surprised as his father when they ran their search for the photographic studio and found it listed for Bicester. Michael jumped when a voice spoke in his ear.

"Hello, Gillman and Soame."

He looked over at his son.

"Hi, er... This might sound a bit of an odd question, but are you the same Gillman and Soame that used to be at 101 High Street, Oxford?"

"Umm, yes, sir, but not for more than a century." The woman's voice had the soft Oxfordshire lilt of a country local. A line of sweat broke out on Michael's forehead. There was a click. Michael looked around to see Imogen standing in the doorway. She had said she was too afraid listen to the call, but evidently she'd been unable to stand the suspense. As she stood there, as nervous as him, her presence gave Michael strength. He beckoned her in.

"Do you keep archives?" he asked as his wife slipped her

hand into his.

"Of course, sir. What is it you're looking for, a school, university?"

Michael's jaw dropped, he couldn't believe he was finally getting somewhere. He nodded at his family with widening eyes.

"That's great. Er, actually I'm looking to find information on a family member who went missing, and, well, all I have to go on is a photograph from your studio. There are four people in what looks like a family group. "

There was a pause and Michael's heart began to sink. Perhaps they only kept corporate records.

"That may take a little longer to look up; only the corporate records have been digitised. What's the relative's name?"

Michael's shoulders tensed as he replied,

"Possibly Catherine Alexander, but I'm afraid I can't be sure."

"OK, well, do you have any other names to go on?"

"Er, sadly not."

"All right, then, a date, perhaps?"

"Not specifically, but from the style of dress I would say Edwardian, pre First World War anyway."

"Well, that helps. The best thing for you to do is bring the picture in. That way we can look through the negatives for a match."

Michael set down the receiver, the anticipation already building like a vice around his heart. Could this finally be a way to find her? He glanced from his wife to his son and felt every bit as nervous as they looked.

"What are we waiting for?" Paul rose, as if to go right that moment.

"By the time we get over there this afternoon it'll be nearly closing time. We'd best wait till tomorrow." Michael was unsure whether that was true, or if he was just a little afraid of what they might – or worse, might not – find.

CATHERINE

London, 1906

On Monday morning Philip got it into his head that the four of us should visit the scene of my arrival into 1906. It was blowing a gale that day, and we should never have gone out if he had not insisted upon it.

As one might expect on Christmas Eve, the city was alive with people. Electric lights twinkled in the windows of Fortnum and Mason's, gift boxes and hampers shimmering beneath in the mellow glow. Women scurried by snuggled into warm coats, hands pushed into fur muffs; children skipped excitedly beside them; men battled along the streets with frowns upon their faces as they puzzled over last-minute gifts for their wives. A series of carriages raced past, crammed with people surrounded by boxes and brimming bags. Rosaline stood at the side of the road as elegantly as she could, with one hand planted firmly upon her hat and the other waving at Philip and me as we danced precariously between the carriages in the centre of the road.

"Do come back to the pavement before you're both trampled to death," she called.

An automobile beeped its horn and growled towards us in its unholy mechanical way. I screamed. Philip swiftly ushered me aside.

"Are you all right?" he asked with genuine concern.

"Yes, I think so," I replied, unsure whether the pace of my heart was down to the automobile or the feel of Philip's hand upon my back. He smiled and I gritted my teeth to fight away the flutter of desire.

"Hurry up, you two," called Arthur from his shelter beneath the arch of the Royal Academy gate. Philip waved at him as though he couldn't hear.

"Right," he said, lifting his hat and running a hand through his flattened hair, "can you remember exactly where you were standing?"

"I don't know," I stuttered, catching my breath as a gust of wind nearly swept me sideways, "it's all a bit of a blur. I think Rosaline would be a better judge."

"Very well, "he said. He turned to her and yelled, "Miss Winston! Would you care to join us for a moment?"

She glared at him and then rolled her eyes.

"Very well, but I think you have both lost your minds." She stepped out into the street and narrowly missed the great rolling wheels of a hansom cab. Mud splashed up and splattered her lovely fur coat. Rosaline exclaimed her disgust as Philip bit his lip and sheepishly shrugged an apology.

"Take care, Rosaline, please," he said with a grin as she made her way to where we were standing. Drivers and passengers were yelling at us to move out of the way, and even Arthur had covered his face with his hands in despair.

Rosaline walked a yard or two further down the road.

"This is it, I'm sure," she said. "When the omnibus stopped we were parallel to the flag." She pointed at the gallery roof.

"Capital!" said Philip, putting his hands in his pockets, swaying back on his heels and taking a good look around, like a sort of casual Sherlock Holmes. He stamped his feet on the cobbles to see if any were loose, and peered down at one that looked chipped. I half expected him to take a magnifying glass out of his pocket and begin to examine the ground. Rosaline and I had to laugh. He sniffed the chilly air and held out a finger as through feeling for the breeze.

"It's coming from the north," offered Rosaline flatly, for we could hardly have missed the gale-force wind.

"Shhh," he said, "I'm listening."

"For what?" Rosaline asked after a moment or two.

"Don't know," he replied. "Well, I can't see anything out of the ordinary," he shrugged, "let's get out of danger." With that he grabbed my hand and tugged me back towards the pavement. Rosaline put her hands on her hips and huffed.

"Perhaps if you had visited the site right after the event there would have been better results," Arthur suggested as we joined him. "It's too long ago now. Any evidence, or whatever it is that you're looking for, must be long gone."

"I believe you're right, but there *is* something here, I can feel it," replied Philip.

"Such as?" Arthur queried.

"I can't quite put my finger on it but my senses are just tingling, although…" his words trailed away. He held my gaze just a moment too long. I turned away furiously. He was not going to get the better of me.

MICHAEL

Oxford — 28th March, 2021

It was a crisp morning and the chill bit through his jacket as Michael led his family towards Gillman and Soame's studios. Usually he would have gone back to the car for his scarf and gloves; today, however, he was too distracted to care.

"Do slow down a bit, love." Imogen reached forward and slipped her leather-gloved hand into his.

"Sorry," Michael replied, reducing speed just a very little and noticing that her hand was shaking. He looked at her and smiled. Her dark hair glinted in the harsh whiteness of the winter sun. He was glad she had finally got round to dyeing it; the warm tones had taken ten years off her face. He gave her hand a squeeze as they reached the door.

Even though the location was different, there was something comforting in the knowledge that at some point in the not-too-distant past, his daughter had also entered the studios of these same photographers. He wasn't sure if he was excited or nervous.

The doormat beeped as they stepped inside. Immediately hot air from the over-door heater blasted on Michael's head. He pulled open his collar and unbuttoned his jacket. A busty redhead stood behind the counter. She looked up as they walked towards her.

"You must be Professor Alexander," she said with a welcoming smile. "We spoke yesterday afternoon."

"That's right. Thank you so much for this," he replied.

"Not at all." She glanced at Imogen and Paul. "How about one of you starts with the customer lists and two of you can get going on the negatives?"

"Great," Michael replied, impressed by her efficiency.

"Excellent, follow me, then," she said, pushing open a side door. Michael drew a breath and followed her.

The archive was large and somewhat cooler than the reception area. A single naked light bulb hung from the centre of the ceiling like a small tubular sun, growing gradually brighter as the power surged into it. All the walls were lined with dusty books and files. Ancient shelves bowed with the sheer weight of boxes piled high and shadows flickered around them like ghosts. Michael was suddenly daunted by the magnitude of the task.

The redhead went over to the far wall and pulled out a hefty ledger labelled 1901–5.

"These are the order books. Please put everything back where you find it. Oh, and..." she tugged open a stiff drawer from a low filing cabinet, "please wear these." She pulled out a handful of cotton gloves and handed them to Paul.

"This is fun," he beamed.

The redhead moved forward and gestured with her arm like a twentieth-century TV model displaying game show prizes.

"These are the private sitters. There looks to be quite a lot, but there's actually only a couple of boxes from that era. They're sectioned chronologically from the date the order was placed." She took down faded box and heaved it onto the table. "May I see the picture?"

Michael took the envelope from his pocket and removed the photograph.

"Handsome bunch," she said, examining the sepia image. "Your ancestor?" she asked, glancing up at Imogen.

"Er…" Imogen shivered and Michael placed a steadying hand on her back.

"Yes," he lied, thinking it was easier that way.

"You look a lot like her," she said flipping the image over. "From the clothes and typeface on the back I'd say try between 1904 and 1910."

"Thanks," Imogen replied, removing the lid from the box.

"I'm Claire, by the way," the girl said brightly. "Anything you need, just call. We're expecting a family in for a portrait at eleven, so if I'm not out front just knock on the studio door to the right of reception."

As they worked through the boxes Michael began to doubt they would find anything. The photograph sat on the table next to where he and Imogen worked. Paul closed one ledger, slid it back on the shelf and pulled out the next. Dust clouded off the cracked leather binding. He wafted his hand in front of his face and sneezed. Michael yawned and rubbed his eyes; they were beginning to sting. Paul plonked the ledger marked 1906–8 on the table with a thump. Imogen dropped the negative in her hand and stumbled back.

"Sorry Mum, didn't mean to make you jump."

But Imogen wasn't paying attention. She was staring at the negative, her whole body shaking like a startled doe. Michael's heart almost stopped.

"Im, what is it?

"Oh my God, Michael, that's it." His wife stepped back to the table and recovered the negative. She held it up to the light again in one jittery hand and held up the photograph with the other. Michael leaned in close and looked over her shoulder. He could smell her shampoo over the faint must of old books; he breathed it in and kissed the back of her head.

The pictures were a match. Imogen turned over the negative and noted down the reference number on the back. "Fetch Claire," she said, but Paul was already on his way.

A minute later Claire was opening the aged ledger and running her eyes over the pages.

"Here we go, number 327, April 7th, 1907. Order placed by P. Boden-Howard.

"Oh," said Michael, disappointed.

"Two copies to be collected and two to be sent to a Miss R. Winston of 52 Russell Square, London," Claire continued, looking up at her audience. "Not what you wanted to hear?" she asked, deflated by the looks on their faces.

"We were hoping for a reference to Catherine Alexander," Michael replied, "Does it list the names of all the sitters?"

"I'm afraid not. But you have two names and addresses to work from. Boden-Howard is listed as resident at Christ Church College, you should find him in the list of alumni."

Of course. Michael relaxed for the first time that morning and began to give in to hope.

"And there should be records of residents for 52 Russell Square as well. You could try the electoral roll," she added.

"Electoral registers won't help, women didn't have the right to vote till nineteen eighteen," Paul corrected.

"And that was only women over thirty," Imogen chipped in. The redhead wrinkled her freckled nose and folded her arms.

"Oh, that's right. The census should be all right though."

CATHERINE

London, 1906

I cannot tell you, dear journal, what a good feeling it is to watch the glisten of ink darken and dry upon your pages. My life so often feels naught but a fantastical dream, but as I write, the words give my journey form and clarity. But I tarry, I shall return to my story.

On Christmas Eve Rosaline and I returned from a shopping excursion to find the house filled with a delicious fresh scent. Standing in the parlour, its tip brushing the ceiling as though reaching for the stars, was a great pine tree. It was placed in a bucket by the window and propped upright by a heavy metal stand that Sissy had covered with brown paper. A huge box of pretty things glinted by its base. My friend clapped her hands in delight and began to pull a roll of red ribbons from the box and tie them to the branches. I had never seen the like.

"Of course. You wouldn't have had Christmas trees," she said, looking sorry for me. "You'll see how beautiful it is when it's finished." She handed me a tatty little box neatly packed with a rainbow of sparkling glass balls. "Just hang them on the branches, wherever you like." As she tied a selection of candles delicately to the more sturdy branches she added, "Next year Father has promised to get electricity installed, and then we can buy one of those modern strings of electrical lights instead."

"They have bulbs small enough?" I asked, trying to picture

the large lights that furnished Fortnum and Mason's window rendered over our tree.

"Oh, yes and far less dangerous than these old things." She prodded a candle, making its branch sway precariously. She then unpacked a set of red stockings from the box of delights and began to tie them at the side of the fireplace. I looked at the childish stitching that said 'Rosaline' and realised that she must have made it herself as a child.

"Did you make them all?" I asked.

"No. Mother made the others when I was ten. As you see, the rest are all executed by a far much more accomplished hand."

I considered how well I had worked a needle at ten years old and appreciated my talent. It was then that I noticed there was a fourth stocking in the name of Eliza. Rosaline caught my puzzled expression and smiled.

"She was eighteen months younger than me. She contracted diphtheria when she was eleven. Mother never really got over her death. I'm sure her poor health grew out of a broken heart. Papa thought so too." I watched my friend as she spoke. "Eliza was very pretty and so musical; she could play the pianoforte far better than the rest of us." As she talked I could see the sadness in her eyes and I thought my heart would break. "Papa too," she added, "finds it painful to speak of her, but he would feel it more keenly if we hid her memory altogether. We always hang her stocking."

I was fighting for composure as my friend handed me a golden star and climbed upon the stool.

"But does anyone ever recover from the death of a child?" she said, almost to herself.

That was the thread that broke me. I sobbed. And once begun, I could not stop.

"Gracious, Catherine, I didn't mean to upset you."

"You didn't, it is only that I..." I could not force the words out but my dear friend could see it upon my face.

"Oh Catherine... you lost a child." Rosaline was down from the stool, wrapping her arms around my shoulders and leading me to the couch before I could speak. "I'm so sorry. You don't have to explain."

"Forgive me for not telling you before," I begged. "It is so painful, I didn't know how..."

The whole story erupted out of me like a volcano and she listened with as much patience as Father Thomas. When I was done she said nothing, she just drew me in and hugged me, letting my tears bleed through the fabric of her gown as an open wound through a bandage. We were still like that when the door handle turned and Philip entered.

"Forgive me the intrusion, I was wondering if you required any assis– oh." He stopped. "I should go."

I cannot describe to you the look I saw upon his face at that moment. Hesitating, he stepped forward and offered me his handkerchief.

"Is there anything I can do for your relief?"

I thanked him and dabbed my cheeks. His chocolate eyes seemed to reflect my pain. For a moment all I wanted was for him to kiss me. Too weak to check myself I simply said, "There is nothing anyone can do. It is all past."

And that is the truth. Though we should not forget our past, we must seize today and live it as best we can.

Philip bowed and took his leave.

After a most lively Christmas luncheon our increased party of some twenty-two retired to the parlour for entertainment. There was a card table for bridge and Leticia played the pianoforte for some of the guests' children to dance to.

"Anyone for charades?" said one of the elder boys. Somehow I was required to join in this game. But if course I was rather useless, I did not know half the things they were performing and some of the gestures were lost on me entirely. After a short while Philip came to my rescue. He suggested we withdraw from the hilarities and take a seat in a quiet corner. There was a moment of awkward silence when I knew not what to say, then it occurred to me that I had learned precious little about him.

"Tell me, sir, why are you not with your family for the holidays?"

Philip gave a sigh.

"There are several answers to that question, and I fear not one of them is remotely interesting."

I narrowed my eyes. Of course such a comment sparked a great interest in me.

"Please, pray tell."

"I would not deny any request of yours, Catherine," he said with a grin that was less artful than I had expected. "Well," he continued, "my sister Evelyn has gone to be with her husband's family in Derbyshire."

"Your sister is the elder?"

"By quite a few years," he replied. "And please don't call me sir," he chastised playfully. He had corrected me on this before but I preferred to maintain the formality between us, however ill it worked. "Being the baby and the only boy, you can imagine I was rather spoiled." His grin became mischievous. "And the reason Evelyn and I have scattered, is that mother and father have gone to winter in Egypt, so the house is all shut up. If I had gone home I should have been alone with a few dusty old servants and a rather large empty house."

"Egypt?" I said, surprised, my mind conjuring up images of all the mummies and statues in the British Museum.

"My father suffers from terrible arthritis in his legs and his doctor recommended the sun would ease the pain. Fabulous place, so many great ruins, and far better weather. The sort of place Arthur should go; steeped in history." As he spoke his soft brown eyes shone with the glitter of candlelight.

"You have been there?" I asked, fighting the urge to lay my hand over his.

"Yes, last Christmas. The parents have been going there now for three years and last year they bought a house in Luxor."

"They did?" I said, astonished. Despite his title it had not really occurred to me just how wealthy his family were.

"I think you would love Egypt. Beauty and mystery is something you both have in common."

The flattery was so utterly contrived that any fluttering in my heart was halted. I raised my eyes to his with more confidence. His smile was broad and easy, but his eyes were pensive.

"There is little about me that you do not know, sir."

"I think there is a great deal I do not know, but I would like to, very much." His voice was low and soft. I turned away. Across the room I caught Rosaline looking in our direction with a disapproving arch in her eyebrows.

"Your husband is very lucky, Mrs More," he added, just as we were interrupted by Rosaline's announcement.

"Time for gifts, everyone!"

A little later she and I were taking a turn about the room when she took my arm and said kindly, "Catherine, do be careful. Philip is a very caring sort, that is why it's so easy to fall in love with him. I'm just not sure he is capable of actually falling in love himself."

"You have no need to worry. Falling in love with anyone is the last thing I have on my mind," I replied, "especially with Philip Boden-Howard. Besides, whatever century I may reside in, I am still married to Daniel." I realised in that moment that I no longer resented my husband. In fact I almost pitied him. If I could have released us both from our vows I would have done so right then, for he must have wanted rid of me just as much as I regretted marrying him. I prayed he was getting on well without me.

"Glad to hear it," Rosaline smiled. "Philip is the last man I would advise any woman to fall in love with."

MICHAEL

Oxford — 28th March, 2021

The sun streamed through the window onto the computer screen. Michael was glad Paul had been able to stay and help him continue their search. He pulled the curtain part-way across to shield them from the glare, and sent a light coating of dust into the warm atmosphere of the study. Sunlight glinted on the particles and created a shimmering beam across the room. Michael dusted the screen of his laptop with his cardigan sleeve.

"There," said Paul as the alumni for Christ Church college appeared. Michael shook his head in disbelief.

"How on earth did I not see that?"

Paul peered at the name and credentials his father had clicked on.

"Oh, him! Dad, he was only your main inspiration!"

"Exactly!" Michael was still shaking his head. "Did I tell you my grandpa was his teacher at Eton too?"

Paul rolled his eyes.

"Only about two hundred times."

Philip Boden-Howard had not only been a student of Mathematics at the university, but he had taught there for several years. His interests had spread further than pure mathematics and out into the realm of theoretical physics, which some at the time found fanciful and eccentric. Had it not been for Dr Boden-Howard, Michael might never have been drawn into experimenting with time travel at all. And if the First World War had not interrupted Boden-Howard's work, then Michael's own projects might have been very different indeed. The irony and the potential paradox did not go unnoticed.

"Well, that makes it easier, anyway," Paul grinned. "Aristocracy are easy to trace."

But as they trawled the records they drew a blank. There were no Catherines at all listed in his household, and no evidence on any census for Hatherley Park. Michael turned to Miss R. Winston of 52 Russell Square. There had been an Arthur Winston listed in the Christ Church alumni for the same graduation year as Boden-Howard. He crossed his fingers and hoped this was going to be the missing link.

Michael opened the birth index on the General Register. Clicked on female, London, and then typed in Winston, R, 1880 +/- 5. It was a long-drawn-out process. *It would have been so much quicker if we could have just looked through the actual books,* he thought, resenting technology for the first time in his life. He sighed as he ran his eyes down the first page. Rachel, Rebecca, Rosaline, Rosanna, Rose. Good grief, there were five for the first quarter of 1880 alone. Michael switched his search to the column at the far end, 'location.' Two were the right district, Rachel and Rosaline.

Paul had settled at the other side of the desk with his tablet. He looked up.

"Here's another Arthur Winston, Dad. Who knew Winston would turn out to be such a common name?"

"What year are you in?"

"1888," Paul replied. Michael moved around the table so he was looking over his son's shoulder. The sub-district for Arthur matched that of Rosaline.

"Well, that's a start. I'll order the birth certificates. Why don't you start searching for marriages, and I'll continue on births in case there are any other likely options.

"Sure."

CATHERINE

London, 1907

For the rest of the holidays I remained determined to avoid Philip's flirtations, and Rosaline seemed equally keen to assist me. Our combined efforts succeeded in preventing Philip and me from spending more than five consecutive minutes alone together. If Philip was irked by this, he did not show it, and so I happily concluded that he was indeed nothing but a flirt. And when Arthur asked us to join him in Oxford for a few days over Easter, we presumed Philip would be elsewhere. We were wrong.

I could have sworn Philip had grown taller and his face seemed even more handsome. He had smoothed his hair and looked elegant and mature. When he kissed the back of my hand, I bit my lip as the soft touch made my stomach flip. I forced my feelings back and set my mouth into a determined line of displeasure, and prayed that he would soon disappoint or vex me in some way that would turn me against him once and for all.

Rosaline and I were installed once more at the Clarendon, with both boys spending as many hours as they could in our company. We took walks through Christ Church meadow, the morning mist swirling about our skirts and chilling our ankles. We talked endlessly, sitting in the tearooms and cafés. We ate at all the best restaurants, walked the halls of the museums and through the grounds of the colleges. It was a perfectly pleasant time, and not once did Philip say or do anything that was in anyway ungentlemanly.

On our last afternoon, climbing precariously into a punt at Magdalen Bridge, I settled myself onto the cushioned seat and laughed at Philip as he pushed and shoved the pole through the thick vegetation of the Isis. He cursed and muttered under his breath as we turned and bumped our way from the jetty and onto the river. His frustration heightened further when Arthur glided past us with ease.

"Don't think I'm going to be out-done by you, Winston, just because you row for the blues," Philip called, as Arthur gave him a cheery wave from twenty yards ahead. It took him several minutes to find his way forward but once he did we were away. The boatman yelled his warnings at us as we raced on. Other punters called their annoyance as we shoved past them, bouncing off their sides and creating waves along the mill-pond flow of the river. I was laughing at first, but as we collided with our third punt and sent them hurtling into the river bank I begged, "Do slow down, we'll knock someone overboard if we're not careful."

"Don't be a fuss pot," Philip said, but when he saw my whitening face he did as I asked. "Oh, my dear, I'm sorry. I didn't mean to frighten you." From the boat in front I heard Arthur's laughter.

"The cricket pitch I shall concede to you gladly, Boden-Howard," Arthur called, "but the water, never." Philip growled at him like a playful puppy.

"Arty, you're too much," Rosaline said as I peered past their boat at the distant club house. There were no cricket matches to be watched that day. I suspect if there had been, we might have missed the river and taken cream tea there instead.

We were all in high spirits when we disembarked, especially after the boatman gave Arthur and Philip a good talking-to. We were still laughing as we stumbled back along the High, so much so that when we passed the window of a local photographer,

Philip got it into his head that we needed a keepsake.

"What better way to remember today?" he said, pushing open the door.

"Really? I don't think I want to," said Rosaline reluctantly. Arthur cupped his hands around the sides of his face and peered inside.

"There appears to be someone free to serve us," he announced.

"Excellent. Come along, ladies," said Philip shoving open the door, "it'll be fun. Do say you will."

"I must look a fright after the river," said I, considering the longevity of a picture.

"You both look exquisite," Arthur said with a wink at me, as he turned to face his sister. "There are bound to be mirrors inside, my dear."

Rosaline looked down at her gown and glanced at the position of her hat from her reflection in the window.

"All right," I said with a grin.

Philip looked ecstatic as we all turned to my friend. "Do say yes."

After a moment's pause, a broad smile spread over her lips.

"Fine," she said, stepping through the door Philip was now holding open.

Ten minutes later we were standing in a large studio before a gentleman in a brown satin waistcoat and sporting a healthy moustache. The gentleman was adjusting Philip's collar and instructing him on where to stand. Arthur was laughing at Philip's expression. He was mimicking the sour-faced look of a man and his wife whose portrait was hanging on the wall.

"Why are they not smiling?" I asked innocently.

"Why not indeed?" Philip replied as his face crumpled into a grin.

"You look perfect, madam," the photographer said to Rosaline. Then he turned to me. He looked me over carefully and said, "I think a quick tidying of the hair might help."

I went over to the mirror and unpinned my hat. My hair was a mess. It was never neat, no matter how well it was done, but the breeze on the river had dislodged the style almost completely. I had to call Rosaline over to help me fix it. I tugged at my blouse to neaten the neckline and smoothed down the front of my skirt.

"There, that's better," my friend said stepping back and admiring her work. She pinned my hat back onto my head and smiled.

"What background would you like?" the photographer asked.

We chose a scene of a country meadow. Chairs were placed in the foreground and Rosaline and I took our positions. Arthur stood behind his sister with a hand resting on the back of her chair and one leg crossed over the other with a swagger and salute. Philip and I began to laugh, forcing Rosaline to turn and look. The photographer gave us an 'I'm waiting' glare. We attempted to regain our composure.

"I think Catherine is right," Philip said as he took up his place behind me, "we should be smiling. This is a beautiful and happy day."

"Agreed," replied Arthur. "Ladies?"

"Agreed," said we.

Then Philip added, "And better a smile than a rod up our arses." The shock of the crudity made the photographer's face turn puce.

We were still laughing as we tumbled back out into the light of day. I tripped over the step and Philip caught me. Lifting me into his arms he spun me about. With the sun and spring air caressing my face I found I was smiling into his eyes as he set me back on my feet.

"You are a truly remarkable woman." His eyes were lit with such fire I thought he would kiss me. But he did not. He stopped abruptly as though catching his breath. "Forgive me," he muttered. Ahead of us I heard Arthur clear his throat.

"Luncheon?" he said. "I don't know about you two, but my sister and I are ravenous."

Rosaline's mouth was smiling but there was a warning in the ice-blue of her eyes that reminded me of my resolve not to warm to Philip.

"No need to worry," I whispered as I joined her. "I'm perfectly safe."

"You just make sure that you stay that way." Her eyes softened and she threaded my arm through hers. "Both of you," she added under her breath.

I do not think she meant me to hear it, but once I had, I could not help but wonder if she had really seen something in his manner towards me that was different from that to any other. Yet I still did not believe him when he promised to write to me. You can imagine, then, my great astonishment when a letter did arrive not a fortnight later. He was all apologies that he had not put his pen to paper sooner, but he had been working very hard on his final exams and had only now found a moment to consider finding some explanation for my situation. He was warm and friendly in tone and most enthusiastic about his work. He talked of papers by scientific men I had never heard of, and used terms I could not comprehend, such as quantum and entropy. And so it was that I took his correspondence to be a part of his project rather than of any intentions towards my person, and gladly replied.

There were two or three more letters over the following weeks, equally friendly yet professional in tone, then, to my even greater surprise, I received another letter which read thus:

I cannot tell you how much I have missed the pleasure of your company, and hope that you will agree to join me at my family home for the summer season. Arthur will of course be there and so it only remains for you and Rosaline to accept. Do say you will come...
Yours etc

I cannot say whether I was simply curious to see his family home and meet his parents, or if I was actually compelled to see Philip again, but, despite my better judgement I was minded to accept.

Rosaline was out. She had gone over to help Leticia with baby Ernest, for Lettie was pregnant again and suffering rather with sickness. I had finished afternoon tea and was sitting in the drawing room watching the comings and goings of the square when I caught a glimpse of her through the trees. I had grabbed the letter and was downstairs before she reached the front door, and hovering in the hall when her outline appeared through the glass panel.

"Gracious, Catherine, are you quite all right?" she said in alarm.

"Forgive me. I... please read this." I said, thrusting the letter at her. Looking at me with slightly narrowed eyes and a raised eyebrow she took the sheet of paper and sat down on the brocade bench by the front door. I watched as her eyes skimmed from left to right.

After a few moments she lowered the letter into her lap and looked up at me.

"Well... Arthur had mentioned going to Hatherley for the summer, but I hadn't expected the invitation to extend to us." She examined my expression. "And if I didn't know better, I would say you are rather keen to accept."

I looked down at my feet and tried to establish the cause of my nervousness. Rosaline continued.

"I do like Philip, you know. I know what I have always said, but I do think him a good sort of man. I merely find it difficult to trust him where women are concerned."

"As do I... and yet... I do find I am curious to see him again."

"So I see."

"And I promise my heart will not be dented by anything he does."

There was a rather long pause as her eyes penetrated mine.

"Then we shall go," she said at last, to my great relief. "But it is you alone I trust with your heart, and not Philip."

And so it was settled. On June fifteenth we were to take the train as far as St Albans where we would be met by his father's carriage.

MICHAEL

Oxford – 10th April, 2021

Michael was on his way down stairs in his gardening shorts and t-shirt. Imogen had insisted he tear his nose away from the computer and get outside for a while. The plan was to mow the lawn and get on with some desperately overdue weeding. They were having a warm spell so Imogen had invited a few friends over for an Easter barbeque later, and she had decided the garden needed a good preening before they dared let anyone sit out there. She called in through the back door.

"Are you coming? I'll have finished the roses before you even come out."

"Be right there," he replied as footsteps came up the drive.

A second later a thick brown envelope slipped through the letterbox and flopped onto the doormat. Michael paused to see if anything else was to follow, but the postman headed back down the path. Edging closer, Michael almost dared not look at the franking on the envelope. He picked it up carefully and read the mark of the public records office.

Instead of going down the hall to the kitchen he turned the handle of his study door and slipped inside. Through the open window he could hear the click-click of Imogen's secateurs. The smell of warm air and flowers made him smile as he sat down in his chair and carefully opened the envelope.

Inside were five certificates. He slid them out onto the desk and unfolded the first. Birth: Name – Arthur Gerald Winston.

Father – Arthur Albert Winston. Mother – Olivia Jane Winston, nee Parks. Father's occupation – doctor. Place of birth – Islington, London.

Michael drew a deep breath and opened the second. Birth: Name – Rosaline Olivia Winston. Father – Arthur Albert Winston. He couldn't believe it. They were a match. Now all he had to do was find the link to his daughter. With a shaking hand he opened the next, but it was the extra one Paul had insisted they should order as well. It documented the marriage of Leticia Gail Winston and Ernest James.

What Michael had underestimated was the historian's intuition of his son. Residence at time of marriage – 52 Russell Square, London. Bride's father – Arthur A Winston, doctor. Michael's heart almost stopped. Hurriedly he checked the last two marriage certificates, one for Rosaline and the other for Arthur, for their residence at the time of their marriages – 52 Russell Square. 'Oh, my God,' he gasped to himself. But where's Catherine? He picked up the certificate for Leticia again. Date of marriage – April 20th 1905, age 21. She could just be another Winston sibling. After all, why would Catherine change her name to Leticia, but Gail? It was all too much.

Now he had the information, what on earth was he going to do with it? Nothing actually proved Catherine was there; and if she was Leticia, then she had married, and might very well have had children. Did he have the right to take her away from her family? The questions swirled around in Michael's head until he felt sick. Finally he picked up the phone.

The line rang out several times. Michael was about to hang up when a breathless voice said,

"Y'ello, Paul's phone."

Michael rolled his eyes.

"Hello, Lewis, is Paul there?"

Paul shared student digs with three other boys in Jericho. Michael didn't really see why his son had wanted to move out and pay rent when he could have stayed at home for nothing, but his son had been adamant.

The boy replied, "Sorry, Prof, I just walked in the front door, his phone was on the kitchen table. Hang on."

Michael looked at the clock: it was quarter to nine. He hoped Lewis meant that he was up early and had been out already, and not that he had only just crawled home. He heard him yell.

"Paul, you up there? Phone."

From somewhere in the house at the other end of the line a woman's voice called back.

"He's in the shower. Who is it?"

Michael raised an eyebrow as he listened.

"Hi, Mil, it's the Prof."

Mil? Now Michael's mind was doing overtime with more questions, only now they were regarding his eldest child.

"Hang on a sec, the water just went off. I'll see if he's finished."

There were more muffled voices and Michael realised the girl had actually gone into the bathroom to disturb his son. *Well, well,* thought Michael, *that does explain a few things.*

"He's on his way," said Lewis and set the phone down.

Michael listened to the thunderous footsteps as Paul ran down the stairs.

"Cheers, Lew," he said as he picked up the phone. "Morning, Dad, everything OK?"

"Why didn't you tell me you were going out with Millie Penning?"

Michael heard Paul draw a breath,

"We're not exactly going out, we're, er... just sort of... well... seeing each other."

"Just sort of 'sleeping together' you mean."

"Dad!" Paul sounded horrified.

"I'm not a total dinosaur, son." Michael heard Paul laugh.

"All right, well, if you want to put it like that. Look, we bumped into each other a few weeks ago in the Turf and we hit it off."

Michael smiled. It was about time Paul found a nice normal girl, rather than some of the politically active anarchists he usually brought home.

"Well, you just be good to her. She's a nice girl."

"And I'm not a nice boy, hey, Dad? You just like Millie 'cause she was Catherine's friend. Anyway, my love life is definitely not the reason you called. So come on, spill..."

Michael cleared his throat and told Paul what he had discovered from the certificates.

"Well done, by the way. That was good deduction with Leticia," he finished.

"Thanks," there was a pause. "Dad, I don't think Leticia is Catherine. I know Gail is her middle name too but it's probably just coincidence."

"It's a pretty unusual name for the period."

"True, but I still don't think... anyway..."

A bee hovered by the study door for a moment then changed its mind and headed up the stairs. Michael watched it leave then looked down at the piece of green paper again.

"So, where do we go from here?"

There was a thoughtful pause.

"I've got an idea. Why don't we take an ad in a newspaper?"

"Asking for information on the Winston family?"

"Exactly. National and local. I mean, Lord knows where the descendants might be now. If anyone's still alive that remembers them, they could be anywhere in the world. Most papers publish their classifieds online now, so it should reach everyone."

"Excellent idea. Thanks, Paul."

"No sweat, Dad. See you later."

Michael had a sudden thought.

"Paul, why don't you bring Millie this afternoon?"

He heard Paul's smile as he replied, "Ok, I'll see if she's free."

Good, thought Michael, *so he does really like her, then.*

CATHERINE

Hertfordshire, 1907

Amongst the rolling green hills the gold of corn danced behind the blue of cornflower and clashed with the scarlet reds of swaying poppies. Nestled between the kaleidoscopes of colour was Hatherley House, a stately rectangle of yellow stone rising from the lakeside and littered with small spires and a great classical portico. A mass of windows glinted in the sporadic sunlight. After what felt like an age since we had passed the gateposts, we finally pulled off the drive and crunched onto a wide expanse of gravel. As the carriage door clicked open and swung back, I was so mesmerised that I did not register Lady Hatherley's presence for a moment.

Philip's mother was tall and heavy set, with a mass of white hair that she wore pinned up loosely like a big fat hat on top of her head. She might have been a large woman, but her manner was so meek and quiet she could hide in plain view. She walked quietly down the front steps, emerging from the vast Hellenistic columns like a shadow behind an immaculately presented footman.

The driver began to unload our bags from the top of the carriage.

"Miss Winston, it's lovely to see you again, it has been far too long," Countess Hatherley said, as we crossed the gravel towards her.

"Forgive me, Mother, I'm forgetting my manners."

Philip bounded down the steps and came over to join us. His

apparel was surprisingly casual: he wore a pair of light-coloured trousers, a matching loosely fitted jacket and a shirt that was open at the neck. Rosaline gave a polite nod of her head and held out a kid-gloved hand towards our hostess.

"It is always a pleasure to see you," she replied.

"Are you going to introduce me to your ravishing friends?" This deep soft voice came out of the dark porch. A scraggy gentleman with unruly white hair tapped the silver tip of his walking cane on the ground and painfully made an effort to follow his son. Philip was about to stop him, but his mother laid a hand on his arm and shook her head.

"Let him come, you know how he hates a fuss," she said, stepping back. "His arthritis is playing up," she whispered to Rosaline.

Lord Rupert, as he has bid us call him, was indeed a proud man. He stood over six feet tall, like a spindly beanstalk. Still handsome, his features were strong and kind with a sparkle of charm in his eyes that no doubt made many a woman swoon his in younger days.

"You remember Arthur's sister, of course," Philip smiled. Lord Rupert bowed as best he could manage then took Rosaline's hand and kissed it.

"A pleasure as always, Miss Winston," he said.

"And this is Mrs More."

Lord Rupert squinted his gentle brown eyes at me as a slow smile touched his lips.

"My dear, it is truly a pleasure to meet you."

"Thank you so much for inviting us," I replied.

"Not at all, child, I am delighted to make the acquaintance of any of my son's friends, but one he speaks of so highly cannot expect to avoid an invitation to join us here for the summer."

I was all astonishment. I had not imagined Philip would have actually said more than a few passing words about me in order to secure the invitation.

"Where is my brother?" asked Rosaline suspiciously.

Philip gave us a wicked wink.

"Playing tennis with Charlotte."

I looked at them both from an explanation but Rosaline appeared as blank as I.

"Surely Arthur has mentioned my cousin? Really?" he said, with a sideways smirk when we shook our heads. "Well, you'll love her, and she's staying for the summer too. Shall we join them?"

Rosaline looked at me for a response. I shrugged for I had never played tennis in my life, nor ever seen a game.

"Why not," she answered.

"Forgive us, Papa, Mother. We shall see you at dinner."

With that Philip was on his way down the gravel path that wound around the side of the house.

The tennis court was outdoors at the back of the house, and exposed to the full blistering heat of the sun. I had not even known tennis could be played outdoors until then. Neither Rosaline nor I were really dressed for the occasion. I in particular found the restrictions of my corset, the tightness of my blouse and the weight of my skirt, rather too unforgiving for such running about.

I still marvel when I contemplate the outward freedom of the Edwardian woman, well educated, free to go where she pleases, able to own property in her own right and to marry, for the most part, by choice, and yet she was as restricted by her undergarments as I have been by the laws of the church and land. Women will never be truly free so long as we are constrained, whether that be in the literal or social sense.

My apologies, I digress.

Out of breath and exhausted in ten minutes flat, I surrendered to the heat of the afternoon and settled, instead, for watching the others play. The game went on for some time, and despite Rosaline's protestations that she needed to be wearing a 'proper tennis skirt,' she was rather good at it. She and Philip made easy work of beating Arthur and little Charlotte.

When I introduce Philip's cousin as little, I do not mean it in reference to her age, though she was only sixteen, but I am referring to her stature. Charlotte was a petite girl of approximately five feet tall, with a tiny waist, a neat, compact frame and what can only be described as flame-red hair. Her eyes were a soft tone of reddish brown, set in a lightly freckled face that seemed to co-ordinate perfectly with her hair. She was pretty, dainty, fast on her feet and was by far the most determined creature I have ever met. I could see from the way she hammered the ball over the net that she would never give in once she had set her mind to something. And the thing she had most set her mind upon, that summer, was Arthur. She barely spared him a moment to himself. She followed him around like a lap dog, attracting everyone's attention and speculation, including Rosaline's.

To my increasing discomfort, her second choice of project seemed to be Philip and me. On several occasions I caught her watching me when I was talking to Philip, and each time, she would flash me a cheeky smirk that lit her amber eyes into a devilish glow of encouragement. It was not, however, until about half way through our visit that she actually passed comment on the subject.

The day in question was some time at the start of August,

and began with the rain spattering a light tune against the breakfast-room window. The greyness of the morning threatened our picnic plans, and Charlotte was sitting opposite me, pouting with disappointment. I watched as she looked up longingly at the heavy sky for a promising patch of blue, but there was none to be found. She sighed for the twentieth time.

"Lottie dear, there are plenty of other things in this house you can occupy yourself with," Lady Mariah offered patiently.

Charlotte opened her mouth as though to reply but then closed it again with a thoughtful pause. She glanced sideways at Arthur. My friend seemed oblivious to his admirer's advances. I suspected he actually rather liked her, but was keeping a cool head about the matter, at least in front of us.

"You could choose a book from the library. It would do you good to sit quietly for once, I'm sure." The countess reached for a slice of toast from the rack.

Charlotte looked over at me with an 'oh, good grief' expression. My attempt at a disapproving response failed dismally and I was forced to suppress a grin when Philip, too, caught my eye and winked. Charlotte observed us both, bristling with mischief.

Despite the increasing frailty of his physique, when Lord Rupert entered a room, the room stopped and looked. He had the presence of a prince and the waspish wit of Oscar Wilde. When I looked at his father, Philip was entirely explained to me. He was the very image of him in manner, feature and intellect, so much so that one could easily envisage what Philip would look like in forty years.

Lord Rupert sat down at the head of the table. I bid him good morning.

"And a very good morning to you, Mrs More," he replied, "Did you sleep well?"

"As well as ever, sir," I admitted.

The hesitation of my answer misled my host into an assumption that was only partially true.

"I do hope this creaky old house isn't disturbing your rest," he said, with genuine concern.

"Oh no, not at all. It is only that I sleep so lightly."

"There are some bangings and thumpings during the dark hours in these old walls, that's true enough. Why, Mariah barely slept a wink the whole first year we were married. Isn't that right, dear?"

The countess looked at her husband from the other end of the table, ignoring a stifled giggle from Charlotte.

"It's so long ago I can hardly remember," she said with a gentle smile.

"Isn't that kind, reminding me of my elderly state," he replied, with an exaggerated look of desolation.

"How old is the house?" Rosaline asked, pouring herself a second cup of tea. She dropped a sugar lump into her cup with a splash that made me jump.

Philip leaned towards me, a little too close. "Surely you're not really scared?" he whispered.

I shook my head and hoped my cheeks were not burning as red as they felt.

"My ancestor, Edward Howard, built the place for his wife in 1639," Lord Rupert replied.

I looked around at the elegant décor and pastel walls. It had not occurred to me to consider the age of the house before, but as my eyes skimmed the Goya portrait that hung over the mantle, I realised just how many generations of Philip's family had passed through those rooms, and likely sat at a table in the same place as we were sitting at that moment. The walls were covered with their images. And yet I had played in the streets of Oxford and sat sewing at my own table long before the first foundation stone of this house had ever been laid. For a moment I felt as though all of history were happening simultaneously. I took a sip of tea to calm my nerves.

"Edward married the then Countess of Hatherley, the only surviving child of the second Earl, Henry Boden. You probably saw Edward's portrait in the ballroom. He's the handsome Cavalier with the long hair and sharp moustache." Lord Rupert's enthusiasm was such that everyone was listening intently. Even Philip and Charlotte, who must have heard the family stories a hundred times, seemed to enjoy his account.

"I should love to have grown up in a place like this," said Arthur, leaning forward eagerly.

"These old walls are as much a part of the family as my own children," said Lord Rupert. "Did you know there are more priest holes and secret tunnels than there are tapestries?"

"Really? How fascinating," I said, surprised that Charlotte had not already given us a tour.

"It made eavesdropping rather a sport," Philip grinned.

"My children were 'all ears' when they were small," Lord Rupert laughed.

"What is a priest hole?" I asked, hoping I didn't sound too uneducated.

Arthur looked at me kindly and said, "It's where they used to hide Catholics and recusants during the Civil War."

"Oh."

I suddenly felt a little uncomfortable as I recalled Arthur's history lessons. "I see. Were there many people who hid here?"

"Oh, yes, several, mostly family of course. We even have some seventeenth-century graffiti in one of the holes."

"It's a heart around the letter P. When Philip was little, he used to say it was for him," teased Charlotte.

Philip raised an eyebrow at her and ran his hand through his hair.

"Catherine is a Catholic, too, Uncle Rupe," Charlotte added.

"Then it's a good thing you don't live in the seventeenth century, Mrs More, or you would be hiding in the dark confines of the inner walls, rather than eating out here at the breakfast table," Lord Rupert smiled.

Rosaline gave me a cautioning look and kicked her brother's ankle under the table, fearing that he or Philip would say something unwise. Whatever Arthur was about to say died upon his lips and instead Philip said, "Ours is one of the few aristocratic families who kept their faith intact, though it wasn't without cost."

"Oh?"

Lord Rupert smiled sadly.

"There was more than one raid on this house at that time. We were even forced out of the park for a short while, but we only lost one family member to Cromwell."

"The family ghost," chipped in Charlotte.

"Ghost?" said Rosaline incredulously.

"Well, sort of. A cousin of the countess was hiding here in 1646. One morning there was a raid and she vanished without a trace. The story goes that she was hurt in the tunnels and left there for dead, eventually dying of starvation. At night she hammers on the walls, still trying to attract attention for someone to let her out." Charlotte's eyes were large and round as she spoke.

"You know very well that the tunnels were searched thoroughly, Lottie. She probably ran away and found safety elsewhere, changed her name and lived happily ever after," said Lady Mariah. "You really do have a wild imagination, dear."

Charlotte shrugged.

"I didn't make it up, Aunt M. I'm only the story-teller."

Lady Mariah shook her head and smiled.

Then Charlotte let out a bright squeak. "That's given me an idea! Let's play hide and seek!"

Rosaline looked mildly alarmed, but the young men were enthusiastic.

"Why not? Seems just the ticket on a rainy day," said Arthur.

"There now, you have your occupation." Philip prodded his cousin in the ribs playfully.

Charlotte rose to her feet and dusted a few crumbs from her lilac skirt.

"Do you mind if I don't?" said Rosaline. "I thought I might write to Father."

"Simon Campbell is more like it," Arthur smirked.

He received another kick under the table.

"Do play, you can hide with me," I said, setting my teacup in its saucer.

"Oh, that won't do at all," Charlotte replied, with a scowl in my direction. "Girls hide and boys seek. We all go our separate ways."

As she walked past Arthur she casually brushed her hand over the back of his arm. Arthur, I noticed, smiled.

"Just how dark is it in there?" I asked nervously.

"Oh very! People have been lost for days," Philip said darkly.

I looked up at him in alarm. Lord Rupert intervened.

"Don't let him frighten you, he's only teasing. We haven't lost anyone in there for, oh, at least five years."

I laughed.

"Ignore them both, ladies, said Lady Mariah. "When we had the electricity generator installed we had the wires run through the passages as well as the house."

"Are you sure you'd rather stay and write your letters?" I asked Rosaline.

"Yes, thank you." Rosaline looked relieved, and for some reason, so did Charlotte.

"Very well. Come along then." Charlotte grabbed my hand and pulled me from my seat.

"Capital," Arthur shoved the last half sausage in his mouth and pushed back his chair.

"Count to a thousand," commanded Charlotte, "and don't forget, Philip, there is always a right way to go."

I found this a rather odd comment but had not the chance to question it, for she tugged me towards the door and out into the corridor. As the door closed behind us she leaned in close to me and whispered, "Confess it. You cannot deny you're in love with him."

Startled, I stared at her.

"Who?" I gasped.

"Philip, of course," she hissed under her breath.

"I… I don't… cannot… I am a married woman," I stammered.

Charlotte towed me behind her along the corridor, still talking quietly. "From what I can see your marriage is over. You do not live with your husband and I do not think you were ever in love with him, but you are in love with my cousin. He feels the same, Catherine, trust me."

Charlotte's assuredness was a great cause for confusion and put me in rather a fluster. If she had not said such a thing when she did, I might never have lowered my guard.

The tunnels were dim, despite the lighting. My dear journal, one cannot begin to describe the blackness that fills them without those lights. As I sit here today in the same house, back in this far more dangerous time, I freely admit that I should fear being in the tunnels all the more if I had not been there before, with the benefit of electric light. I cannot decide if it is irony or, as Philip would say, a paradox. Forgive me. All will become clear on that score soon enough. I shall try to describe events as they happened.

In the hall a large tapestry swung back to reveal the secret door. Charlotte pushed it open and reached inside for a switch. A yellow bulb flickered on and a thin light brightened the shadows.

"This way," she whispered. I followed her down the passage until we reached a fork. "I'll go left. If you go right you will find more passages and a staircase up to the second floor." Then she was gone, disappearing into the dim yellow passages.

Several minutes later I was alone at the top of the staircase. I could hear Charlotte's footsteps come to a stop below as she found her hiding place. I glanced around for my own spot. The bulb on the wall buzzed as I passed it. Everything smelled cold and damp. Somewhere in the main hall I could hear the voices of the boys coming towards the secret doorway. My heart began to pound. I backed against the wall and stumbled into an alcove. The light seemed to shiver in the draught. Though I knew that the bulb could not be blown out, nevertheless I screwed my eyes tight shut, afraid of being left here in the dark.

There was a whisper as the breeze from the open door downstairs ran through the tunnels and rustled about my skirts.

I shuffled back further and realised that I was in fact in another passage. There seemed to be no lights there. I felt along the wall for another switch but found nothing. I moved forward into the darkness, eyes wide to catch any glimmer of light. Sensing a wall in front of me, I reached out and found the bolt of another door. I slid it back and gently pushed it open, breathing in the musty air of the tiny room. This must be the priest hole. I shivered and stepped inside. Far behind me a light bulb buzzed louder, then went out. Plunged into total blackness, I panicked and pulled the door to, shutting myself into the hole.

Distantly through the thick walls I could hear our pursuers' voices, laughing and calling, and then footsteps approaching through the tunnels. They seemed to fade into the distance. Were they following Charlotte's path? Had they missed me? Then I noticed that the other steps, closer, were climbing the stairs.

I held my breath. The consuming darkness heightened my sense of hearing as I listened to the footsteps directly below. I was sure it was Philip, and realised with a start that Charlotte's comment about going right had been a direction, telling him which path to take. I did not know yet whether I approved, but I could not help but feel glad that it was Philip coming my way.

Despite this something in me made my heart beat with terror at the thought of being found. I felt as though I had been there before, as though I were hiding for my life. I swallowed so loudly I thought it would echo. I pressed my back to the corner and imagined how the poor woman who had once been hidden there must have felt.

The room was so small I could touch both side walls at once. A chink of light, thin as a sheet of paper, was leaking in from the wall behind me, and I realised I could see dimly around me. I looked up at the grey walls and saw the faded hint of a heart drawn out in ink. I could not make out the letter in its centre but the sense of it sent a shiver up from the base of my spine and my hair felt as though a brush of ice had been run through it.

Outside, in the house, I could hear an upstairs maid humming as she worked in a room close by. I began to listen to her comforting song and forgot to listen to the footsteps that drew ever closer to my hiding place.

A sound came, so close to me I could have felt the man's breath against my skin.

"Damned light," it muttered.

I gasped.

"Catherine? Are you there?"

Instinct told me I should keep very still. I held my breath. Footsteps began to move past the priest hole and along the corridor. Then they stopped and came back.

"Catherine?" he whispered. I closed my eyes as the door to the passage gently creaked open. It barely skimmed past me. Philip stepped into the darkness. The warmth of his body radiated in the tiny space. My heart thumped so hard I was sure he would hear it. He raised a tentative hand and reached into the black. His fingertips brushed against my hair. The lightness of his touch was like a bolt of electricity. I heard him draw a sharp breath as though he felt it too.

"Catherine," he murmured again. Stepping closer he trailed his hand down my neck.

A hot pulse shot through my body like an arrow to my heart.

"Yes," I gasped. His body was inches from mine. I dared not look at him. My body ached for him. He stepped in closer still and I arched towards him, his lips so near I could feel his breath quicken. I wanted him so much I was shivering. I reached a hand towards his face. Downstairs the bell rang for morning tea. From the tunnel below came a girlish giggle and Arthur's voice hushed it. Carefully I stepped back and looked up into Philip's eyes. They were coal black in the darkness, glinting only from life.

"We had better go back," I stammered, catching my breath. For a moment we stayed there, looking at each other. His gaze seemed so deep I could feel his soul inside me. Then he turned. I thought he would take my hand, but he did not. My heart felt as though it had been ripped out.

MICHAEL

Oxford — 7th February, 2022

Frost glistened on the outhouse window as Michael stared through the dirty glass. *I really must clean that,* he thought, then rubbed his hands over his face. He sighed and a puff of breath plumed from his mouth. He had been sitting there for quite some time. He had lost track of just how long, but it might have been hours. If he was going to do it, he should just get on with it. He knew procrastinating wasn't going to make it any easier or make the thing work any better. Ten months ago he had placed the advert with *The Times* and the *Guardian* with not a single response, well, except for the cranks like that bloke who had claimed he could channel Catherine through his alien spirit guide. *But at least I know what decade I'm aiming at now,* he mused.

He blew on his cold hands, got up, pulled the sheet from cabinet and turned on the power. The lights began to flicker and the air swirled into a crackling spiral over his head and whirled towards the re-locator pad. The floor began to shudder as electricity pulsed through the air, sending a violet bolt fizzing across the room. It bounced off the ceiling and came to a halt, hovering over the pad in the centre of the room. There was a gentle pull and Michael stepped back. But then the signal seemed to fade a little. Slowly, a choking grey smoke began to creep into the room like mist in a graveyard. With his heart in his throat and his breath caught beneath it, Michael blinked and watched.

CATHERINE
London, 1907-8

The rest of that summer of 1907 was blissful, and I was more than sorry to see the leaves turn red and the berries appear on the bushes. But summers must end and winter always comes. There was never another moment like the one in the tunnels, but there were looks and glances that did not get past Charlotte.

On the day we returned to London she grabbed my hand and said, "I know my cousin, Catherine. He may fight it, but his heart will win over his head in the end."

I didn't know then whether I believed her or even if I wanted to, but whatever I might have dreamed of, time had other ideas.

Philip remained at Oxford to further his studies, but Arthur was to take up employment at an excavation Lord Rupert was sponsoring in Egypt. I believe it broke all our hearts to wave him off at Portsmouth. Almost as soon as he had gone, Philip and I took up pen and paper once more. Our letters were more frequent than before and our conversation far easier than I had expected. He enquired about my progress, or lack thereof, with Dr Winston's memory treatment. We talked of our childhoods, our joys and our tears, but not once in all his letters did he enquire about my marriage, nor could I bring myself to raise the subject. Yet a constant guilt nagged at my heart like a wasp at a honey jar. I slept less than ever and my head ached with the strain.

As Christmas approached, Philip announced that he would spend the season with us, but then Lady Mariah contracted malaria and at the last moment he was called away to Egypt. He suggested we might like to accompany him, since it would afford us an opportunity to see Arthur as well, but Rosaline said she could not leave her father at Christmas and Dr Winston would never leave England. One day she took me aside and cautioned me.

"Forgive me for being so frank, Catherine. I don't wish to sound harsh or diminish you in any way, but even if you were not already married, a family like his... despite their kindness and generosity... as lovely as it would be to be readily accepted into their kind of society... I just cannot see it will end well for either of you... You do see what I mean, don't you?"

"Yes, yes, I do," I responded, "and I do not blame you for saying it. You mean that even if Philip and I were utterly in love and I were a free woman, his family would never allow the match." I acquiesced and we did not go. But none of us know what is further down our road and I have learned since to take each day as I find it.

Do not fret for Lady Mariah, dear friend. Thankfully the countess had the constitution of an ox and her illness was of short duration.

Philip was due back at the end of January 1908, and he was stopping overnight in London before returning to Oxford. Regardless of Rosaline's warnings, the excitement of seeing him again had been building in my heart for days, and I had a spring in my step as I meandered through the rooms at the British Museum. When the bell rang in the grand hall to signal the museum was closing for the night, I stepped out into the evening air fully expecting to see Philip at supper.

Whilst I had been inside, the gathering smog of London had dampened the fresh winter air into a bitter taste. The fumes often hung low in the city streets and that evening was one of the worst

I had ever seen. As I walked home, nearly blinded by the grey fog that engulfed me, I heard the clatter of hooves and the grate of wheels on stone as carriages passed me, muffled in the heavy air. After eighteen months I was no longer afraid of the bustling streets, even in such conditions, but as I made my way back to Russell Square my lungs grew tight. My thoughts, as so often of late, were of how I could free myself from my marriage vows to Daniel. Time should have already taken care of that. I was here in the twentieth century and Daniel long since gone from the world. And yet I did not feel able to consider myself a widow.

I tried to draw a deeper breath, but as I did so, something screeched towards me. At first I thought it a motor car, but as I stumbled out of the way I fell into the dazzling brightness of a snow-powdered churchyard.

I blinked as the winter sun burned into my eyes. I tried to focus on my surroundings. The moment the ground stopped spinning I saw the south doors of St Mary Magdalen's, and a flood of panic surged through me. I looked at the familiar graves and the dirt track which was the street. I found myself running to the city gate and slamming my fists against the dreadful wall of the Bocardo, its tiny arrow-slit windows sneering down at me. My heart was breaking. I stumbled along the stinking road to the tatty cluster of shops that crowded the entrance to Horsemonger Street, and stared at the last door in the row, shivering violently. I looked through the window and saw Bessie sweeping the fabric cuttings from the floor. I put my hand on the door handle but the stench of the city nauseated me and all I wanted to do was run. I turned on my heel and felt the icy air drag my hat from my head as I hastened back to the church and through its ever-open doors.

MICHAEL

Oxford — 7th February, 2022

The grey cloak of mist that enveloped the re-locator pad began to thin, and Michael's heart sank as a small grey mouse scuttled out from beneath it. He waited. He held his breath. But nothing else appeared. He ripped out the generator plug and sank down onto the hard wooden chair behind his desk.

"Something must be working right," said Paul, some hours later.

Michael put his hands close to the radiator. He was frozen from spending so long outside.

"Not well enough."

"We can keep trying. You found the fault in the machinery and you fixed it. Now you just need to perfect the recall."

Michael's mind began to tick. His thoughts seemed as loud and regular as the pendulum of the wall clock as it swung rhythmically back and forth at the far side of the living room. *That's it!* he thought.

He bit back a desire to shout "Eureka!" Instead he smiled and said, "You know, I think you're right. I know exactly what needs fixing. And next time I know it'll work."

CATHERINE

Oxford, 1492

Dizzy and confused, I fell to my knees before the church altar and allowed my tears to pour through my prayers. At that moment I knew nothing of the world but fear and confusion. I took a breath and tried to clear my head. As the fog of the journey lifted I found my memory intact, and for once I wished it were not. Never before had I wanted to be somewhere else so much. My fingers clasped the St Christopher around my neck as I looked up at the great gilt cross on the altar. The brilliance of the sun behind it made my eyes sting.

Someone else entered the church, and quiet footsteps drew close behind me. I dared myself to look around. Before me stood Father Thomas, his oversized cassock hanging from his slender arms: he looked like a boy in his father's coat. One smile from his peaceful lips and I gave way to my weakness.

"Father, forgive me." The words scraped from my throat in a dry rasp. The priest drew a sharp breath.

"Catherine? It is. Praise Jesus. Catherine!" The kindness glinted for only a moment before his sky blue eyes clouded over like a rainy day.

"Oh, Father," I whispered. "I cannot tell you how glad I am that you are still here."

I knew not then how long I had been gone from that place, only that when I had quit it summer was high and now the harsh cold of winter bit into my damp cheeks. He took my hand.

"There, there. Come, sit with me."

We sat down on the bench. The previous occasion we had done so had been the day Anne was born. The memory of it struck me and took my breath.

"Will you tell me where you have been all these months?"

I was relieved that it had not been years. I paused to form an answer, for I could not lie to him, nor could I lie before God. He waited with saintly patience.

"London. I have been in London with friends," I mumbled.

"And you are home now, with Daniel?"

I shifted in my seat.

"He does know you are returned?" he asked.

I shook my head. "Not yet. I came here first."

Father Thomas glanced up at the altar cross.

"May I speak candidly?"

I replied with a tiny nod.

"Catherine, your husband has had to endure a good deal of talk. You left without word. People made assumptions, that he had... might have harmed you."

I pressed my fingers to my lips. It had never occurred to me to consider what Daniel might have to face in my absence. The guilt was nauseating.

"Oh, God, pray forgive me."

"Tonight it is not God you must ask for forgiveness. Daniel swore you were with a sick aunt, and whilst I knew this could not be true, I also did not believe Daniel capable of harming you in anyway," he continued. "And there were others, folks who said you had run away with another man."

I squeezed my eyes tight shut. I truly had been a curse upon my husband.

"Then 'tis true?" His look pierced me like a hot poker. "I am aware how unhappy you both were, Catherine, but... you know you could be hanged for this."

"Oh, Father, I have not betrayed my husband..." I blurted. "In my heart there is another, but I knew him not before I left and it has come to naught."

My friend ran a spidery hand through his thinning hair and looked at me closely. "Then what happened to make you leave? Did Daniel beat you?" he asked.

"No, no!" I gasped in horror. "Daniel would never raise a hand to me, only words."

Father Thomas's narrow lips turned up into a thin smile. "Words often cut deeper and heal slowest."

I looked away. "I fear my words equalled his with the sharp edge of their blade. Daniel is a good man, Father, but we do not love each other."

"I wish you had both come to me."

"Do you think he will take me back?" I knew not what else I could do but return to my old home.

"You are married before God and there is a duty."

My body sank into the boning of my corset so it dug hard into my ribs.

"Father, is there not cause, if both parties are so unhappy, that God may see fit to free the husband and wife from those bonds?"

"Friendship in a marriage can grow into something far stronger than passion, Catherine, and I know you and Daniel are capable of that."

"Perhaps, but should that prevent..." I let my words die on my breath.

Father Thomas looked at me intently, his eyes scouring my face for information. Finally he said, "I understand how difficult this must be. The loss of a child is a traumatic event for both parents. Daniel may not admit it, but he feels it as keenly as you do, and you are needed. Perhaps you should work together on getting through the pain, rather than driving the knife further into each other's hearts."

Father Thomas's words strangled me like a hangman's noose, for I knew he was right. Whatever I had been through since, I owed it to Daniel to make this right. Philip was in another time now, and there was nothing else I could do but go back to Daniel or die on the streets.

"Will you come with me, Father?" I whispered in defeat.

"Of course."

MICHAEL

Oxford — 13th May, 2022

Michael was ready. After several long sleepless nights, taking the circuit board entirely to pieces and painstakingly putting it back together with new parts and modifications, he had been ready months ago. But he had made himself wait. He wanted everything to be right, the atmosphere, the equipment and even the date. There was nothing he was leaving to chance. He watched the clock on the living-room wall tick far too slowly, whilst his heart pounded at double speed. Unable to stand the tension, Imogen had gone out and left him to it. Margaret Penning had taken her shopping. The chime rang through the room and Michael moved for the first time since coming home from school.

As he walked down to the bottom of the garden, a pink petal of apple blossom floated down from the tree and past his face. Somewhere a few gardens away a lawnmower hummed, and the smell of freshly cut grass began to drift over the hedges towards him. The evening was a pleasant one. He unbuttoned his cardigan and took the outhouse key from his trouser pocket. His hand shook too much to slip it in the lock, and he was forced to use his other hand to hold his wrist steady.

Finally the key turned and he pushed the door open to reveal the spotless room. He had tidied everything away and painted the walls in fresh magnolia. Even the dust sheet from the cabinet had been washed. He pulled the sheet off and opened the doors to reveal the panel inside. From the drawer of his desk he drew out the new recovery monitor and set it on the table top. It looked like a rather elaborate i-phone, only with two mini antennae. Its outer shell shone like platinum and the keypad glowed green beneath the numbers. He pressed the red button in the top right hand corner and the face flashed on. Dialling a number on this phone, however, would not make another phone ring. This little gadget would connect you to one thing only, the tiny computer that had once hung around the neck of his daughter; he could only hope she was still wearing it.

He keyed in 1907 and the monitor began to vibrate. Michael watched it for a moment as the four-digit number flickered and stabilised. Then, as the machine in the cabinet buzzed into life, he picked up the monitor and held it so he could see the screen and the cabinet together. He glanced at his watch: 17:59. One more minute and he could begin. Tick, tick. The seconds felt agonisingly slow.

18:00. The exact time Catherine had pressed the buttons all those years ago. *Here goes.* As the familiar swirl of energy buzzed around his head and swamped the re-locator pad, he could feel it working. There was a hard pull. Michael stumbled forward, forced to grab the table leg as he tripped and landed on his knees with a crack. The pain meant nothing to him as the monitor slipped from his fingers and was dragged towards the gaping hole of black space that yawned before him. He reached out and grabbed it just in time to prevent it vanishing into the abyss.

Still hanging onto the table, he looked at the dial on the cabinet. Everything looked fine, but the face of the monitor in his hand was barely legible. The numbers were flickering, the seven morphing back and forth into a two, and the zero seemed to run through every number between nought and nine so quickly it made his eyes dance. The nine had vanished altogether. The only constant was the one. Frantically Michael began to press the keys, 1 9 0 7 over and over, but the numbers wouldn't hold. Finally the nine popped back into place and the wormhole around the pad flashed violet. Michael shielded his eyes and blinked through the light.

It was gone.

Once more Michael waited.

Nothing.

Outside there was a sudden shower of rain. Michael looked out at the sky in surprise: most of it was blue, save for a single dark cloud. Damp air drifted in beneath the door. Closing his eyes, he waited.

Still nothing.

The shower stopped as quickly as it had begun. Shaking his head, Michael turned the recovery monitor off and threw it back in his drawer. Feeling sick and exhausted, he yanked out the plug, threw the dustsheet back over the cabinet and shut up the outhouse. His feet felt like lead as he made his way back to the house.

In the kitchen he turned on the cold tap and splashed water over his face. As he lifted the kettle the phone rang. For a moment he thought he wouldn't answer it, but the ring continued and whoever was on the other end was clearly not going to give up.

"Hello?"

"Oh my God, Dad, tell me you tried it. Tell me you had the machine on just now." Paul sounded as excited as a small child on Christmas morning.

Michael's brow furrowed. "Well, yes, but it didn't–"

"You did it!" Paul cut across him.

Michael's heart crashed to a momentary halt, forcing him to sink into the nearest chair. The clock on the living-room wall chimed again. It was six thirty, only half an hour since he had turned on the machine.

"What?" he said, his voice barely audible.

"Sorry. I mean… well she didn't stay, but it was her."

Michael tried to swallow. "I'm not following you, Paul."

The voice crackled in Michael's ear.

"Shit. Dad, sorry, the signal's crap in here. I'm coming round."

"What? Paul?" but the line had gone dead.

When Paul's ancient green Volkswagen pulled into the drive some twenty minutes later, Michael had moved to his study and was wishing for the first time in twenty-eight years that cigarettes were still allowed.

He was on his feet, in the hall and opening the front door before his son had taken his key from the ignition. Michael's hands were shaking violently as he watched. There was someone in the passenger seat and for a brief, wonderful moment, he expected Catherine to emerge and join her brother on the driveway. But the woman had sandy gold hair and as the door swung wide for her to exit, he saw the sleek legs of Amelia Penning step out.

"Hi, Professor Alexander."

"Hello, Millie. I wish you'd call me Michael."

"I know," she said, coming over and kissing him on the cheek. "I just can't get out of the habit."

"Your mother taught you impeccable manners," he smiled wryly.

Paul joined them by the front door.

"Give her back, Dad."

Michael noticed his son's affectionate hand slip around his girlfriend's waist. He would have been happy for them had he not felt so anxious.

"Come on then, you have some explaining to do."

Michael offered them tea as they all settled in the living room, but none of them had the patience to wait for it to be made. As he perched on the edge of an armchair Michael looked at Paul's eager face. He folded his arms and tried to draw a calm breath.

"Sorry if I startled you, Dad. It's just that, well, Catherine was there, at Balliol."

"What? In the lab?"

"No, the college."

Michael opened his mouth to speak, but he couldn't quite focus.

Millie said, "Start from the beginning, babe."

Paul nodded. "Mil and I were sitting out on the Quad lawn with a couple of the guys when there was the weirdest noise, like a scraping..."

"It sounded like a really loud door creaking open," Millie chipped in.

"Yeah, that's it exactly," Paul agreed. "Well, then, and I can't describe the feeling, but it was as though someone was standing right behind me."

Michael fidgeted in his seat.

"When I looked around there was no one there."

"Not right behind you, but you did see her straight away," Millie interrupted again. Paul slipped his hand into hers and squeezed her fingers affectionately.

"I could see a woman watching me through Johnson's... your old office window. There was something about her and the way she was looking right at me that made me get up and walk towards her. From a distance she looked just like Mum, and exactly like the woman in the Edwardian photograph. But close up, when our eyes met, honestly, I thought my heart would stop. Her eyes are exactly the same shade as yours and mine. And the expression on her face, Dad, she looked startled, as though she recognised me. She raised her hand and reached towards me and I was going to say her name, but then there was a flash of bright purple light and I heard her cry out. The next second she was gone." Paul looked at Michael and waited for a response.

Michael didn't know what to say. There was no proof that this woman was Catherine, and yet, just as with the photograph, there was a knowing flutter in his gut.

"It was *her*, Dad," Paul added with encouragement.

Michael began to nod slowly. "The cry. Was she in pain?"

Paul looked suddenly nervous. "No, no... I think she called a name."

"What name?" Michael hoped it was Dad or Paul or Mum.

"I can't be sure. There was that scraping sound again, but... well... it sounded like... Philip."

Michael's heart sank. He had suspected as much. Though he had looked into Boden-Howard's personal history and found no mention of a Catherine anywhere, he felt deep down that his daughter had at least been close to him; perhaps they had even been engaged. The ethics of what he was attempting to do to her burned like flame in his head. He put his hands to his temples and rubbed.

"Thank you."

Paul and Millie were staring at him, bewildered.

"Are you all right? We thought you'd be pleased."

"Doesn't that mean your machine is working properly and you can definitely get her back?" Millie asked naively.

Michael looked up and smiled sadly.

"Yes, Millie, it does. But it also raises the question of whether I have the right to bring her back. Her home is there. She may have married." Michael also knew what had happened to Boden-Howard. If he and Catherine were close, in whatever way, then taking away what little time she might still have with him might be the cruellest thing he could do to his daughter. *Perhaps after... in 1917... but what if she had children?* He looked at his son closely. *I've got a great kid who is here and healthy, shouldn't I just be grateful for that?* he asked himself. *I've neglected him and his mother abominably.*

"Perhaps it's time to stop all this," he said out loud.

For a moment Paul just blinked at him, the disbelief evident on his face.

"This thing has dominated our lives for too long."

"That's not true, Dad, it's been your life's work and we want her back just as much as you do."

"I know, son, and I hope you can forgive me for that. But I think it's time we let your sister go." His voice cracked. "We should let her live her life."

Millie glanced at Paul then moved over to where Michael was sitting. He looked up at her with tears in his eyes as she sat on the chair arm and wrapped her arms around his shoulders.

"Are you sure?" Paul was crying too.

"Certain." Michael's voice was flat. "I'll tell your mother when she comes home. I think she'll be relieved."

CATHERINE

Oxford, 1492

As Father Thomas pushed open the door to my old home, every nerve in my body was shaking. Everything looked the same as it always had. The dark walls covered in bolts of fabric lying heavy on bowing shelves, dim streaks of sunlight glinting over the work bench, and the faint smell of damp walls. I could hear Bessie humming in the kitchen and John was bending over the accounts ledger, his quill scratching at the paper. He looked up.

"Father, good afternoon…"

I must have been quite a sight, for my clothes were all wrong, my hair undone and my face stained pink from crying. He stood up quickly, sending his stool flying backwards and crashing onto the stone floor.

"Mistress More. What on God's earth…?"

Bessie screamed from the kitchen doorway.

"Forgive me, but where is Daniel? I must speak with him at once."

"At Blake's, of course," Bessie stuttered.

That much had not changed at least. I slipped a sideways glance at the top of the open ledger. December 30th 1492.

"'Six months,'" I whispered under my breath. Long enough to cause damage, but not irredeemably so.

As John rushed out to fetch my husband, Bessie threw her arms around me so tightly I thought I would never breathe again.

"Welcome home, welcome home," she murmured, over and over again.

I prayed thanks for such forgiveness and ought to have prayed that Daniel would show me the same, but I could not. Secretly I wished my husband would banish me, for then Father Thomas would have had no choice but to find a way to dissolve our marriage.

There were a few guarded and curious questions from my housekeeper, causing panic to rise higher and higher in my chest.

"You do sound strange. They must have a very different way of speaking in London."

The walls seemed to be closing in around me. Adaptation had come so easily to me in 1906, yet reversing the process was clearly going to take more thought and effort.

"I think I should like to take a moment to refresh from my journey before Daniel returns." I said hurriedly, and escaped to the stairs.

My father's town house consisted of three stories. I reached the very top floor and pushed open the door of the bedchamber I had once shared with my husband. Instantly I could see everything was wrong. The bed had been turned so it rested against the opposite wall. My desk was absent entirely, and the washstand had been placed next to the clothing chest. Only the jar I used to keep flowers in remained where I had left it. It sat like some haunting shadow of me, coated with dust on the tiny shelf by the window, empty and alone. Breathless and with my head thumping, I felt the room spin around me as I fell to the floor.

The next thing I knew was Bessie pressing a cool compress to the back of my neck and Father Thomas kneeling at my feet, holding my hand. I was lying on the bed.

"Thank you, I am recovered," I whispered, uncertain whether I wanted to vomit or cry.

"You are quite certain you are well?" Bessie asked, taking away the compress and feeling my forehead for signs of fever.

I tugged at my frock, wondering how I could loosen my corset, but it was a back-lacer and the effort was futile. Later, Bessie would marvel at my undergarments as she helped me out of them. 'Twas the only thing I was glad to be leaving behind from my twentieth-century life.

"Perhaps a glass of wine, Bessie?"

When she was gone, Father Thomas said, "Daniel is a good man, Catherine, he will be kind."

I was not convinced.

When Bessie returned, I looked at the wine and considered how a glass of water would have served me better, but to drink the water in the fifteenth century would have been to risk my life. There were many things I began to question in my old life, far more than just the state of my marriage.

"Tell me about your friends, Catherine." Father Thomas broke the tension. I was about to decline the discussion, then thought better of it.

"I could not wish for kinder, more Christian friends," I heard myself say. "Rosaline and her sister took me everywhere, to the museums and galleries, even the theatre." Father Thomas raised an eyebrow. But nerves got the better of me and I could not halt my tongue. "And then there is Arthur. He was such fun and we spent last summer at Hatherley Park with…"

"Who is Arthur?" Daniel's voice thundered through the house as the door slammed back against the wall. I almost choked. Slowly I looked up at him. His tunic was new to me and his shoulders seemed a little broader, but the curl of his hair and the curved bow of his lips were just the same. When our eyes met I felt my stomach twist.

"Catherine," he said flatly.

I tried to stand but my legs would not move. His face was cold and hard. Before I was on my feet he had spun on his heel and the door had slammed again behind him. For a moment we could hear him pacing back and forth below, ranting his displeasure to himself. John hurriedly took his leave and Bessie vanished back to the kitchen. Once we were alone Father Thomas looked at me carefully and said, "Give him a moment."

For what seemed like eternity we were suspended in anticipation, nothing but the sound of Daniel's anguish pumping through my veins.

Finally the door swung open again.

"Well…?"

"Arthur Winston," I stammered, attempting to explain, "he is the brother of…"

"And you prefer his company to that of your own husband?" Daniel's face was livid and his lips thin and twisted. "Were you abducted? Were you a prisoner of these people?" His words were spat at me like the venom of an adder.

"No, not at all, Rosaline has been a sister to me."

"And yet you did not send word," he growled. "I thought you dead, Catherine!" His demeanour began to slump. "I imagined you murdered." His fists began to unfurl and I saw his eyes held more remorse than anger. I looked at the gentle lines of his features and the softness of his winter-pale skin. I had cared a vast deal for him once, and he had done nothing to deserve my ill treatment.

"Can you forgive me?" I flung myself onto my knees before him, my eyes fixed on his soft brown boots. He did not move and he did not touch me. I reached up for his hand but he withdrew it from my grasp. "I did not mean to leave, it just happened."

"How can it have *just happened,* Catherine? Was it witchcraft? Was there some kind of spell?" I dared myself to look at him, but he refused to meet my gaze.

"No, of course not." There was a split second where I almost retracted that denial but my new Edwardian reasoning kept me from doing it. "Please let me explain," I begged. "You owe me that much at least."

"*I* owe *you*?" He pursed his lips tighter till they were white. Our eyes locked together. I paused and took a deep breath.

"You recall we had argued…"

"Do you really think I would forget?" Daniel barked.

I swallowed back tears.

"After you left that morning, I was so… distraught. I… ran to the church, to my father's grave…" As I explained Father Thomas sank onto a stool and pressed his fingers together as though in prayer.

"I cannot recall how I got to London…" Daniel was glaring, and I could not tell whether it was in anger or astonishment, "with little memory of who I was or from whence I came. It was a most terrifying thing to be alone in a strange city," I finished.

"Then it was witchcraft!" Daniel shifted his feet.

"I do not think so, my son," Father Thomas offered. "I believe there are two possible explanations. The first is that Catherine was abducted. The criminals later thought better of their crime and abandoned her. The other is that Catherine was so overcome by grief that she ran away in a fever and was unaware of her actions until she arrived in London some time later."

Glad of the Fathers rational consideration, I was about to

reiterate my amnesia when Daniel said, "Then why did she not return once she was free or her humours restored?"

I felt like a disobedient child returned home by the scruff of its neck.

"Catherine?" Father Thomas looked at me.

"I… there was so much sadness here. I believed you would do better without me." This much was true. "Can you ever forgive me?" I grasped at Daniel's woollen-hosed legs. He did not push me away, but neither did he bend to comfort me.

"And I suppose, Father, you are here to tell me that it is my Christian duty to accept this apology?"

"Daniel, it will take time for you both to heal, but you should mourn the loss of your child together. Sometimes God sends these things to make us stronger."

My husband's shoulders sagged in defeat.

"Then it is a good thing I am a forgiving man."

I gasped for breath and sank into a ball at his feet. I pulled my legs up to my chest and felt hot tears burn down my icy cheeks. Whether by God or by Time, I had been sent back to my husband and I knew I must stay.

Daniel grimaced.

"Thank you for returning her, Father." He paused and I could see the effort on his face as he added. "Do stay and dine with us."

When Father Thomas left us some hours later, I felt my heart strangling my throat with fear. I knew not what my husband's true reaction would be once we were alone.

He turned on me the moment the door was closed.

"It is fortuitous for you that I did not tell everyone you were dead."

I swallowed hard.

"Father Thomas explained everything, and I thank you with all my heart." I reached out for his hand; once more he withdrew it.

"Not a single letter!"

"I was not in a position to write."

His eyes darkened.

"How can you expect me to believe that? You say you were with friends, or was that a lie?"

"You know me better than to think me a liar, husband, but it remains that it was im–"

"I do not believe I know you at all, Catherine."

With that he pushed past me and stomped up the stairs. I ran after him, for I knew not what else to do. But the bedchamber door slammed in my face. I went to knock but was stopped short. My husband was crying. I sank to the floor and set my face in my hands.

It was only when Bessie came to bed that I moved. She ushered me into the room I had shared with her as a child. I watched as she opened the linen chest and lifted out a thick blanket to wrap around me. As she did so something bright pink slipped onto the top of the pile. I knew Hannah had kept it, the dress she had found me in that day when I was six, but I had not seen it in many a year. Startled, I went to retrieve it. As the smooth fabric met with my shaking hands a memory shot through my mind.

A woman's hand holding mine, soft and secure. Flowers in bloom on the tree across the street and many automobiles of a kind I cannot have seen before, rushing everywhere. Then waiting in a big white room filled with flashes and deafening sounds. A man screaming, calling my name.

I held the dress to my face. Though the scent was dulled by

dust, something sweet and floral still lingered beneath. The fabric was unknown to me, and the buttons made of something I could not comprehend. My suspicions have been pricked by several memories, but now I knew with clarity; wherever my past lay, it was from a time far beyond my imagination, further forward, perhaps, even than Philip and Rosaline.

I prayed that night, harder than ever in my life before. Whatever Time had planned for me along the road, I begged it to send me back to my Edwardian friends. The answer that came to me made my heart heavy. I had to make do. I had to put my desires to the back of my mind and take each day as it was dealt, wherever and whenever that may be.

I continued to sleep in Bessie's room for many days after. My husband could hardly bring himself to look at me, let alone touch me. Barely a word passed between us. To the outside world we did our best to appear happy together, yet in truth, we spent as little time as was possible in the same room. How convincing we were I cannot say; there were many nudges and whispers between the neighbours when they saw me. And then there was Isabella Blake.

Isabella was a woman of nineteen and the youngest daughter of Daniel's employer. She was not altogether plain, but equally she did not attain the heights of beauty. She had not gone without suitors of her own, but none had displayed the right qualities for marriage. Daniel, I suspected, would have been her perfect match had I not stepped in her way.

"Catherine, dear, it is good to see you looking so well. Have you received word from your aunt of late? Is she fully recovered?" Master Blake was all concern when Daniel and I arrived to dine at their home some three weeks after my return. As I walked up the stairs from the shop floor to the great living room, its windows shuttered and the candlelight dancing a warm glow over the walls, I could not help but recall the clear sheets of glass and the gentle bow of age the house would have in future years.

"Catherine?" Daniel said through the corner of his mouth when I had not answered.

"Oh, Master Blake, indeed she is. How kind of you to ask," I replied with a warm smile.

"Indeed, Mistress More." The remark had a spike to its tone. I curtseyed to Isabella. Her mouse brown hair was wrapped tightly beneath her gable hat and her gown was the same earthy shade of green as her eyes. A smile twitched over her lips but did not travel over the rest of her features.

Supper passed pleasantly enough, but I had grown used to the lighter delicacies of Rosaline's world. The supper Mistress Blake served was as good as any I had eaten in those times, but my stomach ached so when we had finished. We retired to the warmth of the fireside. The gentlemen fell into matters of business whilst the ladies chattered on more trivial subject matter. I longed for a conversation of greater substance.

As my mind wondered from the ladies' latest favourite, I watched Daniel standing with Master Blake. His hair was dulled from lack of sunshine but the mellow light made it glint like polished bronze. He caught me looking and shifted his stance so I could not see his face. I began to envisage Arthur and Philip leaning against another mantel, puffing cigars and laughing at their own jokes. I closed my eyes to ease the tearing at my heart.

"Are you all right, child? You seem out of sorts." Mistress Blake had leaned forward in her chair and laid a hand over mine.

"Forgive me. The fire is so warm and my stomach so full, I fear sleep is attempting to take a grip." Daniel shot me an exhausted glance.

"Perhaps a turn about the room would be refreshing." Mistress Blake gestured to her daughter to stand and walk with me. Isabella obeyed, but only with a dark glare of resentment. As we began to walk I felt the gaze of my husband come to rest upon me. For the first time in since my return I was pleased to find his expression was not cold. I smiled gratefully back and his eyes warmed. Isabella stiffened at my side.

"So," she whispered, "Daniel has forgiven your adultery."

I could not believe her affront. I stopped and stared at her with an open mouth.

"Is that what you think?" I hissed. "I can assure you that is not the case. I have never betrayed my husband."

"Really?" she said. "Then tell me why he finds it so hard to tolerate your presence."

Mistress Blake was now staring at us. I urged Isabella to begin walking again. She obliged, but her grip on my arm tightened.

"He was distraught when you ran away. People accused him of all sorts of unthinkable things."

"I am aware of that, Isabella. Causing him pain had not been my intent."

"And yet that is exactly what you did."

"Madam, this is a matter between me and my husband." I broke away from her. She grabbed my wrist.

"He has told me all about this Arthur and his sisters," she hissed. I was horrified that he had spoken so intimately to anyone, especially another woman.

"You have no right to question me so."

"Is that what you think? You abandoned him. What gives you the right to come back and claim him now?"

By then all eyes in the room were looking our way. The anger that bubbled in my heart at that moment almost made me slap her, but instead we each stood our ground. The silence was broken only by the roar of the fire. A log of wood cracked and spat an ember onto the hearth. I flinched as it came close to my feet.

"Isabella!" Mistress Blake was on her feet and prising her daughter's hand from my wrist. "Get to your room!"

"Mother, I am not a child and she..." Isabella sobbed, "she does not deserve a man like Daniel."

I glanced over at my husband. He looked like a lost boy, his eyes moving from her to me and back again, and I knew; I was not the only one in our marriage to find affection in another. Yet where I had no chance of happiness, Daniel did. The weight on my back lifted just a little but the vice of guilt around my heart tightened.

"Isabella, do as your mother says," Master Blake bellowed at his daughter. She spun about and fled, tears flowing down her cheeks.

"Oh, Master Blake, I am so sorry," I said, my own eyes filling with tears.

"Catherine, you have done nothing. I will speak with my daughter when she has calmed down," Mistress Blake soothed.

"I think we should go home." Daniel strode to my side, violently clenching my hand in his.

As we walked home in silence I allowed his grip to hurt me without complaint. The pain of his anger was a relief after the weeks of icy silence.

The shop door crashed shut behind us and Daniel swung around to face me. But when our eyes met his expression was not fierce – it was defeated.

"She was here and you were gone. I did not mean to… she was kind and I knew not if I should ever see you again." For a moment I thought he would break down and cry before me, but he held steady.

"It is my fault," I offered.

"Perhaps Father Thomas has a point, we are both at fault."

His grip relaxed and the blood throbbed into my fingers. I stretched them. "Forgive me," he said, looking at my hand.

I shook my head. The ceiling creaked as Bessie moved about upstairs. We both glanced up.

"I should have been kinder to you after the baby. I was angry at God and myself, not you. I resented the child for trapping us into this marriage. We ought never to have…."

"There is little point in regret, we cannot change what we did. And were we not happy at the start?" I whispered, my legs beginning to shake with relief.

Daniel took my hand back, but this time with care. He led me through to the living room. The fire had been recently damped down and the grey smoke curled into the room with a pleasant smell of burned wood.

"Do you love her?" I held my breath for I could not tell how I wanted him to answer.

He looked at me intensely. Eventually he nodded.

"I do. Catherine, can you ever forgive me?"

I leaned against his chest and he folded his arms around me, holding me tight. I felt his cheek press against my head. I pushed him back a little and looked up.

"Then we are equal in our feelings and there is nothing for either of us to forgive."

His eyes clouded and the dark walls seemed to tower over me.

"Then Isabella was right. You do love this Arthur."

"Not him. But there *is* another, a friend of his," I said. "And I do not think I really knew my own heart until this moment." The tension in my body gave way as he kissed my forehead.

"And you wish to be with him?"

"I doubt that could ever be, even if you and I *were* free, but yes, yes I do. I am so sorry, Daniel." It felt good to admit such thoughts out loud.

"Then we *are* equal. How are we to go on?" he whispered.

"I know not, but we must think of something." That night I returned to my husband's bed chamber. Though we never consummated our marriage again, it was a comfort to slumber at his side.

Every option had been discussed. My husband was well versed in law, but our obstacle was not the legalities of the land but those of the church. Daniel and I had spent hours sitting together talking upon our marriage bed, until the ropes beneath us sagged and needed redrawing. In many respects Father Thomas was right; the friendship that developed between Daniel and me was stronger than our passion had ever been. But we were not so easily satisfied. Finally we approached Father Thomas to ask for an annulment, but there were no grounds and he would have none of it.

As the weeks passed I could see Isabella growing more impatient and Daniel more forlorn. They had not spent any time alone together since my return, and the desire between them was both irritating and painful to watch. The more desperate they became, the more I longed for my other home and the chance to see Philip again. But it was not until months later, when summer had been and gone, and the nights were drawing in to their shortest point once more, that the answer finally came. And it was an observation unwittingly made by Father Thomas himself that brought it about.

We were standing by the church door after evening mass, a layer of frost shimmering on the frozen ground at our feet.

He said, "I am so gladdened to see how well you two have worked out your differences. Whatever happens in your lives now, only death could break such a bond."

I looked up at the thin moon hanging like a nail-paring over the roof of Balliol. The air was so cold my lips were stiff, and my cheeks felt like porcelain. As we took our leave, thoughts were racing and formulating in my mind. I folded my arms to keep warm.

"You are very quiet, Catherine," my husband noted.

I stopped walking and looked up at him. A bat flew low over our heads and swooped up over the roof of our home.

"What if one of us were to die?" I said calmly.

Daniel looked startled.

"What?"

I swallowed and tried again.

"I mean to say. If one of us were gone from this place, presumed dead, would we not both be free?"

"Isabella would not leave her family."

"I did not mean you."

I could see the thoughts run through Daniel's mind. He shook his head.

"No, Catherine. Where would you go? How would you live?"

I had already considered this.

"Death would be rapid and neat, and you and Isabella could be wed before the year is out. Let us say my aunt is sick again, I go to her, only this time I too succumb to the consumption and leave you a widower. I return to my friends in London and begin a new life, and all is well for us both." There was no way on God's earth I would to admit to him that I had no hope of finding my friends. I would be out on the streets and risking my life.

"This time I will leave in broad daylight and no one will have cause to think ill of you."

All I could do was pray that Time would be kind enough to make my deepest wishes come true and return me to Rosaline's world just as soon as I was away.

"All I ask is that you keep Bessie on at the house and get help for John."

Daniel was still shaking his head.

"That is still bigamy, Catherine. You, I and God will all know the truth of the matter, and I cannot lie to Isabella."

I had thought of this also.

"You will not have to. We shall tell her together before I leave. If we swear on the Bible to release our vows, whether we have the blessing of the church or not surely God will forgive us and we shall be free. I have heard of such things in London," I said, recalling King Henry VIII from Arthur's history lessons. "In our hearts we will have betrayed no one and to God we have declared our intent. I believe there will be a time when actions such as these will be accepted in law. If we are wrong, then God will judge us when we face him, but I do not think he can punish us for being true to our hearts."

My husband looked at me long and hard, his eyes shining with silver reflections of moonlight.

"And can you lie to your friends?"

"Do not fret yourself over that, I shall do well enough."

"Very well," he concurred at last.

Only the very wealthiest households possessed a Bible in 1493. How I wished I could have just reached for the little printed copy that sat upon my bedside table at 52 Russell Square. As it was, in order for us to make our proclamation before God, Daniel and I had to gain access to the church and in secret. There was a brief period during each day when most of the monks were at the friary, the priests were out on visits and most folks were too hard at work to stop by. Isabella had been brought in on our scheme and had amiably agreed to create a diversion.

On the arranged day, a little before noon, a horseman arrived at our door with a message for me. He had of course been sent by my own husband, but to the world he was come from my dear sick aunt. Shortly afterwards I watched Isabella enter the south doors of St Mary Magdalen's, her hair scraped tightly beneath her cap and her face a little more flushed than usual. As she disappeared into the stone interior I made my excuses to John. The message from my aunt could not wait. I must speak with my husband immediately.

When I entered Trimble and Blake's, my husband was hunched over his desk at the back of the room. He looked up and set down his quill. In his eyes I saw the same torrent of emotions that ran through my own heart.

"I beg your forgiveness, Master Blake. There is something I need to speak with my husband about," I said.

"Of course, Mistress More."

Daniel rose to his feet and gave a short bow to his employer and said, rather too loudly, "Come, Catherine, pray tell me, what is so urgent that you must interrupt my work?"

"Oh, husband, I have received the most disturbing account just now, regarding the health of my beloved aunt," I said, as we pushed open the door and stepped out into the street. Together we hurried to St Mary Magdalen's.

Inside the church, the air was cool and refreshing, and the gold cross on the altar glowed beneath the sun's bright rays. A woman was on her knees in prayer, but when she heard us enter she rose. Relieved to see that Isabella was alone, I bowed as she passed us by. Her green eyes held a hint of anticipation and her lips quivered when she smiled. I admired her bravery. She was not a sinful woman – a little hot of temper and inclined towards simpering vanity, perhaps – but she had a good disposition and would have very little to confess. Daniel and I would have to work quickly. Isabella approached the priest and requested that he hear her confession. I dared to turn around and was glad I had, for I caught Isabella flash a wink in our direction before drawing the curtain. I closed my eyes and squeezed Daniel's hand. He kissed my forehead. This was it.

The Bible was resting upon the lectern. The cover was heavy oak-brown leather, and the lettering on its front was laid in glittering gold leaf. I laid my right hand atop and Daniel did the same. As his fingers touched mine I drew a breath. My husband turned to look at me and we both began to utter the prayer we had been rehearsing all week. We were quiet, efficient and as true of heart as either of us had ever been in all our lives.

"Our Father, forgive us our sins. We seek thy permission to allow us to depart this church today as friends and not as husband and wife. At thy mercy we declare that from this day forward we shall no longer be bound to one another in holy matrimony, but are, by thy will, free of the vows that we made to thee in good faith and in error. We pray thou grant us this freedom and forgive us our trespasses against thee. We swear to thee our sincerity in our regret, and our promise never to take such a path again without full and lifelong intent."

After this, I continued alone.

"I, Catherine Gail More..." I hesitated suddenly, for I had no notion where that middle name had come from. I had never known it nor heard it in my life before, and yet there it was. Daniel stared at me urgently; I swallowed hard to moisten my throat. "I, Catherine Gail More, release this man, Daniel More, from our marriage vows and declare before God that he is free to marry another."

A breeze whipped in through the open church door and swirled around us. I shivered and raised my eyes to the eaves above. Footsteps were approaching through the churchyard. Daniel hurried on.

"I, Daniel More, release this woman, Catherine..." he paused. Tears welled in the corners of his eyes. "Gail..." he said carefully. Outside, someone was coming closer. Daniel began to shake. "More, from our marriage vows and declare before God that she is free to marry another."

I wanted to wipe his tears away.

Something blew in through the door and we both flinched. Hurriedly we ended our pledge together.

"We beg thy forgiveness and trust in thy mercy."

We crossed ourselves and knelt before the altar. "In nomine Patris, et Filii, et Spiritus Sancti, Amen." In my heart I prayed for a sign that we were forgiven.

Something fluttered over my head and landed upon the fold of my cap.

"Gracious, it is a butterfly. Keep still a moment."

A sob caught in my throat. "It is a sign from God!" I gasped.

Daniel raised his hand and let the creature step onto his finger. The footsteps outside reached the south door, and the voice of Father Thomas could be heard speaking with Sarah Goode, the butcher's wife. Daniel slowly lowered his hand so that I could see the butterfly. It was blue as a cornflower, just like the creature I had seen on our wedding day. Slowly it opened and closed its wings.

"It's a rare one," Daniel smiled in wonder.

Behind us the curtain to the confessional slid back and Isabella scuttled away without any further acknowledgement. I swallowed hard, forcing my tears back down my throat. Father Peter emerged from his alcove.

"What have you there?" he said, observing our unusual positions. He walked towards us. I prayed my eyes were not pink and my cheeks not blotched. Outside I heard Mistress Goode take her leave and Father Thomas entered the church. I began to feel as though the butterfly were inside my stomach, for I knew I could not lie to my friend.

"'Tis a butterfly, Father, it just landed upon my w–" Daniel hesitated, "Mistress More's cap."

"Well, isn't that a little miracle right there," Father Peter said to Father Thomas as he came towards us. "What on God's earth can it be doing wandering in here when it ought to be out in the fields enjoying this sunshine?"

"I cannot think," Father Thomas replied, looking in my direction.

With that the creature fluttered its wings with greater rapidity and drifted off towards the door. Father Peter bowed and bid us a good afternoon.

"Well, well," Father Thomas added. "Catherine, Daniel, good

day to you." He looked us over with suspicion. "I hope all is well."

Daniel offered me his hand and we stood.

"I am afraid my aunt's sickness is returned and I must away to London once more, Father."

The priest looked at me closely, scrutinising my expression.

"And there is nothing to be done to persuade you otherwise?"

I shook my head.

"She is in need of urgent care," Daniel answered for me. Father Thomas nodded slowly. For a moment his eyes drifted towards the lectern and rested upon the Bible. I tried not to notice. Daniel shifted his feet. I thought my heart would never take its next beat.

"I see. If it is all settled, then I wish you well."

"I leave tomorrow."

Father Thomas suddenly looked old and I hoped he was not unwell. He smiled but the gesture did not quite reach his eyes.

"Promise me you will take care of yourself," he said.

I was a little taken aback, for I had expected chastisement.

"Yes, Father."

He took my hands in his and looked deep into my eyes. I had to fight for composure.

"I think I can guess what you have done and where you are going. I have failed you. I could not help. Can you both forgive me?"

Now I was all astonishment. I felt my cheeks flush from shame, for I had planned to leave my old friend without confession. I opened my mouth to speak.

"Do not tell me, child. I must not know. What you do is your business, I am only sorry that I could not have mended it for you myself."

"Father, I..." Daniel began.

"Shhh," he urged, letting my hands go and placing a finger over his lips.

"Then do not worry, no matter what you may hear," I said. "Do not be sorry, there is nothing you or any other living soul could have done."

"You still wear your St Christopher," he said, eyeing the gold chain about my neck.

I nodded and reached for the pendant. Though it was no bigger than a coin, the gold was thick and the weight heavy for its size. I had been wearing it the day William and Hannah Harris found me wondering the streets and I would not have taken it off even if God himself had demanded it.

"Do not lose it," he added, and I knew he meant my faith.

"Never, Father."

And that was all that passed between us on that subject. Sometimes, dear friend, I wish I could see him just once more. To look into those wise eyes and thank him for all he has done for me, but I think that shall never be, now.

The following morning was a frantic one. The packhorse Daniel had hired was delivered early and I had not finished dressing. I ran a comb through my hair and twisted it into a roll at my neck. Daniel had been up for hours. I had heard him rise and though I had barely slept a wink, I could not bring myself to crawl from my bed. Time passed as always and the stable boy's knock on the front door told me I must hasten.

I looked out of the window and down at the street for the last time. Daniel was tightening the straps upon the horse's pack.

I watched the muscles ripple beneath his shirt and admired the line of his back. I prayed that Isabella would love him better than I. Lifting my gown I tied a money pouch around my thigh and took one last look about the room. The jar on the table by the window was brimming with bright forget-me-nots. I had placed them there the previous morning so that Daniel might remember me, at least until they withered and died. I shivered nervously.

"Goodbye," I said to the room and turned quickly away.

Outside, Bessie was sobbing into her apron and when she hugged me she clung to me like a mother sending her son off to sea. I wondered if she suspected I was not coming back.

"There, there, Bess. I shall miss you too."

"You really should not go unescorted. I wish you would allow me to come with you," she said, fiddling with the tie on my horse's pack.

"I shall be fine, Bessie, don not fret for me, please. Besides, I need you to look after Daniel whilst I'm away."

Daniel slipped his arm about my waist and pulled me towards him. For a moment we held each other, then he said, "I pray God keeps you safe on this journey and your friends keep you well on your arrival."

"And you," I said, holding my nerve, "make sure Isabella takes good care of you."

I could feel the beating of his heart against my bosom as he held me close. But the hour could be delayed no longer. I allowed him to help me onto the horse. As the groom turned my horse about and led me away I glanced back to wave. Daniel was grasping at Bessie's hand, and I dared not look back again, for fear of changing my mind.

London, 1493

The city had always been kind to me, and I saw no reason to expect anything else of it this time. But as the pleasant fresh scent of the grass ebbed away and the dust track beneath my feet turned hard, the familiar stench of the river was near drowned beneath the stink of people. I had never been to London in the fifteenth century, and the chilly reality of the squalor-filled streets was a shock.

Nothing looked familiar. A boarding house had been recommended to me, but upon enquiry I found there was no room and I was forced to look elsewhere. I must find a room or I could truly be in mortal danger. I took my belongings from the saddle strap and let the horse and groom go, wending my way past the endless nunneries and monasteries that filled the city with clergy, but not piety. I wondered if I would be forced to join a convent. I prayed it would not be so, but as I wandered eastwards the winding streets grew narrow and dark, haunted by living shadows. Scraggy children with blackened skin and sooty rags grasped at my skirts, begging for food. There was a constant hum of flies hovering above the filth-ridden, broken-down slums. Dozens of people seemed crammed into each timber home, like cherries in a paper bag.

One child, her hair matted into flattened ropes around her face, offered to take me to a reputable boarding house, for a small fee. She was not more than nine years old but her manner far outreached her years, and I presumed from the stains on the back of her tattered frock that she did more for a farthing than I wanted to imagine. She grinned at me with yellow teeth and led me down a back alley. I stopped, afraid of where we were going. My bag was growing heavier. I set it down and rolled my aching shoulders.

"It ain't far, mistress, just round the corner there." She

pointed to the end of the tiny street where the buildings began to widen out once more.

"What is the name of this establishment?" I asked warily. She shrugged her bony shoulders.

"Dunno. It sez over the door, mistress... It's nice, I promise."

I let her continue, glad to feel the weight of my purse where I had strapped it against my thigh. I knew my funds would not last long. I needed somewhere to stay, and then employment. I decided to trust the girl.

"What's your name child?"

"Sarah, mistress. There, see."

She went past the last building and out into the waning daylight of a broader street. As I drew closer I realised I could see the white stone of the Tower just across the way. I had walked from one end of the city to the other. The ominous walls of the enclosure made me shudder and the girl laughed.

"Creepy place, ain't it? Can yer imagine the 'orrible crimes them inside has done?" she said with the kind of macabre enthusiasm only a child can have.

"No," I replied mindfully, "and I do not wish to." Images swirled before me of all those who were yet to die there. I thought of the axe as it would fall upon the neck of my husband's poor cousin Thomas More, and considered whether I should write and warn him. But I suspected such a thing would do more harm than good. And would it change anything? Should I change anything? I decided that if God let it happen, then it was the way it was intended to be. Changing the past or future was potentially a dangerous thing.

"This be it, mistress," Sarah said, walking boldly up to a wide friendly doorway and crashing a knocker against the wood.

I looked up at the sign that had been crudely placed over it;

Madame Legard's Boarding House. I was contemplating what sort of a woman Madame Legard would be, when the latch scraped back and with a grinding groan the door opened to reveal a tiny woman, no bigger than Sarah. Her hair was a brassy blond, piled on her head with wooden pins sticking out in all directions. Her eyes were bright and her cheeks, though pinched thin, were a healthy shade of pink.

"Sarah, how are you today?" There was no trace of the foreign accent her name had suggested. "Would you like a bit of bread and cheese?" The woman smiled to reveal a missing front tooth. Sarah nodded eagerly.

"I brought yer a guest." Sarah looked extremely pleased with herself. Madame Legard squinted at me.

"You shall 'ave to get a bit closer dear, my eyesight ain't that good."

I was not more than five yards away from her, but I obliged. As I stepped closer I saw that her complexion was enhanced by cosmetics; rouge was rubbed in to brighten her naturally pale tone. Her eyes were surrounded by a spider's web of fine lines and the colour of her hair faded to grey towards the roots. "You're a pretty one, if you don't mind my saying so, mistress. How long do you plan to stay?"

"Thank you," I said, wondering what sort of boarding house this might turn out to be. I suspected it did have a reputation, but for its occupants profession, rather than piety. "How much do you charge for the week?"

She glanced around the street and waited for an old man shuffle past before saying, "We can work that out later. I work on a needs must basis. You tells me what you can afford and I tell you 'ow much I need to take to keep you."

"Told ya she was nice, didn't I, mistress," Sarah said, slipping past Madame Legard and vanishing down a corridor.

"Don't mind 'er, she's a good little wretch, really."

"Does she have a family?" I asked as the landlady directed me into a dusty-looking living area. Cramped into a tiny space were several rickety stools, two rather threadbare chairs and a dresser that had seen better days. Placed in the centre of it all was a small table covered with a faded green cloth. The attempt at homeliness was amiable but wanting.

"Take a seat, Mistress...?"

"More," I replied, wishing I could dust off the stool before sitting down.

"I see," she said squinting harder and scrutinizing my gown. For a moment I thought she would pry further but she did not, instead she said, "Her Pa's dead and her Ma... well, let's just say she ain't fit to take care of herself, let alone a kid," she added. "Sarah does all right, I feed her when she'll let me."

"Where does she live?" I don't know why I asked, I already knew the answer.

"Wherever she falls asleep. Would you like food? I've got broth on the stove, or there's bread and cheese. It's stew for dinner," she said displaying the gap in her teeth again.

"I'm fine for now." I said. "Would you mind showing me to my room?"

"Of course. You can share the big room with Mistress Tyler and Mistress Jones if it pleases you, or the small room is free if that suits better," she said, leading me to a twisted staircase that creaked and leaned so much I was afraid to walk up it at first.

"Oh," I said. "How many people live here?"

She scratched her head and the entire pile of hair moved – I could swear there was something living inside it.

"Right now there's the two ladies as mentioned, then there's

Mistress Arundel in the front, she's a funny one, widowed young but never managed to re marry, you shan't see much of her. There's Master Schmitt and Master Smith in the back, they arrived together if you catch my drift, lived here for three years now, nice chaps, and well, now, there's you." She stopped at the top of the stairs. "The big room's up there," she pointed at another stairway, "or–."

"I think I should like the small room, if you don't mind," I said firmly. I wondered at an establishment that housed men as well as women, but decided I had little choice for now.

"As you like." She ferreted in her petticoat pocket and fished out a heavy black key. "It's that one." She indicated the door opposite. I took the key from her and let myself in.

When the door closed behind me I dropped my bag on the floor and looked at my lodgings. The dim light that glinted through the tiny window somehow managed to brighten the dirty lime-washed walls. I ran my hand along the heavy beam that ran through the sloping ceiling. It would do for a night or two until I found work, or better, Time took pity on me and moved me on. I opened the window and looked out at the Tower peering over the rooftops and drew in a breath of putrid air.

"What hell is this?" I asked myself, as a drunken man staggered across the street and vomited right below. I pulled the glass shut again and slumped down onto the narrow bed. It creaked and shuddered as I shifted my weight. There was nothing else in the room but a crooked chest for my clothes, a wash bowl and jug and shoved beneath the bed was a yellowed chamber pot.

As for my fellow boarders, Madame Legard was right; I never did see Mistress Arundel. I heard her though, through the wall. She cried at night, sometimes all night. The two men were very nice. There were noises from their room too, but no one said anything about that. I discovered the two ladies were not permanent residents and Mistress Jones moved on before the end of the week, but Mistress Tyler stayed for two months complete. I never did discover her sin, but she had been turned out by her father and had been desperate for a place to go. In the end a forgiving cousin took her in. It was unusual to find such a residence in that time. Madam Legard offered a service to those in need, who could afford it of course, who did not wish to finish their days in gaol or on the streets. I was very fortunate to have found Sarah to guide me to her.

I began to look for work right away. I never could be idle for long and with no books to read I grew impatient for a needle and thread.

"What are you good for, Mistress More?" Madame Legard asked, when it came to rent day at the end of the week.

"Will that do?" I said, extracting a coin from my money pouch.

"Still no work?" she said, hesitating. "You know we can wait a few days if you would rather?" Her kindness still astonished me. I shook my head.

"I'll find something tomorrow, I can feel it."

"As you please," she said taking the coin and dropping it into her petticoat pocket.

I had tried all the tailors in the city, from what I could see.

"You know, there's other ways to make a penny," Sarah offered as she accompanied me down the street the following morning.

I looked at her in horror. The thought of what she was implying made my skin crawl, not so much for myself but for her. I wanted to protect her, so she would never have to serve a man's temptation again. How a mother can abandon her child to such a fate I cannot comprehend. I watched her hair as it swung in a filthy roll down her back and over the dirt on her ancient tunic, and thought how easily that could have been me. My heart tore at the thought of it. I know not where my true parents are, or if 'tis their fault, but I know I could not willingly abandon a child of mine. That night, when I tossed and turned on my sagging straw mattress, I considered how lucky my life had been in comparison to Sarah's. I had to help her.

"I'll pay for her board, and we can move into the big room now Mistress Jones has gone," I said to Madame Legard over breakfast.

"A good heart you have, but she'll not come. Don't you think I haven't tried. Let her make her own way, feed her once in a while, that's the best thing you can do for 'er," she said with a kind smile. I almost hated her honesty. Part of me would have preferred not to see things as they really were.

"I can at least try," I said.

"You do as you wish, Mistress More, if it makes you feel better, but I tell you, she'll not come." And she was right. The look of shame that crossed that little girl's face when I suggested it made me feel smaller than her.

The morrow brought with it a violent storm. Lightning kept the sky bright and the rain poured down like a widow's tears. A crack of thunder shuddered the clouds and Sarah grabbed my hand. "Run, miss, it's only just across the street," she said and dragged me through the splashing mud towards a grey shop front. We pushed open the door with a clunk and stumbled into the drapery.

"May I help?" A skinny man with a thick foreign accent swung around to face us.

"Forgive the intrusion, sir. I am looking for work and my friend here informs me you are in need of an assistant. I have experience with all manner of fabrics. I can read, write and keep good books. I am an excellent tailor and ran my own..." He put his finger to his lips to silence me.

Master Rosenberg was sallow, with heavy-set eyes and a long thin nose. He peered at me with piercing grey eyes for what felt like an hour, examining my face and attire before finally taking my hands in his and turning them over. He ran a manicured fingernail over my slender fingers, feeling for the calluses worn from the pressure of scissors and the prick of needles.

"A hard worker that knows how to handle cloth," he said finally. "Did you make this gown?" he gestured at my dress.

"I did, sir. Back in Oxford I made—"

"Very well, you start tomorrow."

Once more I thanked heaven for my good fortune.

I found I was comfortable at Madame Legard's. And I did not wish to abandon Sarah as others had done, though I knew one day I would. I earned my board with little effort but for my aching feet. The wages were not much but I got by. My evenings were my reprieve, so long as Madame Legard felt like talking a while, and I finally found a way to help Sarah. I taught her to sew. She was a willing pupil and excelled with a needle and thread, far better than I could have hoped.

Sometimes I imagined that she was the little girl Anne would have become, sitting by my side and learning our trade. For a while, my existence continued as such. Days drifted into weeks and blurred together. At night my dreams flitted from Daniel to Philip, wondering what better life one had forged in my absence, and longing for a life with the other that I knew could never be.

I know not how long I continued that way, but it was autumn when it ended.

MICHAEL

Oxford — 5th September, 2025

Just the ticket for the mother of the bride, thought Michael, as he watched Margaret Penning enter the little chapel. Her faded strawberry blond hair was pinned into a French pleat, and the tailored turquoise suit flattered her ample figure. Michael was standing at the altar end of the front pew with his remarkably calm son and Tom, his best man. *Tom looks more nervous than Paul,* considered Michael. In fact Tom was practically green. Michael hoped the lad wasn't going to be sick. That really wouldn't go down well with the other guests and certainly not with Millie when she arrived.

He looked down at the black and white tiles of Balliol Chapel floor. *It's like walking on a sanctified chess board,* he mused. Looking up, he caught Imogen's eye and smiled at her. She replied with a teary wave. Her appearance took his breath, just as it had that morning, when he had zipped her into her elegant lilac dress, and just as it had on the day he married her, almost thirty years earlier in that same chapel. As their gaze locked he saw the same mixed emotions behind her eyes that swirled in his chest. Ecstatic as they both were for Paul and Millie, there was that nagging loss of their daughter that never stopped beating in their hearts, especially on such occasions as this. For a moment his mind wandered and he imagined what Catherine would have looked like on her wedding day, or dressed in one of the Cadbury-purple cocktail dresses Millie had chosen for her bridesmaids.

He closed his eyes for a moment as Millie's best friend Grace entered the church clutching a bunch of bright irises and gripping the hand of the pageboy. *That could have been Catherine, if it weren't for me,* he thought sadly.

Heeled footsteps clicked over the tiles towards him. Michael put on a casual smile and greeted Margaret.

"Good afternoon, Maggie, you look lovely." Right behind her were a middle-aged couple he couldn't quite see. He attempted to look over her shoulder as she stopped in front of him and said,

"Thank you, Michael, and don't you gents look smart?"

"Thanks," said Paul, looking her over with the eye of a future son-in-law, "you look pretty hot yourself."

Margaret posed and pouted like a supermodel, then laughed.

"Naughty boy," she said. "Now, they were just taking a few last photos at the house before setting off. The car was all ready and waiting so there shouldn't be any delays. Geoff said ten minutes or so."

Geoff Penning was Margaret's husband, Millie's stepfather.

"How you holding up, Paul?" Margaret asked, examining his pallor for signs of nerves.

"Great, thanks," he replied enthusiastically. "It's Tom that's nervous about his speech."

Margaret gave him an impressed smile,

"Excellent. I was surprised how calm Millie was this morning, as well. She seems more excited than anything else." Margaret gave Paul's hand a quick squeeze. Paul grinned and excused himself to greet some more of his guests.

Margaret stepped aside to reveal the couple. The man looked to be sixtyish, with a shining bald head and thick bushy eyebrows. His high cheekbones and aquiline nose were contoured in precisely the same way as Margaret's.

"Michael, this is my brother David, and his wife, Sue."

Sue was a petite woman with sandy hair that might have been formerly red. Her eyes were piercing blue and despite her fifty-plus years, they remained as bright and clear as though she were no more than twenty.

"Pleasure," Michael said, shaking hands with them both. "You must be Ellie and Heather's parents." Michael had met Millie's cousins once or twice when they were girls. He particularly recalled one afternoon, not long before Catherine disappeared, when he had collected his daughter from the Pennings house and they had all been there, playing together on the front lawn. They were grown up now, of course; though it was not until Millie had shown him a photograph of them all on her hen night that it struck him just how grown-up Catherine should be too. In his mind she was still a little girl of six, not a woman of twenty-two.

"That's right."

"Where are they?" asked Michael, looking around for them.

"Outside in the Quad, grabbing a bit of this lovely late summer sun."

"Ah, can't blame them for that. Not often we get days like this in September."

"Not in this soggy little county anyway," said David with a laugh.

Michael's father had always described Oxfordshire in the same way. He liked David instantly.

"Millie tells me you're *the* Professor Michael Alexander," said Sue, as Imogen joined them. Michael stared at her in surprise.

"I'm sorry. I've never been called a '*the*' before."

"Oh don't mind Sue, her Grandpa was rather a fan, that's all. He had a bit of a fascination for time-travel," David said, with a warm smile.

"Really?" replied Michael, his heart sinking. He saw Imogen shoot a warning look in his direction; he hated to be reminded of his past and had, on previous occasions, been known to retract sharply from any conversation that brought it up. He forced the corners of his mouth into an upward tilt as Sue continued.

"Oh, it was only a hobby, but I know he read your book. In fact I think my dad still has it."

"Gracious," said Michael, astounded anyone had actually bought a copy. "It must have a bit of dust on it now, it came out sixteen years ago, before…" his voice trailed.

Sue shifted her sandaled feet.

"I'm so sorry. We shouldn't have mentioned… it must be very difficult for you, especially today." Her cheeks were turning a furious shade of red. Suddenly Michael felt sorry for her.

"No, no, it's all right. You meant well."

"Sometimes it's nice to talk about her," Imogen offered, kindly.

"You must miss her very much," David added, then flinched as his wife jabbed him in the ribs.

Imogen smiled. "Every day. How much did Millie tell you?"

Michael wanted to run up the aisle, through the Quad and vanish down some narrow side street. Sensing this, his wife slipped her hand into his and held him steady.

"We know you never stopped looking," David said to Michael.

"Really?" said Michael for the second time in the conversation. "She told you that?"

"Well, yes. But, oh, please don't think we would ever say or… look, they…" Sue nodded at Paul, "just mentioned that you had never given up hope."

"Ah," muttered Michael.

"We would never mention your research to anyone. Though

Sue's Grandpa would have-"

"Loved to hear all about it," Sue finished her husband's sentence.

Michael glanced at his watch and then up at the door. *Hurry up, Millie.*

"Show them the photograph, honey," Imogen said brightly. "You know, we really believe it's her. It's amazing, really, to think of our daughter living in another time."

Michael adjusted his tie.

"Michael?" Imogen said. "Michael, you have it with you, don't you?"

Michael started, his wife's voice finally penetrating his thoughts.

"Sorry?" he stuttered.

"The photograph of Catherine." Imogen wore an expectant glare.

"Oh, yes." Michael went over to the pew and fished in the breast pocket of his jacket.

He had been keeping the photograph in his wallet since the day Paul had found it. His eyes wandered over the sepia surface, resting briefly on Catherine's face before he offered it to Sue.

Sue ferreted around in her pink leather handbag for a glasses case, from which she extracted a pair of pink-rimmed spectacles. Taking the photo card carefully in her slim fingers she pushed the glasses up the bridge of her nose and peered at the little group of strangers. Her flushed cheeks paled and her mouth opened. Michael looked at her, puzzled. He was about to enquire if she was all right when she exclaimed, "It can't be!"

Outside there was a scuffle in the chapel arch and Heather appeared in the doorway, waving to the organist to strike up the music. Michael desperately wanted to continue the conversation but it would have to wait. Sue pushed the photograph back at Michael and he noticed her hand was shaking as he took it from her. He opened his mouth to speak but the couple were already dashing off to their seats and Imogen was tugging at his hand to take his place.

He looked up from the photograph just in time to see the proud grin on Geoff Penning's face as he stepped through the chapel door with his step-daughter on his arm. Michael winced at the deep stab of regret as he realised he would never have the chance to give his own daughter away.

CATHERINE

London, 1493

One night, too cold to undress and my feet throbbing with wear, I kicked off my shoes, crawled onto my bed and pulled the thin blanket over my body. My St Christopher pressed against my throat. I twisted it out of the way. A cold draught fluttered through a crack in the frame of my window. I tugged up the blanket and shivered. Mistress Arundel was sobbing into her pillow next door and somewhere outside someone was screaming. I closed my eyes and scratched at my bug-bitten legs, picturing Philip's face until I drifted into a restless sleep.

When I awoke the sun was not yet over the horizon and I blinked up at the naked moon. I stared at what I thought were stars and tried to make sense of my surroundings. My head was thumping hard and my eyes dazzled by a sparkling mist of bright greens and violet. As the spinning sensation eased and the Earth's turn settled into a natural rotation, I rubbed my face with my hands. The stars had receded into dull distant specks and were replaced by the yellow glow of the gas lamps along the street. My room at Madame Legard's Boarding House was gone, and instead I was slumped against the rough brick of some tall building. The air smelled cold and above my head my view was obscured by the swirl of chimney smoke. I stood and looked down at my bare feet and the state of my crumpled gown, dusted myself down as best I could and prayed I was somewhere close to safety. I could be thankful at least that I had not been deposited in the middle of a busy road.

London, 1916

At first I was unsure which way to walk. To one side were the cream stone walls of a great building looming out of the early dawn light; to the other, a row of tall town houses, the back of which I had been sleeping against. I listened to the gentle lap of the water and took in the sour aroma that drifted on the breeze. I would know that stench anywhere; I was only a few yards from the Thames.

I made my way around the side of the building and crossed over the road to the river's edge. My breath plumed out into the chilled morning air like smoke from a cigarette. I shivered, pulling my shawl tighter about my shoulders. Across the river a light flashed in a window at Lambeth Palace and the boats on the water were beginning to hum with life. In the distance I heard the roll of an engine and the beep of a horn. Looking back at the grand steps and high Corinthian columns behind me, I recognized the limestone facade of the Tate Gallery and breathed a sigh of relief. I was in Pimlico, and whatever the date, it could not be too far from Rosaline and Philip.

I drew a long deep breath to gather my thoughts and check my memory was as intact as it had ever been and began to walk along Milbank, past the Palace of Westminster and up Whitehall.

I had only ever been to the Tate Gallery by carriage with Rosaline, but I knew where I was. I did not stop to think of anything but seeking out my old friends, nor did I care that people stared at me as I walked by with my shoeless feet and my sleep-crumpled fifteenth century clothes. It was only when I reached the open space of Trafalgar Square that I began to fear London was not exactly as I had left it.

A line of growling scarlet beasts surrounded the square; horseless omnibuses spluttering like angry dragons waiting to pounce. I had never seen so many at once. A young man in a smart khaki uniform passed me by. He doffed his cap and flashed me a wink. I tugged at my gown and hurried on.

By the time I reached the bottom of Russell Square my feet were black and aching and the city was full of life. Two more men wearing khaki uniforms walked by; one looked weary and the other so very young. I did not know what all this meant but a sense of unease began to gnaw at my stomach. I sighed gratefully as my eyes met with the pink bricks of the Hotel Russell. It was broad daylight by then and the sky was dotted with fluffy white clouds.

As I made my way across the street to number fifty-two, a couple were walking towards me. The woman looked elegant in a long flowing navy-blue coat, with a fur wrapped about her shoulders. She was tall and slender with greying blond hair piled under a wide-brimmed hat that shadowed her features. The gentleman tipped his hat at me, revealing a deeply receding hairline in what had once been very thick hair. My heart stopped. He looked about a decade older than when I had last seen him, but I could not mistake the gentle, slim features or the rhododendron-bush beard of Simon Campbell. He must have seen me falter for he too stopped, grasped the elbow of the woman he was with and held her still.

"Are you all right, madam?" Then, after a pause he cocked his head slightly and asked, "Do I know you?"

I could not speak. The woman lifted her head a little so the light caught her face and I almost fell to my knees.

"Can it be? Catherine?"

I nodded, timid and silent.

"It is you! My dear Catherine, how *are* you? Where have you been?"

Rosaline was suddenly upon me. She flung her arms around me and hugged so tight I could scarce draw breath. Tears were rolling down my cheeks as she set me back from her and took in my attire.

"Gracious, what happened to you?"

I had not yet found the strength to answer any of her questions. Dr Campbell caught me as my knees finally buckled.

"We were just about to take a stroll but we can forgo. Come, let's get you home." Rosaline slipped her arm through mine and led me up the short path to her front door.

I watched curiously as Doctor Campbell extracted a key from his coat pocket and slid it into the lock.

From down the hall another familiar voice called, "Back so soon, madam, is all well?" I staggered back a little as the figure of an elderly man stepped out from the dining-room doorway.

"Markham," I whispered hoarsely, finally finding my voice. The aged butler narrowed his sharp eyes at me and blinked in great surprise.

"Sweet Jesus, it cannot be, Mrs More? You have not aged a single day. He scowled at me through a squint. "In fact I could say you almost look younger than when we last saw you."

My friend laughed softly at the irony of his unwitting observation. Rosaline picked up a small bell from the hall cupboard – the same cupboard that had always been there, only the Nippon vase was gone and in its place stood a spiky dark green plant in a plain white pot – and summoned the maid.

A moment later a woman scuttled in from the direction of the kitchen and tripped over the mop bucket, which I can only assume was where she had left it.

"Sissy!" I gasped. The maid had gone from a slip of a girl to a scrawny, long-faced woman with flecks of grey scattered through the dark curls of her uncovered hair.

"Where is your hat, Sissy?" Markham said, with a sigh.

Suddenly I was laughing out loud as relief swept through me. Thank heaven some things never change.

"Fetch us some tea and then run a bath for Mrs More, dear," Rosaline instructed the maid, "our friend has come a long way to see us today; she is tired from the journey and needs to rest."

As she spoke I noticed the fine lines that had once crinkled lightly around Rosaline's eyes were now deeper and more permanently set. "Will you be staying a while?" she asked, shooing Dr Campbell up the stairs towards the drawing room. I watched the familiarity of her gesture and registered the simple gold band that adorned her hand. She had married Simon after all. I was most delighted for her. "How silly of me, how can you possibly know how long you will be with us?" she added with a broad smile as we sat down on the drawing room couch. "But you will stay with us whilst you are here, won't you?"

I nodded sheepishly, "You remember Dr Campbell, of course," she smiled.

Simon gave me a short bow. "Of course she does, dear. She is a time-traveller, and it may have been only yesterday when she was with us last."

"Thank you, Dr Campbell, but I believe Rosaline meant to enquire whether my memory was intact. It has not always been so when I have been travelling," I offered with mild amusement. The look upon my face however must have been more like shock, for my friend then offered an apology.

"Forgive me, Catherine, my husband is aware of your situation, I hope you don't mind."

I shook my head and smiled. "Of course I do not mind. He is your husband." This was not a question but it came out as such.

Rosaline blushed and Simon cleared his throat.

"I finally came to my senses in 1914 and made an honest woman of her." He beamed lovingly at his wife as she rolled her eyes at him.

"1914?" I said, attempting to date my surroundings.

Rosaline cast her eyes over me. "Then you have only just arrived?"

"Yes, not two hours since, I should hazard."

The hall clock struck nine-thirty. Rosaline furrowed her brow thoughtfully.

"Today is Monday, February 21st, 1916. *Where* did you... er... arrive?" She asked, clearly considering the possibilities.

When I told her she raised an eyebrow and said, "Good thing you found a landmark."

I laughed again. "Definitely less of a problem than my last visit."

She nodded with another roll of her eyes. "It certainly is that." Something curious flickered in her eyes, but then her face relaxed into a broad smile. "Oh, it is good to see you, Catherine."

I was about to enquire after Philip and Arthur when I noticed the distinct absence of one particular family member. His hat had not been upon the hall stand, no coats or jackets rested there either and his newspaper was not laid out on the side table.

"How is your family, Rosaline?" I asked carefully.

My friend lowered her eyes and her fingers began to work her wedding band around and around. I noticed Simon shoot a glance towards a photograph on the mantel.

"Leticia is in excellent health. She and Ernest have four children now, all well and thriving. You will not believe how tall little Ernest has grown, you'll barely recognise him, he's eleven now." Her voice was quavering and I could see she was leading up to something unpleasant. "I am sorry to have to tell you, but father is no longer with us. He has been gone these five years. It was nothing lingering; his heart simply gave out in the end."

"I am very sorry to hear it," I replied, reaching over and resting my hand over hers.

"Oh, he was a good age," she added, with a half-smile. She was clearly about to continue when we were interrupted by a clatter at the drawing-room door. We three all turned in time to see the door swing open to reveal Sissy carrying the tea tray, with the cups and saucers intact but the sugar bowl tipped on its side, with the contents spilled out over the tray. She began to apologise profusely as Rosaline took it from her and set it down upon the coffee table.

As Sissy fretted over the spilled sugar and made attempts to scoop it back into its bowl she looked up at me.

"Forgive the impertinence, Miss, but I'm dying to know, was it a boy or a girl?"

Rosaline and Simon glanced at each other with wide warning eyes. For once my friend seemed incapable of forming a response. I was not entirely certain whom Sissy was addressing but it seemed to be me.

"I… I'm sorry… I have no…"

"It was a girl, Sissy, thank you for your interest. Now, please go and run that bath, and watch how hot the water is, won't you?" Rosaline intercepted.

As I watched her leave the atmosphere was sharp as a knife. My heart was pounding and Rosaline looked nervous.

"You know, I nearly scalded my feet last week, she made the water so hot." She forced a laugh. Simon rose suddenly and excused himself, vanishing to the study as quickly as his feet could manage, leaving Rosaline and me alone.

My dear friend came to sit beside me on the couch and poured the tea. I knew from the amount of sugar she piled into each cup that there was more bad news to come.

"Please, Rosaline, do tell me what it is, the suspense is driving me to distraction."

She paused, her hand halfway to the milk jug. The frankness of her expression when our eyes met was the only thing that could have made me believe her words.

"When you were last here you were heavily pregnant."

"But I… that was nine years since, and I was…" I did not finish my protest for I could sense the twist coming.

Rosaline continued. "I can see that it has not happened for you yet, but even without the difference in your age I would have known it. It was some years ago that you were last with us, but not so long ago as you think. It was in 1910, and at that time you asked me, or rather I should say, it was your own words that warned me, not to speak of future events. I was unsure what to make of such a statement then but now I see exactly what you meant. I don't think we should talk of what is past for some and not yet occurred for others. Such a conversation would cause too much confusion. Forgive me, Catherine, but this is where this topic must end."

I breathed in deeply and attempted to digest what she had said. All the while she watched me expectantly. The news that I was to have another child was shock enough, but to know that I had visited a time out of the natural order was most distressing.

"Well, if you think it best, then I concur. But, please tell me…" for a second she looked horrified, "how long was I here, then?"

"Oh," she breathed in relief, "not long, less than a month. If I can give you one piece of information then let it be this; that you have nothing to fear."

I sat back against the arm of the couch and rested my head on my hand. This was indeed news that could keep my heart steady, but that such a comfort needed to be said at all disturbed me far more than had she kept the thought to herself. Do not think me ungrateful, dear journal, believe me, the comfort those words have brought me since has been greatly appreciated, especially here and now.

"Are you all right, dear?" she asked when I did not respond. "Was I right to say?"

I returned to my regular composure and smiled.

"Yes. Thank you."

She swallowed visibly and added, "Oh dear, there is more I must tell. We are at war, Catherine. Our country is at war with Germany and it is a war like no other. I shan't bombard you with details now, you must be exhausted and confused enough, but you must be wondering about Arthur and Ernest. This bloody war has taken them away to France along with half our men. All the able ones it seems are to be drafted in."

I sat bolt upright, my hand shaking so much the teacup rattled in the saucer. I had never heard Rosaline use such language before and the sound of it then made the news all the more distressing.

"They are safe as yet," she added, observing my alarm, "but I cannot assure you they will stay so. Too many of our men are killed and too many more are needed. This thing is bigger than any of us ever dreamed possible and there is no end in sight."

After this news I found I dared not enquire after Philip, I could only trust that if something terrible had happened, she would have told me. Instead I gulped down the scalding cup of tea and rasped, "Forgive me, but would you mind if I took my bath now?"

"My dear, not at all. Simon and I shall take our stroll and leave you to it."

"If we may continue this conversation later," I asked, "I should very much like to be told more about current events."

"Of course, dear," she smiled. "Take your old room. It is pretty much as it was. Oh, and you may take anything you like from my wardrobe. Your sewing box is where you left it."

I gave my thanks and withdrew from company to soak in a soapy tub of very hot water. Despite the heat of it I cannot stress to you just how delectable a good bath can feel when your bones are weary and the news has been disturbing.

Later, after a more detailed conversation with my friends, my mind was agog. I thought she would be shocked at my divorce, but Rosaline took it in her stride. I was the one left reeling from all her news. The whole world seemed to have gone mad with war and little of it made sense. I cannot even begin to explain the complexities, dear friend. But know this: that Great War of the twentieth century was one that would destroy a generation and for no good reason that I could see.

Rosaline did have some brighter notes to tell though. Arthur had married Charlotte Boden-Howard. They met again in Egypt on Lord Rupert's archaeological dig, and had quite the romance it seems. But when war broke out they returned to England. Now she was left behind with their young son and Arthur was in France. He had joined up right at the start, 'Back before Christmas,' he had said. But that was more than a year since. I was shown a photograph of Rosaline's wedding, a delightful family group with Charlotte on one side looking graver than she ought, Arthur on the other in his uniform and greatcoat, and little Albert standing to attention between them. The boy was the spitting image of his father, not a sign of the Boden-Howards visible in his features. He had been three when it was taken and now he was near five. Arthur must have missed them so. I asked if I might write to him.

"Oh, yes, dear. He would love that," Rosaline smiled.

Yet still she said nothing of Philip. I cannot say for certain which I feared most, that he should have married someone else or that he had been lost in the war. Perhaps both prospects were of equal abhorrence to me at that moment.

There seemed to be so many preoccupations and distractions about and since no one had volunteered the information and I had not had the nerve to enquire, I still new naught of Philip some five days after my arrival. I could hardly eat for the worry of it.

On the first Friday morning of my stay I awoke from a fitful sleep to the inviting smell of slightly burned toast and frying eggs. As I pushed back the curtains to reveal a gloriously sunny day I resolved to find my courage and ask after Philip. But from the moment I set foot upon the stairs other events thwarted any attempt. I had no sooner opened my bedroom door when the telephone rang loudly in the hall.

I could not comprehend its workings and no matter how many times it went off I could not get used to the ring. Telephones were a rare possession, so much so that it was almost only ever the hospital that used it. Unusually, on that morning it rang twice. The first call was to summon Dr Campbell to the 4th London General to assist with a train of wounded soldiers that had just arrived at Waterloo.

When I arrived at the breakfast table I found Dr Campbell stuffing a slice of toast into his mouth quicker than his jaw could chew, and Rosaline holding a cup of tea to his lips so that he could take a sip whilst buttoning up his shirt.

"You know, if we lived closer you would be able to come home at night," my friend said. "We could take a house in Denmark Hill." This was a proposition Rosaline had put forward on more than one occasion, but Dr Campbell wouldn't hear of it.

"I doubt there will be time to sleep tonight, anyway," he replied, as Markham appeared with his surgical bag.

"Sir, the cab is here."

"Very good." Simon grabbed a second slice of buttered toast, took his overnight case from where the maid had left it and dashed out of the front door.

"Well, goodness knows when we shall see him again. Sometimes he's gone for days when the trains come in."

"There must be a lot of men for it to take so many doctors," I said naively.

"My dear, too many to dare count."

That was when the telephone rang a second time. I looked at it with a start.

Rosaline picked up the receiver. "Dr Campbell's residence." There was a pause as she listened, her thin mouth relaxing into a light smile. "Oh, Charlotte dear, what a pleasant surprise… Yes, yes of course you may… No, we haven't as yet… yes, I'm sure we shall… oh, that is excellent news… yes my dear I shall… That would be lovely… Sunday it is, then." She set the receiver back in its rest on the wall bracket and turned to face me. "Well, it seems Charlotte will be joining us for Sunday dinner," she said brightly.

I could only assume Charlotte was already informed of my presence.

"Excellent," I said, pleased. I liked Charlotte and I was curious to see how such a vivacious and flighty girl had turned out.

"Bertie, too of course, I'm sure you'll get along famously with him. Oh, and she has received a letter from Arthur."

"That is good news. He is well?"

"As he can be, I suppose. She says his spirits seemed high and he's uninjured, which is the best we can ask for right now."

Behind her relief I could detect disappointment that she had not received her own letter. She need not have concerned herself with such thoughts however, for her letter did arrive by the second post. It was a good letter too, though there was one section that caused concern. Those words are engraved in my mind.

'The guns never let up. I even dream of the sound when it isn't there.'

And though there was no morbidity or mention of those he had lost, it was implied when he wrote, 'Do send me more paper, I seem to run out so fast and there are letters I must write to comfort those I can.'

I did not quite follow the implications at first, but when I read it over later, I saw what he meant. Arthur was writing to the families of the soldiers killed in his regiment. I cried myself to sleep that night, for more reasons than one.

Forgive me, I have digressed, and I think I must take you back again to that morning.

It was turning out to be a most unseasonably pleasant day. We had no fixed plans so, after breakfast, I decided to cut myself a dress from some newly purchased fabric. Rosaline had wanted to buy me an outfit off the peg but I couldn't let her spoil me so. The fabric was cheaper. But the very moment I had laid out the cloth over the dining table, Rosaline came in holding out a hat and coat for me.

"I think we should go out today. It's too nice to stay indoors and there's plenty of time for sewing when it rains."

"But the sooner I have a couple of gowns of my own the sooner I can begin to take in work again," I protested, but she added,

"Do let's go out, dear. It's not often the sun shines so warmly in February."

"Very well," I grinned. "Where shall we go?"

"I thought perhaps we might walk into town. There's a café you haven't tried in Leicester Square that makes the most delicious macaroons."

"All right," I said, accepting the hat and coat. The borrowed outfit I was wearing was respectable enough, and who would notice me, anyway?

Before luncheon we ventured around the corner to the National Gallery. I paused at the top of the steps and looked out over Trafalgar Square and Whitehall. The sun blazed over rooftops and glinted in windows. Automobiles and carriages clattered by and people were going about their everyday business. Everything seemed almost normal, save for the khaki uniforms. Rosaline leaned over my shoulder and said,

"It's a nervous world down there. Shall we go in and forget all about it?"

I knew what she meant, and yet I was glad to be in it.

We strolled along the corridors just as we had many times before. I found the art calming until we came to the Rokeby Venus. I adored the works of Velasquez and this piece was one of his finest.

As I stood admiring it my friend said, "You can hardly tell it was damaged at all." I looked at her, bemused. "Of course," she added, "you were not here. It was attacked by a suffragette just before the war and had to be taken down. The whole gallery was closed for a while because of it."

I was clearly missing a vital piece of information.

"What's a suffragette?"

"Oh, my dear," said my friend, resting her hand on my arm, "you'll love them! Women who fight for equality with men. If you had been here, I think you might have joined them!"

There had been rumblings of such things in 1907, but nothing I had heard then compared to the determination of these women in the few years that followed. The right to vote! My goodness, the thought lit my heart. The restrictions placed upon my sex had near suffocated me in both the centuries in which I had lived. And here was a movement to unlace the restraints so that we might strip off our corsets and breathe freely.

"Could such a thing be possible?" I gasped.

"Not yet, and this war has hindered the progress, but I think the day will come, and before this decade is out."

"I think I need to sit down for a moment," I said. But as I turned towards the bench I near fell backwards in surprise.

Before me stood a tall slim gentleman in a neat, almost sober-looking tweed suit. His hair was in the same ragged state I knew so well, only now flecks of grey dappled his temples. His astute brown eyes were as warm and bright as ever, and the wonderful, heart-warming grin, that lit up his face and the room with it, almost made me weep. It took a great deal of control for me not to reach up and kiss him.

"My dear Philip, how are you?" said Rosaline, looking almost as pleased to see him as I. As always he bent and dropped a kiss on the back of her kid glove.

"Very well indeed, Mrs Campbell, and better still now I have the pleasure of seeing you today."

Rosaline rolled her eyes in her usual way. But as his gaze lowered to meet mine, the grin upon his face eased into a most disconcerting expression.

"Why did you not tell me Catherine was here?" he asked without breaking his stare.

"You're near impossible to contact these days," she chided, "and besides, she's only been back since Monday, barely enough time to take in all the changes."

"Mrs Campbell, that is almost a week!" he retaliated playfully.

If Rosaline had told Charlotte of my arrival, then neither of them had informed Philip. I was confused and desperately disappointed that no one had thought he would care enough to know. Swallowing the fluttering nerves in my stomach I found my voice.

"Philip, how good to see you." The light behind his eyes warmed further and I was forced to choke back tears. "I'm glad to find you safe." The relief in my tone was blatant.

"You thought I'd gone to war?" He was clearly flattered at my concern.

"I feared it, yes," I replied, "and I have been too afraid to enquire."

"Forgive me for not explaining, Catherine, but... I... well... I was not sure when... or..." Rosaline mumbled in an uncharacteristic loss of composure. Realisation hit me.

"Philip, the last time I saw you, when was that?"

He turned his head a little and eyed me sideways.

"I can never forget." There was an odd crack to his voice as he spoke and he watched me carefully until the truth of it dawned upon him. "1910," he said slowly.

"I have not been there yet, sir," I said, praying he would forgive me any ignorance of past events.

He stepped back a little.

"Then you really have not…?" His eyes flickered towards Rosaline with something resembling desperation. I thought my heart would tear for not knowing what had transpired six years ago that made them react so.

"No, she hasn't. She's been through a lot since we last had the pleasure of our friend's company, but she's not had the experiences that brought her to us then." There was a warning tone in Rosaline's voice that sent a shiver down my spine.

Philip's eyes widened further as he considered the implications.

"Oh, how blind could I have been? When you saw us last you were aware of all this?" He opened his arms and gestured at the world around us.

"Now so much makes sense." He looked at me with the most unfathomable expression. "You knew what was to come." He gently scanned my face. There were faint shadows around his eyes that gave him the same tired look I had seen in so many since my return. "I wish you could tell me, Catherine, if all you said to me then was the truth, or if you had hidden more than this war from us."

"Now it's your turn to forgive me, Philip," said Rosaline and we both turned to stare at her. "Catherine did… or will… give some indication that something… unpleasant was to come, but in her own words, we are best to remain unaware of our own futures."

"You have nothing to apologise for, Catherine said as much to me also, but… well, you can see why I had not entirely… why I found it so difficult to… I shall say no more."

As I watched Philip's mind click everything into place, I

knew then that he understood far more than I, and the fear that something I had not yet done that had altered his opinion of me in his past, made my head spin. I wondered if I could fix it when the time came and what the implications would be.

"That is precisely why I think it best not to discuss Catherine's last visit," Rosaline continued, glancing from Philip to myself.

"Perhaps we should take tea?" I offered desperately.

"That is a very good idea," Philip said with a slow breath and a widening smile.

He offered us his arms like a bird opening its wings, and Rosaline and I accepted his escort as we made our way to the little teashop Rosaline had been telling me about.

Moments later we were seated by the window and the waitress came to take our order. I caught the flirtatious look she gave our companion. Philip gave her a flash of his best smile and she blushed and tripped over the nearest chair leg. Rosaline raised her eyebrows at me and we both began to laugh.

"Poor girl is probably missing her chap," Philip said defensively. "It seems everyone is off to war these days."

"And you?" I said tentatively. "Do you not wish to join the campaign?"

"Philip is working at Whitehall, his war is here," Rosaline answered rather quickly.

"Oh, I said," without comprehension.

"I work for the government, Catherine," Philip explained. "There are important things I can do for the war effort here. They snatched me from my teaching post at Oxford within days of the war breaking out."

Somewhat bewildered, I nodded. Philip's hand was so close

to mine on the table that we were almost touching; his fingers twitched but then he withdrew his hand and sat back. I wanted to cry.

"What sort of things?" I asked.

"I'm afraid I cannot say."

"Oh," I replied again, unsure whether this was the truth or simply something he did not wish to discuss with me. I could not expect all my friends to welcome me back openly after such a length of time, especially if I had done something awful to lower their opinion of me.

Rosaline saw the sting of tears in my eyes.

"Government jobs can be rather secretive," she said, "all very hush-hush, especially with the war."

"Exactly," said Philip. "There are a lot of sealed lips these days."

For a moment I thought he was jibing at me, but then he added, "You never know who might be listening, and there are too many enemy ears flapping about."

At that moment our scones arrived accompanied by a large pot of soothing tea. Suddenly Philip's eyes twinkled and he sat back in his chair looking at the pair of us. The change made my heart skip.

I think I preferred the more casual dress of his youth, but he looked so handsome in his suit that I believed it impossible for him not have a wife or at least a fiancé. I looked down at the scone I was smothering repeatedly with jam and wondered if my face were the same colour as the strawberries.

"It is truly good to see you, Catherine." Philip's voice was so soft I dared myself to raise my gaze to look at him. His eyes met mine and I felt Rosaline shift a little in her seat. After a long moment she cleared her throat.

"Philip still holds his reputation for being the most eligible bachelor in town. Though, and I'm sure he will not mind my telling you, he is now a far calmer and steady prospect for a good woman."

Astonished and feeling my face burn even more I exclaimed 'Ah!' so unexpectedly that both of my companions jumped. Relieved I had the presence of mind to think of it at that moment, I quickly changed the subject.

"I have some information for you, if you are still interested in me," I stuttered and stopped for a moment. "That came out wrong," I said attempting to regain my composure. "I mean… my situation," I finished with a dry rasp.

But Philip was grinning.

"Of course," he said only to me. Then looking almost as embarrassed, he said, "Do fire away."

I began to speak of my recent experiences with time. I confirmed the consistency of the sounds and colours that came with each journey and the spinning sensation that made my head light and my stomach turn. I told them of how my memory was less and less affected each time I travelled. I told them of how I had been taken from the smoggy streets of London and arrived outside St Mary Magdalen's. The more I spoke, the more I was at ease, and the more intrigued my friends became.

"Well, indeed," said Rosaline finally.

"Excellent," said Philip, sitting back again and folding his arms thoughtfully across his chest. "That really *is* very interesting."

"Now don't get carried away, dear, you have war work to do you know."

Rosaline attempted to look disapproving but failed miserably. My friend certainly had softened towards Philip.

"And your childhood memories, before you were six, have

you recovered anything else?" he asked.

I shook my head.

"Nothing, but I did recover the dress I had been wearing *that* day and the fabric was of a most peculiar kind, I have not ever seen the like of it..."

As I gave my description, Philip and Rosaline drew in closer and closer until I was done.

Philip nodded slowly, examining my expression.

"I was making good progress with my time travel research, but then this infernal war came along. But, well, you're here now. When this thing is over I'll try again, and then perhaps we can find a way to keep you here."

I think my whole body must have reddened at that. Certainly my heart warmed so much it seared my insides.

"You continued to study my case?" I gasped.

"Of course," he replied with an oddly sheepish smile. "You are an anomaly that presented me with an incredible opportunity for study."

Then he glanced up at the clock on the wall and rose hurriedly, excusing himself. He muttered something about a meeting, and suddenly he was gone.

As Rosaline and I strolled home she took my arm and said, "He never stopped searching, you know."

"For an answer to time travel?"

"For you," she said.

I stopped and turned to her, amazed.

"He was interested in time travel, of course, but it was all for you. To get you back."

"But I thought..."

"Surely you must have known how he felt, Catherine, even back then," she continued.

I shook my head.

"I saw the way you looked at him today, you feel it too…"

"But he is so much better than I," I protested, "you said as much yourself."

"Catherine, can you forgive me? It was meant in good faith, but I was very wrong to say so."

"I know you meant it, and you were right."

"No, no, that's just not true." Rosaline curled her lips into a sympathetic smile.

"But he is a lord and I am nothing but a penniless wretch who spends her life living off the kindness of others." I began to cry.

"Oh, my dear," she said slowly, "that is far from who you are. You are the kindest, most hardworking creature in the world. You have simply had a life of most unique circumstances. That he is a lord is of little relevance. He doesn't care about the class difference between you and nor do his family, especially now with this damned war. Even after… look, what happened in 1910, it was very confusing and disconcerting for him, but even then… and now… I know he still loves you. Why do you think he has never married?"

"I prevented him from finding happiness in marriage?" My head was spinning.

"Gracious, please don't think of it that way… I didn't mean… Catherine, I should like nothing more than to see you both happy."

I could barely take it in. I had dreamed of him for so long, with no prospect of happiness, that I barely accepted my own feelings. And now I was discovering that his heart matched mine. I knew not how to react. All I could do was hope.

MICHAEL

Oxford — 5th September, 2025

What a day it had been. The ceremony had been lovely, the food delicious and Tom had succeeded in not throwing up before his Best Man speech. Millie looked beautiful and Paul ecstatic. Michael sat back in his chair, his belly full to bursting and still a slice of cake to eat. He unbuckled his belt and loosened it onto the next hole. Imogen returned from the Ladies just in time to catch him in the act.

"I told you those trousers were too small. You should have got the bigger size," she teased.

"They were fine till I ate dessert."

"Well, don't eat any more or they might split."

Michael grinned.

"Just remind me not to try bending over."

Imogen smirked fondly and shook her head.

A waitress came to collect the plates. Behind her the room was buzzing with chatter and circulating people. Michael looked over towards the table where Sue and David were seated. Now all the formalities were over perhaps they could finish the conversation that had been brought to such an abrupt end earlier. Sue noticed him and waved.

"Shall we go over?" Imogen asked. Michael nodded. "I'm dying to know what that was all about at the chapel, aren't you?"

"Definitely," he replied, relieved to see Imogen as enthused with curiosity as he was.

Michael glanced over at their son. Paul was standing with Tom and a couple more of his old school pals, his hand gently resting in the small of his wife's back as they talked. Michael smiled and stood up, wincing as his top button dug into his stomach. He wondered if he could unfasten it without being noticed. As he twisted it through its hole, Imogen raised an amused eyebrow. Bathed in the stream of late afternoon sun her warm eyes looked like melted chocolate. She had lightened her hair shade of late too and the rich chestnut complemented her complexion perfectly. *She looks young again today,* he thought, as she began to weave her way around the tables and milling guests.

"Lovely wedding," said David as Michael eased himself into a recently vacated chair.

"Isn't it," agreed Imogen, seating herself next to Susan. Michael was about to speak when the two women spoke simultaneously.

"I hope you don't mind…"

"About that photo…"

They laughed.

A waiter approached with a bottle of white wine, and David covered his glass with his hand.

"Would you prefer beer?" Michael asked.

"Oh, I'd love one, thanks."

Michael asked the waiter to fetch two pints of Old Speckled Hen. Imogen invited Sue to continue.

"Would you mind if I took another look at the photograph? I'm sorry if I worried you earlier, it's just… well… I could swear I've seen it before."

Michael extracted his wallet from his back pocket and handed the picture over to Sue. They all edged forward, eagerly peering at the sepia card. Sue slipped on her glasses and gave it a proper examination. Michael saw Imogen was holding her breath and slipped his hand onto her knee.

After several moments, Sue put the picture down on the table and removed her glasses.

"Well, I never!" she said at last. "I'm ninety-nine per cent certain that my father has that exact same photo in an old family album. That," she pointed a pink polished fingernail over the blond man, "is my great-grandfather."

Michael's heart felt as though it had been stabbed and Imogen froze.

"I'm sorry, say that again," Michael spluttered.

"Are you quite sure?" David asked his wife.

"Absolutely certain. The woman in front, I think, is his sister Rosaline. I'm afraid I'm not sure of the other two, but Dad will probably know."

The revelation flattened Michael like a bulldozer.

"Arthur Winston is your great-grandfather?" he said after taking a good swig of the amber liquid the waiter had just delivered.

"That's right." Sue looked almost as dumbfounded as he did. "How did you come by this picture?"

Michael explained how Paul had found it and the detective work they had done to name the characters in the silent scene. David and Sue were fascinated.

"Wow," said Sue at the end, "Philip Boden-Howard. Now you say it, the name does ring a bell. My great-grandmother was a Boden-Howard. You know, if Catherine married him, we could actually be related. Distantly of course, but... good God, that's a complicated thing to get your head round." She rubbed the bridge of her nose where her glasses had been. "And gracious, Catherine looks just like you." She was looking at Imogen now.

Michael wanted to know everything.

"Have you any idea what happened to her?" It was a long shot and he knew it, but he had to ask.

"I'm afraid not. I didn't even know her name. Philip was a relation somewhere along the way, a cousin I think. I wish I'd paid more attention to Grandpa's stories now."

Imogen leaned forward again.

"Sue, do you think your dad would meet us? I... We'd love to talk to him about what he remembers. Perhaps you could all come to dinner next week sometime?"

"I'm sure he would. But he's pretty frail, I'm afraid, he went downhill fast after Mum died. He's in a retirement home. He'd love it if you went to see him, though."

"Oh, I see. Well, only if you think he's up to it." Michael watched the disappointment creep over his wife's face and knew he looked the same.

"I'm visiting him tomorrow. I can talk to him then, and we could arrange to go together next weekend if you're free. He's perfectly with-it mentally, just pretty incapacitated after his stroke."

"If you're sure," Imogen smiled.

"I bet he'll be delighted."

And so it was settled. On Monday afternoon when Michael came home from school he found a light flashing on the home voicemail. The message was from Sue.

'It's all arranged, Dad can't wait to meet you. We'll pick you up at ten thirty next Sunday.'

Michael's heart raced. Anticipation was going to drive him crazy for the rest of the week.

CATHERINE

London, 1916

Charlotte appeared utterly unchanged. Her complexion was a little darkened by her years in Egypt and her freckles had merged and multiplied, but her stature and figure were just as petite as ever. Her eyes maintained the brightness of youth and she was by far the most optimistic of all those of my acquaintance. She was like a welcome breeze on a hot summer's day.

When our Sunday appointment came she ran up the stairs, burst into the room and gasped, "Good afternoon all, do forgive us, Bertie and I were having a race."

The child who followed her through the door had bounded up the stairs with all his mother's enthusiasm, but came to an abrupt halt when he laid eyes upon me.

"Say hello, Albert," Charlotte added.

The boy was a perfect cherub. Golden curls framed his bonny face and his eyes were the same bright blue as his father's. He looked so young and delicate. He straightened himself as tall as he could get, came over to stand before me and offered me a formal hand.

"Good day, my name is Albert."

"Well, good day to you, sir, I am very pleased to make your acquaintance," I said, shaking his hand. "What a darling boy, Charlotte."

"Thank you," she replied. "This is Aunt Catherine," she told him.

I was flattered; I had never considered I should be termed anyone's aunt.

"You're very pretty," Albert said with a grin that so resembled Arthur's, I thought my heart would break.

"Why, thank you, you're very kind."

Charlotte did not stand upon any such ceremony herself. She threw her arms around me and hugged me.

"I'm so very glad you're back," she said, releasing me and examining my face. "Don't worry, darling Rosaline has filled me in, I shan't spill any beans." Her red hair glowed warmly as the sun streamed in through the drawing-room window, and I recalled her playing tennis the first day we met.

"Gracious," she mused aloud, "it just won't do, you know. You still young and pretty and us getting all old and grey."

She grinned as she spoke, but her meaning hit me like a slap to my face. I have been plagued with nightmares ever since that day. Visions where Time pulls me this way and that, ravaging my friends until they are all dead and gone, and leaving me with still too many years to live through all alone. Just to write down the notion makes the hairs on the back of my neck prickle.

"Mustn't grumble," Charlotte was saying to Rosaline, "no good wallowing in self-pity when most of us are in the same boat. That won't help keep up the lads' morale. Besides, Bertie keeps me occupied when I'm not busy."

"I wish Lettie could be as brave as you," Rosaline replied.

I had seen Leticia only briefly since my return, when she popped in to collect a prescription for cough mixture. She had fluttered about like a moth at a street lamp and not stayed more than five minutes.

"When did she last hear from Ernest?" asked Charlotte.

"Not for a week now. The regiment were on the move. She gets so agitated when she doesn't hear."

"Of course she does, but there's no point dwelling on it. She should find herself an occupation."

"You mean a job?" Rosaline asked with some sarcasm.

Albert had dug out a wooden train from a box of children's toys that Rosaline kept in the corner of the room. He began pushing it back and forth along the floor by the hearth, clattering the wheels over the floorboards as they rolled.

"Why not?" Charlotte replied. "I'm not saying she should suddenly turn into Florence Nightingale, but perhaps something in an office or at the Royal Mail. There are so many vacant posts to fill with all our men away. It just might help distract her, and she can do her bit at the same time."

"Do you work, Charlotte?" I asked in surprise. She was the niece of an earl: I hardly expected her to say yes.

"Mummy is a spy," Albert replied for her.

"Thank you, Bertie, my day would be far more exiting if I were," she laughed. "I'm a translator for the War Office."

"Goodness," I replied, feeling rather inadequate and unsure what that was.

"My sister-in-law puts us all to shame," Rosaline added.

"Don't be silly, darling. I just do what I can. And you're a doctor's wife. You have plenty to keep up with."

"Excuse me, Aunt Rosaline, may I go and play in the garden, please?" Albert asked, with his father's most persuasive smile.

Rosaline rolled her eyes.

"Yes, dear, of course you may. Just don't go in the flower beds, the daffodil shoots are just starting to come through."

Albert carefully picked up his train and took it back to the toy box, looked around shyly and said, "And could Aunt Catherine come too?"

"Oh, now, I'm sure Aunt Catherine would prefer to stay inside where it's warm and…"

"I'm happy to keep him company," I interjected. "Of course I shall come outside with you, Albert." I looked from Charlotte to Rosaline. I had not yet full comprehension of that war. "You two have much to talk about and I am rather ill-qualified to contribute anything helpful to the conversation," I offered. I was also feeling rather dejected that Philip had not joined us.

Charlotte smiled kindly. "Well, Albert, you are a lucky boy. Be good for Aunt Catherine, won't you?"

"Of course, Mummy," he replied, grabbing my fingers tightly.

"Thank you," Charlotte mouthed as I was tugged out onto the landing.

Outside the remains of a light frost glinted over the small lawn. The daffodils were indeed beginning to peek through the soil, and a line of snowdrops hung their dew-coated heads low along the borders. Albert rescued a ball from behind the privy and suggested we play catch. He was a good aim and had a strong arm for such a little boy. I, on the other hand, was not so capable. The ball was slippery and wet and my heels sank into the damp grass. When I failed to catch it for the second time the ball skidded away and bounced into the flowerbed.

"Oh dear," said Albert putting his hands upon his hips, "Aunt Rosaline will be cross."

"I fear you're right." I cringed as a snowdrop stem snapped.

Albert knelt down by the flowerbed and reached for the broken flower. He examined it solemnly.

"I don't think we can save it now," he said as though he were a doctor with a dying patient.

I smiled. "No, dear, I don't think we can."

Suddenly he beamed and offered the flower to me. I curtseyed.

"Why, thank you, sir, I'm honoured."

Albert looked pleased as punch when I knelt down beside him so that he could push the flower into my hair. He stood back and admired the white bell.

"Thank you," I smiled.

"It looks even whiter now, because your hair is so dark," he mused.

"Or perhaps my hair looks darker because the flower is so white," I replied mischievously. He considered this for a moment.

"Both," he said finally. I could feel the damp grass begin to seep through the fabric of my skirt and petticoat. I was about to stand up when he said, "Do you know my daddy?"

"Yes, I do. He's a very good friend."

He tilted his head to one side. "He's in France now, fighting the Germans."

I forced a smile. "I know, Bertie. He's a very brave man."

"Do you miss him?"

I pressed my fingers to my lips and tried to keep my voice steady. "Yes, I do, we all do."

"Mummy misses him too. She cries at night. She thinks I don't hear her but I do."

He was standing straight as a soldier, but his bottom lip quivered and his eyes welled with tears. My heart tore for Charlotte and I knew if Albert cried it would break me. I wrapped my arms around him.

"Your ma is just trying to be strong, like you."

"I wish he would come home and then she won't cry any more."

"Oh, darling, he will come home when the war is over, but you have to be brave for her until he does."

The stiffness in his body gave way. He wrapped his arms about my neck and buried his head in my shoulder. He did not give in to tears, but he hugged me so tight I could feel his heart beat against my chest.

"You must miss him too," I patted his back. He nodded into my neck.

On the path I heard a scuff of a shoe against stone. I opened my eyes and looked up to see Philip leaning heavily against the wall. He adjusted his collar with a sniff, put his finger to his lips to silence me, and waited quietly for Albert to loosen his embrace. When the boy relaxed I set him down and smoothed back his hair.

"There now," I said as Philip made a move as though he had just arrived.

"Ah, there you are Bertie; let's have a look at you then."

Albert spun around, his forlorn expression melting instantly into a gleeful smile.

"Uncle Philip!" He almost ran to him, but halted and saluted instead.

Philip returned the gesture. "Gracious, Bertie, how you've grown."

"A whole inch, sir," he replied.

"As much as that, goodness, in such a short time." Philip ruffled Albert's hair but smiled over at me. I lowered my eyes and clambered to my feet. There were huge dark patched over my knees where the dewy grass had penetrated through. Philip noticed and smiled. I wanted so much to kiss him.

"It's not *such* a short time, Uncle Philip. It was on my birthday."

Philip stared for a moment, thinking it through.

"Good Lord, Albert, you're quite right. I've neglected you abominably. Do you think you can forgive me?"

"You have important war work to do," said the lad and Philip looked sheepish.

"Well, how about I promise to visit you more often?"

"I'd like that," Albert said, offering Philip a handshake. "And you'll visit Aunt Catherine, too?" he added as he watched Philip's eyes flicker towards me once more.

"I most certainly shall," he said, to me rather than to the boy. "It's always good to see you, Catherine."

My cheeks began to burn from the heat of his gaze.

"I hope you will keep that promise, sir," I said.

Philip did honour his promise. We began with luncheon once a week, but as time passed once turned to twice and then thrice until finally no day could pass by without us spending at least an hour or two in each other's company.

MICHAEL

Oxford – 13th September, 2025

Park View Retirement Home was in Hertfordshire, a drive of about an hour and a half from where Michael and Imogen lived. Michael cursed Sue and Dave's eco-car as it smoothly drifted along at fifty-five miles per hour. *There was something to be said for good old fashioned petrol,* he thought to himself rebelliously, *at least you could get there in a day.* He glanced at his watch for the twentieth time in five minutes. Imogen sighed and looked out of the window.

"Nearly there," said Sue over her shoulder.

David was driving and Sue had been asleep for the last thirty miles or so. She stretched lazily and added, "Don't worry if it takes Dad a few minutes to settle down. Once his mind is focused he can speak pretty well."

"When did he have the stroke?" asked Imogen.

"Oh, about three years ago now. At first he couldn't speak at all, but now he's just slow. Poor love, it really frustrates him."

"I'm not surprised, it would me," Imogen replied.

Michael caught sight of a sign ahead. The board was large and white with a picture of grand house to one side of the name.

"Is it a nursing home, then?" Imogen enquired.

Michael wished she wouldn't ask such things but Sue didn't seem to mind.

"It's more a like a pensioners' village. Dad has his own little bungalow, but there are nurses on site constantly and the residents all go into the main house for meals and such."

"It sounds lovely," Imogen said and Michael turned slowly to look at her.

"Planning for my retirement, are we?" he teased.

Imogen hit him lightly on the arm. "Well, you are three years older than me!"

They turned onto a long gravel drive that led up to a stately home.

"The bungalows are in the gardens behind the house," Sue explained as they pulled up in the parking area.

Michael noticed the car next to theirs was a Bentley and wondered just how much it cost to live in such a place.

"What a beautiful house," Imogen said.

"I know, isn't it?" Sue's reply seemed rhetorical.

CATHERINE
London, 1916

I had long since lost track of my actual age in days, months and years, but May 13th is most certainly the anniversary of my birth, however long ago that may actually be. On that date in 1916 I presumed myself to be somewhere in the region of three-and-twenty. The morning was to be spent with Rosaline at the British Museum, and Philip was to meet us for luncheon in the café across the street. The day was anticipated to be pleasant and uneventful. What transpired was quite the opposite.

Rosaline and I were in the Egyptian Mummy Room. Coffins of bright colours and gold glittered behind glass. The scent of must lingered beneath cleaning fluid and polish. A striking face I had never noticed before seemed to look out at me from the wooden lid of an otherwise ordinary coffin. She had flame-red hair, a pale complexion and her eyes were a piercing shade of emerald green. She was mesmerising. After a moment I realised Rosaline was calling to me.

"We should go; it's almost one."

"Very well, I shall catch you up in a moment." I replied.

I wonder what would have occurred had I gone with her when I was asked. No matter now, it is done.

Rosaline's footsteps vanished into the distance and I found myself alone in the room. I am not squeamish and a few dead bodies do not make my heart quiver; however, at that moment I began to feel ill at ease. I looked back at the beautiful face of the Egyptian girl, so long dead and now trapped behind a sheet of glass. A cold shiver twitched up my spine. I turned to go, my pace quickening with each step and the air seemingly growing colder around me.

Then I heard it, the shrill scraping of stone against stone, familiar and terrifying. I hastened my pace further and skidded around a corner but the sound grew louder until it banged upon my eardrums. I could not let Time take me. I did not want to leave. I was not quick enough. With a vivid flash of violet I was dragged out of the British Museum and left standing in a sunlit room heavily lined with books.

I needed to catch my breath and wait for my head to cease spinning. I sat down in a plush chair of dark-green leather and stared around what appeared to be a study of some kind. In the centre of the room stood a large desk upon which was a selection of what I can only assume were pens, except I could see no well in their nibs to take the ink. There was a large book on the desk, its cover shut to display a picture of a woman in Edwardian clothes and the words 'votes for women' emblazoned above her head. I picked up the volume and turned to the first page. Inside was a list of publication dates. Nervously I scanned down to see the years 2015, 2018, 2020. My heart felt as though it were tearing in half. All I wanted was to get back to Philip. Fighting back tears, I walked over to the window.

Outside was an impeccably kept lawn where many young people were lolling about in clothes that I can only describe as indecent. Some had plates of food on their laps, others were reading, alone or in groups. It was warm outside and the sun beat down on them mercilessly, reddening their skins like lambs sizzling on a spit. I pushed open the window and breathed in the grass-scented air and stared. The quad itself was so familiar to me, from the garden wall and the black wrought-iron gates, the yellow stone of Oxford towering up at its side, right down to the characterless construction opposite. For a moment I expected to see my younger self playing, a small child amongst the adults, yet somehow belonging.

A young man nearby got to his feet and began to walk towards me. He looked about the same age as me. A pretty girl with golden hair that flowed freely down her back had been sitting by his side, holding his hand. There was something about them both that gripped me with déjà vu so powerful I could scarce draw breath. Aware that my travels do not always fall in Time's linear order, I began to wonder if this were in fact the date from which I had originally come.

The man had dark hair that shone with a hint of russet, and just like mine it had a gentle wave that made his fringe flop slightly over his eyes. He stopped dead, just a few feet from my window, staring in at me with round blue-green eyes. My face began to burn and a clammy chill spread over my skin. I stared back at him with my own blue-green eyes and felt an overwhelming desire to reach out and touch him. I wanted to call out but I had no notion what to say. His lips parted and he raised his hand towards the window. Then, from absolutely nowhere, it began to rain. He looked up at the sky and there was a crack of thunder, but not from outside. It came from behind me and once more I felt the swimming pull of Time and the image of him began to fade. Someone called my name and I cried out for Philip.

The next thing I knew I was lying on the ground by the front steps of the British Museum, and a kind gentleman in a bowler hat was kneeling at my side. The man took off his hat and began to waft cool air at my fiercely burning face, and for a moment I thought I might be sick. But the nausea passed and my surroundings began to still. I pulled myself up so my back was leaning against a stone column and took the glass of water that was being offered to me by a familiar-looking woman. I noted her dress. I had no idea what time had elapsed in my absence, but it could not have been long, for the woman was wearing the same frock I had noticed when we had entered the building that very morning. I slumped back in relief. It is quite shocking how I have grown accustomed to these changes in time and learned to adapt to them.

The man with the bowler replaced it upon his head and offered me a hand.

"Are you all right, madam? You must have fainted."

"Forgive me if I frightened you all," for I had drawn quite a crowd by then, "but I think I shall be fine now. It's just that it's a little warm today." That much was true: the weather had been unseasonably pleasant, but I should hardly say it was hot. I allowed the gentleman to assist me to my feet and was dusting myself down when to my great relief I heard a cry.

"Rosaline, she's here!" Philip's voice sounded like an angel calling me.

The relief flooded through me so fast I almost swooned. Philip's arms were around my waist and holding me up before I had chance to say his name. "Let's get her to the tea shop."

Since then I have considered very hard who this mysterious boy in the Quad might have been. As I write this now, something in my memory has clicked into place like the cog of a clock about to strike. And perhaps one day soon it will. Yet, despite all the years of wishing to remember my early life, I found in 1916, just as I do today, that I no longer desired that knowledge. For I am quite certain I do not belong in Philip's time, and not to be with him is the last thing I should ever wish for.

"Tell us what happened," Rosaline said soothingly some ten minutes later, as she dropped a second cube of sugar into my tea.

It seemed I had been gone a little over an hour, and had caused quite a panic. I cannot say whether it was by chance or sheer determination that I had returned to them so quickly, but I can tell you that I have never in my life been more gladdened to see a person as I was when I saw Philip bounding up the steps towards me.

We did have our lunch, albeit with a more dramatic conversation than we had expected, and the excitement did not end with my little escapade.

As I finished my scone a carriage rattled past the window, making the glass shudder. I glanced up at it, for I was still on edge and the noise startled me. As I did so I noticed two young women sitting at the window table. They were leaning in close to one another and talking quietly, as though they were a pair of German spies. One, with dark hair cropped short in a rebellious modern style, was quite blatantly starting at Philip. At first I truly thought they might actually be spies. I was about to say something to my friends when she stood suddenly and stalked towards our table. Rosaline looked up at her with a start and Philip was about to enquire if he could help her when she thrust out her hand and dropped a white feather on his plate.

"Coward," she spat, then spun on her heel and stormed back to her seat. There she snatched up her coat and, as cowardly as her own accusations, grabbed her friend and left the tea shop, slamming the door behind them.

The waitress rushed over apologising profusely and took the feather away, but the damage had already been done. Others in the café were looking our way and whispering. One or two were looking at Philip with just the same expressions as the girl had done. Philip tried to appease the waitress, saying it was not her fault, and Rosaline, who seemed to understand this dramatic gesture, felt the need to say, rather loudly, that Philip does his bit for the war just like everyone else.

As the commotion died down and people began to return to

their business, Rosaline suggested we take a stroll.

Once outside, I found the courage to enquire what the feather meant.

Rosaline slipped her arm through mine and Philip drew a sharp breath. I had never seen him so rattled about anything.

"Many women seem to think that all our men should be at the front, fighting. They fail to consider that some must stay behind and contribute from here," Rosaline offered when she realised Philip would say nothing. "They hand young men white feathers as a sign of their disapproval. They think their intimidation will drive them to join up."

Horrified, I knew not what to say. I did not want Philip to go to war, and I did not see why he should, when he had such important work to do here.

Philip stopped in his tracks and turned to me.

"It's nothing more than we can expect. We have all had them at the office, and more than one. We just have to get used to it."

But I could see he was not used to it and the matter bothered him far more than he was ever going to admit.

The very next day we were sitting in Westminster Palace gardens. The last of the May blossom floated down from the tree on the bank side and a pink petal came to rest in my hair. Philip leaned over and gently removed it. He had been quiet all through lunch and I could see his nerves were on edge. As he retracted his hand he let the back of his fingers brush lightly over my cheek. He closed his eyes and drew a slow breath. My heart pounded, for I was certain he was going to tell me that he was giving up his job and going to France.

He began to fidget with the chain of his pocket watch. I

stared at the inscription on the back of the gold disk, the italic initials of his grandfather. He flipped open the back and snapped it closed again hurriedly. I couldn't bear it. I raised my eyes to the South Bank of the river and stared out blindly.

"Catherine, please look at me," he said, reaching for my hand.

I had removed my gloves, for the day was warm. The feel of his skin against mine made my heart skip. I forced my gaze to meet his. The smattering of grey in his temples had thickened over the short time I had been back, but his eyes were as bright and alive as ever. To my surprise he was smiling. My lips quivered to match his. He looked at me for a long moment and then said, "Marry me, Catherine."

For a moment I did not comprehend. I had been about to beg him not to join up, but now he had taken my breath. His smile wavered and he tightened his hold on my hands.

"Say something, please," he said, and I realised he was nervous. "Darling, after what happened yesterday, I knew I couldn't let you go again. After everything that has happened between us, everything you have been through... I..."

All sense of propriety left me then, and I flung myself into his embrace and sobbed.

"I will... I will marry you," I cried as he pulled me in close and pressed his lips into my hair. "I love you," I stammered, for the first time. The relief of the confession made me cry harder.

I could barely breathe as he slipped his hand into his breast pocket and took out a ring. I looked down at the gold band and gawped at the cluster of gems. I had never seen anything so beautiful. Philip slipped it onto my finger and then kissed me so deeply I felt I should faint.

"Once this damn war is over I promise I will find a way to

hold you here, with me... if that is what you wish," he whispered moments later, as his forehead rested against mine.

Passers-by were staring at us, and some even tutted at our public display. But the war had relaxed the morals of many women and made exhibitionists of many more. And now I was his and neither of us cared what anyone thought.

"Of course," I said, kissing him again.

A little later I was admiring the ring.

"It was my grandmother's" he said. I looked up in surprise. I could not imagine when he had found the time to go Hatherley and obtain it. He read my mind. "I've had it in my possession for six years," he admitted. "I asked mother for it then, but you were gone before I had chance to make you the offer. She refused to take it back and told me to keep it for when I found you."

Startled I said, "But how... what happened? You mean your parents will not mind that I am of no great family?"

Philip didn't know whether to kiss me, laugh at me or comfort me.

"Darling, after everything that has happened to us all in the last few years, they will only be glad that I am finally happy."

"Oh..." I gasped, as the realisation hit me. "Your parents know? How I... the way Time... and they believe you?"

Philip did laugh then.

"Yes. I've never been able to hide anything from Mother, any more than she can keep anything from my father."

"And your sister?" I said in alarm.

"No, just Charlotte."

"Well, thank goodness for that. I shouldn't like my situation to be completely public knowledge."

Philip kissed the back of my hand.

"Your secret is safe with, well… the dozen or so that know."

"I sincerely hope you are better at keeping state secrets," I laughed.

"I thought perhaps September at Hatherley for the wedding," he said. "My parents would love it if we were married in the family chapel."

"How absolutely perfect."

I could not believe how delighted our friends were at the news. I had thought Rosaline might still harbour some objections, but far from it. She hugged me tight and cried with joy, giving us both her deepest blessings. And if his family objected they never owned it. Lady Mariah even wrote to me with her congratulations.

MICHAEL

Oxford – 13th September, 2025

"Hello, Sue, David," said a chirpy receptionist as they went inside.

Michael stared at the sweeping staircase that flowed up from the wide entrance hall, and the shimmering tapestries and great paintings that covered the walls. The smell of beeswax drifted up from the parquet floor. The woman at the desk pushed a visitors' book towards them and Sue picked up a pen to sign them all in.

"He's in a very good mood today, hasn't been able to sit still all morning for the excitement."

"That's because he has special visitors today," Sue said.

"So I see," the receptionist replied, eyeing Michael and Imogen with interest.

When Sue had finished writing the woman turned the book around so she could read the names but then looked disappointed, as though she had been expecting someone famous. "Go on through, he was sitting on the patio with Reg last time I checked."

They made their way into a bright, airy day room. The ceilings were vividly painted with classical allegories and the panelled walls indicated the former status of the house. Above the great fireplace hung a portrait of a Cavalier, sporting long wavy hair and an impeccably pointed moustache and beard. Michael was drawn to look at him. His warm brown eyes seemed to welcome him to the house. Opposite was a pair of large French doors which swung open onto a pleasant, well-kept terrace.

Sue led them outside to a small table where two elderly gentlemen were playing what looked like snap. The frailer of the two was a willowy man with a fine head of white hair and sallow skin. As they approached he stood up and bid them good day.

"Well, that's my cue to be off," he said. "Have a good afternoon, Richey."

The other man scooped up the cards with his one good hand and slurred a bright greeting at them. As he looked up with his lopsided smile Michael was taken aback by the brightness of his blue eyes. Despite the man's advanced years they were clear as a Spanish sky. His skin was pale and papery but his build still had the solidity of one who had played a lot of sport or served in the military. Michael recalled Sue saying her grandfather had been in the RAF, and wondered whether Richard had followed in those footsteps.

"Michael, Imogen, this is my father, Captain Richard Winston."

And there's the proof, thought Michael as he smiled and shook Richard's right hand, then winced, finding the old man's grip remarkably strong.

"Call me Richey, everyone else does." The retired officer spoke with painfully slow care.

Michael accepted the need for patience and agreed enthusiastically when Richey suggested they take a walk back to his bungalow.

"Well, you can walk," the old man added, "I'll be zipping along in this thing," and patted the side of his mobility scooter.

It was a lovely day, but the September air had a bite and the breeze was getting up. Michael took in the vista of the extensive grounds as they headed across the pristine lawn and towards a cluster of small bungalows.

"I've changed my mind, you can send me here whenever you like," he said to Imogen as she threaded her arm through his.

"We can give the house to Paul and Millie and move in tomorrow if you like," she replied. "This place is immaculate. No more cooking, someone else to do the cleaning and laundry, and I think I could live with a garden this big if someone else is mowing it!"

David laughed as he overheard them. "Fabulous price too, if you're a paying guest."

"That's true," Richey grinned mischievously, "I'm a bit privileged, my grandmother was a Boden-Howard, as I suspect Sue already told you. This was their estate. Like many great families, the upkeep of running a place like this got too much, so after the Second World War they turned it into a hotel. Then about ten years ago it got turned into what you see now. When my wife died my very kind cousins offered me a home here, rent free!"

"Gracious," Imogen said, raising her eyebrows at her husband, "that's very kind of them."

"Indeed."

They wound through the maze of paths to the last bungalow in Swallow Drive, at which point Richey fumbled around in his jacket pocket for his door key. Michael could barely contain his anticipation. He swallowed his excitement and tried to tell himself not to get too many hopes up. Whatever Richey knew about Catherine might only be a fragment that could give them comfort. It might not actually lead them to finding her.

Inside, the bungalow was small but perfectly adequate. There was a decent-sized living room. There wasn't much to the kitchen area, just a couple of low cupboards, a small fridge, a microwave, a toaster and a kettle. On the worktop sat a tea tray loaded with a cup, saucer and sugar bowl. There were two doors leading out of the room but both were closed. Richey offered them seats on the luxurious three-piece suite as he eased himself into an extremely cosy looking La-Z-Boy with a sigh.

"Sue's told me all about your daughter. She sounds like she was a lovely little girl," Richey said as he looked along the bottom row of a crammed bookcase.

There were almost as many books squeezed onto the shelves as Michael had in his study, but the bottom shelf seemed to consist of a combination of oversized books and photo albums.

"Sweetheart, would you take out that one there, please?" Richey pointed at a heavy-looking antique album, "and that one."

Sue did as she was asked and pulled out a blue book.

"No, the red one next to it," Richey said, pointing at a leather-bound book that looked even older than the first. Sue tugged it out and took the books over to Michael and Imogen.

"I don't quite know how to say this, I know it sounds utterly ridiculous, but I'm quite certain my father knew your daughter. I thought long and hard this week about what I was going to say to you, and finally I decided to let Catherine tell you herself."

Michael and Imogen both looked up with a start, and even Sue and David seemed taken aback. Richey waved his good hand at the larger book and said, "Open it, please. The picture's about three pages in."

Sue shuffled in next to Imogen on the sofa. Michael followed Richey's instructions and turned over the leaves of the Edwardian family photograph album. Exactly as expected, three pages in, was an identical copy of the picture Michael kept inside his wallet.

"My grandfather, Arthur, is the fair-haired gent, and his

sister Rosaline is sitting in front of him. The other man is Philip Boden-Howard. He was my grandmother's cousin. And the woman whose shoulder he is resting his hand on was a lady my father always referred to as his dear Aunt Catherine."

The sentence seemed to take forever for Richey to get out, but Michael forced his patience to remain steady. At his side he could feel Imogen shaking. He extracted a hand from beneath the album and squeezed her arm. She glanced at him gratefully. Sue was staring at her father.

"How can you be sure she's the right Catherine, Pops?"

Richey shrugged.

"I'm afraid I can't, for certain. But there's plenty of good evidence. At the time the picture was taken she was known as Mrs More..." he pointed at the other book.

"Mrs?" Imogen gasped. "She looks too young to be married."

"She was young, but like I said, she should explain to you herself."

"I don't follow," Michael said, passing the album to David, who had come over from the armchair to get a better look.

"Open the journal," Richey said.

"Journal?" Michael gawped at the faded binding of the second book, and ran his fingers over the dry, cracked cover. Breathing as steadily as he could he opened the volume and looked at the yellowed pages.

Inside the front cover was a loose sheet of paper, Michael looked up at Richey.

"Go ahead, read it." The old man nodded his bald head and blinked back what Michael suspected was a tear.

Michael carefully opened up the folded sheet of paper and smoothed it out over the page beneath. For the first time Michael laid eyes on his daughter's adult handwriting. Imogen leaned in close,

"Gosh, what an elegant hand," Imogen said. "Read it out," she urged her husband. Michael's throat rasped as he began but as he went on he found he grew comfortable with her words.

> *Thursday, 28th April 1910*
>
> *Dearest Rosaline,*
>
> *It seems impossible for me to repay all the kindness you have shown me over the years and for my part, this may well be the last opportunity I have to express my gratitude, therefore I do so with all my heart. For you, however, this is most assuredly not our final meeting. Though it will be several years hence, you shall see me again. I beg your forgiveness for not explaining the particulars, for I believe it would be detrimental to all concerned, should future events be known. It is for this reason also, that I must ask you to promise that you will keep this journal, unopened and unread, at least until my next visit has passed and you are sure you shall never see me again. Which brings me to Philip. You will see there is a note for him too. I ask you to give it to him with my love. He is a truly good man and he will prove that to you in time.*
>
> *Thank you once again. I wish you great happiness.*
>
> *Your friend always,*
>
> *Catherine B-H*

"Do you have Philip's letter?" Michael asked.

Richey waited for Imogen to blow her nose then said, "I'm

afraid not. But did you notice her name?"

Michael looked at the letter again and shook his head,

"I'm sorry, please explain."

"She signed her name B-H, but in 1910 she should still have been Mrs More. My aunt Rosaline knew just one thing of the future, that Catherine would one day marry Philip Boden-Howard. Rosaline told my father years later that she had opposed the attachment between them until she read that letter, then she changed her mind."

Michael folded the letter back into its quarters and found his eyes drawn to the writing on the first page. In the same hand, it said,

C G B-H
The Year of Our Lord 1646

"You see, Aunt Catherine was a time traveller," Richey offered, "I think there can be little doubt who she really was."

Michael was speechless and Imogen was pale.

"I want you to have it," said Richey.

Michael blinked.

"Really? Are you sure?"

"It should belong to you. Rosaline gave it to my father when she was old and sick, like me. She made him promise to keep it until he saw Catherine again. You two are as close as I may ever get to fulfilling that promise, and I'm convinced, with her help, you can find her."

Michael flicked through the book.

"Why are there some pages missing at the back?" he asked,

seeing several sheet stubs.

"It seems she tore them out," Richey replied. "The very last entry explains."

"So none of you ever saw her again?" Sue couldn't refrain from asking.

"There was the one last time that she referred to in the letter, and then, I'm afraid not. But both my father and Aunt Rosaline thought very highly of her."

Imogen was on her feet and hugging the old man before he had chance to finish his sentence.

"Thank you, thank you, so much. I can't tell you how much this means to us."

Richey caught his breath through an embarrassed laugh and said, "You deserve to know what happened."

Michael's hands were shaking so much he could barely see the page any more. He gritted his teeth and fought back tears.

"Are you all right, Michael?" Imogen asked, rubbing the side of his face with the back of her hand gently. He shook his head.

"I'm sorry. It's just a bit of a shock, that's all."

"Understandable," Richey said quietly.

CATHERINE
London, 1916

My dear journal, the evenings here are drawing in and I find that I am tired more often than I am not and yet still I do not sleep. I cannot decide if it is my pregnancy or my captivity that is the cause. At least I have you to help me while away the hours. Now I do believe we were in 1916.

As the summer bloomed the war in England seemed to close in tighter than the humidity in the air. Everything felt oppressive. Rosaline, unable to stay on the sidelines any longer, decided to volunteer as a nurse at the 4th London General. She lacked formal training, so she began as the girl who turned down the sheets and gave a kind word to the soldiers, but she had assisted her father and husband for so many years that she found the training came easily to her. She was soon on her way to becoming a proper nurse.

I did not consider myself capable of such a noble occupation, but thanks to my education and a little assistance from Charlotte, I took on a position as a French translator in the war office. For the first time in my life I was something other than a tailor. And working in the same building as Charlotte and Philip, I was happy. We were all so busy in our efforts to help king and country, that none of us noticed poor Leticia.

It was mid-August, about five weeks from my wedding date. I had the morning off and found a rare moment alone in the house, save for Sissy. I was passing my time in the drawing room, hemming a new pair of trousers for little Albert, when I heard a dreadful racket coming from downstairs. I ventured onto the landing to see the outline of a woman peering in through the glass panel of our front door. The moment she saw me at the top of the stairs her bell-ringing grew more frantic. I wondered why Sissy hadn't come to answer it, but then I heard the door slam from the kitchen and realised she must have been out hanging the laundry. I ran down the stairs and turned the handle, nervous about whom I might find waiting outside. As the door swung back, it revealed Leticia, hatless, gripping a young boy's hand so tight his skin was white, almost as white as the face of his mother.

"Leticia, what on earth is the matter?" I said, aghast. I had never before seen her in even the slightest disarray, and there she was with her blouse buttoned up wrongly so that there was a gap at her bust, her shoes did not go with her skirt, and her eyes were raw from crying.

"Heavens, Lettie, tell me what the matter is!"

"Where's Rosaline?" she stammered, wrenching the arm of her youngest child as she dragged him over the step and into the hall. As she released his hand he pulled it to his chest and rubbed his bloodless fingers, glaring at his mother with malice.

"I'm sorry, she's at the hospital."

Leticia stared blankly for a moment then said, "Of course. Ronald, go and play in the parlour." The boy bolted out of sight. "Don't touch anything," she added as an afterthought, "especially the piano."

"Come up. Can I get you some tea?" I offered, dreading what news she might have had that disturbed her so.

"I don't know. Perhaps I should come back later."

I couldn't let her go out again in that state.

"Please, Lettie, I'm sure if you sit down for a few minutes… and I would appreciate the company," I lied.

Hesitantly she followed me up to the drawing room and perched on the edge of the settee. I rang for Sissy. In the parlour the lid of the piano banged open.

"I said don't touch that!" she yelled.

Ronald might have been the same age as Albert, but he was the precise opposite in temperament. I never imagined a child could be so unruly. Notes began to plonk out, heavy and slow. "Ronald!" Leticia was screaming now. I laid my hand upon her arm and the moment she felt my touch she collapsed into tears.

"Oh, God, Catherine," she said at last. She flipped open her bag and extracted the telegram I had already been expecting to see.

"Is he..." I couldn't bring myself to say it, but she shook her head and offered me the letter.

"Where are the girls and Ernest Junior?" I asked, suddenly considering Leticia's other children.

"At home, but I couldn't leave Ronald, they can't control him."

Neither can you, dear, I thought, but kept it to myself. Downstairs there was a smash of china and Leticia closed her eyes in exasperation.

"Ronald, what have you done? Get up here now!"

When there was no immediate response we both rose and went out onto the landing just in time to see Sissy rush out from the kitchen with a mop and bucket.

"Sorry, madam," she said sheepishly and began to mop up the spilled flower water.

"Was that you, Sissy?" I asked, praying for the child's sake that it was.

"Yes, Miss, I'm very sorry. I was just sweeping the hall when I caught the vase with the end of the broom."

I almost laughed. Instead I said, "Sissy, we rang for you. Please fetch us some tea."

The maid looked even more flustered for a moment, then bobbed and scuttled away.

I unfolded the telegram and read the words.

> '...We regret to inform you that Major Ernest James has been wounded in the line of duty...'

I was so relieved I could barely speak.

"Lettie, this isn't so bad, he is hurt, but he is alive,"

"Read on," Leticia tugged out her handkerchief and began to dab at her eyes.

> '...His condition is unstable and he is unable to be moved at this time... We will inform you when there is further news.'

"I think I should go home," she said, taking the telegram and folding it back into a square as though it were precious. "Maybe there's more news."

I tried to comfort her.

"I do not think there will be anything else so soon. But, my dear, this is not all bad, just think, he is still alive and as soon as he is well enough they will send him home."

She looked up at me with a spark in her eyes that unnerved me.

"Oh, yes, he must come home right now. Get him home,

Catherine. Philip can swing it. Tell him to get Ernie home."

I swallowed hard.

"If he is too unwell to travel, perhaps he is best to stay where he is for now."

She began to shake violently. Her hands fluttered about so much she dropped her bag and her eyes were so bright and round she looked like a startled doe.

"Please, promise you'll try."

How could I refuse, though I knew it would not help? What Philip did manage was to obtain better word of our friend's condition. It took near a fortnight to get to us and when he told me the severity of the injuries I was little surprised of the delay. Ernest had lost a leg and had been so lacerated by shrapnel it was a miracle he was alive at all.

MICHAEL

Oxford — 13th September, 2025

My God, what a life she led. Michael hadn't moved in over an hour. He flipped back a page to the beginning of the entry. *Almost 379 years ago to the day she sat at a desk somewhere and penned this.*

"You'll strain your eyes in this light," Imogen said as she drew the living-room curtains and flicked on the lamp behind him. He mumbled an affirmative but didn't raise his eyes.

He knew Imogen was dying to read the journal too, but Michael was the faster reader and she had generously given him first chance. The moment they got home he had opened the journal and ever since she had been fussing around him. She had made him tea, dusted the house, hoovered upstairs and prepared their supper.

"I'm just waiting for the Yorkshire puddings then it'll be ready," she said, dropping a kiss on his head as she passed.

Michael glanced up from the page and smiled.

"Thanks, Im." He hesitated. "You know, she didn't remember us. I don't know which I would have preferred, that she remembered us and missed us, or that she'd forgotten and was blissfully unaware of our existence." Michael's heart had broken almost from the first sentence.

"Not at all?" Imogen stopped still by the door.

"Well, there were subconscious memories she mentioned, more like dreams but not... I should have just let you read it, I'm sorry. It's not her fault. The trauma of what happened... it must have sent her into shock. She was so little." Tears were rolling down his face now. Imogen pressed her fingers to her lips. Michael could see her whole body was shaking. He held out his hand to her but she walked away. He set down the journal as tears stained the page and soaked into the long-dried ink. In the kitchen he could hear the oven door open and his wife pulling the plates out from the oven base. There was a clatter followed by a rare outburst. He was up and through the door in an instant.

"I'm so sorry, Im," he said wrapping his arms around her.

For a second Imogen stiffened then relaxed.

"I don't blame you," she whispered, "I never did. I blame myself for not waiting with her. I should never have left her until you came."

Michael set her back and looked into her eyes. She had always said she didn't blame him but she had never before admitted to blaming herself.

"What happened in that room was a freak accident," he said slowly. "There's no way she should have been able to get past the security. Everything was set, Oliver confirmed it."

Imogen tugged a tissue from the box on the counter and dried her eyes.

"I know, but it doesn't stop the guilt."

"You and me both, love," said Michael. He searched for a distraction. "Now, shall we have this dinner?"

Imogen watched as he picked up the tea towel and pulled the Yorkshire-pudding tin from the oven.

"I wonder how Paul and Millie are getting on?" he said with forced brightness.

"Oh, I forgot, a postcard came yesterday, I put it in the letter rack."

"What, already? That was fast. Let's have a look, then." Michael allowed his wife to take over serving and picked up the card. For the second time that evening, he read the writing of one of his children.

'Dear Mum and Dad, the weather's great and Brazil is fabulous. You guys should think about taking a trip over here, you'd love it. We did Corcovado yesterday (the picture). Amazing! Heading out to the Pantanal tomorrow. See you in a few weeks, Love, Paul and Mil.'

"I'm glad they waited till after Paul finished his PhD, even if Millie did have to use their honeymoon as part of her medical placement," Imogen said as Michael set the postcard back in the rack. He knew she was keeping the conversation away from Catherine and he was glad of it. There would be enough to talk about once they had both read her memoir.

"Not that he has a job yet."

"I know, but he'll get something, and Millie will be a doctor in another year and… they'll do all right."

"More than all right."

"They'll be surprised when they get home, though," Imogen added calmly. She grabbed the oven mitts and picked up the dinner plates.

"No kidding," he replied, pleased she was now smiling, and followed her into the dining room.

CATHERINE

London, 1916

To have been married twice at the age of three and twenty seems a little indulgent, however, I cannot regret my marriages, not even the first. My wedding to Philip Boden-Howard was on a Tuesday, the fifth day of September in the Year of Our Lord 1916. We were very lucky to be allowed to take two days off together, but it is incredible how generous people can be at such times.

I think I may have failed to mention Philip's other girl. It is not from intent, I can assure you. She was perhaps the only thing that brought back the wildness of that Byronesque, carefree youth I had first known. I say *she*, for that is how Philip described her. And she was an elegant machine, I cannot deny, but I had thus far avoided travelling in her. Alas, on the day before our wedding I ran out of excuses and was forced to submit.

They pulled up by the front door of 52 Russell Square with the soft roar of a sleeping lion. Philip had taken the roof down to give me the full effect of her beauty. As I came out of the house he was standing next to her with a broad, proud grin on his face, her white exterior shimmering in the morning light like a wedding dress as though *she* were his bride. He had his hat in hand and the door open ready for me to take the step up and climb in.

I stood and stared for a moment. There are automobiles and there are shining charismatic beasts like her. She really was something else. The wheels were an intricate mesh of white spokes and black tyres, and she seemed to watch me with her large round headlamp eyes peering out from her square black face. On her nose was a sleek figure of a winged woman leaning out like the figurehead of a ship.

"You think she's magnificent, too, admit it!" he said with a laugh as I walked down the front steps towards him. I admit I was intrigued but could not quite banish my fear. I nodded in agreement as I took his hand.

"If you don't hurry we shall be late," he said as Markham heaved our suitcases onto the back seat.

I rested my hand in Philip's and a small crackle of electricity sparked between us. My heart skipped a beat as I allowed him to help me into the bottle-green leather seats.

"Better make sure your hat is pinned tight or the wind will have it off in a jiff," Philip said mischievously.

"I shouldn't worry about that, madam, sir is about to put the top back up," Markham suggested with a wink at me, but Philip would have none of it. Not even when Rosaline clambered into the back seat, squashed in with our luggage and protesting about the threat of inclement weather, would he allow us the comfort of a roof.

It was only when the rain actually began to spit at us, not half a mile out of the city, that he finally acquiesced.

"Spoil sport," he said to the sky as he pulled over and wound up the canvas.

"And not too fast," Rosaline added, as the engine began to rumble again and we pulled away into the road.

"You love riding in the Ghost and don't you try to deny it," he said, glancing back over his shoulder. We swerved a little and Rosaline grasped the back of my seat. I let out an involuntary squeal, causing Philip to swerve even more.

"Darling, I'm sorry; I didn't mean to frighten you," he said, unsure whether he really had.

But I was laughing too much by then for him to take me seriously.

"Why is this a ghost?" I asked, trying to calm my breathing, for my chest was tight from the motion and speed.

"That's the type of car she is; a Silver Ghost. Bought her in 'fourteen, just before this infernal war broke out…" his voice trailed away. "Still, let's not talk about that today," he added. "Can't let the Boche get the better of us, hey?" His voice was tight and for a brief moment his face clouded.

Ever since the incident with the white feather at the tea shop he had been growing more and more frustrated, and after we found out about Ernest it escalated further. I should perhaps tell you that at this point Ernest was still not home, and there had been no word of when that might change.

Philip flashed another look at Rosaline.

"Absolutely," she agreed, attempting enthusiasm.

"But I thought she was a Rolls Royce," I said, still confused.

Philip laughed. "She is, that's the make, but Silver Ghost is the model. I'm sure I've told you this before." He glanced at me sideways.

"Probably," I replied apologetically. I have to admit to not really paying much attention when my husband talked about his motor. "Keep your eyes on the road, please," I added with a nervous nod, gripping the dashboard as we swung slightly to the right.

"Oops," Philip grinned, but did as he was told.

After an hour or so we turned off the country road and onto a familiar, tree-lined lane. The leaves were just beginning to turn from green to gentle russet. As we drove up the long gravelled driveway I smiled at the distant house looming up over the hill. Its Grecian centre stands Parthenon proud, flanked by long low galleries and bookended by the turreted towers like the protective rooks of a chess set. Hatherley Park has my heart now more than any other place on this earth, save for in Philip's arms.

By the time we arrived the rain had paused and I was pleased to see Lady Mariah waiting for us on the drive with a cheery wave.

"Hello, old thing, good to see you." Philip said, bounding out of the car, throwing his arms around her and lifting her feet from the ground. Blinking her bovine eyes and laughing softly, she gasped, "Hello, Philip! Do put me down."

Her son laughed but his smile was full of admiration as he obeyed. She smoothed down her skirt as he said, "Now, don't pretend you are not pleased to see us, mother. Where's father?"

"In his study, he'll be out presently, just as soon as he realises you have arrived."

Philip gave a knowing nod.

"It's good to see you again, Catherine, and you too, as always, Mrs Campbell," she added with a distinctly Victorian air.

"Did the others arrive safely?" Philip enquired as I bobbed a curtsey

He and Rosaline were forever telling me not to do such things, *'terribly old fashioned'* they always said, but then I always presumed that is exactly what I was.

"They ought to be here by now," he added.

Simon was unable to get away from the hospital and was reduced to taking the milk train the following morning, but Leticia, Charlotte and the children should all have arrived before us.

"Oh, yes, dear," Lady Mariah replied, but the question was unnecessary, for right at the moment a barrage thundered down the steps and into Philip.

Children always loved him and it pained me then that I might not be able to give him any of his own. But he had insisted there were enough children in his family and that it was of little consequence. I knew that it did matter – it mattered a vast deal to the heir of a noble title – and yet he had proved himself determined not to marry at all unless it was to me. He insisted that his sister's boy would make a good Earl if necessary, though I suspect he had failed to mention this issue to his parents.

As Ernest Junior stood with his mother at the top of the steps, Eleanor, Martha and the ever-incorrigible Ronald danced around us, excited at the chance to stay in such a grand house and happy to be out of London. It seemed a good excuse for everyone to forget the outside world for a day or two. Bertie, I noticed, joined in too. He seemed happier and more inclined towards mischief than I had ever imagined he would. I hoped Ronald wasn't having a bad influence upon him.

Charlotte was her usual self and threw her energies into managing the children's activities, for it was apparent Leticia would not. Leticia was by all accounts in a delicate state between terror and tranquillity, a situation which no one wanted to risk unbalancing.

We had a smattering of other guests also. There was Charlotte's father, of course: her mother had died giving birth to her, but Sir Benjamin Boden-Howard was very much alive. Philip's sister and brother-in-law were there, along with their delightful fifteen-year-old son, Rupert. And finally there was Philip's old house-master from Eton, Dr Joseph Alexander, and his wife. The peculiar thing was, I could swear to have met them both before. Dr Alexander was tall and broad-shouldered; his hair was thinning on top and nearly white where it remained. His eyes were striking, a fresh watery mix of blue and green, 'ocean blue', his wife called them when she noted they were a near match for mine. She was most surprised when I remarked that I had never seen the ocean and was therefore unqualified to agree. She was a demure, kind lady somewhere in her fifties. She was slender and soft-featured, though her bone structure suggested she had been a remarkably pretty woman in her youth, and her visage maintained the better part of it, with large hazel eyes and lightly freckled skin. Aside from her tendency towards talking too much of her two grown-up sons, I like her a vast deal.

The only person absent upon our arrival was Lord Rupert. He had not ventured outside with everyone else to greet the bride and groom, but had instead only waved from his study window. I was startled by his wan appearance. Of course, I had not seen him in nearly ten years and had been prepared for some difference, but not such a dramatic alteration as this. Philip ushered the children inside and led me a little way down the long gallery to his father's study door. When we knocked, the voice that greeted us was thin and airy.

"Come in, come in," he said with a pale smile as we pushed open the door. "Let me look at you, my dear."

He was grasping the back of his chair tightly. I glanced at Philip and saw the worry in his eyes. I felt the fragility of the old man's touch as he drew my fingers to his papery lips. Each breath he took seemed to drain ever more of his energy.

Later that evening, Lord Rupert retired to his bed so soon after dinner that I suggested Philip go to him and see how he was doing. My husband readily agreed and left me in the company of Mrs Alexander.

As she chatted I could not help but notice that her hair, a faded shade of chestnut brown, had slipped from the confines of its fastenings, and its height had diminished considerably since the start of the evening. She would periodically adjust the pins in attempt to maintain the style.

"Oh, do tell me how my hair is," she whispered. "It matters not how well I tie it up, it is simply incapable of staying in place." I smiled at her confession.

"I suffer the same imperfection myself," I said comfortingly. "It looks just fine, and I am sure no one has noticed but you."

"And you," she replied.

"Ah, but that is only because you had told me to check it."

Mrs Alexander seemed happy with this conclusion.

"It's the natural curl in it, that is responsible," she said.

"Certainly it is," I agreed, "and it is just the same for me."

She patted my hand. "He has been ill for a while, you know."

For a moment I was unsure to whom she was referring, and then it dawned upon me.

"Why did Lady Mariah not say?"

"You know Lord Rupert, he has the determination of an ox when he wants to. Where do you think Philip and Charlotte get their stubborn streak from? They are Boden-Howard to the core."

"But if he had said something, we could have postponed our wedding until he was feeling better."

"My dear girl, do you not see? He doesn't believe he *will* get better. All he wants is to see his son happy."

"Then we could have brought the date forward," I offered.

"Well, you are here now, and you may be lady of this house sooner that you had thought."

I was horrified.

"That is not why I… I love Philip… is that what…"

"My goodness, no. Forgive me, that is certainly *not* what we think. Dear girl, not at all."

Her mortification was convincing, but the notion that others might see me as someone who would marry for titles and wealth bit deep into me. Perhaps the thought would not have bothered me so much, had my first marriage been born of love and not convenience.

After a moment's awkward silence she said quietly, "I am always inclined to say the wrong things. I don't mean to, but sometimes my words come out in the wrong manner. Do say you forgive me, I meant nothing by it, I can assure you."

I happily reassured her that no offence had been taken and I was just glad of her honesty over poor Lord Rupert's condition.

When Philip returned from his father's room he was quiet and pensive, and when I asked him how he had found his father, he confirmed Mrs Alexander's observations. Lord Rupert had insisted upon explaining his will to his son. Though the entire estate was entailed upon Philip, he wished, and had requested, that certain elements be passed over to other family members. Philip had not questioned this and I knew my husband well enough to believe he would have done so regardless of his father's intentions. The earl had also insisted that we were not to allow morbid thoughts of his illness to dampen our celebrations.

The following morning began in a hub of excitement. Charlotte, eager to take the Ghost for a spin, had volunteered to meet Simon at the station. This was first and only occasion where Philip could find no excuse to prevent her.

"You be sure to treat her well," he said, as Charlotte leapt into the driver's seat and waited for Philip to crank her up.

"Like you're careful," she replied with a sharp wave and a 'Woooohoooo!' as she tore out onto the drive.

The tyres crunched on the gravel, sending pebbles flying out behind her and battering the paintwork. Philip cringed and covered his hands with his eyes.

I was not with them at this point, of course. I was up in my room watching through the window. I was not supposed to let Philip see me again until the service. I had breakfasted in my room with Rosaline but had been left alone for a few minutes whilst my friend claimed to be running an errand. There was a knock. I turned around to see Albert standing in the open doorway.

"Is Mother going to be back in time?"

"Oh yes, she'll be back in half an hour," I replied, patting my bed for him to come in and sit down.

He jumped up and sat cross-legged on the blanket.

"I bet Father wishes he could be here," he said, bouncing up and down slightly on the soft feather mattress.

I looked at the boy: his bright blond curls were so long they were almost in his eyes.

"I'm sure he does, just as we wish he was here, too," I replied, and prayed Arthur had received our letters. We had not heard from him for a fortnight and had hoped for a telegram to wish us well. Somewhere deep down I secretly hoped he had obtained leave and would surprise us all by arriving any minute, and I think Philip prayed for it too.

A moment later Rosaline returned bearing a small cluster of beautiful ivory flowers. I had never seen their type before. They were fluffy in appearance with large round heads so crammed with petals they seemed to be bursting out like a fountain of silk.

"Peonies," she informed me as I raised them to my nose and breathed in the sweet powdery scent. "Lady Mariah had them brought from the hothouse."

"I love them, thank you."

"You're going to look so beautiful," said little Albert as he bounced off the bed. "I had better go get dressed before Mummy comes back," and with that he vanished into the hall closing the door behind him. I pressed my fingers to my lips.

"He will break hearts, that one," Rosaline observed, "just like his daddy."

I nodded, pulled the sheet from my dress and sighed with contentment.

MICHAEL

Oxford — 23rd October, 2025

Paul set down his sister's journal and looked up at his parents. He was sitting in the armchair in the living room, with his wife perched on the arm and reading over his shoulder. Michael was eager for a response. He and Imogen had come to terms with their daughter's life now. They had had six weeks to mull and talk it over before Paul and Millie got back from honeymoon.

Paul shook his head and said, "Wow!"

"That's it?" said Michael. "Is that the best you can say, wow?"

"It really was her, that day, in your old office, on her birthday!" Paul was shaking his head in amazement.

"I can't believe she was still wearing the St Christopher after all that time and had no idea what it was for." Millie was staring at the pages with wide eyes. "And I can't believe she and Philip married on the same date as us!"

Michael hadn't even noticed this little paradox.

"Good Lord, you're right," Paul gaped.

"And what happened next? Where did she go? And the baby? It can't just end like that, it's like some kind of bad movie where they just leave you hanging for the sequel." The questions continued to tumble from Millie.

"That's all we have," apologised Imogen.

"And I suspect all we will ever have until we find her." Millie glanced from one of her in-laws to the other.

Michael watched Paul rub her back with his hand.

"Unfortunately, I agree," Michael replied.

"But what about Philip? She never knew what happened to him." Millie was clearly upset.

"That may have been for the best, dear," Imogen said, "to lose one's husband at any time would be hard enough, but so soon after marriage…"

"War is a dreadful thing, and she was sadly far from alone," Michael attempted to comfort them.

"The lost generation." Millie was fishing in her pocket for a tissue.

Michael let the silence ease the moment.

The clock in the hall struck eight. Michael saw Millie yawn. They had arrived home from honeymoon only that morning, and the long flight and jet lag was catching up with her.

"Lordy, if I feel like this after only a three-hour time difference, what on earth must it have done to Catherine over centuries," she mumbled, through a stretch.

"Oh, good grief," Imogen said, "I hadn't even thought of that."

Michael had, but he hadn't wanted to worry anyone. Time could have had all kinds of effects on his daughter's body that they didn't yet know about. All he could do was hope that the reason the journal stopped was because he had found her, and not because time took its final toll. He had considered the dizziness and nausea she talked of, and he had thought about the post-travel headaches and the insomnia she often suffered, especially towards the end. He wished with every part of his mind and body that he was not harming her with every attempt he made to locate her.

"What now, then, Dad?" Paul asked.

Michael smiled wryly.

"Start again," he said. "Fire up the machine and try to open a doorway for her." He looked at his wife as he spoke. They had agreed that now they had found out where she was, they had to try again.

"Cool," Paul said with a flash of hope in his eyes. "I'll help."

And for the first time Michael didn't resist.

"I'd like that, son. But don't get your hopes up; it might take some trial and error."

Imogen looked relieved the conversation was over.

"So... let's have a look at your holiday pics before you go, then," she said. "You turn on the viewer and I'll make us some custard."

"Custard?" said Paul.

"To go with the treacle sponge, dozy." His wife playfully tapped him on the back of his head. "I'll come and help," she said, following Imogen into the hall.

CATHERINE

Hertfordshire, **1916**

The sky was clear and a burst of late summer sun was warming the day up nicely. The ceremony was scheduled for noon and the priest had been there since ten o'clock. I was quite taken aback by just how many things had been available to Lady Mariah. She had acquired the most delicate Nottingham lace for my dress and had it delivered to me in Russell Square in plenty of time for me to make it up. She had found a magnificent supply of food for the wedding luncheon and even had a cake made in the village with special icing and white roses placed on top. And I couldn't believe how beautiful she had made the ballroom; there were lilies and roses everywhere, in vases, urns and hanging over the fireplace like a Christmas garlands.

At eleven thirty I was in my room with Rosaline putting the finishing touches to my attire. Buttoning up my gown I felt, for once in my life, so utterly elegant that I could have been Cinderella on her way to marry her Prince. As was the fashion then, the skirt was slender and fitted. My veil flowed down my back into a beautiful train that drifted about behind me like a fine spider's web, glistening in the morning sun.

Rosaline finished pinning on the flower ring that gripped my veil to my hair and stood back to look at me.

"My dear, if you don't melt him to tears today, you never shall."

For the second time that morning, I tried not to cry. She

passed me a handkerchief and chided me, "Don't you dare, or you'll set me off."

Rosaline looked as elegant as ever. She was in a daringly short lilac tea dress that finished above her ankle and made her feel as rebellious as Charlotte had looked driving away in Philip's car. I glanced at the clock on the mantel.

"Charlotte really ought to be back by now. Surely the train couldn't have been that late."

Rosaline made an attempt at reassurance.

Down the hall we could hear Lady Mariah, fretting over Lord Rupert and somewhere downstairs Leticia was yelling at Ronald. I examined myself in the mirror one last time then wandered over to the window. On the front steps below I could see Albert watching the driveway for signs of the Ghost.

There was a knock on my door.

"It's open," called Rosaline.

We looked around to see Lady Mariah standing there with tears in her eyes. Her face was pale and for an awful moment I thought something had happened to Lord Rupert, but then I saw his stooped frame coming down the landing towards us. His breathing was so laboured I could hear it from where I was standing.

"Oh, my dear, you look so beautiful," Lady Mariah whispered, pulling a handkerchief out from her sleeve. "Rupert was wondering, in the absence of your own father, if he could do you the honour of walking you up the aisle?" She took his hand as he reached her side.

Giving in to tears, I threw myself into her arms.

"Oh, yes, I would love that." I sobbed. I heard Rosaline sniffing behind me and downstairs, I heard Albert cry out "Mummy!" in a joyous tone.

I ran to the window in time to see the Ghost tearing back up the drive. Charlotte waved frantically at her son and Simon could be seen checking his watch.

Philip called, "Come on, Lottie, you've got ten minutes to get ready, where the hell have you been?"

As the car crunched to a halt and Simon got out I noticed the solemnity in his countenance, but then Charlotte leapt out of her seat and bounded past her cousin as cheery as ever.

"I'm afraid that's my fault. I was held up and had to wait an hour for the next train," Simon offered, regretfully.

"You get to the chapel and I'll be down in a jiff," Charlotte called over her shoulder as she bolted into the house. "Sorry, Catherine, I won't be a sec," she added when she saw me watching, then closed her door behind her.

Not twenty minutes later, I stood in the doorway of Hatherley Park Chapel. The scent of peonies and furniture polish somehow made everything feel safe. I tried to not to notice the empty spaces where absent friends should have been. Philip turned as we entered. His lips parted into a gasp then curled into a huge smile that sent my heart soaring. For once in his life his hair was smoothly combed and his suit was so well-fitting he looked taller and slimmer than ever. In his lapel he wore a single white rose, which later that night, he would trace over my stomach and naked breasts.

It felt like an age walking towards him. My consolation was the wonderful gallery of sunlight that streamed through the vast panels of clear glass and lit my dress and face. I felt as though I was floating down the Nile at dusk and the lanterns on the banks were leading me home. So glad was I to finally be marrying Philip that I found my pace quickening with each step. Poor Lord

Rupert had to pause to catch his breath. But when he placed my hand in that of his son he looked, for a moment, twenty years younger. How ecstatic I felt I cannot begin to describe. The last time I had walked up an aisle to be wed I had done so alone and my nerve had been unsteady. This time I had the real blessings of family and I could not have been more certain. When Philip took my hand I felt the world vanish and there was naught but the two of us together.

He had a cheeky glint in his eye throughout our vows and when it was over he swept me up into his arms and kissed me so passionately I blushed. Scooping me up he carried me out onto the small lawn where a photographer was waiting to capture our perfect day in sepia. He set me down then pulled me tightly against him. For more than a moment we held each other. I felt his cheek, cool and damp against my own, and I realised we were both crying. Something landed on my veil.

"My goodness, hold still, you have a butterfly on your shoulder," Rosaline said quietly.

Philip carefully let me go and, through the fine lace I saw its delicate blue feet and pale folded wings.

"It's a common blue," said Philip in amazement.

But there was nothing common about it.

"It's just like the one you described when you and Daniel..." Philip was smiling.

I thought of that last time Daniel and I had been in St Mary Magdalene's and I thanked God.

"I think it's a blessing," I said just as it fluttered its wings and danced away.

Luncheon was a delicious array of every good thing we should not have had, when so much was hard to come by. Everyone seemed to be enjoying themselves immensely. The gramophone sent bright music floating around the room. Children danced and glasses clinked.

There was one person, however, who did not appear to be entirely sharing in our joy. Just as we began to retire to the drawing room, I noticed Simon take Rosaline aside. Then I saw him beckon over Charlotte and Leticia. Behind me the children broke into laughter, but the sound seemed suddenly shrill. From his jacket pocket Simon withdrew an envelope.

For a moment I thought it was for Leticia then I saw Rosaline's knees give way. I barely noticed the footman refill my wine glass. The smile on Charlotte's face froze into a fixed, cold stare. She took the envelope and slipped a fingernail under the flap. Mrs Alexander was telling me something, but I never heard what it was. I reached for Philip's hand. He looked around, and in a second we were at Charlotte's side.

"I'm so sorry," said Simon. "I didn't want to spoil your day, but I couldn't keep it to myself any longer. It came this morning. They couldn't find Charlotte. Someone in the office told the telegram boy to come to me. He only just caught me at the hospital…"

"Thank you," Charlotte rasped.

She was shaking so much she cut her finger on the envelope. Leticia laid her hand over hers and helped her remove the single sheet of paper from within. Lady Mariah took Albert's hand and led him from the room,

"Come along, children, we have games to play." Her dry voice echoed in my head. The record ended and the gramophone needle began a rhythmic clunk. I heard Lord Rupert slump down into a chair and Philip slipped his arm around my waist. It was as though everything around us ceased. We could all see the black frame around the envelope rim. Charlotte blinked to see the words. She rubbed her fingers over her eyes then pressed them to her lips. I never could bring myself to look at it. I only stared at Charlotte as she forced herself to read it aloud. The words drifted over us, half of which I did not even register but those that did pierced the room like a bullet to the heart. *'...it is our painful duty to inform you...'*

How hard this is to write, dear friend. Forgive me my tears.

Charlotte's eyes glazed and her breathing tightened. Rosaline was crying silently and for once Leticia was still as a frozen river. Her face was white and dark rings hung heavy around tired eyes.

In the short time I had known him, Arthur had treated me like a sister, just as I loved him as a brother. But I had not grown up with him as they had, and at that moment I felt outside them, my heart breaking at a distance. How angry I was then, that Time could tease me and yet I could do nothing to go back and make this not so. And poor Charlotte. Bright, strong, sweet Charlotte. She knew not where to put herself. For a moment I thought she would faint but instead she just sank to her knees, wracked with sobs. Philip knelt at her side and held her close.

For so long no one spoke. No one moved.

"Where is my son?" Charlotte raised her red swollen eyes to me. "Fetch Bertie, please."

I do not recall how I got to the other room. I cannot remember taking his hand or leading him back to his mother. All I can see in my mind is Albert, his father's bright blue eyes looking up from his little face, knowing what had happened and understanding his father's death in a way no five-year-old should ever have to.

The atmosphere was so black that I felt my heart would crumble into the darkness.

❧ ☙

Forgive me for abandoning you last evening, I found I could not go on. We all loved Arthur. And there was a thunderous cloud over all of us, but the storm did not cease there. Almost as soon as he could be taken to his bed that afternoon, Lord Rupert fell swiftly into a feverish sleep from which he never awoke. The wedding party quickly dispersed. And though I wished Rosaline would stay with us at Hatherley I knew she could not allow Leticia go back to London alone. My husband himself was forced to return on the Wednesday morning, but I remained with Charlotte, Albert and Lady Mariah. Poor Charlotte walked around the house like a ghost, staring into the empty spaces and eating like a sparrow. I could not begin to imagine how wretched she felt.

My father-in-law held on for three agonizing days. I telephoned for Philip the moment it was over. It broke my heart when I saw how ill he looked upon his return. He was in agonies that he had not been present at his father's side, but it could not have been helped.

What I had not considered – until I informed the servants of the news, and they bowed, curtseyed, and called me Your Ladyship – was that I was now Countess of Hatherley. It grated upon me to feel so elevated at the expense of others, and after all, I was no different to the servants beneath my clothes. And in all the commotion we none of us thought to announce our wedding in the papers. It seemed wrong, anyhow, to make a celebration at such a time.

Not a week later we were all back at work, even Charlotte. She looked thin and drawn but her countenance was as chipper as ever. There were times I wished she would give in and be angry or hurt, but she never did.

"What can we do?" she said. "This war will continue whether

we like it or not, and there's no time to sit and wallow in self-pity. If we did that, the world would grind to a halt."

She was right, of course, she was only one widow among many, and I prayed hard that the day would not come when I would add my name to that list.

There was one piece of news that was like a spark of light through the blackness. Leticia received it in the sitting room of our Mayfair flat. She was quiet and completely still. She had finally received word that Ernest would be back on English soil by the end of the week. When Philip gave her the letter she sank onto the sofa so serenely I thought she had been paralysed. For such a long time she sat there staring at the crumpled sheet of paper, grateful tears rolling down her cheeks in silence.

But this glimmer of hope only seemed to make things even harder on Philip. I had watched the guilt slowly eat away at him, from the moment we had met in the National Gallery all those months before, but now it was near unbearable to see. Losing Arthur had broken him, and the thought that his friend had given his life for his country, whilst he remained in London in the safety of an office, was too much for him to bear.

The day we went to see Ernest in the hospital was the final straw. He had been sent straight to Queen Mary's Convalescent Home in Roehampton, which was where they sent the amputees.

From the outside it looked just like a great manor house, but inside the rooms were filled not with grand furniture but with bandaged men and fussing nurses. The stench of carbolic was nauseating. We were shown into an endless ward lined with metal-framed beds, each containing some poor wretch with vacant shirt sleeves dangling down, or flattened sheets.

Two beds from the end we saw him. If I had not known where he was to be found I would not have recognised him at all. His face was thin and his moustache gone. His eyes were faded and watery and its left side was still bandaged. The visible burns were healing well but the scarring would last for the rest of his life, imprinted like a brand to remind him of the war. His right side seemed relatively unscathed, save for the gap where a leg should have been.

"I can still feel it, you know," he rasped.

The nurse told me later that the explosion had caused shrapnel to pierce his side and puncture a lung.

"The leg," he explained, looking down at the stump of thigh that remained. "I could swear I can still wiggle my toes."

Philip tried to laugh.

"Good to see you, old chap," he said patting Ernest on his good shoulder.

"You too, old man. How's Whitehall?"

"Doing what we can."

"Congratulations, by the way, Lettie said you finally got round to marrying this lovely girl." He beckoned me to come closer. "Nurse Cliffy over there reckons I'll be all right to go home by Christmas," he continued, "and at least this thing gets me out of going back to the front."

His stump moved a little and it made me jump. "Sorry, Catherine. It's all right, you know."

"We brought you some grapes," I said feebly. Ernest gave a lopsided smile and I wondered what the rest of his face looked like beneath the bandages. At least his eyes were spared.

"Lovely, thanks. Be a sweetheart and pop them in the dish," he pointed to the small stand by his bedside and I did as I was asked.

"Some lovely girls here, you know. Nurses are absolute peaches, especially Cliffy. She's the best, knows just what to say when the nightmares come."

I had no idea what he meant but I saw Philip flinch.

"Lettie said she was coming yesterday, did she get here all right?" I asked quickly.

"Oh yes, bless her. She comes every Tuesday without fail."

There had only been two Tuesdays since his return and the first had been the day he arrived.

"Of course she does," Philip said with a forced smile.

Ernest sighed and closed his eyes.

A nurse came over and said politely, "He tires very easily. You might be best to leave him now."

"Thanks, Nurse…"

"Clifford," she replied, "the boys call me Cliffy."

Philip shook her hand warmly.

"You do an excellent job."

"We do our best for our boys."

I watched her as she walked away. I could see why the soldiers liked her. She was a comely girl, a little stocky perhaps, but she had a peaches-and-cream complexion and her hair was the bright red of a fox's tail, peeking out from beneath her bonnet. She had a bounce in her step that made the boys watch her as she made her way around the ward.

Philip was silent as we got back into the car. I dared not make him speak, for I knew what he was about to say. In the end I gave in and said it for him.

"You're going to France, aren't you?"

He took one hand off the wheel and ran it through his hair.

"I have to, darling. You do see why, don't you?"

I did see, but it didn't make it any easier.

"When?"

"I don't know. Soon."

"Before Christmas?"

"Maybe. I'll speak to people tomorrow." He reached over and took my hand. "Darling, I can't sit back here and let it all happen. They're running this thing abominably. The methods are archaic. I can't just stay here and be a part of this disaster from the back row. I cannot be a party to all the things that are wrong with it any longer, I have to go onto the front line and stand side by side with our men. I have to try."

I could see how he felt and I understood the sentiment. I did not know to what methods he was referring, but I had heard the rumours. This was a war being fought by aged generals who knew nothing of the brutality men like Arthur and Ernest had faced. It was worse I think for Philip, though, for he knew exactly what he was going to; at least they had been spared that.

MICHAEL

Oxford — 30th January 2026

Michael looked at the page of teenage scrawl and decided he couldn't be bothered to decipher it. There had been a move of late to return to hand-written work. The education minister was worried kids were not learning how to write properly any more. Michael feared he was right. He circled the text in red ink and wrote *"please rewrite legibly"* in large clear letters. The kid – he turned to the front cover – Devon Matthews would have to wait for his grade till next week, after he had done his homework properly, *and he'd better not think he'll get full marks for it,* he thought as a key turned in the front door.

"Hi, Dad." Paul's voice called out from the hall. Michael heard his son hang his coat on the rack and turn the handle to his study door. "You ready?"

Paul was commuting to London during the week now and usually spent every free minute at home with his new wife, but tonight was different.

"As I'll ever be," Michael replied.

"Well, come on then, let's get this show on the road."

Paul had already collected the outhouse key from the hook before Michael caught him up in the kitchen.

"Are you sure you're ready, Dad? You seem a bit hesitant."

Michael shrugged. "Bit nervous, I suppose."

He had been tweaking the machine for weeks until he had finally had to admit it was good to go. He could find no fault with anything, the calculations seemed accurate, the wiring was sound, and all there was left to do was test it out.

"It'll work, Dad, and you know it."

Paul was right, Michael did know it.

"I think that's why I'm nervous. For the first time in seventeen years it feels…"

"Tingly, right?" said Paul with a laugh.

"Something like that."

Michael unlatched the back door and let Paul out first. It was dark and damp as he followed him through the overgrown grass.

"When did you last cut this?" Paul asked, looking down at his wet shoes.

"Er… It got a bit neglected. It shouldn't grow much till spring now, anyway."

Paul shook his head and unlocked the outhouse door.

"Anyway, I don't know what you're worried about. This time it isn't about getting her back; it's just making sure everything connects," he reminded him.

"Yeah, I know," Michael agreed. "I just… I don't know… *need* it to work. Then next time we can fire her up for real."

Paul switched on the generator and flicked the light switch. The room blazed with a yellow glow.

"Did you come up with a name for her yet?" he asked. "I swear that's why she never worked in the past, she's gotta have a name."

Michael screwed up his face. "Well, yes, but you won't like it."

"Come on then, out with it."

Michael cringed. "A.G.W.V."

"*A.G.W.V.?* What kind of a name is that?" Paul blinked at his father as the bulb overhead came to full power.

"Artificially Generated Wormhole Vortex," Michael offered.

"Couldn't you have thought of something that rolled off the tongue a bit better, like… I don't know, TARDIS," Paul sighed, as Michael fired up the A.G.W.V.

"See, I said you wouldn't like it. I thought we could call her AG for short."

They watched the lights flicker from red to green.

"Is that really the best you can do?"

"Well, you think of something then. That's exactly what she is, anyway, an artificial generator for…"

"… a wormhole vortex," Paul and Michael finished simultaneously.

"It's just not exactly… catchy," Paul added.

"I can't call it after a fictitious police box from an old TV show," Michael defended.

The machine began to hum loudly as Michael pushed the re-locator pad into the centre of the room and switched it on. Paul extracted the new recovery monitor from the desk drawer and checked it for signs of life. The screen flashed green.

"I wasn't suggesting that, Dad. Never mind," he shook his head in amused despair, "we'll think of something eventually. Just preferably before we patent it."

The keypad on the recovery monitor began to flash up the words "enter location".

"It's all working. Shall we?" Paul asked, handing his father the small phone-like device.

Not only did the monitor now latch onto the home location and form a link with AG, but it also contained a mini camera and sound recorder.

"Be my guest," Michael said, offering his son the opportunity to dial a date and time into the machine. Michael watched him punch in 30/JAN/2026, today, and then 19:35, ten minutes into the future.

"Ready?" Paul said, his fingers hovering over the vortex dial.

Michael stepped onto the re-locator pad and said, "Hit it."

A second later the room swirled. Lights flashed in his eyes so brightly that he was forced to close them. Violet streaks whipped around him and finally a black tube appeared over his head and engulfed him. Another second later he was standing at the other side of the room behind Paul, watching his son staring at the pad, stopwatch in hand. Michael couldn't see the seconds ticking by but he knew Paul could. Michael cleared his throat and Paul spun around.

"Oh, my God, we did it! Right to the second!" He was jumping up and down like a kid at Christmas.

Michael's head was thumping and his stomach felt as though it had been turned upside down, but he also felt every bit of his son's excitement.

"To the second?" he asked, for confirmation.

"Absolutely." Paul ran over and hugged him.

Michael hoped he wouldn't vomit on him, but the motion sickness eased rapidly. He pulled the recovery monitor from his pocket and checked the screen. He had kept his finger on "record". It was flashing with the right time and date and when he pressed playback there was burst of purple light and then the counter zoomed through the minutes in a millisecond, so fast it seemed nothing more than a blurred flash.

"Now it's all down to locating Catherine," he said to Paul with a grin so broad it made his cheeks hurt.

"We'll have her home in no time," Paul replied.

CATHERINE

London, 1916

Philip left for Cambridge to embark on his officers' training the same day as Ernest was released from Queen Mary's, six weeks before Christmas. He joked about going to "the other place" and how it went against the grain to be there instead of Oxford, but none of his wit could ease my heart. Even though I knew Philip had not yet gone to war I felt as though I had already sent him to the front. I would not wish that feeling upon any woman; to know one's love is out there in mortal danger.

I wanted to give him my St Christopher but he had refused to take such a treasured possession. And when he had gone I found I had never felt so alone in all my life. I knew not what I would do once he had gone to France.

A day or so later, Rosaline and I paid a visit to the Jameses.

Everyone was so quiet. Even Ronald seemed subdued. Each time his father made a sudden move he flinched as though he were about to be struck. Ernest was so vastly changed that at first I could not find words to speak. I had intended to tell him how well he looked, and considering his injuries he assuredly did, and yet the scarring on his face was so striking one could barely resist looking at it. The skin over his burned cheek was so twisted that it puckered in shades of purple and white, and the line that ran from the side of his eyes to his ear made him look as though he was wearing one side of a pair of spectacles. The absence of his leg was barely noticeable in comparison. What disturbed me most, however, was the knowledge that his face had not taken the worst of it; beneath his clothes his body must have been a painful and ghastly mess.

He was not as chipper as he had seemed in the hospital, either, and he was so very on-edge. Each time a door creaked or one of the children moved, his eyes darted around the room as though he feared for his life. Once, when a distant housemaid dropped something, he covered his head with his arms and cowered, shaking violently. Leticia had to perch on the edge of his chair and stroke his good arm until the episode subsided. I felt as if I was intruding, so I suggested I take the younger children out into the garden. The weather was not too harsh for the time of year and the sky was a crisp welcoming blue.

At that time Eleanor was nine, Martha seven and Ronald six. Eleanor was always a quiet girl and reminded me of Rosaline rather than Leticia; her countenance was so similar that I imagined she was exactly how Rosaline had been at that age. Martha and Ronald, however, were wild. Martha would tease and torment her brother until he pushed her away or screamed in her face. I'm certain she only did it because she knew it would drive him to distraction. But on this occasion they seemed to be playing well together. So amicable was their game that I allowed my mind to wander and home in on a conversation I could hear inside the house. The back door was open and the housemaid was gossiping to an errand boy.

"There hasn't been a moment's sleep in this house since Mr James came home. It's every night."

"Doesn't the mistress do anything to help?" the lad replied.

From where I was, I couldn't see them, but from the sound of their voices I should have said he and the maid were of a similarly young age.

"Oh, yes, she goes to him all the time, she's tried tea, cocoa, hot milk, she's even tried holding him and rocking him, singing lullabies like he were a bairn, but you just have to wait it out till he stops."

"I heard there's a lot come back like that. Mrs Jones says it's so terrible over there that they get plagued by 'orrible nightmares."

I didn't know who Mrs Jones was, but I prayed she was wrong.

"Well, *he* surely does. It's no wonder the mistress hasn't slept a wink since he got back."

"I'n't your Charlie in France?" the boy asked.

"Since June," the girl replied, her voice losing its chattiness. "Went the second he turned nineteen."

I stopped listening then, for Martha had kicked Ronald and Eleanor was attempting to prise them apart. Ronald was tugging at his sister's hair and Martha was yelling at him to let her be the cowboy for once. I rubbed my hands over my face and marched over to assist Eleanor.

"Be quiet, you two, and play nicely. You know your Papa is unwell, you will upset him."

They both stopped and looked at me. Martha aimed one last sly kick at her brother before surrendering to the intervention. Ronald's malice ebbed from his face and he nodded sadly.

In the carriage home I told Rosaline what I had overheard. My friend said sadly, "I've seen it myself. It will ease in time. God only knows what horrors he saw over there. But he had better not talk about it too much or they might send him for electric-shock treatment."

My eyes widened. There have been many barbaric things in this world, but surging electricity through a man already terrified seems to me one of the worst I have ever heard. I had hoped the visit would be a distraction from Philip's impending departure, but all it did was heighten my trepidation.

Christmas came and went with too much rapidity. Philip got three days' leave. So many days leading up to that short time and all so painfully slow, yet those seventy-two hours flew by faster than a sparrow escaping the rain. I had thought it would be a sad occasion; rattling around Hatherley surrounded by a frozen empty park, but there was no time to be melancholy. They had promised us two more days in April before his deployment, but they seemed so far away. And there was much to discuss. The army wanted to requisition the house, and though I still saw Lady Mariah as mistress of the estate she had, upon her husband's death, been relegated to dowager. The responsibility now fell upon my husband and me.

"Can you not prevent the army taking it?" I asked when Philip and I were alone. I was sitting at my dressing table and untying my hair. Philip came to stand behind me, his shirt unbuttoned and his warm brown eyes watching me in the mirror.

"Possibly, if we were living here. But as it is, I must go to war and you have your own work to do in London. Unless you would prefer to be here? I shall not mind either way."

"No, you're right," I said, "I have to do my bit, too. I couldn't bear your being away at the front and my doing nothing but sitting around the house. Perhaps your mother could come and live at the flat with me until it is over?"

"Thank you," he whispered into my hair as he bent down to kiss my neck. I gasped as his hands slid below my under slip and cupped my breasts. For a moment I enjoyed his touch until I could wait no longer. I turned to face him and began to unbutton his trousers.

I hope I did not make you blush, dear journal, for I was

blushing myself as I wrote.

I cannot tell you just how much I miss my husband. At this moment I would settle for the sight of him across a crowded room, just to know he was safe.

The following morning we sat down to breakfast, resolved to ask Lady Mariah if she would agree to my plan. But she would have none of it.

"You are a sweet girl, Catherine, but I think I would go mad living in London. And the last thing you want is to be stuck with the company of your mother-in-law day in day out."

"Not at all," I began to protest, "I enjoy your company very much."

"Then what do *you* suggest, Mother?" Philip said with a furrowed brow. I took his hand beneath the table and held it tight.

"I shall go and live with Evelyn. The army should have the house whilst you're gone, Philip. And when you come back, you two can begin your lives here together in earnest. It's just not the same for me here without your father, and your sister has already asked me to go and live with her." Her lips were quivering but I could see the determination in her eyes. "Ultimately it is your decision and we shall all do as you wish in the end, but I think this is for the best. I shall be comfortable with my daughter and the army will have a great house to train its soldiers in."

Philip sat there, his thumb caressing the back of my hand, his eyes dulled and his tea untouched. Finally he looked up at the portrait of his father over the hearth and said, "You're right. If we are all agreed, then that's how it shall be."

Just short of six months after his training began, on the dank dim day of April 17th, 1917, Philip and I sat in Mrs Henderson's tea shop opposite the British Museum for the last time. Every moment is engrained in my mind.

The rain was hammering a tune on the glass behind him, and his uniform seemed to weigh heavy upon his body. The smell of damp clothes and warm cakes filled the room. I glanced over at the coat rack. Several greatcoats were hanging there and my heart ached for all the other girls in that room who were facing the same fate as I. I did not wish to cry. I could not bear to have his last day in England tainted with tears. Behind him condensation rolled down the inside of the glass as though defying my wishes.

I bit my lip. I could feel my legs shaking below the table and I feared if I were to stand they would not hold me. The room was buzzing with chatter. On the table next to us a young man held the hand of the girl opposite. She was smiling so hard I thought her face would crack. The man looked weather-worn and his uniform needed a good clean. His right arm was in a sling and I could see how glad they were just to be together. The waitress brought a pot of tea and placed it between us. Philip smiled up at her as she turned away.

"Mother seems to have settled in well with Evelyn," he said, conversation not coming with his usual ease.

"Yes. I'm glad," I replied, the words catching in my dry throat. I felt for my pendant and found it as always resting just below the neckline of my blouse. I pulled it over the fabric and let it fall on the outside. As I reached around to unclasp it, Philip leaned forward and gently took my wrist to prevent me. "Please take it," I said. "I want you to have something of mine with you."

Philip lowered his eyes. I shall never understand the true reason he would not take it, but he said, "It was your father's, you must keep it."

"My father's?" I was taken aback. I had never said such a thing. It had been around my neck my whole life but I could not tell you how I came by it.

"I mean, it must have been your father's. Either way, it's too precious to you for me to risk losing it."

"But it is all that I have to give."

"No, it isn't. I have your heart and that will always be with me."

I swallowed so hard I thought I would choke.

"I have this too," he said, fumbling with the lapel pocket of his uniform. I watched as his shaking hand took out our wedding photograph. "You see, right over my heart." He dropped it back inside and patted the fabric covering it.

"Very well," I conceded.

As I poured us our tea my engagement ring slipped around so the stones were facing down. I turned it right again and Philip tried to relax into a smile.

"You have lost too much weight lately," he said, "You should get the ring made smaller or you'll lose it."

He was right, I had lost weight. Worry and fear were eating me away.

"I shall never lose it, and besides my wedding band holds it fast," I replied and he leaned over the table and kissed me lightly on the lips. Two elderly women tutted from a table nearby, but we didn't care, and neither did anyone else.

In all my life I have never clung to anything as tightly as I did to Philip as we rode in the hansom cab to Waterloo station. Nor have I ever been so desperate for a single moment to last forever, as during those last few minutes on the platform.

People were crammed into the vast station, spilling over every square inch like bees in a hive. The clock in the centre ticked onwards with cruel torment, forcing us towards the second we were dreading. I could barely feel my body and my heart felt as though it had been frozen in cotton wool. Each beat in my chest pounded against my corset as if it was trying to break free and go with him. Uniforms were a blur around us. Men and women just like us. Hats and coats brushed against us and shoes clunked on the floor with heavy echoes. I neither saw nor heard anyone but Philip. We held on to each other in a close embrace until a whistle screeched. A train tooted and steam began to rise. I dreaded stepping onto the platform. The smell of burning coal made me cough.

He kissed me slowly. Someone caught his elbow as they scurried past. There was no apology.

"I have to go," he said and I heard the guard shouting for all to board.

"It's not long enough. Two days wasn't enough," I said as he pulled me onto the platform and paused by the open door of the train.

Other soldiers were boarding and other women were standing on the concourse at my side, some waving handkerchiefs, others crying into them. A child at my side called, "See you soon, Daddy," and a man turned from the top of the step and blew him a kiss.

The doors began to slam closed, windows were pulled down and hot breath steamed in the air as farewells were said or sobbed. A second whistle urged us on. I thought I should stop breathing as Philip stepped up onto the train and a guard shoved the door closed behind him. He dropped his bag and pushed through to the window. He leaned out.

"I love you, Catherine."

I waved furiously. "I love you," I called, but the words were stolen by the creak of the train as it heaved away from me. I mouthed it again praying he had heard, praying for the moment he would return.

"See you soon," he mouthed and I stood silenced, staring out as the great bulk of metal clunked over the tracks towards the coast. A woman to my left gripped my arm and began to cry. I put my arm around her shoulders and there we stood together, for how long I know not. The train had long since gone and the platform had emptied save for a few stragglers by the time we moved.

"Will you be all right?" I asked her.

She nodded.

"Sorry," she said. "I've already lost my brother and now my fiancé is going, too."

"It seems all our men are in France," I said and offered her a cup of tea, but she declined and excused herself. I never knew her name.

I made my way home, shut the door to our flat and sat on the edge of the bed we had barely left for the previous two days. I kicked off my shoes, lay down upon it and breathed in the scent of him from his pillow. The sun sank into the night. I closed my eyes and relived those blissful hours we had spent there. Our bodies entwined, so close, so deep, so much love.

I must have fallen asleep eventually for I woke as dawn was breaking. I forced myself to get up, wash and dress. I forced myself to leave the flat and walk the streets and sit at my desk and work. I wished, sometimes, I could have been more like Charlotte. Even Leticia seemed to have gone on better than I, in the end. Days slipped by and I could barely make out one day from the next. All I seemed to do was drift from the flat to work and back again, over and over.

MICHAEL

Oxford — 7th February, 2026

A car door slammed in the driveway and Michael looked up from his daughter's journal. He had been intending to study her last known movements, but had found his eye wandering back to the two letters written on the last pages of the book. Both were from Rosaline to Catherine, but it was the first that pained him most.

> *June 27th 1917*
>
> *Dearest Catherine,*
>
> *Forgive me for not waiting for more time to pass as you asked, but after all the dreadful news that we have received of late, I found I could not refrain. I pray that one day I may give this journal back to you myself and that you shall hear it from my own lips, but if it is not to be then I must tell you somehow, and this is the only way I could think of.*
>
> *The telegram came not a week after you left. Philip is missing, presumed dead, and it happened the very same day as time got the better of you. When they could not find you, Charlotte took the telegram. She's such a brick. She took the news to Lady Mariah herself. We had not yet told Her Ladyship of your disappearance and she was most distraught when she heard that you too were gone. All I could think to do was to offer her your journal. I was certain you would not mind. And*

today, a week later, she has sent it back and now I too have read it and I am glad.

All our hearts are broken, so many loved ones taken from us.

I believe I know where you are and what you are going through, I hope with all my soul that you are safe and well. Simon sends his love,

Your loyal friend

Rosaline

Dear God, Catherine would be devastated to know her absence had caused so much pain, Michael considered, *and it's all my fault. Yet how can I leave her there to be faced with such loss?*

The front door clicked and voices could be heard in the hall. Michael listened as Imogen welcomed in Paul and Millie.

"Your dad's in the study," Imogen said. "Go on in, he's been waiting for you all afternoon."

"Thanks, Mum. Any chance of a cuppa?"

"I'll help," Millie offered.

Michael set the journal down on his desk and watched the door open.

"Sorry we're a bit late," Paul offered, "Maggie called round just as we were putting on our coats."

Michael rolled his eyes. "No matter. You're here now." He stood up to go.

Paul laughed. "You're even less patient than I am. She was driving me nuts, but you know what Maggie's like, once she gets going there's no shutting her up."

"Oi!" Millie entered with a plate of cookies. "That's my

mother you're complaining about." She jabbed her husband playfully in the ribs and offered Michael a choice of chocolate chip or walnut. Paul raised an eyebrow at her and she giggled. "Well, OK, it's true, she can talk for England."

Michael declined the cookies: he was too anxious to eat. He picked up the journal and headed for the hall to collect his coat.

It had been snowing for three days and it was going to be sub-zero in the outhouse, at least until the electricity crackled enough to heat it. He had almost postponed this attempt, but he just couldn't wait any longer to try again. He had already delayed once: last weekend he had had a bad cold and Imogen insisted he shouldn't spend time in the freezing 'shed', as she called it.

"A week won't hurt," she had told him, "it won't make any difference to Catherine, and I'd rather you didn't get pneumonia in the process." He had conceded and so here they were.

The outhouse was indeed freezing; there were even icicles forming on the inside of the window. Michael hoped that AG would not be frozen or frost-damaged. Paul placed his cup of tea on the desk and opened to drawer to retrieve the recall device. There was an unhealthy rattle as Michael fired up the machine and he found he was holding his breath. Finally it began to hum with its usual regular tone.

"Thank God for that," said Paul, "for a second there I thought she was going to need defrosting."

"Me too." Michael took a swig of his tea and scalded his tongue. "Ahh!" he exclaimed, and put the mug down.

He watched the steam rise from the liquid in a tannin-scented swirl, and breathed a sigh of anticipation. He began to check all the dials, push all the appropriate buttons and finally switched on the re-locator pad. Paul and he settled back together, leaning their backsides on the desk and folding their arms. Neither dared to utter a syllable or break their concentration. Paul watched the recall box buzz into action and waited for his father to give him a nod.

"OK, punch in the date," Michael said, too nervous to do it himself.

Paul went back to AG. "What do you think this time?"

As Catherine had noted in her journal, events in her life did not always happen in linear order. Michael had begun a few weeks ago with the date of her very last entry in 1910, and had not seen a flicker of response. The day both Catherine and Philip had gone missing in 1917 seemed the next most significant option, but from the journal they could not tell the precise date, only that is was the beginning of June. This was their second attempt to hit it.

"Surprise me," Michael said.

Paul pressed the keys and June 5th 1917 flashed onto the screen.

"All right?"

Michael shrugged. "Good as the last one."

He hadn't expected to feel so hopeful this time, but the desperation was rising in his chest as strongly as ever. Paul, too, was shaking as he stepped back from the machine. AG's hum grew louder. Michael drew a slow calming breath and they waited.

The now familiar vibrations of the forming wormhole sizzled in the air, and finally the re-locator pad began glow. Michael glanced at the recall box on the desk. They were not planning to go anywhere themselves: the recall was to warn of any incoming signal.

Nothing.

Michael stared at it harder as though his pounding heart might make it work.

Nothing.

He glanced at his watch. Ninety seconds.

Nothing.

Tick, tick, tick... two minutes... three...

Paul saw something on AG and gently tapped one of the dials a fraction to the right.

A light.

Michael couldn't believe what he was seeing. The recall box was flashing bright electric blue. 'Incoming' burned on the screen in hard clear letters.

"Shit!" said Paul, and rubbed his eyes in disbelief.

Michael grasped his son's shoulder and they turned to face the re-locator pad.

The violet glow grew brighter and brighter until it was a blinding white light.

CATHERINE

London, 1917

My final days in 1917 were spent busying myself with any distractions I could find. It was some seven weeks after Philip's deployment when time found me floundering. I was on my way home from work when I decided I could not bring myself to go back to the empty flat. Instead I decided to pay a visit to the Campbells. I had no idea whether they would be in, but the occupation was better than going home alone.

It was the start of June and the days were long and lingering. The sun was glimmering over the city as I set out from Whitehall and crossed the street into Trafalgar Square. An omnibus beeped its horn at me as I mindlessly stepped into the road. A cool breeze was blowing in from the river, bringing with it the stale pungent aroma of the murky water. My mind flickered back to when I was living at Madame Legard's, and I considered just how dreadfully the river stank before they cleaned it up. Something seemed to crackle near my ear and I flinched. Then I heard the scraping call of Time.

All I could think of was Philip. I tried to run. But then his image blinded me, blocking my vision of anything else. He scrambled, clambering over a muddy wall. He launched into an open field amidst lines of men. Hundreds of filthy, weary men, fired with passion and crying out. Philip's cheeks puffed as he blew hard into a whistle. Its screech was drowned out. The sound of thunder rolled all around him. He was running. Hurtling towards a twisted sneer of spiked wire on the horizon. A constant boom of lightning strikes hurt my eyes and I realised it was not a storm.

I screwed my eyes shut and stumbled over the curb, falling against the warm paw of a great bronze lion. I rested my head against it and hoped I would not pass out.

I saw Philip fall. I saw the men around him fall. There was an explosion. Dirt blasted out in front of him and he went down. I reached out and felt the edge of the lion's mane, praying I could catch him, and I saw my husband reach out a hand to meet mine. His clothes were dark with dirt and blood. Glistening red drops splattered over his face. Our hands could not touch but I felt the tips of his fingers brush against mine. I could not help him. I felt him go. I let myself go. I tumbled into the hidden doorway of Time, for if Philip were gone, then there was nothing left for me to be afraid of.

MICHAEL

Oxford — 7th February, 2026

A deafening sound blasted through the outhouse. The floor swirled with a filthy mist and the putrid smell of burning flesh. Dirt shattered through the electric swirl and coated Michael and Paul as they stood. The walls shuddered and something hit the light bulb overhead. It exploded. Jagged shards of glass showered down. Michael ducked and pulled Paul to the ground with him. Something hit the floor hard in front of them. Michael lurched forward feeling through the mist, crawling on the floor towards the body.

Oh, God, Catherine, please be all right, please be all right, he thought over and over as he patted the ground. The dust began to settle and Paul clambered to his feet. Someone outside was running towards them. Then there was yelling and hammering on the door.

"Let them in," Michael gasped as his hand finally touched the fabric of his daughter's sleeve. Half blinded by the flashes, he blinked through the blackness of the now quietened room and called out, "Im, get me a torch. Hurry."

He heard Paul stumble into the door and pull back the bolt. Millie mumbled something as she threw her arms around her husband. Michael tried to focus on the room and not on the light that drifted in from the house at the other end of the garden. Imogen dashed off to do as she was asked.

"It's all right now," he whispered and he pulled the limp body towards him. The body was shivering ever so slightly.

Thank God she's alive, he thought. But as he lifted her into his arms he felt the weight and size of her, then the texture of the clothes. He felt the shoulder of the body and just as Imogen's padding footsteps came back towards them over the grass he touched the short hair of a man. The torch flashed on and beamed down at them.

In his arms was a soldier, badly hurt. Blood covered his face, obscuring his features completely. Millie was pulling away from Paul and by his side in second. She felt the man's neck for a pulse.

"He's alive," said Michael, feeling the soldier's weakening heart beating against his embrace.

"What the hell have you done?" Millie gasped. "Who the hell is he?" Her expression was one of utter horror.

"And where's Catherine?" Imogen cried in desperation.

Paul took a tentative step towards them.

"Philip?" he asked as the man groaned.

"Jesus!" Michael gulped, "it is, it's Philip Boden-Howard." The man groaned again.

"How the hell…?" Millie gently turned him onto his back as Michael lowered him onto the ground. She yanked open the soldier's torn jacket and winced at the wound in his chest. Around the man's neck his dog tag glinted through the blood.

"Call an ambulance," Millie urged.

"What on earth are we going to tell them?" Paul sounded stunned.

"I don't care, but this man's been shot and I can't get the bullet out myself. He needs surgery and fast. I think there's shrapnel in his leg too. Shit!" She was pressing down on the wound hard. "I can't stem the bleeding, call an ambulance, now!" she wailed. "And fetch me a towel."

Imogen flew back towards the kitchen and Paul extracted his phone from his trouser pocket.

Michael was shaking as much as Philip now. Millie looked at him.

"You're in shock," she said, not taking her hands away from Philip's chest. "Paul, take your dad inside."

"They're coming," Paul said, hanging up the call.

Michael allowed his son to wrap his arm about his shoulders and help him to his feet. As they reached the door he paused and said, "Will he make it?"

Millie glanced up at him and shook her head.

"I don't know. The bullet missed his heart, but he's in pretty bad shape."

Michael nodded in a daze.

"Michael," Millie said from behind them. Paul helped him turn around. "We know where he came from. If you hadn't got him out of there he would have been dead for sure. At least now he has a chance."

Michael was too numb to cry, but for the first time since he had first lost Catherine, he was glad of the time machine.

CATHERINE
Oxford – March, 1646

The first thing that hit me was the stench. My head was spinning and all I could see was a dim light. My stomach lurched. I clapped my hand over my mouth to prevent myself from vomiting and breathed slowly. Delicately I made my way towards the light and found a candle resting upon a writing desk. I moved my hand from my mouth and a second wave of nausea washed through me. I wondered whether it was the putrid air or the vision of Philip that had turned my stomach so.

As the room came into focus I realised I was in someone's bedchamber. The walls were lined in heavy wood panelling and the bed covered in the finest silks. I ran my hands over the smooth crimson fabric and felt the fine gold thread catch against my fingertips. I laid my face against the cloth and let it cool my clammy skin. Lying back I looked up at the great silk canopy overhead. Beneath me the drawstrings creaked and the smells in the room began to separate.

By the bedside and again upon the desk there were pomanders filled with rose petals; frankincense burned in a dish on the window ledge. I rose from the bed and went over to the window – there the underlying rottenness in the air became a feast of revulsion; sewage, animals and filth mingled in with human sweat. I tried to shut the window but to no avail. Cupping my eyes to shield them from the flickering candlelight I attempted to peer out into the blackest night. A muffled jumble of voices rose up from a room below and a crow screeched close by. I flinched and withdrew into the room.

Footsteps clicked along a corridor outside. I could see nothing to conceal me but the curtain. I was fortunate that the window ledge was set deep enough for me to perch upon. Climbing up I pulled the curtain to at the very moment someone opened the door.

The footsteps were heavy, like a man's, and yet when I risked a peek through the narrow slit between the drapes, I saw that the shoes were heeled, and tapered at the toe. The person went to the desk, scraped back the chair, and settled down there. I heard the tap of a quill against glass and the scratch of a nib on paper. Cool air came in at my back and I began to shiver. Quietly I pulled my feet further back from the edge of the sill and hugged my knees for warmth. I wanted to adjust the curtains and cover the tiny slit, but I dared not move. The incense made me want to sneeze. I pressed my tongue to the roof of my mouth to hold it in.

The scratching continued for some time. My thoughts began to wander back to my darling Philip. As I witnessed the battle scene over and over in my mind I tried to force the image away. I focussed upon the room, on the sounds and shapes that shadowed over me but the vision would not dissipate and yet I did not feel that my husband was dead. Silently I cursed Time for all its games and swore to God that I would not let it beat me.

A spider unfurled hairy legs and scuttled down the glass towards my hair. Instinctively I ducked, and the creature landed instead upon the sleeve of my blouse. Had he not been so large I might not have flinched and dusted him away. Catching the curtain with my elbow I saw the spider vanish into the room on a shining silver thread. The person at the desk stopped writing. I screwed my eyes tight shut and prayed they would not come over.

The chair scraped over the floorboards and a quill was laid back in its stand. I cowered away pointlessly and waited, grasping the pendant around my neck and praying to St Christopher to guide me out of there.

There was a low grumble.

"Damnable maid must have opened the window again."

I realised the person was a man after all. *Dear Lord, let him leave the window alone,* I prayed, but St Christopher and Time had other plans.

The curtains swished back and I opened my eyes to see a remarkably attractive man, aged about forty. His deep brown eyes widened and he took a step back.

"Heavens above," he spluttered. "Who the devil are you?"

I shrank back into the open window until I could go no further without falling through. The man's dark hair hung long and loose about his shoulders. He sported a thin moustache, an arrow of a beard and his neck was half hidden by a deep width of fine lace collar.

"Cavalier," I whispered, marvelling at my presence of mind at such a time. I bit my lip as the word slipped out.

The man raised an arched eyebrow and offered me a slender hand.

"Perhaps you should get down from there before you catch your death," he said with a lopsided smirk.

I did as I was bid and, as elegantly as I could, climbed out of the window ledge. The man's twinkling eyes drifted over me and his eyebrows rose further.

"It has been a long time since a woman has stolen herself away in my chambers, madam. I can only presume that you were not lying in wait for me, but rather hiding from someone else. Am I correct?"

Fighting a girlish urge to giggle, I nodded slowly.

He reached out and gently touched my shoulder. As his skin met with the fabric of my coat a crackle sizzled in the air and startled us both.

"Well, well we do seem to have caused a spark," he said, flashing a grin that warmed my heart so much I could have kissed him. "I can see you are not one for conversation," he added, his gaze still roving over my clothes with an increasingly perplexed expression. "Perhaps I could offer you a seat for a moment whilst you gather your thoughts into some kind of excuse, for I would very much like to hear it."

As I accepted his offer and settled myself into the chair by his desk, I found my eyes did not wish to leave his dashingly handsome face. There was a remarkable familiarity to his countenance: even the crinkles that wove out from the corners of his eyes made me feel certain I had seen him before. My mind rationalised that I had never set foot in the seventeenth century before, and therefore that could not be, and yet there he was looking so very familiar.

I glanced over the table. The inkwell was full of dark liquid and the quill was stained at the tip. A small droplet of black had splattered onto the wood and glistened in the candlelight. A parchment lay on its back, the contents of the letter within hidden from sight. Over the fold was a shining wax seal of deep scarlet embossed with a family crest. My eyes fixed upon it and before I knew what I was about I had turned it so that I might read it better. It too resembled something I had seen before, but I just could not quite place it. The man put his hand over mine and prevented me from moving it any closer. A gold ring glittered on his little finger.

"It is a letter to my wife. What business is that of yours, madam?" His voice was colder than before. I snatched my hand away and made an attempt at apology.

"Forgive me I… I only thought…" Then it struck me. "Oh!"

The ring upon his finger bore the same crest as the seal, and I knew that ring as well as if it were my own, for my husband wore one just the same. He narrowed his eyes. I moistened my lips and swallowed to relieve the dryness in my throat. Now I knew him.

"It's you..." *from the painting.* "You are..." I needed to think fast.

"Hatherley at your service, madam," he said with a flourishing bow, the mischief returning to his manner.

"Lord Hatherley?" I stuttered. *Edward Howard, from the portrait in my husband's home.*

"Third Earl thereof, in a manner of speaking, anyhow," he replied with increasing amusement. "I see you are aware of my reputation, madam. Pray, do not let it alarm you. I can assure you I am a happily married man."

"Then, 'tis all rumour?" I replied, finding his wit contagious.

"There is always an origin to a rumour, but alas, that fire has long since been dampened. I give you my promise, madam, I am a man of honour and fidelity."

I began to laugh.

"You are so like..." *my husband; your many times great-grandson,* I finished in my head.

"Like whom?"

"A man I once knew, a dear friend."

"I see," said he, folding his arms and suppressing a grin. "Now, are you going to tell me who you are, or do I have to call for the guard to escort you from Christ Church and away from Oxford for that matter?"

Oxford! I thought with horror. If I was in Oxford, and this was the seventeenth century, then I might have just been dropped into the most fearful moment in England's history.

I could not say for certain whether he would carry out this threat, nor whether it would be an altogether bad thing if he did; but something in my heart said I was better to be in his protection than removed from it.

"I am Lady" I stood "...Winston," I said, thinking quickly, for I could hardly use my real name. Pressing his lips to the back of my offered fingers he looked up at me with brown eyes and I felt the stab of Philip's absence right to my core.

"Lady Winston, are you unwell?" he asked.

I sat back on the chair and wafted my glowing face with my hand. He stepped over to a closet, extracted a fan and offered it to me. It was not hot in the room, and the fire was not lit, but I felt flushed and light-headed. I took the fan and opened it gratefully.

"I am well," I replied, not at all sure that I was. "I am merely exhausted from my journey. I have come a long way to be here." *Further than should ever be possible.*

Hatherley cocked his head to one side and waited.

"Do go on," he said, when I did not immediately oblige.

"I…" I made a rapid judgement and took a risk, "I am in the service of Her Majesty and I have been sent to…erm…"

"The queen is well, I trust?"

"I… oh, yes, sir… I mean to say, she… oh…"

"She what?"

"The thing of it is… I find myself in the correct room after all. I was… er… sent to… find you for… you are a trusted… I mean…" Hatherley was looking more and more amused as I rambled on, "You… I… Her Majesty said I should come to you as you were so well liked and trusted by…"

"The king?" he enquired.

I nodded, wishing I could find a way to ask the date, and

desperately trying to recall my history lessons with poor dear Arthur. Hatherley frowned.

"I do not recall seeing you about court."

"I am only recently of the queen's... er... bedchamber. I was sent to her not five months since."

"Then you have come a long way. 'Tis a tedious journey from France."

"Yes, it is," I replied.

Hatherley's expression darkened with a level of mistrust that near terrified me. I did not wish to be arrested and thrown in gaol.

"And you have a message for the king, from his wife?" he asked carefully.

My hand fluttered nervously to my pendant. Hatherley registered the chain carefully, his eyes taking in the rings around my fingers also.

"I do... not, sir. Not a letter... only word, to urge him to make his escape and flee to France where he will be safe." The explanation escaped my mouth before I had time to think it through.

"I see. Well, messages not written down cannot be intercepted. How wise of Her Majesty to think of it. But she must know that France is impossible."

I nodded slowly.

"Yes, she does, sir; it was but a vain hope. Her real intentions are for me to assist the king in any way that I can, and she informed me that you were the one to approach."

Hatherley's eyes hardened to the colour of coal and smouldered like the embers of a phoenix in ashes.

"She must trust you a vast deal, My Lady," he said at last.

"Answer me this and I shall believe you." He walked around me steadily, eyeing my every move.

If my dress were not suspicious enough my behaviour must have been quite extraordinary.

"Are you a Catholic?" he asked.

I was staggered. That was not the question I was expecting. I glanced around for a way out. It could be a ruse to catch me out, but I knew my husband's family had always been Catholic too, and I knew this man had been loyal to the king.

Seeing no other way but to answer him, I stood up tall and looked him directly in the eye.

"Sir, I am of the true faith, as are you."

He stopped before me and held my gaze fast. The candlelight reflected in the brown of his eyes and made swirls in them like melted chocolate. I knew then that I would trust him with my life.

"How did you get in here? The city is sealed and only those with a pass may get through."

"I am very inconspicuous, sir, as many women can be. You are of course aware of our abilities." I was referring to the numerous women who had spied for the king during his time in the city, and I prayed that Hatherley understood my meaning. *Thank you, Arthur, for being so thorough in your teachings, and for encouraging me to continue to study history.*

Hatherley brushed his hand over his moustache, the family ring on his finger flashing in the light.

"And to prove I am sincere I am to say this…" *Think, brain, think…* "Her Majesty thanks you for your efforts and assistance to those who have needed shelter." I prayed that Hatherley would already have taken into his home the recusants Lord Rupert had so proudly told me of. I looked up at him with hopeful eyes. "You follow, I presume?"

"I do, madam. I see very clearly now, you are indeed in the confidence of the queen, for she alone knew of our," he lowered his voice, "family guests. I also see that the message which you bring is to be revealed to no one but the king."

"That is it exactly, sir, I am so pleased that you understand," I said, astounded at my good luck. *Thank you, Jesus.*

"Pray, though, tell me," he continued, "wearing… such a gown as this…" he gestured at my anomalous attire. "You must have drawn a few eyes. This is not the common dress of a lady to the queen, this is… I know not."

"This is all the fashion in... Prussia, sir..."

"Prussia, indeed?" He raised an eyebrow, and I do not blame him, for I would have done the same.

"I am all stealth, sir, as you see," I blundered on. "I am here and I came entirely unnoticed. Had I been certain that this was your room and had you not returned at the very moment you did and startled me, I should have left you a note to meet me in...the Cathedral... though that matters little now." I could scarce believe the words that tripped off my tongue. I could only hope that I would not actually be required to convey any messages or assist in anything that might get me killed.

"So I see. And what for what purpose do you require my services?" He raised one eyebrow with flirtatious cheek.

"To convey me to the king, sir." *Oh, Lord, stop me.*

"Very well," he replied, "I should be happy to make your introduction, though it may take a day or so for me to find the appropriate moment. The king is, I am sure you appreciate, a little preoccupied at present." He bowed and I dipped a low curtsey.

"Of course," I agreed.

"And, I suggest we find you something more appropriate to wear."

"How?" I asked, concerned that his wife might actually be in the vicinity and I was at risk of being discovered in her husband's bedchamber. Hatherley read my thoughts.

"Sadly for me, my wife is safely at home, in Hertfordshire. However, there are women here at court who could be persuaded to part with a gown or two in the name of the king.

The gentlewoman we approached for assistance was not so gentle as I would have expected, for a woman at court. She was a sharp-eyed creature with hard features coated in heavy cosmetics. Her hair was flame red, her countenance severe and she looked a man in the eye as though she were his superior. When we first sought her out, she was in a small room in the midst of what appeared to be a clandestine meeting. Hatherley, apparently, was a party to it yet not directly involved. As she came to the door to speak with us I noticed the way others eyed at her with suspicion, and when I asked who she was my companion merely said, "It is of little consequence and best you know not."

And when I asked why people looked at her so, he replied flatly, "Her hair, it taints her as a Scot and many distrust her for it."

"Yet she is English?"

"Mostly."

"And she is for the king?"

"Most certainly."

"Then why do they question her integrity by the colour of her hair?" I was incensed.

My companion turned to look at me. "You must have been too long in France, madam."

"Perhaps," I acquiesced, for what else could I say?

A short time later we were back in his chamber, awaiting her arrival. Hatherley slammed the window shut and adjusted the curtains. The droplet of ink on the table had dried into a dark stain and the candle was near burned to the wick. He took another from the desk drawer, replaced it in the holder and lit it. I watched as he went about tidying. The mellow light flared through his hair, making it glow warm like rosewood and picking out the occasional sliver of silver. He caught me looking and curled his lips into a sideways smile. I was about to make my apologies for staring when the bells of the Cathedral rang out to mark the eleventh hour, and with the first chime came a rap at the door.

"Welcome, my lady," he said.

When she entered I saw she was laden with heavy fabrics and her face wore an expression of mild disapproval. Her own gown was plain and dark, yet her collar was elaborate and expensive.

"You have a screen?" she asked Hatherley, laying the gowns on the bed and extracting a small box from her petticoat. He shrugged and shook his head.

"I am alone here," he said. "There is little point dressing behind a screen when there is no one to see."

"You have no shame for your servants?"

He shrugged again. "As you see, madam."

The woman sighed.

"Very well, close the door and face the wall," she instructed.

Hatherley did not protest.

The gown she selected was of midnight blue and trimmed about the cuffs and collar with the same style of lace as her own. She shook her head at Hatherley.

"Edward, you really ought to be more discreet in your choice of mistress."

Hatherley spun around, only to be hissed at and instructed to turn back immediately.

"Madam, you are quite incorrect. This woman is a cousin of my wife's, and a lady to the queen. She has come here to assist in our mission."

The woman raised her orange eyebrows at me and smirked.

"Whatever you say." Her tone dripped with sarcasm. "She is comely, I shall give you that. I am sure I can find some use for her, if you cannot."

"She is discretion and stealth itself," he replied, ignoring the implications of her comment.

I assumed she too would turn around, but when I realised she would not I began to strip down to my undergarments until I was standing in no more than my corset and under slip, at which she openly stared. Finally she said, "Most peculiar," and handed me the gown.

I continue to be grateful that in times such as these, people do not ask too many questions. As I tugged on the dress with a little assistance, I felt light-headed once more and was forced to sit down.

"Forgive me, I had a long journey and I have not eaten for some time," I apologized. The woman's eyes pierced into me for a moment and then she said, "I do not think it is exhaustion or hunger that ails you."

"You think I am sick?" I asked in alarm.

"Ha!" she laughed and shot an accusatory glance towards our friend in the corner. "You are a married woman, are you not?" Her eyes were flickering over my figure. I nodded, with no notion as to where this line of enquiry was heading. "And not for long, I presume," she added with a wry smile.

"A few months, but what has that to do with... oh!" I could not believe I had been so blind. The woman began to laugh.

"When were you last with him?"

"A few weeks past, but so much has happened since and... oh, sweet Jesus,"

I pressed my hand to my aching forehead. This was not the time or place to be with-child. If I were to be as sick as I had been with Anne, then I would be of no use to anyone, least of all myself. I needed to go home.

"Well, you have time yet to do your duty and return to him before your confinement."

"If that were but possible," I replied, feeling all strength wash out of me.

"He is not at home?" Hatherley asked, from the other side of the room.

"I am afraid neither of us is. He is away at war, fighting for his country."

"For the king?" Hatherley asked almost rhetorically.

"Of course," I replied, praying that the acknowledgement might not have consequences at a later date. Though it was indeed the truth, the king for whom my husband had signed away his life was a very different man from the one who resided then at Christ Church. King Charles had not proved to be a good king; he had abused his people and their trust abominably and I knew not if I could, in all conscience, fight for his cause. And yet equally I could not condone the radical actions of the parliamentarians. Cromwell and Fairfax had been ruthless and just as corrupt as the king himself. Most poignant to me, of course, was their puritanical attitude towards religion. I was a Catholic and was thus, by no more than my faith in Rome, their enemy.

I wondered at God and Time for putting me in such a position, but it mattered not. I had made myself an ally to the king and decided there was nothing to be done but follow the course through.

"Then he is a better man than my worthless husband," the woman said, beginning to help me fasten up the gown.

For a moment I was at a loss, then asked, "Your husband does not fight?"

She shook her head with sour distaste about her mouth.

"Ran like the wind and the coward that he is... There," she said at last, stepping back to check my gown.

Attitudes towards men who do not go to war do not vary across the centuries it seems.

"There is a small sewing kit in the box," she said, "but I think this fits you now – for the time being. I believe you shall pass unnoticed very well." Her tone suddenly thawed from its icicle sharpness. "Very well indeed."

MICHAEL

Oxford — 7th February, 2026

The ambulance siren screamed into the night. Michael sat with his back against the vehicle side and an oxygen mask over his face. Millie was at his side holding his hands. He looked down at them: they were rusty brown with the dried blood of the man who lay on the trolley next to them. The paramedics had been asking all kinds of questions, and Michael was sure they suspected him of shooting the solider. The man checked Philip's saline drip again and smoothed back his hair. The woman kept glancing in their direction warily.

"Were you playing at some kind of war re-enactment?" she asked through thin lips.

Millie shook her head.

"They were conducting a scientific experiment, how many more times do I have to tell you? He," she indicated Philip, "wasn't even meant to be there. He just… kind of got in the way." She cringed at her own words and Michael gave her hand a gentle squeeze.

"Well, they made a right royal mess of it, then," the woman said as they ran a red light, leaving other traffic standing at the junction.

The man began talking into his headset, telling the hospital Philip's condition.

"I'm afraid you'll need to fumigate him too, his clothes are riddled with lice," he said, scratching his hand and attempting to wipe some of the blood from Philip's face.

They took a sharp turn and Michael felt his insides swing around the corner. He reached for his oxygen mask and took it off.

"I think I'm all right now," he said unable to take his eyes off Philip.

"Are you sure?" asked Millie.

"I will be when I know he is," he replied.

"Is he family?" asked the girl. She had already taken Philip's details but had been concerned when none of them could give a date of birth.

"My son-in-law," Michael replied." The girl glared at him so hard her grey eyes looked like slate beneath the florescent light.

"Why didn't you tell us that before?" she said, more to Millie than to Michael.

Millie shrugged. "I thought we did."

The girl shook her head. She opened her mouth to ask something else but they had pulled up at the John Radcliffe and the doors were flung open. Moving fast, the girl was outside and sliding out the wheel ramp for the trolley to come down. After that everything happened very quickly.

Before Michael even knew what was going on he was sitting in a sterile-looking room with his family, waiting for Philip to come out of surgery. When a nurse asked where their daughter was, as she ought to be informed of her husband's condition, Michael had been forced to admit that she was missing. Fortunately Millie was recognised by another junior doctor and everything seemed to have been smoothed over, for the time being.

"God knows what kind of trouble we'll be in if he dies," Paul said to his wife.

Michael hadn't thought of that, and right at that moment he couldn't even consider it. Philip was in theatre fighting for his life, Catherine was still lost out there, and all Michael could do was hope.

Imogen was standing by the window looking out into the night. Michael tried to think of something to say but couldn't. He looked for a distraction and saw a pile of magazines on the table opposite. He got up and went over. They all looked rather geared for a female market but he picked one up anyway and took it back to the sofa. The cover had a picture of some third-rate celebrity he had never heard of splashed all over it with the slogan, 'Izzy's baby shock,' printed in bold black letters beneath it. He sighed and opened it to reveal a contents page. As he scanned down the options he heard a noise in the corridor outside. He paused, listening hard but no one opened the door. He shut the magazine and closed his eyes. He hated hospitals; they always smelled like a sour combination of strong bleach and death. He let his mind wander and wished he could fall asleep. The clock on the wall above his head ticked loudly, echoing through the silent room.

Somewhere down the hall there was an emergency and people were running down the corridor and into a room one or two doors down. Michael tried to listen to what was happening but there were too many voices to distinguish one word from another.

"Go and see if you can find something out, please, Millie?" Imogen asked from the window.

Millie got up and Michael heard the door click open and closed.

He wasn't sure if he had drifted off or if she had really been gone for ages, but it felt like hours before she returned. And when she came in she was not alone. Michael opened his eyes and stifled a yawn. The room was stuffy and when he looked at the clock it was ten to two in the morning.

The man accompanying Millie was a tall Asian wearing a Sikh turban. Michael stood up to greet him.

"This is Dr Singh," Millie introduced. "He performed the operation on Philip."

The doctor smiled, turned to Michael and spoke in a surprisingly strong Irish accent.

"The bullet in your son-in-law's chest cavity was very deep, but thankfully it missed his heart and the lung damage will heal nicely. The shrapnel in his leg was pretty extensive but we got it all out and there shouldn't be any lasting effect. Everything else was superficial. He's stable now, but he'll be unconscious for some time yet. I suggest you all go home and get a good night's sleep. He won't know a thing for at least six or seven hours. I'm afraid we had to sedate him rather heavily."

"Why's that?" Imogen turned to face the room for the first time since they had arrived. The doctor's brow crinkled.

"He was in danger of waking at one point during surgery and began to, well, he screamed. It took us all a bit by surprise. We couldn't get him to settle with normal anaesthesia after that, so…"

"I see," cut in Michael. "But is he going to be all right?"

The doctor nodded. "Everything went very well. He's lost a lot of blood and there will be a few scars, but he'll be just fine. Your son-in-law is a very lucky man."

"He just needs a lot of rest and good care," added Millie. Michael sighed again, this time with relief. Imogen joined him by the sofa.

"That's good to hear," Paul said, shaking Dr Singh's hand. "We'll take very good care of him."

"Excellent, but he will be staying here for a little while yet." Dr Singh paused uncomfortably, "I'm afraid there's something else..."

A quiver of unease rushed through Michael.

"Yes, Doctor?" Michael was dreading the words he could see coming.

"It's protocol with any gunshot wound that we call the police. Dr Alexander," he gestured to Millie, "has informed me that this was some kind of science experiment that went wrong. I understand it was a complete accident, I really do, but the police will want to speak with you and see the weapon."

Michael stared.

Weapon?

"But we don't have... of course," he said slowly.

Dr Singh didn't move. "There is one more thing." The doctor winced at his own words. "Mr Boden-Howard seems to have acquired lice. You might want to report that to the shop he hired his uniform from, which is very impressive by the way, though perhaps a little too authentic."

"We will, don't worry," Paul said as Michael searched for the right response.

"Look, I know your daughter is missing and this must be a very difficult time for you all, but this kind of experiment should really be conducted in a more secure environment and er... you understand I had no choice in the matter, I had to...."

"Yes, thank you, Doctor, we understand." Michael offered kindly, "Just let us know when we can see Philip."

"I can let one of you in now for a few minutes if you like, but as I said you won't get much response."

Michael sat at Philip's bedside and watched his chest rise and fall steadily. The breathing tube hissed gently with air and the constant bleep from the heart monitor made Michael feel more at ease with his son-in-law's condition. The chest wound was covered with sterile healing gauze and a box had been placed over the injured leg to keep the sheets from touching it. They had cleaned him up really well and Michael could see that this was undoubtedly the man from the photograph. His face was pale and his hair looked terrible but he was a very handsome man. Michael shivered at the thought of what Philip had been through. He leaned over and gently touched his arm.

"We'll look after you, son, don't you worry. And when we get Catherine back…"

Michael stopped. Philip's hand had twitched.

"I'm sure you must be a good man, Philip. I trust my daughter to have made a good choice."

The hand twitched again. Michael waited, hopeful of Philip waking up. But after ten more minutes of nothing, a nurse poked her head round the door.

"Time to go now, sir," she said quietly. Michael got up to leave. "The police would like to talk to you," she added as he closed the door behind them.

"Thanks," Michael replied. Two officers were waiting a little way down the corridor. One was a burly black man with a shaved head and the other, Michael thought, *looks about twelve.*

CATHERINE

Oxford, 1646

Hatherley found me a room close to his under the same pretence as he had given the flame haired woman. I was a cousin of his wife's, and though the truth of the matter was more complex, I could safely admit to being family without lying further.

From the very first night I began to dream of Philip. As time went on and the dreams became more and more vivid and I began to believe that Philip was perfectly alive somewhere in France. I saw him in a bright clinical room filled with flowers and surrounded by fussing nurses in queer, unfamiliar uniforms. It pained me, knowing that he would assume me to be at home, waiting for him, when instead I was trapped in a city I barely recognized.

Oxford was a fortress, barricaded in and sealed off from the rest of civilisation and everything was at its worst. The streets ran brown with rot. The incessant rain washed the slime of excrement and waste along the streets like a rancid river. One dared not venture anywhere without a scented handkerchief pressed to the mouth and nose. Colleges were requisitioned for magazines or supplies. Professors were relegated to dank back rooms and the students were all but gone. Homes I had known a century and a half before were either gone or turned to slums. Fire had cleared some of it not long since, but what remained was crammed with strangers, military and outsiders shoved in with the reluctant city folk.

I was most fortunate to find my health good and the sickness of pregnancy so mild I barely noticed it. I felt a little guilty forcing Hatherley's man to fetch me a tub of heated rainwater every Thursday evening, but I am certain bathing is the reason I remained well whilst many around me succumbed to sickness. Hatherley had even warned me against it.

"It cannot be good for your child. Your skin might become water logged or you will scrub it away. You will throw your good health out with that water, I am sure of it."

But I did not take heed. Nor did I cease in my faith. Hatherley even risked himself to fetch me a rosary after he found me praying in my room with nought but my fingers to count my prayers. And as promised, he took me to the king at the first opportunity, three days after my arrival. I knew not what I would say, I just hoped it would not be something that might endanger my head, for I did not wish to lose it.

By then I had found out the date. Dear Arthur had taken great pains over the Civil War. Perhaps as a Christ Church man he had found the details of the city's occupation of particular fascination. Thanks to him I knew exactly where and when I was. Though England was supposed to be at peace, the truth was far from it. It was only a matter of time before the war began to rage again and King Charles would face the unthinkable, yet I could not reveal these future events to a single soul. Such knowledge, dear friend, is a great burden indeed and has left me with such great guilt, even though I know full well it would have done more damage to speak of it than not.

When my moment came to see the king I had been sitting in my room and looking out of my window. The rain had abated briefly and the sun had burned a blue hole in the sodden grey sky. Beneath the city stink the faint aroma of damp grass filtered through, and a bird was singing close by. With the meadow to my right, Corpus and Merton to my left, the view would have been idyllic, had it not been for the chilling boom of cannon fire in the distance. 'Twas a cruel, cold sound that made me wonder what terrors my darling Philip must have faced on the front line in France.

The cannon were not so close as to cause us panic, but the repetitive sound of shot against stone echoed around the city, taunting us. I almost leapt from my skin when a knock came at my door. I called out that it was open. Hatherley entered with his hair loose over his shoulders and his best smile upon his face.

"My lady, this might be a good time to approach the king if you are ready, and I see that you are." His eyes skimmed my gown flirtatiously and I gave him my best disapproving glare. He laughed. "Forgive me; I never could resist a beautiful woman, especially when she is as fresh faced and comely as you."

I could not hold my countenance and laughed.

"Of course not, sir, how could I blame you?"

"Modesty is highly overrated," he replied. "Honesty is a far greater virtue."

I cringed. I had barely told him a single truth since the moment I arrived.

"And you, sir, are honesty itself," I replied with a blush and a prayer that I was right. He held out his hand and I took it.

The dome of Christ Church gates was yet absent and the quad only enclosed upon three sides, but the familiarity of it still gave me comfort. I wondered for a moment where we were going, but then I saw him, walking about the lawn in the company of another gentleman.

"The king is taking a little exercise and is not averse to receiving a pretty guest who is here for his benefit," Hatherley said meaningfully.

I knew what he meant. The best place to introduce a

conspirator was out in the open where no one would suspect a thing, especially from a woman. Though I had married an earl and met many grand gentlefolk in the twentieth century, the idea that I should be presented to royalty had never occurred to me, and I found myself not a little intimidated. It is against my nature to feel so unnerved, though perhaps it was more the situation than the man.

"Come along, child, let us not tarry or the moment shall be lost," Hatherley urged when I stopped and adjusted my skirt.

As we approached from the other side of the lawn the king turned to face us. His hair was receding from his forehead but the colour remained dark brown. His beard was lighter in shade than his hair and it tapered down into a sharp point in contrast to his moustache, which twirled upwards into a sort of wide hairy smile. He stopped and halted his companion.

He was slight man of no great stature, shorter than I even in his heeled shoes, yet there was something about him that made one feel his presence keenly, as though he were six feet tall.

"Try not to stare, madam," Hatherley whispered as we came before him. I felt my cheeks flush and could have hit my friend for saying such a thing whilst in earshot. "Your Majesty," he said and bowed before the monarch.

"Lord Hatherley," the king acknowledged, and awaited our approach without moving so much as an inch. He was so still he could have been a statue.

Once up close I saw his features were soft and his eyes seemed sad and quiet. I might not have approved of the king's behaviour towards his people, yet I could not help but feel warmly towards him. He waited patiently for Hatherley to make his introduction.

"May I present Lady Winston. She is the cousin of my wife."

The king finally broke from his stillness and offered a hand for me to kiss.

"Your Majesty," I said, curtseying rather too low, "it is an honour."

"Yes," he replied with a feeble smile, "but one that is all mine."

I felt my cheeks glow even hotter and wished I knew what I was going to say next.

"My lady has been in France, Your Majesty." Hatherley looked the king directly in the eyes as he spoke.

"I see, how lovely for you. Tell me, Lady Winston, was the weather preferable to that of Oxford?" The king waved his hand and began to walk once more.

The two men set off with him. Hatherley shot me a sideways glance to do the same. I wondered why neither had introduced me to the other gentleman. He was a younger man but of similar countenance to the king. He was a perhaps a little more muscular in build but there was most certainly a family resemblance.

"The rain here *has* been rather incessant," I replied nervously.

"Her Ladyship found France very informative," Hatherley prompted. The king's gentle eyes ran over my profile.

"I am pleased to hear it. Perhaps she would like to share some of her recently acquired knowledge," he said.

I glanced at the other gentleman and wished he could be dismissed, but the king made no effort to do so. Clearly he was a man to be trusted. I supposed he might have been Prince Rupert.

"There is little to tell but for me to convey the queen's best regards and encouragement, Your Majesty. However, it was also thought that perhaps some assistance might be required in your service."

"Ah, I see. I am always in need of loyal servants. The

assistance will be most appreciated. Was there a particular task you had in mind?"

Having had two full days to consider forthcoming events, I still said the first thing that popped into my head.

"You are to leave here shortly, are you not?" I said, watching for the king's reaction.

He paused momentarily and examined my eyes as if searching for my soul. He gave a mild nod.

I drew a breath and continued.

"It is my... forgive me, Her Majesty's idea, that you should take the dress of a servant and leave here incognito in as little company as possible. You should be accompanied by a gentleman whom you trust implicitly, for instance..." The name of the man whom had actually undertaken this task had yet to find its way to the front of my memory. Hatherley inadvertently came to my recue.

"Ashburnham, Your Majesty. He has a pass to leave, he would be perfect."

That's the chap, I thought with utter relief. *Thank heavens I am not solely responsible for the king's actions.*

"Exactly," I agreed.

The king's hand was shaking ever so slightly as he raised it to his face and stroked his beard pensively. Slowly he began to nod.

"And how am I to acquire these clothes? Shall we have them made?"

I bit my lip and said, "Why, sir, though I am perfectly able to tailor such garments myself, even if I were to have a horse trample them, they would still appear new. It would perhaps be best if we procure existing livery from a trusted man servant." From the corner of my eye I saw Hatherley flinch. I noted the king's slight stature and considered that this might be easier said than done.

"If you are not in a position to take them from a man of your own, then I shall be happy to procure them for you," I offered tactfully. For a moment I held my breath, but I need not have feared, for the king's expression was of considered approval.

"The queen is a good judge of character, my lady. Now you will excuse me, my companion and I have some other business to discuss." The king gave a quick tired smile.

"Your Majesty," Hatherley said with a bow.

"That went well," he said when we were back inside. The Cathedral bell tolled and I felt my heart beat too fast.

"You are shaking," he added, taking my hand and leading me back towards my room. "You should rest a while. It will not be long to wait. Rest assured, it will be I who gives you instruction when the time comes, take no word from any other lips. But are you sure you want to obtain the garments yourself? I can have a trusted lady fetch them for you." I knew he meant the anonymous redhead.

I considered a moment and thanked him gratefully, but said, "I am good with a needle, sir, and an excellent judge of size. I shall obtain the garments and alter them accordingly. I have the sewing box that our friend brought, it will come in for good use, and the less people know about this, the better I feel."

"Very well, my lady." He stopped to look at me with an admiring shake of his head. "You are truly remarkable." His eyes were bright and kind. "For now, feel free to walk about in the garden, but take care not to stray too far, it may not be safe."

"Which uniform do you suppose would be best fitting?"

Hatherley pondered.

"Of a mid rank. Nothing so grand as to be noticed and nothing too lowly as to be separated from his master."

My mind began to race. I was about to commit a crime, but it was my own fault, and is it still theft if it is for the king himself? I nodded again and left him at the door.

It is remarkable how a woman with unimaginative hair, no colour on her cheeks and wearing as plain a frock as she can find, may walk by even the most observant person unnoticed. I had seen laundry hanging in the gardens that morning and had spotted amongst it some suitable attire for the king to travel incognito. The college was a vast maze of rooms and corridors even then, and I was forced to follow a maid for some minutes before I smelled the fresh aroma of clean linen. The maid disappeared around a corner and I pushed open the door to the first room. It was crammed with soap barrels. The strong scent caught in my chest making me cough. Footsteps clipped outside. I clapped a hand over my mouth. The door handle dipped. I backed away, scraping my ankle against a barrel. The sharp pain made my eyes water. I held my breath. There was a moment of silence then the footsteps continued on. I unclasped my mouth with a gasp. Slowly I peered out into the corridor. The way was clear once more.

Pressing my ear to the next door I could make out the hiss of steam from a hot iron and the rattle of a mangle. I had hoped to find the room empty but had prepared for the probability I would not. I looked at the bed sheet laid over my arm and smiled.

"Who is responsible for the clean bedding?" I said, marching into the room. Three women stopped and stared.

"My lady," the room chorused. I was in no mood for pleasantries, or at least that was the expression I had set upon my face.

"I asked a question," I said coldly.

The woman at the mangle was about my age. Her clothes were drab and stained with street dirt along the hem. She had her sleeves pushed up to reveal bulging arms and red cracked hands. Her eyes were grey as slate and darted about, hoping someone else would reply. No one did. Of the other two, one was a mere child but the one in charge of the press was older and braver. She gave a swift curtsey and nodded her head towards the mangle. The grey eyed woman raised her straw blond head and confessed, "That'd be me, my lady, is there a problem?"

It was highly irregular for a woman of my standing to venture into the servants domain and I felt the tension of the women burn as hot as the fire for the irons.

"There is a stain on this sheet that I do not wish to identify," I replied knowing full well that the only mark on it was the hair oil I had put there myself not half an hour since.

"I am truly very sorry, my lady," she stuttered. "Beg your pardon. I'm sure I didn't see it or should not have sent it up."

"Yes, yes, just do not let it happen again. Now give me another so I may have my maid make up the bed."

The woman took another from the pile and exchanged it for the one I was returning.

"Whilst I am here, I believe you have a livery for Lord Hatherley's gentleman. His Grace was not satisfied with the man's state of dress this morning. Perhaps I could make myself useful and take up the clean set." I added as though it was an afterthought.

From the corner of my eye I saw the elder woman smirk. I had heard the rumours regarding the nature of my relationship with Hatherley; this woman thought me far too familiar with him, but I did not care if it got the job done.

"Yes, my lady, of course."

The girl brought me the only livery she could find, presuming it was the correct one. I cannot tell you to whom it truly belonged.

Against my grain I did not thank her. I simply took it and stalked out as though I were the queen herself. Behind me I heard the grind of the mangle as it began to turn again, and when they all thought me out of earshot I heard them mutter something unpleasant about my manner. Once out of sight I tugged the sheet from beneath the clothes and covered them over until I reached my bedchamber, where I hid them at the back of my closet. Even the maid would not look there.

Things were so tense at court that I hardly saw Hatherley from one day to the next, until finally, on the six and twentieth day of April, the moment came for our plan to come into action.

The sun was barely glinting through my window when a quiet knock came at my door. I had been dreaming of Philip again and the sound thumped through my heart like the bullet that had pierced his chest. I sat bolt upright and gasped. The sudden move made me nauseated and I dared not move for a second or two. I did not wish to call out for fear of drawing attention, so I held my breath and hoped he would not grow impatient. There was a scratching sound from the door and a note slid beneath the wood. I pulled a shawl about my shoulders and hurried to the door. Turning the handle quietly I heard light steps stop and return.

"May I come in?" Hatherley whispered, glancing over his shoulder. I nodded and let him pass. Once we were inside and the door closed behind us I picked up the note and glanced over it.

Dress and come to my room as soon as you wake, H.

"Forgive me," he said. "I thought you sleeping too soundly

and I could not risk making more noise."

"It is to be today, then?" I said, knowing the answer.

Hatherley looked me over. I was wearing an ancient nightgown of his, my hair was loose and ruffled and my skin crumpled from the creases in my pillow. He suppressed a smile and I tried not to notice.

"You are well, I hope?" he said considering the contours of my figure.

By my calculations I was in the region of ten weeks along and the evidence of the child remained a secret beneath my day clothes, but in my nightgown a gentle swell could be seen.

"I thank you, yes." I replied with nervous hesitation.

"Good, good," he smiled. "I shall not burden you with the particulars, but we must have His Majesty out of the college and through the city gates before dawn tomorrow." His voice was low and hushed. "There will be no servants to accompany him as an entourage would draw attention, and 'tis safer if they do not know." Those around the king claimed to be loyal but barely a soul dare be trusted. "You have the clothes, I presume?"

I nodded.

"Excellent. The discretion of your arrival here is precisely that kind of invisibility that is required today. You are to take the clothes to Mr Hudson. He will be waiting in his chambers at ten this evening. Do not be late."

"Of course."

My stomach twisted with rising fear and the moment Hatherley was gone I was sick.

The time passed slowly as it always does when one is waiting for the hours to tick by. I conducted my day as I normally would and after supper retired to my room on the pretence of reading a book. I had not long then to wait, for it was nine thirty, and all I needed to do was retrieve the clothes and make my way to Hudson's chambers.

When I arrived there was another gentleman already outside the door. He saw me coming and moved as though to walk away but when he saw the bed-sheet over my arm he squinted and examined my face a little more closely.

"Lady Winston, it is good to meet you at last," he said with a flourishing bow. When I looked blank he continued, "Ashburnham, at your service."

I curtseyed.

"Though we are all at the service of another tonight," he added. I glanced about but we were quite alone.

"Indeed," I replied just as the door opened and Hudson bid us enter. The king was already there, along with Hatherley and the mysterious red-haired woman. She unnerved me more than the king.

"You, my lady, are a sight to behold," the king said as I approached with his new clothes. "You shall be rewarded handsomely when I am properly restored to the throne."

As I gave him my thanks I felt the now familiar stab of guilt. Ought I to have warned him, told him not to trust the Scots? But had I spoken out, who would have believed me? Or would I have been tried as traitor or a witch? I cannot tell you. But what I did know was that what was happening that night was exactly how I had read it in the history books, so all I could do was pray that was how it was always meant to be. I bit my tongue and waited for a moment to be given further instruction. It came in the form of a dismissal.

"You have been very good, Lady Winston, you may leave us now," the king said with a quivering smile, and I pitied him.

I saw no one else that night, not even my maid. I sat up in my room, the candle blown out and only the scent of incense to sooth me into the small hours. I did not have confirmation of our success until mid-afternoon the next day, when Hatherley sought me out in the Master's garden.

"This day is a pleasant one," he said as we took a turn about the lawn.

"Then, 'tis all done?" I enquired carefully.

"Safely," he replied with a wink. "Not an hour past midnight."

"In good time, then," I replied as he took my arm and threaded it through his, just as Philip had so often done.

"Timed to perfection." He patted my hand and added, "You did beautifully, my lady, just beautifully."

I grinned.

The sun was out and the warmth of it pleasantly tingled on my face. Hatherley paused by a cluster of bluebells and picked one.

"We cannot say for certain how long he will be safe," he said, offering me the flower.

Not long at all, I almost said out loud. Tightness strangled my chest for a moment. *God give him* strength.

"And Oxford, sir? How safe are *we* here?" I knew the answer, of course.

"I fear this is no place for any of us now. This city will be forced to surrender sooner than any of us would like. You should apply for a pass now and take your leave before it is too late."

"I did not arrive with one, sir, perhaps I could leave the way I came." That was more a prayer than a suggestion. Hatherley shook his head so that his hair fell over his eyes.

"No, you must leave by a legitimate route, and no one gets out of this town without the right papers; security is tighter now than ever. I could not live with myself if anything should happen to you." The sincerity in his voice made my heart ache. He ran his hand through his hair to reveal streaks of grey beneath the upper layers.

"And you?"

He smiled and without reply asked, "Are you back to France?"

I shrugged. For the first time I was truly afraid of what would become of me next.

"I know not," I replied hesitantly. "I hope to see my husband again soon," and that was assuredly the truth, "but until then I think I must stay in England, where I can at least be near him if he needs me."

It hurt me to speak so, for France was surely closer to Philip than anywhere, and yet I knew I had to stay on these shores.

MICHAEL

Oxford — 8th February, 2026

Shit, shit, shit, shit, was the only thought that ran through Michael's mind as he walked towards the waiting police officers. The twelve-year-old, on closer inspection, was closer to thirty. He had a baby face with soft blond hair and stood at no more than five feet six, but there were thin lines around his eyes, and now that his hat was removed Michael noticed that his hairline was receding. Michael was relieved when the young man informed him they were not going down to the station, at least not until morning anyway.

"Step inside, sir," said the elder, who Michael noted had the build of a boxer but the face of a movie star.

Michael was being shown into an office. On the walls were various certificates, a photograph of a woman shaking hands with the Prime Minister and a painting of a meadow. He squinted a fraction so that his view of the painting sharpened. *I must get new glasses,* he reminded himself. He didn't recognise the picture, nor did he find the name of the artist familiar, but the landscape he knew well enough. Bales of hay, rolled up like spiky carpets were scattered across a lush field, trees of all shapes and sizes broke the line of the horizon and a deer looked out at the artist from the far distance. It was Christ Church meadow.

The older officer settled himself behind the over-sized desk and pushed a photo frame away from his line of sight. Michael tried to smile calmly.

The younger one pulled up a chair from the corner of the

room and joined his colleague.

"Take a seat, Professor Alexander," he said.

Michael did as he was told and sat down opposite them.

"I'm Detective Inspector Wilkes and this is Sergeant Simmons," the bald man gestured to the not-so-twelve-year-old. "We will need an official statement, of course," he added, without giving Michael chance to respond. Michael nodded.

"Good. But for tonight I think we can manage here, it's very late and we do understand you would prefer to remain with your family." There was a brief pause and Michael felt the urge to fill the gap.

"Thank you," he said, unsure what he else he should say.

"You know, there's quite a file on you," DI Wilkes said, sitting back and folding his arms across a remarkably broad chest. His head shone like polished bronze beneath the yellow glow of the overhead light. *Wouldn't like to face him in a dark alley,* Michael thought with a shudder. There was another pause.

"Er... regarding my daughter's disappearance, I presume," he offered.

Sergeant Simmons nodded but DI Wilkes didn't move a muscle, he just watched Michael for what felt like several minutes before continuing.

"You said the injured man is your son-in-law, and yet your daughter has been missing since she was six years old. That seems very young to get married."

Michael felt his stomach growl. It was so late it was early, and he was getting hungry for breakfast. He clenched his muscles to prevent the noise.

"I can only find record of one daughter, so unless your son is a most unusual kind of bigamist, I should say that is an impossibility. Would you care to explain?"

The truth or not the truth, that is the question. Michael wished he could think of a valid lie.

"Well?" The DI unfolded his arms and leaned forward over the table. "Or would you prefer that we head on over to the station right now?"

"No," Michael said. "My family and I never stopped searching for Catherine, and recently some information came to light as to her whereabouts. She is... er... alive and well." Michael cringed, *though technically only when you take into account various quantum theories,* he added in his head, "and we wanted to bring her home."

"I see. And you made contact with her when?"

Michael's stomach growled audibly this time.

"We, er... haven't, as yet. But we did manage to contact her husband and he was going to help us." He winced at his white lie.

DI Wilkes narrowed his dark eyes. Michael thought he looked like jaguar ready to pounce. The officer pursed his lips.

"Go on," he said, clearly intrigued.

"He, er... turned up unexpectedly, out of the blue... and..." Michael paused to align his thoughts. DI Wilkes didn't wait.

"Professor, we are perfectly acquainted with the nature of your daughter's disappearance. I've read yours and Mr Brown's original statements, amongst those from various students and several rather interesting news reports. Oliver Brown is, I believe, still at the university?"

Michael rubbed his hands over his face. There was a tap at the door.

"Come in," the DI instructed.

A middle-aged nurse popped her head round the door.

"Would ya all like a cup o' tea?" she asked with a thick northern accent.

"That would be very nice, thank you," DI Wilkes smiled. "Oh, and could we trouble you for some biscuits too? The professor is hungry."

The nurse smiled brightly and somewhat flirtatiously at the handsome officer.

"Aye, I'm sure I can rustle som'et up."

Michael forced a smile of his own.

When the door had clicked shut again Michael answered the DI's question.

"Yes, though he's *Dr* Brown now. He's... er... still a friend of mine."

"Good, then I'm sure he won't mind assisting us with our enquiries."

Depends if you want him to tell you what really happened, Michael mused. He knew that despite having initially blabbed to the press, Dr Brown was now very sorry for having spoken out. He had since come to believe that what happened that night was best kept to themselves.

"I'm sure that would be fine," Michael said. Sergeant Simmons, he noticed, had started to type on his phone, Michael raised an eyebrow. The DI followed his gaze.

"Simmons is recording the interview," he said. Michael opened his mouth into a silent "Oh."

"What I find most interesting about all this, Professor, is that I can't find any record at all for a Philip Boden-Howard. There's absolutely nothing in the database. He has no credit cards, no bank account, no transport, no house, mortgage or rented property. He has no phone, no internet access. By all accounts Mr

Boden-Howard does not exist."

Only because you're looking in the wrong century.

"Oh, really? That does seem odd," Michael said.

The sergeant was shaking his head now and the light on his mahogany-coloured forehead was bouncing from one side of his shaven stubble to the other.

"What I would like to know, Professor, is that if your son-in-law was in a position to contact you, why did he not just bring your daughter home right away? Surely once he realised he had located her missing family he would have wanted to share this with his wife as soon as possible."

Shit, shit, shit, shit, Michael thought again.

"Well, you see, it's... a bit... er... complicated." He was grasping at straws. "Catherine doesn't remember us. She... whatever happened to her... it caused some kind of episodic amnesia that left part of her memory, the part before she went... er... missing... and, well, Philip..." Michael knew he was drowning fast.

"Really, you do surprise me. I'm all ears, Professor."

Saved by the nurse, what a lovely woman, he thought as she tapped on the door and entered without waiting. She was bearing a tray with three mugs, a jug of milk and a selection of packet sugars. Most gratefully received however, was the plate of biscuits. She set down the tray and retreated, glancing with interest at Michael. Half way back to the door she stopped abruptly and turned back.

"I'm sorry," she said, "but you're Michael Alexander aren't ya?"

Surprised, Michael swallowed a mouthful of biscuit and said, "Yes, do I know you?"

The DI opened his mouth to interrupt but the nurse jumped in first.

"I don't mean to butt in. I just, well, I wanted to say you've made me dad's life worth livin' again. He was in such a state after Mam died, depressed, ya know, but then you went to visit the 'ome and 'e's been bright as a button since. I know it's all nonsense but it 'an't half cheered him up."

The DI tilted his head back with an intrigued expression and Sergeant Simmons stopped messing with his phone and looked up. Michael tried to shrink further into his chair.

"I'm sorry, I don't quite follow," he said, taking a sip of tea.

"Oh, excuse me, where me manners," she said, offering him a pudgy hand to shake, "Nurse Amy Shaw. Me father's 'Arry Copes, lives at Park View, next door to Richey Winston. Ever since you went to visit last autumn there's been nowt but time travel on me dad's brain. I think the adventure of it's given the old lads a new lease of life."

Michael tried to blend into the leather seat. *Oh floor, swallow me whole.*

"How did you know it was me?" he croaked.

"Oh, I were there at t' same time, visitin' like. I saw ye's leave."

How does a nurse afford that place? Michael considered, then checked himself for being so presumptuous.

"Well, thank you, Amy, but we really must get on," said the DI.

"Oh yeh, sorry," she said, flashing a cheeky wink at Michael.

"Thank you, it was a pleasure," he said smiling back, though every muscle in his face seemed to wobble from the effort.

When she had gone, Detective Inspector Wilkes looked

rather too well satisfied.

"If we search your property, I presume we'll we find that same cabinet you once kept in your university lab?" he said after several moments of starring Michael down.

"I'm also assuming we'll find it's now working perfectly well. And if I get those clothes Mr Boden-Howard is wearing checked, I will find they are authentic, complete with actual First World War lice?"

Michael set his tea down on the table. *The game's up,* he thought with a weary sigh.

"And will we get the same story as the lovely nurse Amy Shaw just gave us if we pop along to this retirement home and pay Mr Copes and Mr Winston a little visit?"

"Richey's a sick old man, I don't think that'll be necessary." Michael ran his hands over his face.

"Then I suggest you start talking, Professor, save us the trouble of all those interviews. We will find out the truth, whether you confess it now or not."

Michael surrendered.

"You can search my home if you like. The cabinet's in the outhouse. It's not really a cabinet..."

"Really? We hadn't realised," the sergeant cut in with a mouthful of custard cream and sarcasm.

Michael glared at him for a moment. *Little point avoiding it now. Here goes...* he thought and proceeded to explain.

CATHERINE

Oxford, 1646

Getting out of the city proved to be disturbingly easy, though somewhat time consuming. In order to avoid arousing suspicion, I waited more than a week before applying for my exit pass and thereafter was forced to ponder upon where I should go for a further four weeks before its approval. At length the papers came, and not a moment too soon. Tension in the city was so high that it felt as though we were all about to plummet from a great crumbling cliff. War councils had been held. Fairfax was ready to storm the gates, and a proclamation had been issued declaring all those connected with the king's disappearance were enemies of the state. I was a traitor to my country and yet loyal to the crown. How could this be? How could I have become so embroiled? It matters not now it is over. What matters is that I stay safe for the sake of my child. Here is how it unfolded.

It was Hatherley's plan that I agreed to in the end, for I could think of naught myself and his offer was too kind to refuse. The idea was that I should leave Oxford in the company of the Marchioness of Hertford. I was to travel with her until the first night's rest stop, from whence I would go by stage as far as Hatfield under the guise of one Mrs Crathorne. I would then write to my "cousin" Elizabeth Boden-Howard to request a visit. Upon the receipt of an invitation I would then go on to Hatherley Park and remain there until word came from my husband to instruct me otherwise. The very second my papers came I went to inform Hatherley.

"My lady, you look very well, very well indeed," he said in his usual flirtatious manner. "They are here, I take it?" he added, once the door was closed behind me.

"Indeed," I said with a curtsey and the irresistible urge to grin. It was hot in the room for the windows were tight shut, and the rain beat a steady rhythm against the glass, blending with the distant cannon fire. He sat down upon the edge of his bed.

"I shall inform the marchioness at once and you shall leave tomorrow," he said. "I am sure she will be most relieved to find you can both escape this place at last." Her pass had arrived several days since, making her impatient for the arrival of mine.

"I cannot thank you enough, sir, your assistance is most gratefully received," I told him.

"Not at all, my dear lady, your service here has been most welcome. Now are you clear of your instructions?"

The potent scent of frankincense drifted over from the lamp by the bedside and I began to feel a little giddy. I tried to draw a deeper breath, for my clothes were now tight over my belly and I would have been happy to take a knife to them to relieve the constraint, but my pregnancy needed to remain concealed until I was safely away. Hatherley patted the bed at his side.

"Do sit down. It is very stuffy in here, I admit, but I cannot bear the stench from out there," he said, waving a hand in the direction of the window. I did as I was asked and settled next to him.

"Thank you, sir. I am most clear. Lady Winston will vanish and Mrs Crathorne shall take her place. Your wife is expecting my letter in a week or so and then I shall be accepted to Hatherley Park, where no one will know the truth but Lady Hatherley herself."

He smiled at me in the gentlest manner and patted the back

of my hand.

"You really are a remarkable woman," he said softly. Then in a flatter tone, "As yet you are safe, your name has not been called into question. However, until you hear from your husband you must promise me that you will remain at my home."

"You are too kind, sir. Of course I shall do as you wish," I replied and wondered just how long that might actually be before Time would strike again and pull me away.

I was about to leave him when he went over to his desk drawer and removed a small purse.

"Take this, it is not much but it will give you extra security."

"Sir," I spluttered, "I cannot. You have already given me sufficient funds for my journey."

Hatherley would not take a refusal. He pressed the purse into my hand.

"Then give it to my wife when you see her, if it suits you better. But take it now or I shall worry."

I raised my eyes to meet his and saw the pleading in them. I could not refuse. "Just be careful of highwaymen," he added, and I laughed at his fretting.

"You are worse than a mother, sir. I shall stitch it into my under slip," I said with a grin. I stood and for a moment we just looked at each other until finally I knew I must take my leave. He grabbed my hand as I moved away and tears began to roll down my cheeks. The salt water stung the heat from my face and I could resist no longer. I fell into his arms. He embraced me tightly and kissed my forehead.

"I fear I must go," my heart was breaking. There have been too many missed goodbyes in my life and those that have been said were too painful to live through twice. For a moment I felt I was back at Waterloo and Philip was pulling away from me.

"Be safe. My lady and I shall see you soon enough I hope. I shall be home by Michaelmas and by then there will be two of you to greet." He set me back and looked down at my belly. Deep inside me there was a flutter. I must have looked startled for Hatherley said,

"Are you well?"

To which I replied,

"Indeed, sir, we both are."

The journey was rough and uncomfortable. The rattling of the carriage shook my bones until I grew concerned for my child, for the coaches were not so well sprung or smooth as those to which I was used. I never thought I would say it, but right then I would have given anything to be speeding along in the Ghost instead. But the journey was over soon enough and before I had time to catch my breath I was entering the doors to my own home. I cannot tell you how queer it felt to arrive at Hatherley Park two and a half centuries before I had last left it. To be simultaneously in such familiarity and yet so far from it. But at that moment I could only be glad to be a good distance from those barricades at Oxford.

From the outside, Hatherley Park is near identical today, in the year 1646, as it will be in 1917, though there are no tennis courts and the fountain is not installed. On the inside the house is as welcoming as ever. Her rambling halls and great rooms are brighter and the decor more gilded and elaborate. The dining suite copied from Versailles is not yet bought, of course, and many of the paintings upon the walls have not yet been executed, but there is one work of art here that I know very well, the one of Hatherley himself. The brilliance of the artist's talent is more apparent than when I first examined it, for the paint is still fresh and the brush strokes clearly marked.

Each time I look upon Edward's face I pray for his safe keeping. Perhaps my prayers are unnecessary, for at least I know he survives this war. I know it because I saw his tomb in the chapel in the twentieth century. I have run my hands over his effigy and read the date of his death that will not occur until some two decades hence, and yet I cannot help it, for I miss him. I miss him because he is so like Philip, but most of all I miss him because he is a good and kind man.

We did not have to wait until Michaelmas to hear from him, either. Though we have yet to receive him home, there have been letters, some to his wife and some addressed to us both. There was one, however, that was addressed to me alone. It came on the fifth day of August and was delivered by the hand of woman I recognised. She was from Oxford and though I had never had the pleasure of an introduction, I knew her red hair in an instant. She did not stay more than two days here and though she gave her name as Lady Skelton, I am quite certain that was a lie. Whoever that good lady really is, Lady Hatherley received her with a trusting welcome. The letter was afterwards burned at the author's instruction and I am well aware of the risks I am taking by recounting its contents in your pages now. Should I be caught, I shall burn you and my life will be destroyed by the flames, but should I escape, as I hope and believe I must, then you shall come with me and no one of consequence to this time will read my words. The letter I speak of went something thus:

> *Dear Mrs Crathorne*
>
> *I trust this letter finds you well. I have the unhappy task of informing you that a warrant has been issued for the arrest of Lady Winston. Her name has been discovered, by what method I know not, in connection*

with the king's escape from Oxford in April and her life is in danger. I know you are great friends and hope, if you have the means, that you shall warn her of this situation and suggest that she should hide. There are safe locations for her and she need only consult those close at hand for instruction.

I hope this news is not too distressing for you.

Best regards, your loyal servant,

H

The servants were told I had left Hatherley Park before dawn the next morning. And so here I am, as you find me, hiding like a fugitive in the old nursery at Hatherley Park, on the 21st day of September in the Year of Our Lord, 1646. Five weeks of hiding like a ghost in the attic, pregnant and without my husband. But my friends here are honest and kind and I am well looked after. And you have been here to help me pass my days. Lady Hatherley gave you to me a month since, with the idea that I should perhaps like to keep a journal in my confinement. I am certain she did not intend for me to speak as freely as I have, but 'tis done. And now what shall I do to occupy my time? Perhaps Lady Hatherley can fetch me some books to read. I shall miss you, dear friend.

C G B-H

MICHAEL

Oxford — 8th February, 2026

Detective Inspector Wilkes was staring at him with such a blank expression that Michael wondered if he had dozed off. Sergeant Simmons, on the other hand, was gawping with an open mouth and eyes so wide they made him look even younger than twelve.

"Look, I know this all sounds insane," Michael said.

"You're not wrong there," said the sergeant. It was the first thing either of the officers had said in over half an hour.

"But I swear that's the truth of it. After all these years of trying to replicate and perfect it, AG..."

"AG?"

"The Time Machine Simmons, keep up," the DI replied impatiently.

The phone in Simmons' hand flashed and he began to tap something into the screen. Michael wondered if there was something wrong with the transmission of the interview. He watched him warily as he continued.

"As I was saying... AG works. We *actually* got the thing to work. Not just to activate but relocate a person from one time to another, completely successfully." He was beginning to grow excited. It was the first time he had really reflected on his achievement.

"Well, not quite," DI Wilkes said, with a more pragmatic view.

"Oh, well, yes, all right. It wasn't Philip we were aiming for, and..." Michael paused pensively.

"Something wrong?" the DI asked as he took the last custard cream from the crumb-littered plate.

"I er... well, I was just wondering how Philip was brought through. He doesn't have a recall device, so, well... it doesn't make sense. Catherine was very clear in her journal; she tried to give him the St Christopher, but he refused to take it."

"Sir, you'd better take a look at this." Simmons passed the phone to his superior.

The DI scrolled the screen slowly for a moment, his eyes growing more curious as he read. Finally he raised a black eyebrow and said, "Looks like you have some mysteries to solve yourself there, Professor."

Michael's mind raced. *What the hell is that supposed to mean?*

"But the crux of it is, we can get her back now and safely," Michael finished, suspiciously examining the DI's expression, "assuming you allow me to keep the machine and continue with my work."

Detective Inspector Wilkes scratched the side of his head and considered Michael carefully.

"As far as I can see, you've done nothing illegal. This message here," he turned the screen around so that Michael could see the tiny page of writing, "are the records of Lord Hatherley. I can't quite believe I'm about to say this, but your story appears to check out. We'll need to speak to Boden-Howard when he wakes, of course, but if he can corroborate your story then I see no reason to take this further. Your methods of experimentation, however, do need to be more secure. You understand we'll have to get someone to examine this... AG," he winced a little as he said it, "but if... and that is a definite, non-negotiable *if*, you can get your equipment into a properly supervised laboratory and continue your work in a *safe* environment, then I'm not about to stop the progress of what can only be described as a monumental scientific discovery... invention?" he question himself.

Michael shrugged. "Both," he suggested with a gush of exited relief. "I promise I'll get everything sorted to whatever standard you like, so long as we can continue."

DI Wilkes actually smiled.

"I should say you saved Lord Hatherley's life tonight, or is that a hundred and nine years ago?" The DI got to his feet and stretched his legs. "A mind-bender this one, for sure," he said with a cock of his head. "I think we're done for tonight. We've got everything on audio, but we'll still need you to pop along to the station tomorrow and sign a transcription for our records. No hurry, any time before six will do."

"Of course. Thank you," Michael said gratefully. He was about to leave when the DI said, "Just one request, Professor."

"Of course, what is it?"

"That I..." Simmons waved at him, "*we,*" he corrected "can come along as see it working, when it's all fixed up."

Michael grinned.

"When it's ready for a public demonstration I will personally send you an invitation."

CATHERINE
Hertfordshire – 19th October, 1646

Forgive my hand. It is so dark in here I can scarce see the page to write on. I have a candle but the wick is getting low and the light that glimmers from it is no more than a tiny flicker. I have been in here for some hours now. The air is musty and despite the cold draught from the corridor I find it stuffy. Forgive me, I should explain. The baker's lad came this morning telling tales of Fairfax's men. They are not a mile from here and they are searching for certain people who are accused of collaboration. The lad knew not whom, but there were no chances to be taken. Lady Hatherley came right to me the moment she heard of it and I have been hiding in the priest hole ever since. I snatched up my quill, a bottle of ink and the candle from my bedside. Fortunately Lady Hatherley brought me a little sustenance before she pushed the cupboard over the door and I was shut in.

I know not how long I shall remain here. I can get out into the corridors, of course, and for a short while I paced there as silently as I could, but the fear that I should be heard began to disturb me and so I settled down here, on the damp stone floor, with you. I have of course been shown these dark corridors by other friends in a later generation. You are aware of this already. But last time I was here it was not fear but desire that burned inside me. 'Tis a queer thing, that despite the utter blackness, I find comfort in being here. It is as though I can feel Philip close by and as the darkness closes in, it wraps around me like a blanket and takes me into his arms.

I dreamed of my husband again last night. He was laid out still in that same queer room I had dreamed of before. A tube ran from his nose like a cow's rope, there were patches on his chest and a needle pushed into the back of his hand and bandaged down with a peculiar kind of ribbon. His eyes were closed but behind the lids they danced with dreams, and I prayed that they were of me. A man came in and sat by his bedside. He had a tired face with a worn-out expression and watery blue eyes tinged with pink. I could not tell if he had been crying or simply had not slept. There was something about this man that made me want to reach out to him.

My memory stirred, and a door long since closed clicked open in my mind, but the light behind the door was only a glimmer and the images behind it a blur. I tried to push it open further but it would not shift. I asked the man to help me but I could not make him hear. I was screaming and sobbing but he never once glanced my way. My husband's hand twitched and the man was up in an instant, begging him to wake. When I awoke there were tears streaming down my cheeks and my pillow was damp from crying.

What does this mean, my friend? Only that Philip is safe? Or was there something there that I must discover? There are so many doorways in this world, why do some open too easily and other refuse to budge?

A most remarkable thing has happened in the minutes since I last set my quill to your page. I looked about me in this tiny room recalling the last occasion I was here, with Philip, and I thought of the heart drawn on the wall. I looked for it, I even raised the flickering candle up to locate it, but it was entirely absent. I have checked thrice.

Oh! How could I be so blind? It is I! I am the one who draws it. Philip was quite right all along, it *was* for him.

As I put my quill to the wall I found the heart scratched easily enough, but I had chosen a rough part of the wall and when I tried to write my husband's initials the P ran and I was forced to leave it at that. And now I think of it, there was only that one letter. I am happy with my work. My heart is forever yours, Philip Boden-Howard.

It grows ever colder in here. The damp begins to bleed through my gown and chill me to the bone and my baby begins to protest at my discomfort. It has been a long day indeed.

Sweet Jesus, I hear knocking upon the front doors!

The visitor is impatient.

There are voices, male voices. Dear Lord, help me!

Lady Hatherley is called for now. The Butler sounds afraid.

People have come inside the house. I do not think they waited to be invited. I can hear her footsteps upon the stairs. Should I go into the tunnels?

I cannot, the baby is kicking me so hard she is making my head light. *Shhh, baby. Please calm.* I cannot move. I tried to stand but my belly is so big and I have sat too long. I do not think I can get up and even if I could my legs are shaking too much to carry me.

There is shouting now. Lady Elizabeth is shouting, I cannot tell what she says.

She draws closer. Men are calling out over her but I can hear my friend's voice, she is saying, "You may search all you like, but Lady Winston has never been to this house in her life, my cousin is in France."

What shall I do? Is the sound of the quill too loud?

They grow closer still and Elizabeth's pleading has ceased. She cannot stop them now. I can hear her crying.

There is someone in the tunnels below. Heavy footsteps clunk against stone and they are making their way to the inner stairwell. Other voices are calling to each other. It is all swimming in my head now. The man in the tunnels has called for assistance and I hear him.

He has reached the fork where the hidden passage lies.

A creak on floor boards too close by... Pray God, help me!

There is someone in the nursery. I must blow out the candle.

MICHAEL

Oxford — 9th February, 2026

The nurse took the tube from Philip's nose and watched his breathing stabilise. The poor lad had slept most of the previous day but now he was coming to. Michael felt Imogen's hand on his shoulder.

"Go on," she whispered, as the nurse turned to face them. Michael went to Philip's bedside and winced at the sight of the shrapnel scar by the lad's right ear. It wasn't long but it had been deeper than the doctor had first thought.

"He's going to be just fine," the nurse said, "if he keeps improving like this you can take him home in a week or so."

"Thank you," Imogen replied, as Philip rubbed his ear. "The shrapnel scars, will they be..."

"Permanent?" the nurse cut in.

"But they will fade?" Imogen's voice cracked a little.

"Absolutely. Our laser tissue removal is fantastic now, but it will take time."

"How long?"

"Maybe up to a year, but we can't start until he's fully healed. Eventually they should all be gone, except the one at the top of his right thigh. That one was so deep it will always be a bit of a mess, I'm afraid." She was half speaking to Philip and half to Michael and Imogen.

Michael didn't even want to think about the great bullet wound in his son-in-law's chest.

"I'll leave you now, but don't stay too long. I don't want him tired out."

"Thank you," Imogen said again.

When they were alone, Michael perched on the edge of Philip's bed; the staff didn't like you doing that, but he felt he needed to be close when he explained where he was. Imogen settled into the chair at their side and gave him a nod to begin.

"Philip?" Michael said slowly as the young man's eyes closed for a second.

Philip blinked a couple of times and then focussed a cloudy gaze on Michael's face.

"Do I know you?" Philip rasped. "Can I smell peonies?"

Michael drew a shaky breath. "Yes, you can. My wife brought them for you."

Philip tried to turn his head but it clearly hurt him. He winced and turned back to Michael.

"That was very kind of her; they remind me of my wife. I'm not in France any more, am I?"

Michael shook his head. "No, son, you're in hospital in Oxford."

Philip moved suddenly as if to sit up, but he sank back quickly, his breathing tight.

"Be careful, Michael," Imogen said, her hand fluttering at her throat.

"I'll be all right in a jiff," Philip coughed. "I could just do with a spot of tea, that's all," he said with a brighter smile. Imogen got up.

"I'll go and fetch you a cup," she said.

Michael watched her go.

"How did I get here?" Philip asked when the door had closed.

"I brought you."

"You rescued me from the field?" Philip looked bemused.

"No. I... well, yes... oh Lord... I can't think of any better way to say this other than bluntly."

"Go on, sir. You seem like an honest sort of chap to me, and I'm in no position to argue, regardless. But please answer me something else first." The lad's expression had shifted to a one almost of realisation.

Michael paused and drew a breath. "Of course."

"Your wife, she reminds me of... well, she reminds me of Catherine, *my* wife. Who *are* you?" Philip's voice was wary but his eyes had sharpened their focus.

Michael took an extremely deep breath. *Here goes...*

"Catherine is our daughter." He watched Philip's stiff lips soften. *Well, he's not freaked out, anyway,* he thought. "I brought you here by activating A... my time machine." He paused again, but Philip's only reaction was to grow more interested. "I was trying to bring Catherine home, as I have for the past seventeen years. But somehow, this time I got you instead."

"Must have been a disappointment," Philip grinned, then was forced to cough again. "The Bosch did a bang up job on me," he gasped. Michael was impressed by the lad's resolve.

"I'm afraid they did a bit, yes. But... look, I know you're aware of Catherine's er... unusual... lifestyle..."

Philip laughed.

"Now there's an understatement."

Michael began to laugh too. Feeling more relaxed, he allowed his back to slump and folded his arms.

"Well, I'm not sure if you're aware, but she kept a journal and, well, Imogen and I have it now, and..."

"I do hope I was in it," Philip said.

"Starring role, I can assure you. The point is, we know all about you and our daughter and we are more than happy that we could..."

"Save my life?" Philip's eyelids were beginning to droop despite his attempt at liveliness. "I knew about her diary but I never looked inside it." He winced at a pain somewhere. Michael smiled at him worriedly.

"Perhaps we should let you rest a while. We'll come back in a couple of hours."

Michael got up from the bed but Philip's hand reached out and grasped the sleeve of his cardigan.

"Please stay. I don't know anyone else around here."

Michael nodded and sat down in the chair. The door clicked and Imogen returned carrying a cardboard tray and three teas in disposable cups. Steam curled from the holes in the cardboard lids like the chimneys of a tiny power station. Michael was about to thank her when he realised she was not alone.

Striding in behind her were Detective Inspector Wilkes and Sergeant Simmons.

"Good morning, Professor. Lord Hatherley, welcome back to the world."

"Not exactly back to it, sir," chipped in Simmons, "he's never been in this time before." DI Wilkes glared at his colleague before turning to Michael.

"We need to speak with Lord Hatherley. Would you and Mrs Alexander mind waiting outside, please?" It was an instruction, not a question. Imogen passed Philip's tea to the sergeant's outstretched hand and did as she was told. Michael was about to follow her when Philip spoke.

"Before you go, Professor."

"Yes, son?"

"Please tell me the date."

Michael told him, and watched comprehension dawn on Philip's face.

"A hundred and nine years! Dear God, no wonder poor Catherine got so confused. I don't know how she ever got used to it."

"Well, I think that answers our first question, sir," said Simmons as he pulled out his phone.

CATHERINE

Hertfordshire – 19th October, 1646

Forgive me, dear friend, I did not mean to alarm you. It is three hours since I was crouched in the priest hole behind the old nursery wall. Here is what transpired.

In the corridor close by, where an electric light bulb had once blown out and plunged me into darkness, another man was searching for me. This time there was no excitement, no tension of hidden passion, only the same glimmer of light seeping beneath the nursery door. This predator was cold and unforgiving. His feet stomped hard on the ground. I clambered to a standing position. An icy breeze swept around me. I pressed myself further into the corner. Blackness engulfed me. There was movement in the nursery. I held my breath and waited. Male voices called out for Lady Winston. Behind me; banging along the inner wall, growing ever closer. Outside, a woman was weeping, and Lady Hatherley was instructing the men to leave her home. Footsteps right outside the priest hole.

"Sir, this chest has been moved of late," a man's voice said.

"Shift it back."

"It was moved for sweeping, the maid must have forgotten to return it."

"This floor has not been swept for weeks, madam."

"How dare you!"

"I said move it, lad."

Scraping, dragging.

"Nothing there, sir."

Behind me; shouting.

"Hoy, I am close. There must be a door on your side."

"I see it, look here!"

Voices from all sides. A heavy slam against wood. A stumble in the corridor.

"Ah! There is a space here!"

A scuff right beside me.

Another slam.

I closed my eyes. My baby kicked so hard I cried out. A hand reached down. My head began to spin. The floor began to spin. The bolt gave way and the door swung open. It crashed against my body and I stifled a scream.

Again a slam. Blackness, then bright, bright, violet light.

Oh, what an April fool Time has made of me. It taunts me, yet it is kindness itself.

Hertfordshire - *1st April,* 1910

Nothing came at me. No one was there. With my head pounding and my feet unsteady, I fell out into an empty room. Toys, too modern for the gown I wear, cluttered the floor. Dusty white sheets covered the furniture. A familiar rocking horse grinned at me, and outside I heard the gentle spatter of the fountain. I stumbled towards the window, laughing and gasping at the fresh spring air. If I were not so heavy with child I might have danced for joy. I pushed open the smooth glass pane and breathed in the twentieth century.

Behind me; a scuff. I spun around, fearing for my life.

He was leaning against the door jamb, his face as white as

the dust sheets. He rubbed his fists over his eyes like a small child waking from a bad dream. So much I wanted to run to him, but I could see immediately that this was not the man I had married: he was younger. His eyes were bright and the shadows of war were not yet present. We stared at each other like estranged lovers. Philip's gaze flickered over me, lingering at my round belly, and my heart sank. Of course! It all made so much sense now.

His wariness when we first met again in 1916, his initial distrust and desperate need for my reassurance that all I had said, this day, had been the truth. On that occasion he had lived through today already. How I wish I could ask *my* Philip what I had said to him, how I wish he had told me. I know not what I shall say, yet I must explain. Tell me, dear friend, tell me what to do. This child in my belly is his, but how can I expect him to believe me? Why would any man believe a woman in such a predicament, and how do I explain myself without informing him of his own future? Does it matter? Which would damage our lives more – if I were to lie, or to give him the answers? Why should he trust me?

The silence was piercing. I tried to form a sentence but nothing would come. I did not even know how to address him. Husband? He is not yet so. My love? He was but unaware. Friend? He has always been.

"My God, Catherine!" he said eventually.

"Philip, forgive the intrusion. I was... Time... it brought me."

"So I see." His eyes filled with confusion but his soft mouth turned defiantly into a kind smile.

Philip is home for Easter and I am lucky for it, or I might have had much worse to explain to his parents. He has not sent me away, thank God. I have been hidden once more, away from his family and the servants, until he decides what to do. I have delayed an explanation, but it cannot be for long. The light begins to fade and the clock on the mantel tells me I should be hungry, but I have no appetite. Father Thomas would tell me that truth is best. If the telephone were installed I should sneak down stairs and call Rosaline, yet I know what she would say: follow your heart. And I know I cannot lie to Philip.

It is close to dawn and I have done it. Philip returned to me after supper with a plate of the best roast chicken dinner I have ever tasted, and I found I was ravenous after all. He sat down in the window seat and watched me devour it. All the while I could see the nervousness in his eyes and yet not once did he press me for an explanation until I was ready.

Long ago, in 1916, I had told Philip of my former life with Daniel. Back then I had felt his comforting words had almost been too knowledgeable, his actions one step ahead of me, and now I see why. He had heard it all before. Tonight he laughed with me when I eavesdropped at Daniel's classroom door, and cried with me through the birth and death of my Anne. Everything flowed easily until it came time to explain how I got here, in this state. His body grew tense as I spoke and his lips tightened.

"You know what I am, Philip, and I know you understand how this works for me. When I left Madame Legard's Time took me to you, several years hence. When you last heard from me in 1907, our... friendship... had grown strong, but we had not allowed it to develop into something deeper. That changes in our future. I love you, Philip, I always have and always shall."

For a moment he opened his mouth but no words would come. There was relief on his face, yet fear flickered at the back of his eyes.

"Things do not always happen in the right order for me," I continued. "We, this baby and I, are from your future. I dare not explain when or what happens in between for fear of altering our paths, but I hope you trust me just as I trust in *you*, for I know that in the future you love me too."

A nightingale began to sing and we both turned in its direction. I made my way over to the window seat and perched next to him.

"I have been trapped in 1646 for the past few months and have missed you more than I can say." I decided to keep one detail of this latest adventure for *my* Philip, for now I am certain that one day I shall find him again, and he will hold me close and laugh when I explain the carving in the priest hole. This Philip looked at me intensely. All I wanted was for him to wrap his arms about me and kiss me until all my breath was gone. I lifted my hand to his young face and trailed my fingers down his unshaven cheek. His eyes locked with mine for a moment, then lowered to my swollen belly.

Instinctively I laid my hand over my baby. That he wanted to believe me I could tell, but I cannot blame him for doubting. Perhaps he always will, or at least until the child comes, and then he will see in her face that she is his. He shook his head.

"And your memory is intact?"

I nodded.

"My travels no longer seem to affect me in such a way. I seem to have grown used to it. Though my early childhood, I fear, will always be gone."

Philip chewed on his lip. It seemed like an age before he spoke.

"I can do nothing but put my faith in your honesty." He

gazed deeply into my eyes. "I think perhaps I have always loved you, too, but I never thought it would come to anything."

I was taken aback by his confession.

He sat back, pensive for a moment.

"I have an idea," he smiled cautiously. "My parents are going out tomorrow morning and I am to head to London. They were to drop me off at the station, but I shall wait for the noon train and insist they leave without me. The moment they are off the park grounds we will smuggle you out of here."

"Where am I to go?" I asked, trying to recall when he purchased the lease for the flat in Mayfair. Sadly it was not yet.

"The Winstons, of course. I'm staying there for a couple of days myself, before I return to Oxford."

"And they will welcome me?"

Philip grinned for the first time since I had tumbled back into his life.

"Always, my dear," he said in a falsetto tone. I prodded him in the ribs.

"Don't make fun of Rosaline; she is good to us both."

"I know," he said, getting up to take his leave. "Now sleep well. We'll have some interesting explaining to do when we get there, so you'll want to feel refreshed. Oh, and I'd better find you something to wear, too. I hope you don't mind my sister's hand-me-downs. I'm sure there's something here we can adjust for your, er, shape."

I prodded him again and this time he laughed.

"Good night, Philip," I said.

"Good night." He clicked his heels like a Roman soldier and left me alone.

I was exhausted, and I thought the moment he left, sleep

would take me away; yet here I am talking to you whilst this child does somersaults inside me. But I have a terrible headache that has not abated since my latest journey, and my eyes finally begin to droop, so I shall attempt to close them. Good night, faithful friend.

MICHAEL

Oxford — 9th February, 2026

The police had been gentle with Philip, and did not stay for nearly as long as Michael had anticipated. When he and Imogen returned from lunch they found Philip wide awake and sitting up with a dish of raspberry jelly in his hands. The nurse had turned on the television. He was gawping at the screen with the spoon hovering like a zeppelin half way to his mouth. There was some dreadful daytime soap opera playing. It must have been set in the midlands as most of the characters had Black Country accents. The peonies on the bedside table were blooming and the whole room smelled of them. Philip didn't look over when they came in. He seemed catatonic.

"Are you all right, son?" Michael asked carefully. *This must all be a dreadful shock to his system.* "Would you like me to turn it off?"

"Hugh? Oh, I'm so sorry," he said, shaking his head as though he had woken from a trance. "I just, well, this thing is *fantastic*. Terrifying, but fantastic!"

"This is a terrible show, it's not a very good example of modern living," Imogen said as Philip finally put the spoon of jelly into his mouth.

He swallowed politely before replying, "Really? Well, I am rather glad about that."

Someone in the corridor clattered a trolley past the room and Philip's eyes shot to the door. Michael noticed how he cowered from the sound. *What that poor lad has been through, it's a wonder he's even sane,* he mused, as Philip regained his composure and scratched at the scab on the side of his ear.

"You shouldn't scratch, love, you'll make it bleed," Imogen said, taking the TV remote from Philip's hand as he pressed every button in an attempt to turn it off.

"Sorry," he said. "Shan't do it again, Ma'am." With a wink he saluted and his lips broke into a heart-melting smile. Imogen tapped him playfully on the back of his hand.

"Cheeky boy," she said, shaking her head. She reached into her bag and drew out Catherine's journal.

"Philip, there's still a lot we need to explain," Michael said, "and a few questions I'd like to ask you. Would that be all right?" he asked. "Only if you feel up to it, of course."

"Fire away, I'm perfectly fine – well, aside from the great gaping hole in my chest, but what can one do?" Philip said, gently patting the shoulder above his wound.

Michael was worried that Philip was being a little too chipper. *I hope this hasn't all been too much for him,* he thought. He was reassured when Philip replied.

"Really, I shall be just fine. You can't be married to Catherine and be surprised by anything. Not that I expected to time-travel myself, but I had hoped, before this... *that* infernal war came along, that I might come up with some decent theories of my own. I wanted to stop her travelling, she *wanted* to stop travelling, but I guess there's no need now. You already have the answers."

Michael's heart began to beat in a more regular and less stressful manner as he examined Philip's face. The boy was utterly sincere.

"Some of them, I hope," he replied.

"Please, tell me how you got that," Philip said, looking at the journal. Imogen settled into the chair by the bed and Michael perched on the arm of it.

"Arthur's grandson," Michael replied somewhat cautiously. He wasn't sure exactly how much detail was necessary at this point; too much could confuse the lad and make things harder to accept.

"Oh!"

For a moment Michael could see Philip's mind working overtime. *Even for a genius like him it's going to take some getting used to,* he thought. But Philip seemed to accept the response without further question.

"I saw it on her dressing table once but I didn't read it. She asked me not to."

"We want you to have it. Her words are so much better than ours."

Imogen passed it to Philip. The young man took it gratefully and ran his hands over the battered leather cover.

"She said she would let me read it one day, I just never considered that it would be like this. I thought it would be her that... well, never mind."

"I know," said Michael.

Philip looked suddenly very self-conscious. "Oh, of course." He blushed a little. Michael decided to change the subject.

"Perhaps I should explain how she went missing in the first place," he said.

"I shall hazard an educated guess and say that she was six years old when it happened," Philip replied. Then he noted that Michael looked slightly crestfallen, and added, "Please, do tell me."

Michael blinked back a tear, forced his voice through a wave of emotion, and began.

Oxford – 11th February 2026

Philip was doing remarkably well. The doctors said they might be able to take him home on Monday. He was chatting away to Paul and Millie when Michael and Imogen arrived. Michael was pleased they were all getting along so well; he could see why his daughter had fallen in love with the lad. As Philip waved them in, Michael noticed the journal resting innocently on the bedside cabinet. Philip had just finished reading it for the second time. Michael had been worried at his reaction at first, whether it was all just too much too soon. *But it doesn't seem to have done him any harm,* he thought, as Philip bid a friendly goodbye to his brother and sister-in-law.

"We'd better run, Dad, but we'll catch you later," Paul said as Millie kissed Imogen on the cheek.

"Don't forget dinner at ours tomorrow," Michael said as Paul put on his coat. His son laughed.

"We won't. Oh, and Philip's had a good idea," he added, then vanished out of the door. Michael turned to the lad with a questioning smile.

"You know, I'm getting rather used to all this pampering and all these visitors," Philip said, "though I'm not sure I shall ever get used to that box." He pointed at the television.

Michael nodded.

"Wait till you go to the cinema! The special effects they have these days will blow your mind."

"Not literally, I hope," he grinned, and scratched at the scab by his ear. Imogen slapped his hand away, "Oops," he said, smiling even more broadly. "They didn't even have talkies at home yet," he added to Michael.

"Gosh, I suppose not. It must all be like a crazy dream at the moment," Imogen said, her gaze drifting over her daughter's journal. She picked it up and held it on her lap.

Michael went to close the blinds; it had been dark for hours but no one had thought to shut out the winter night.

"Tell me, did you ever doubt her story?" Imogen asked carefully.

"Not the time travel, strangely enough, that all just seemed to make sense. But I confess there was a moment or two when... I'm ashamed to admit it, but in 1910, when I hadn't seen her in three years and there she was, standing in my old nursery, wearing a dirty seventeenth-century frock and eight months pregnant, I couldn't help but question..."

"Her condition, you mean?" Michael asked. Philip lowered his eyes.

"I'm afraid I did wonder."

"You can hardly be blamed for questioning the child's paternity. They were extremely unusual circumstances," Michael offered.

"Thank you," Philip said gratefully. "But the doubt was in my mind alone, my heart never wavered."

Imogen sighed.

Michael smiled at her; it was like one of those sappy romance novels she seemed to like reading.

"Of course, I knew she was telling the truth for certain when I went back to get my grandmother's engagement ring. Catherine was wearing it, and yet there it was, still in my mother's jewellery box. There was no way it could be in two places at once. Well... not normally."

Michael nodded thoughtfully.

"I hope you don't mind my asking," Imogen said, "but why did you go and get the ring from your mother?"

Philip looked hurt.

"Please don't think I did it through doubt. I asked for it because I meant to propose. Whether the child was mine or not, I couldn't see Catherine alone and an unmarried mother; the shame would have been so damning for her. I loved her then as I do now. I had to try."

Imogen sighed again.

The ceiling light flickered. Michael's eyes were temporarily drawn to it. From the corner of his vision he saw Philip shift his position in the bed.

"Would you like me to bring you anything?" he asked. Philip shook his head.

"All good, thanks."

You've been talking to Paul too much; you're starting to sound like him, Michael thought. Imogen was stroking the journal as if it was a sleeping cat. He took it from her and set it back on the table.

"You look very well," Imogen volunteered. Philip smiled over at her then drew a breath.

"Thanks. Look, I think I know how to get her back. The only date that makes sense is just before her twenty-fourth birthday, the date of her last entry. She was supposed to meet me and didn't come. She vanished into time and no one back then ever saw her again. I think she came here... er... comes here, oh, you know what I mean. Anyway, I've read the journal and it all makes sense. I can go back and fetch her. If I explain things I'm certain she will come with me."

"She was supposed to meet you and never showed?" Michael repeated, feeling as if he was missing something vital.

"Yes, we had arranged to meet at the café near the British Museum. That was when I planned to propose."

"You can't go back, love," said Imogen, "you're not well enough." She looked up at Michael. He wanted to back her up, but the proposition did seem to make sense.

"Maybe not yet," Philip replied, "but I'm on the mend, all the doctors agree. I will be up and on my feet in no time."

"Twenty-ninth of April 1910. We tried that date already, son," Michael said. "It didn't work."

Philip flashed them his most endearing grin.

"That's because you didn't have me. I know exactly where to find her *and* I have the means of transport."

Now Michael was really curious; he had not yet established how Philip came through the wormhole. Philip pointed at the bedside cabinet. "Imogen, would you be so kind as to open that drawer for me."

"Of course, love," she said. "What am I looking …oh!" She stared into the drawer. "But how did you get it? I thought…" she stuttered. Michael peered over her shoulder, unable to wait any longer.

Three small items were neatly laid there. At the bottom was a photograph. It was hard to tell through the dark stains of dried blood, but it appeared to be of a wedding group. Michael shuddered. Sitting on top of it were two small shining items: both had been cleaned recently. He put his hand in the drawer and pushed aside the bullet-twisted soldier's dog tag and picked up the glinting gold disk.

"They took it off me when I was in surgery," Philip said, as Michael turned back to face him.

"All right, son. It seems we have a plan."

CATHERINE

London – 25th April, 1907

Last night was the most romantic of my life. Though, perhaps I should take a step back.

I am installed in my old room at 52 Russell Square. Rosaline hugged me so tightly when she saw me, I thought my belly might pop right there. Philip and I made our explanations and she took them in with astonishment.

"This is a most unexpected surprise," she exclaimed when I was done, "and a most welcome one."

"Even under the circumstances?" I asked, indicating my swollen belly, for I was then already past eight months along.

"Well," she said with an unconvincing frown, "I ought to refuse you entry to my home, you wanton floozy," then she laughed and looked at my wedding band, "but you are a married woman. I wonder if being married in the future, even if it is your past, still makes you an unmarried mother today," she babbled. "Gracious, I knew your life was complicated, Catherine, but this really is the icing on the proverbial cake!"

Philip rolled his eyes at her, but as he ran his hands through his hair I saw the tightness of his expression. *Oh, please trust me, Philip,* I prayed, *for I cannot bear it if you do not.*

"I have decided not," I replied, holding out my hand for her to examine my wedding ring. She looked curiously at my engagement ring and then at Philip. If he had not recognised it, I am certain Rosaline did. I can only presume she had seen it worn by his grandmother before she passed away.

"Very nice," she said kindly. Philip I noticed looked a little uncomfortable but he said nothing.

That was three weeks since.

Arthur and Charlotte are in Egypt, of course. It is most extraordinary to think of him still alive out there. I wish with all my heart I could see him; if I were not so heavy with child I swear I would board a ship and do just that. Simon comes around daily and I am even more pleased to see silly little Sissy than I was in 1916. Leticia and Ernest are well. I have seen them but once in this time, and 'tis so strange to see the children so much younger than before, and Leticia is pregnant with Ronald. I do amuse myself with the knowledge of that child and wonder if perhaps if I should warn her to be stricter with him. But that is not my place. Dear Lord, no wonder my head aches.

Philip stayed with us for two nights before returning to Oxford, and I was most grateful when Rosaline invited him to come each weekend for as long as I am here. This week he had pressing family business to attend to at Hatherley Park, yet he came after all, late yesterday afternoon.

Dr Campbell joined us for supper at seven, after which a most pleasant Sunday evening was passed in the parlour. Rosaline had entertained us at the piano and we all laughed at Philip's wit, until exhaustion got the better of me and I excused myself to bed.

The night was still early so I was surprised to hear footsteps on the stairs not fifteen minutes later. There was a knock at my door. Assuming it was Markham, fetching me some tea, I bid him enter. But as the door creaked open I saw it was Philip. His face was shadowed but as he stepped tentatively into the room the moonlight caught in his hair and lit his eyes. His expression was soft and nervous.

He pushed the door quietly closed behind him and for a moment he just stood there, his eyes locked to mine. I pulled myself up to sitting and turned back the blankets. His eyes flickered to the space at my side and then wandered slowly over the curves of my rounded belly. As he began to loosen his necktie the rising heat from my body flushed my cheeks. His hands shook as he unbuttoned his shirt. I slid over the bed and stood before him. Laying my hands over his, I steadied him. Slowly we unbuttoned his shirt together. Our hearts hammered so hard I could feel them both, mine against my ribcage and his against my hand. His body was more slender than I had seen it before, but his tone just as smooth and firm. In the silver light he seemed so very young, more so than I had imagined. I was mesmerized.

My hair was loose about my shoulders and my nightgown was tight over my belly. He ran his fingers along the side of my face and threaded my hair behind my ears. So very gently he trailed his hand down my body. I felt his power over me run through every ounce of my flesh and pulse through every vein. I shivered as his hand slid over my heavy breasts and into the small dip where my waist had once been. Then he kissed me, timidly at first, then, as I grew hungrier for him, with great passion. His lips covered mine, then my neck, my throat, until he unfastened the ribbon at the neck of my night gown and kissed ever lower over the top of my breasts until I groaned for more.

"I love you," he whispered as he pulled me back onto the bed. Behind me he folded his arms around me and pulled me in close, one hand resting on my belly. I could feel the hardness of him and yet he did no more than hold me, hold us. Our child squirmed beneath the palm of his hand, as though she knew her father's touch, and I felt him jump as the movement startled him. I smiled and placed my hand over his and he pressed his lips to my neck. In that embrace we slept, I more soundly than ever in my life before.

When I woke he was still and I thought him sleeping. But as I stirred a little he wrapped his embrace tighter and said, "Let's not move just yet. It's still early."

The sun was well over the horizon by the time he was forced to rise. He had missed the first train and would have to rush for the second, for he had to be back in Oxford before one. As he dressed he saw you, this journal, sitting upon my dressing table. He wanted to open the cover and see inside, but I would not let him.

"Some day," I said.

He flashed me a mischievous grin and said he would sneak a peek when he next came. I slapped his wrist and put you away in my drawer. I cannot let him read these pages, not yet, not for years perhaps. He paused to look at me for a moment.

"You know, you really are a remarkable woman, Catherine." His words echoed those of his ancestor and I found myself smiling at the memory. "How you cope with all that you have gone though is truly incredible. I don't know what I would do if my life were so complex." At that I kissed him deeply to hide my tears. "I hope one day I can solve this for you," he whispered into my hair.

And now he is gone to Oxford and I shall not see him for another five days. How I was loath to part with him, and how I long to see him again. Of course, there may well be two of us for him to visit by the time he returns, for this child must be due any day now. I cannot say the idea of giving birth does not scare me half senseless, but I am as excited as I am nervous. And now that I am in the hands of old friends, friends with medical knowledge, I am most assuredly more at ease.

MICHAEL

Oxford — 28th March, 2026

15:30

"Are you sure you're ready for this?" Michael asked for the fifteenth time.

Philip raised his eyebrows at Paul and replied, "Absolutely. Let's get it done."

Michael drew a nervous breath as AG hummed louder and the lights began to synchronise. He looked at his son. Paul was perched on the table edge, drumming his fingers together as if in some kind of rhythmic prayer. They were all nervous. Imogen and Millie had been instructed to wait in the observation room. He could see them peering in through the thick triple-glazed panel of his shiny new laboratory.

The last light flicked to green and Michael turned back to Philip. The lad nodded and stepped up onto the relocation pad like a baseball player stepping onto the plate. Michael passed him the recall device. Philip looked at it.

"Do I need this?" he asked, "I already have…"

"I'd rather you had it, just in case anything goes wrong," he said.

Philip slipped it into his costume pocket. Imogen had ordered him an outfit from a vintage store. Michael had suggested borrowing something from a museum but no, she wanted the fun of spending a small fortune instead. He ducked to avoid a violet swirl of light. The time vortex crackled and fizzed.

"April 28th," Paul said, watching the monitor. "If you want to go a day early you'd better hit the button now."

Philip screwed his eyes tight shut and then he was gone.

Michael watched the empty space for a moment and then stepped back to join Paul.

"And now we wait," Paul said.

"Five, ten minutes, tops," Michael replied with a nervous shake in his voice. On the desk behind them was Catherine's journal. Paul reached around and picked it up. Michael watched his son as he turned past the stubs of the missing page to the last entry in Catherine's own hand.

> *London, 29th April 1910*
>
> *Forgive me, my dear friend. Yesterday I saw Philip at Mrs Henderson tea shop and now everything has changed. In a moment of panic I decided I should destroy you. I began to tear out your pages to throw in the fire. But I could not do it, and now the pages are folded and tucked inside my gown, ready to be reunited with you at the other side.*
>
> *Adieu*
>
> *C*

"I hope that means she's coming home," Paul said. Michael put his arm around his son's shoulder.

"With all my heart I have to believe that," he said.

15:40

The last second ticked by and the alarm on the monitor began to flash. Michael held his breath and crossed his fingers. Paul jumped up and ran over to the re-locator pad.

"In-coming!" he bellowed, and began to dance about like an excited school boy.

Michael could barely think. He stared at the pad, willing the flashing particles to swirl into a wormhole. Then they did.

The scream tore through the room like a freight train. Philip tumbled out of the void and fell forward. Michael rushed to help him. The unconscious woman in his arms was waxy and grey. Philip could barely hold her.

"She needs help, fast" Philip said, as Michael and Paul relieved him of his load. They lowered Catherine gently to the floor. Behind them the lab doors flew open and Millie rushed in.

"What happened?" she cried, feeling for the young woman's pulse.

Philip was flustered and the journey had disorientated him. It took him a few seconds to focus. Michael put his hand on the lad's arm and told him to take a breath. Philip obeyed.

"She came to meet me at the café as planned. She was already waiting there when I arrived. She looked terrible. I asked her if she was all right, and she told me the baby was coming." He spoke through lips almost as pale as Catherine's face. "Will she be all right?"

"Call an ambulance!" Millie cried, pushing back Catherine's skirt. Paul fumbled for his phone.

Imogen was hovering by the door. Michael held out his hand and she began to walk towards him.

"She's fully dilated," Millie said. "The baby's coming and she's going to need help."

Philip looked down at his wife nervously.

"Why did she pass out, was it the journey?" Imogen asked.

Millie shook her head.

"I don't think so, but it can't have helped. I don't know how she did it, but she was holding back. Any normal woman would have been unable to resist the urge to push by this point. Jesus, her pulse is low!"

Imogen buried her face in Michael's shoulder and he kissed her hair.

"Is this our fault?" Philip asked in a stilted voice.

Millie shook her head.

"I can't say for sure, but I think she may have been in trouble already."

A siren screeched through the streets towards them, shattering the nervous silence that filled the room. Before any of them could react, two paramedics were running into the room and heaving Catherine onto a trolley.

16:57

The doors to the waiting room swung open. Michael turned from staring out of the window. Millie came in wearing a white coat and an unfathomable expression. In her hand was a wad of crumpled paper. Michael glanced at Philip. The poor lad was sitting on the sofa, his face as miserable as a wet Sunday and his eyes so dark they seemed like caverns in his head.

"Well?" said Imogen in a thin voice.

Millie drew a breath.

"She has pre-eclampsia. I'm amazed she hadn't passed out before... she could have had a fit or collapsed at any time... she's lucky..."

"What's that?" Philip voice was a shock to them and they all turned to look at him.

"Her blood pressure's dangerously high. If she'd been here all this time we would have had her in hospital under watch weeks ago, and probably whipped the baby out well before today. It explains the headaches she mentions towards the end of the journal."

"Oh," he said, "then this is all our fault?"

"Stress can be a factor – all this time travelling, all the situations she was in may have contributed – but with the history of her first pregnancy, it may well just be something Catherine's inclined to."

"I had high blood pressure when I was pregnant with both my children," Imogen volunteered.

Millie just nodded and continued.

"The baby's heartbeat is weak and Catherine hasn't regained consciousness. We've taken her down to theatre for a c-section..."

"Are they going to be all right?" Michael asked, unable to take the pressure any longer.

Millie's lips quivered into a small smile that didn't reach her sad eyes.

"We'll know more very soon," she said. "I should get back, they're letting me attend."

"Good, that's good, someone she knows is with her," Imogen said.

She hasn't seen Millie since she was six years old, thought

Michael, but kept it to himself.

"And, er... she had these stuffed down her dress," Millie added, passing the wad of paper to Michael.

As she left them he unfolded the pages.

"Oh!" he whispered.

"What is it, Dad?" Paul asked.

"The missing pages from the journal," he replied. Philip still didn't move.

Paul stood up to read over Michael's shoulder and Imogen tried to read sideways. In the end she gave up and said, "Please, read them out."

Michael obliged.

London, April 28th 1907

My back aches and I have asked Sissy to draw me a bath, but I cannot wait another minute to tell you of my day. I have certainly experienced some bizarre things in my life but this has be the most peculiar yet.

I was taking a walk towards the British Museum this afternoon. I had a dreadful headache and the baby had been so restless that I could not sit about any longer. I was approaching the front gates when to my great surprise I saw Philip on the other side of the street, standing outside our favourite café, Mrs Henderson's. He was pacing up and down by the doors, glancing down the street anxiously as though he were waiting for someone. My heart sank, for he was not due back in London until tomorrow. Though I was afraid to know it, my curiosity was so strong I just had to see whom he was meeting in such secrecy. I lowered my head away from his gaze and went to hide behind the conveniently wide gatepost, but it was too late. He saw me and to my great astonishment, his face lit up with relief and he waved me over.

'Twas only when I reached him and looked right into his eyes, that I noticed the change in him. This was not the young man with whom I had spent the night a few days ago, this was the man I had kissed goodbye at Waterloo. The grey in his temples seemed even more pronounced than I recall. He wore a scarf high about his neck despite the warmth of the day, and I could see a shadow in his soft brown eyes. He seemed to hesitate, his hands stuffed in his pockets as though they might fall off should he extract them. He stared at my shape as though it were the first time he had seen me in this condition. I wanted to reach up and touch his face but he sniffed, wiped his eyes quickly and said, "Damnable dusty road."

I was so confused that I knew not what to say or do, so I waited for him to speak. He ran his gloved hand through his hair and suggested we go inside to take tea and cakes.

The café was busy and the noise seemed to bother him. Clattering spoons on saucers, forks on plates, chairs scraping on the floor, inane chatter, it all seemed to set him further on edge. The waiter seated us in the corner table by the window. Philip took the seat facing the room; he usually allowed me that privilege. He removed his coat but not his gloves and scarf. As I watched him he began to tremble, withdrawing his hands beneath the table. I did not let him. I took his hands in mine and with increasing nervousness asked, "Will you not take off your scarf? It's so hot in here."

He opened his mouth to protest but it was indeed too stuffy and hot.

"Promise me you will not be alarmed?" he said, as he unwrapped the cream silk from about his neck.

Unsure I could speak, for I could already see the tight scar that cut along his neck from his ear, I nodded and squeezed his hands. He winced. I looked down and saw another scar peeking out from his sleeve. Gently I pulled off his gloves to reveal a gnarling twist along the back of his left hand. The waiter came to take our order and Philip stared blankly for a moment before making his request.

"Tea and macaroons please."

I had never known him order macaroons before, I was not even sure that he liked them. He scratched at his collar as though something were irritating him. The ladies at the next table got up to leave and I saw how he flinched when one knocked the table with her knee and sent a knife clattering to the floor. Then I knew. I had seen that kind of skittish reaction in another. I had seen it in Ernest James after he came home from the war.

This really was my Philip, somehow come back for me. I presumed somewhere in the future he had finally discovered a way to take me home. I pressed my fingers to my lips to prevent them from quivering and I swallowed my tears, for I had to let him explain. He scratched at his throat again and I could have sworn the pendant about my neck began to tingle with heat. We stared at each other warily. The smell of almonds mingled with the steam from the tea and my stomach grumbled. I had not realised I was hungry. Philip *stirred two lumps of sugar into his tea instead of one.*

"Forgive me, Catherine," he said at last. "I know you were not expecting me until tomorrow but the man who will come home to you then is not me. Well, it is me, but a considerably younger version," he said with a frown. I raised an eyebrow at him.

"I am long past surprises, Philip, and I am not afraid to hear whatever it is you're trying to say."

He relaxed his tight shoulders and his hand steadied as I took a bite of macaroon.

"I should have known you would see right away," he said. "You know all the signs of a time traveller, I suppose." Someone nearby glanced in our direction, but Philip glared at them and they turned away again.

"I simply know you, my love. You are the man I married."

He smiled for the first time since we entered the café.

"Thank you," he replied. "I must look so much older than..."

"The other you? Well, a little. But I love you as you are at twenty-three and I love you as you are at thirty." I could swear to you he blushed, but certainly he grinned and just as broadly as ever I have known.

"You flatter me too much, Lady Hatherley," he said shaking his head.

"What I cannot fathom is how?"

Philip looked at his macaroon and pushed it away.

"I don't even like these," he said, glancing towards the cake tray on the counter.

"We can order something else," I said, putting his biscuit onto my plate, "but please do not procrastinate further, the suspense is driving us both insane." I felt the baby kick hard and my back twinge. The dull ache intensified. I shifted my position as he waved at the waiter and had him fetch a slice of Bakewell Tart.

"In short, your father..." Philip said, watching me carefully.

"I'm sorry?"

"Your father is responsible for getting me here." He reached inside his collar and extracted a St Christopher pendant that matched mine exactly. I stared for a moment then shook my head.

"But... how?" I asked. "You wouldn't take it. I tried to give it to you but you wouldn't take it." I reached inside my own blouse and pulled out its twin.

Simultaneously we exclaimed our pain. I unclasped mine hurriedly, for it was glowing white hot, and set it on the table. I felt naked without it, for 'twas the first time in my life it had not been around my neck. We both watched as it began to vibrate gently where it sat. Philip let his fall against the outside of his shirt and suffered the heat.

"You did give it to me," he said.

"When?" I asked with increased suspicion. I held my breath for the answer.

"Tomorrow," he said, so matter of fact that I stared.

"I don't understand. How can I have given it to you tomorrow when you did not have it in...1917?" Even I was struggling with the concept now.

"Yes, I did. I wore it every day until we met again in the British Museum."

"Then where did you keep it?"

"In an old sock at the back of my chest of drawers, until the day we parted at Waterloo."

"Gracious," I said, "I'm not surprised I never came across it, then." We both laughed and any remaining tension ebbed away.

As he drew a breath Philip's eyes took on a more serious glint. The pendant vibrated itself towards the edge of the table and I was forced to remove it and put it in my purse.

"Catherine." He leaned forward and took my hand again. "Your parents, your real parents, they have been looking for you all this time, since you were a little girl. You were born in the year 2003. You father was... is a brilliant physicist at Oxford, at Balliol, to be precise. He invented this machine, a time machine and you... this pendant was his. It's a like a key, a recall device. You took it from his laboratory when you were six years old and..."

I stared so hard, trying to comprehend, that my head thumped even more than ever.

"Forgive me," he said, catching his breath, "I'm going too fast."

No, it's fine. Please continue, it's just... please continue."

His eyes scoured mine. "Are you sure?"

I nodded.

As Philip explained my life to me I saw that heavy

door in my mind once more. His words pushed at it like the north wind. I felt it creak open and grey images began to leak out.

"He worked in a school for a long time after you disappeared," Philip was saying.

I closed my eyes and in my mind I reached out. My fingertips brushed against the imagined wood, barely touching it, then, suddenly my palm was against it. I shoved hard. The door swung wide and visions of my family flooded through in vivid technicolour.

"I have a brother," I interrupted.

"Yes," said Philip with a startled blink, "you remember?"

"I do," I said. "His name is Paul, and my mother, she... she teaches French and... her... her name is Imogen and she has the exact same colour hair as me, only there is a curl of grey in her fringe and ... Oh!" I felt the tears pulsing in my eyes and I fought to keep my composure.

"Should I go on?" he asked with concern. I nodded again.

He told me all about my father, how he much he loved me and how he had never given up on finding me. I rubbed my hands over my face.

He told me how my father had saved him and now, somewhere in the year 2026, the machine is working again and I can go home. Oh, how odd that sounds, the year 2026, and home! He told me how I could have gone back all this time, if I had only used the St Christopher and set it to the right date. All the times I had touched it, twisted it between my fingers, I had been re-setting it. Perhaps I had somehow subconsciously turned the dial so that it would keep leading me back to Philip. But where is my home, then, if not with him?

There was another more powerful twinge in my back and I drew a sharp breath.

"Are you sure you're all right?" he asked.

"I'm fine, I insisted. "What do you mean, go home?"

"To them," Philip replied with a tilt of his head.

"No, I cannot go... I cannot leave you. I want to be with you." Panic began to set in and I had the urge to run.

"I came here to take you back. I shall be going with you."

I took a sip of calming tea and said, "To stay? To stay with me, in the future?"

As he was about to reply, someone tapped upon the window behind him. He flinched and swung around. I looked up to see Ernest James peering in through the condensation. He waved, and I prayed he would not come in. Philip gave him a bright wave back and I wondered at his bravado. Ernest doffed his hat then tapped at his fob watch and scurried on.

"That is how I knew where you would be today," Philip offered when Ernest was gone. "Ernie swore blind he had seen us in here on... well... today, and I swore blind he must have been mistaken."

"Time is full of quirks," I said with a smile. "But you did not answer my question."

Philip lowered his eyes and I thought he was going to tell me he would take me home and leave me there, alone, but he looked up slowly.

"Of course to stay with you. Darling, I cannot force you to come. I see that you have a choice."

"Explain," I said, beginning to feel weary.

"You may stay here, with the younger me, marry him, have seven happy years with him. Perhaps even have more children, but you know what is to come after, you know how and when it will end. Can you live contentedly knowing that? Or, you may come back with me, take a chance on beginning a new life there, with your family."

I was confused.

"How can you be certain we shall only have seven years?"

Philip's eyes darkened and I realised the light outside had begun to dim. Heavy storm clouds were forming and through the window I could see nothing above us but grey.

"The war will still come, Catherine. In four years, the war will still come."

"That may be so, but you do not have to fight, this time. With me and the baby here for all those years with you, you would not leave us, surely."

Philip was silent. He looked away.

"Do you not think that is how it will be?" I asked. My stomach seemed to flip over and I had to bite my lip to prevent a cry escaping.

I cannot say for certain, but I believe my feelings

on the subject would remain the same."

"Then you would still be saved by my father, and you would still be able to come back to us."

"Do you not see? If you stay here, then all that has happened to us will never happen. And more things may alter than we could ever anticipate. It would be like ripples in a mill pond, flowing out further and further. We may damage more than our own lives."

My brain was throbbing hard behind my eyes. I wanted to scream.

"How do you know it would not be for the better?" I muttered.

"I don't, but I know what has passed. You parents, your father has dedicated his life to getting you home. Our future should be with them."

"I had a father, and he is dead." I slammed my fist upon the table and the whole room turned around to stare. I knew my temper was not my own, it was the frayed logic of a heavily pregnant and confused woman, but I could not prevent myself.

"No one can take that away. William Harris was an excellent father to you." Philip was saintly calm and at that moment I could have hit him for it. "I'm just saying that they are good people and I believe they deserve the chance to get to know their daughter again, and to meet their grandchild when he comes."

"She," I said quietly. "I am certain it is a girl." My anger crumbled. "And you? What of your parents? Do you not wish to be with them?"

"I was with them, for seven more years I shall be with them, but now my father is dead and my mother believes me killed." He tilted his head with a moment's puzzlement, but dismissed whatever the thought was and continued. "My mother was stronger than she seemed, you know. And she has Evelyn and young Rupert."

"Would she not wish to know that you are still alive, would you not wish her to know that?"

"But I am not. If you stay here and alter my past I, as I am before you now, may not exist at all. I am not afraid to go back to that field and die. I am not afraid to go back to the front line and fight. But I believe God, fate, science or whatever it is that controls this universe, took me out of that moment and gave me to your father so that I could come back here and take you home, to them. I want you to have that chance, and, selfish as it may be, I want to be there with you, with our child, and not just another white gravestone on another pitiful field."

I did not understand. I attempted to stretch my back a little.

"What gravestone, what field?"

We paused whilst the waiter cleared our plates and poured us more tea. Philip fidgeted with his hands.

"After the war they... it doesn't matter. What matters is you. Look, there's something I omitted from your father's story."

I watched him as he twisted his heated St Christopher around in his fingers. "They... they have your journal," he admitted.

I gawped. "I beg your pardon?"

"Your journal, it... it's a long story, but save to say,

it found its way into your parents' possession and..."

"Oh." *I blushed as I thought of all my confessions to you, dear friend.*

"At the back there are two letters, both from Rosaline to you. I know my mother... well, she was just fine and..." he sounded doubtful. "Young Rupert will inherit, and if he does not, then the journal may well never make it to your father and none of this will have ever happened at all. I will be dead and useless to you and you and our child will be left alone, and I cannot bear the thought of that." He was beginning to sound desperate. He took my hands with tears in his eyes.

I shook my head.

"How can I abandon such friends? How can I leave Rosaline without word again? Now I know the cause and I have removed it from around my neck, I can end this travelling for good."

"I should have brought the letters," he said, lowering his head, "then you would see."

He is quite right, of course. Why should my friends need me? I already know that they lived their lives perfectly well in my absence for the six years until our next meeting. And I knew my continual presence could alter their lives as well as my own.

"Could we not come back and visit?" I asked, full of hope, but I knew the answer.

"Perhaps, but, well... you did not."

"And you know this from the letters?"

"Yes."

"Why would we not?"

"Perhaps it was not necessary," he said, half comfortingly, though I could see the question had touched a nerve in him.

"Then I am a poor friend." I thought better than to pursue that train of thought, for both our sakes.

"Maybe we cannot, or maybe after the baby comes we decide it is best not to. Maybe we decide the past should remain as it was."

"Perhaps," I conceded. "And you would give up your life for mine?"

"I would not be giving it up. I would be starting it in earnest, with you and our child."

He let go of my hands and sipped his last mouthful of tea. "I don't expect you to come right this instant."

"Then when?" I asked with mild relief.

"Tomorrow."

I sighed.

"Why must everything be tomorrow?"

I got up to leave. Philip rose, too. I pulled on my coat hurriedly and stumbled to the door. I needed air and I needed to be alone.

He did not attempt to follow. He simply said, "I shall be here tomorrow morning at nine sharp. Do come."

I did not turn around.

As I made my way home the clouds lowered over the city and engulfed the streets in a dense fog. The damp air clung to my throat and throttled the emotion in my heart. In the echoing privacy of the foggy streets I found I could cry freely, and once begun I could not stop. Wheels screeched past and for a moment I thought Time was calling me on, but it was just a carriage. I began to pray for guidance, but images of all those I have loved seemed to dance in like ghosts in the mist. Now I am at home and still I am at a loss. But my bath is drawn and growing cold. I must soak a while. Perhaps it will ease the pain in my back and the pounding in my head. Goodnight, dear friend.

17:10

Michael was unsure he could go on, but when he looked down there was only a single page left.

"Why did she not say she felt unwell yesterday?" Philip said quietly.

"We have all put her through hell," Michael replied. He blinked the moisture from his eyes and continued.

London, April 29th 1910

I slept very ill last night. My head still aches and the pain in my back grew worse with each hour until the realisation came upon me. I do not know how I could have been such an imbecile. The baby is coming, and coming soon. My waters broke with the dawn and now I have so little time left. I have made my decision and I must get to Philip before it becomes impossible. I shall entrust you to Rosaline, my good friend. I have written her a note which I shall leave here upon my writing desk, with you beneath it. Enclosed is a packet for Philip containing the St Christopher.

Do you approve? Now I must dress and pray I can get to the café in time.

17:11

Michael turned over the page but the other side was blank. Philip lowered his head into his hands and sank further into the sofa. Imogen sat down at his side. Michael took the journal from his wife's handbag, opened the tattered cover and placed the creased white pages in their rightful place, next to the yellowed stubs inside.

"There was a note with the package." Philip's voice was barely audible. "I can remember every word of it. She said, 'My Darling, forgive me. One day you will understand. Please take my father's pendant and wear it always until we meet again. In it is my heart, it is yours. All my love, Catherine.'"

"Oh darling," said Imogen, wrapping her arms around his shoulders, "she will get through this, she must."

Michael looked once more at the letter Catherine had left for Rosaline, then closed the completed journal and hoped with all his heart that she was right.

18:32

Michael sighed and stretched his neck. No one had been to see them in well over an hour. His stomach gurgled. It was almost dinner time and though his stomach seemed to think he was hungry, he didn't think he could eat. He glanced at the clock on the wall. *Seconds tick so slowly when they're watched,* he thought, as the big hand clunked on to mark another minute passing. Philip shuddered and closed his eyes.

18:51

Down the hall a baby had been crying for several minutes. At first Michael had hoped it was his grandchild, but clearly it was someone else's. He wished its mother could calm it; the noise was beginning to stab at his already fraught nerves. Paul pulled the blind down over the window and began tapping his fingers on the sill. Michael winced and was about to complain, then decided it didn't matter.

19:02

Imogen was pacing up and down now. Michael grabbed her cardigan sleeve as she passed him by for the fifth time. She opened her mouth but couldn't bring herself to protest. She flopped back onto the sofa. Philip reached out to her and held her hand. Michael closed his eyes.

19:07

Footsteps were drawing closer, but Michael didn't dare let himself imagine someone was coming to them. Everyone almost jumped out of their skins as the door handle turned. They all watched it. It seemed to move in slow motion and Michael almost ran over and wrenched it open himself. But then it creaked and Millie walked in with a bundle of soft blankets in her arms. Michael thought his heart had stopped as they waited for her to speak. The smile on her face was watery and her eyes were pink from crying. Michael couldn't stand it. She walked over to Philip.

"This is your daddy," she said to the bundle. The blankets stirred and the tiny face buried inside yawned and blinked open its eyes.

Philip stared at it for a moment, unsure what to do. Imogen nudged him.

"Take her," Millie said. "She's perfectly fine, she's been thoroughly checked over. You have a strong, healthy baby girl."

Imogen sobbed and Michael came over to her side. Philip held out shaking arms and waited for the bundle to be placed in them. Once she was settled he pulled her close and kissed her forehead. The baby wriggled and he looked up at the room with an astounded expression of utter pride, then he frowned once more.

"And Catherine? How is my wife?" The words came out so brittle they seemed as though they could shatter like glass.

Millie looked down at him and with careful words said, "She's in a stable condition at the moment, but she's not out of danger yet. She's still very weak."

"May I see her?" he asked, eagerly standing up and almost forgetting the delicate bundle in his arms. The baby screwed up her face and began to cry. "Oh, what did I do?" he asked.

Clearly not much experience with children, Michael mused.

"Allow me," Imogen said, taking the baby from him.

"Of course you can," Millie said. "She's still out for the count, though."

20:16

Michael entered his daughter's hospital room with Paul and Millie, cup of coffee in one hand and a large pink rabbit from the hospital shop in the other. Imogen was walking about with the baby, rocking her back and forth. The infant was whimpering. Philip was sitting in the chair holding his wife's hand. *Still asleep,* Michael thought sadly. *God, she looks so fragile.*

"May I have a turn?" he said.

"Poor little mite's a bit fretful, I think she wants her mum to wake up," Imogen said. There was a groan from the bed. They all looked over.

"Philip?" Catherine whispered. Millie went over to check on her then rang for the nurse.

20:45

The attending physician looked up and smiled.

"I think you're a very lucky girl," she said, though Michael was unsure if she was talking to Catherine or the baby.

Catherine lifted a feeble hand.

"May I hold her?" she asked.

Philip was cuddling their now quietly sleeping daughter. Kissing Catherine gently on the mouth, he laid the baby in her arms.

Michael entwined his fingers with Imogen's as they watched. Catherine looked up at him. Michael felt his heart would break.

"Father... Papa..." she paused, unsure what to call him. "Dad... there were letters from my friend Rosaline. I should like very much to read them."

Michael glanced at his wife. Imogen reached down to her bag, extracted the book and offered it to her daughter. Catherine shook her head. "Would you read it to me please?" she asked, looking directly at her father.

Michael beamed.

"Of course," he replied picking up the first letter.

When he had finished he paused, wondering whether this was all a bit too much, but then she asked him to continue.

December 24th 1942

   My Dear Catherine,

   It has been many years since we last saw each other and now I am old and fear you would not recognise me. But I am well and should not complain.

   There are so many things to tell you. When you left us we were in the midst of a vicious war and now we are dealing with another. Life is hard once more but we get on with it, as we must.

   Simon passed away last June, he had been sick for some time so it was a mercy in the end, and so now I rattle around this house without him. Christmas is always a time when we most miss those we have lost, I think, and I feel it most keenly today.

   Forgive me, Catherine, I don't mean to dwell on my sadness. I've had a good life and have no right to complain. This house does not have all the memories for me though, as Simon and I moved to Richmond in '23 when the Markhams retired. We found the quieter life suited us better. The house is a good size for the two of us, and of course Sissy came along too – she is probably breaking something in the kitchen as I write. We overlook the park and as I sit here in the living room I see there are children playing there. It is a comforting sight; so many of the children have been sent away from London, to spend the war in the safety of the country. London has suffered so much of late.

   Leticia and Earnest are well. They are coming down for New Year along with Martha and her family. They have a whole brood of grandchildren, though Ron is yet to settle down. But he's joined the army now and gone to fight in Italy. We can only pray for his safe return. Ernest Junior joined the Police Force and has done very well for himself.

Albert is of course all grown up too. He is in the Royal Air Force, based in Yorkshire. He has a lovely wife, May, and son Richard, who is just adorable, he's four now. Sadly Bertie couldn't get leave for Christmas but we shall see him in the New Year, God willing. May and little Richard are to come for Christmas and will be arriving this evening. I am so looking forward to seeing them. Charlotte is to come too. We all hoped she would remarry after the war, but she never did. She carried on regardless as always, but underneath I know her heart was shattered, poor love. It is so hard on her now, seeing her son off to war and leaving a child behind at just the same age as Bertie was when Arthur went to France. Bertie looks so much like his father that each time I look at him it breaks my heart. He has that same laid back cheek of a smile just like Arthur's; you know the one.

Lady Mariah is ticking along well at 96. She is really quite marvellous for her age. I had a Christmas card from her as always. She never could bring herself to move back to Hatherley after the war, though her spirits were raised after she read your journal, and for some reason she has always insisted that Philip is out there too, with you. I hope with all my heart that she is right. But, no matter where you are, with you both gone from here the estate and the title passed to young Rupert, Evelyn's boy. He has done the best he could with the place, but it seems to have lost its soul somehow.

Well, my dear, I don't believe I shall ever have the pleasure of your company again, but I hope that one *day this letter finds its way into your hands.*

I pray you made your peace with time and found happiness, 'whenever' you are.

Your dearest friend,

R

"Thank you," Catherine said.

Michael noticed how very tired she looked and her eyes were filled with tears.

"Perhaps we should go now," he suggested. "Leave these three alone for a while."

Catherine nodded gratefully. Then with a hint of desperation she added, "You will come back in the morning?"

"Of course," replied Michael, holding back his tears. "We won't ever leave you for long again."

Paul opened the door. Michael paused and asked, "I don't suppose you've thought of a name for the baby yet?"

Catherine and Philip glanced at each other with contented smiles.

"Rosaline," Philip replied.

ROSALINE

Oxford — 7th May, 2049

The water was cool and refreshing. Rosaline loved the feel of it as her body glided through the pool. As her fingers touched the side she popped her head up and looked out through the glass panel window of the university baths. The sky was stained with rusty splotches and streaked over with pink. *Sunset already.* She looked round for the clock on the far wall as she climbed up the steps; 20:10,

'Shit,' she muttered, wrapping one towel around her slender body and then drying her face with another. There was a small flash from the chair the towel had been laid on. Rosaline leaned over to see who was calling, dripping a spot of water onto the screen of her phone as she did. The image of her mother flickered through the small prism of liquid.

"Answer," she said. "Hi, Mum." Catherine's miniature form appeared on the seat of the chair.

"Where are you? At the gym?" Catherine's voice sounded excited.

"Not quite, I'm at the pool," Rosaline replied, "What's the news?"

"What makes you think I have news?" her mother could barely contain her excitement.

The hologram flickered again so Rosaline leaned over and wiped the screen dry. As the image stabilised she said,

"Sorry, I'm running late, I'm going off sync at nine, so you're just going to have to end the suspense and tell me."

"Ooh, where are you going?"

"The premier of As You Like It."

"How lovely, that'll be fun."

"I hope so," Rosaline said, imagining the theatre in her mind as she unplaited her hair ready for the shower. "So…what's the news?"

Catherine's hologram beamed.

"Gramps is getting a Nobel life time achievement award."

Rosaline looked at her mother's image and grinned back.

"That's brilliant. When's the presentation?"

"September twelfth."

"Great. Book me a spot. Tell him congratulations. Now I really am sorry but I had better run, I only have a two hour doorway."

"Ok sweetheart, call me when you get back."

"I will. Love to Dad."

"Love you back," Philip's voice called from somewhere in the distance.

Rosaline grabbed the phone and terminated the call as she belted towards the showers.

Forty minutes later she was in the wardrobe rooms at Balliol College straightening the hem of her gown whilst Marla, the costumier, pinned-up her still wet hair. The corset was pinching at her ribs and the bust was slightly twisted. She had been in such a hurry that despite the dress having been tailored for her by her own mother, it felt as though it were meant for someone else.

"Almost done," said Marla aiming a powder puff at Rosaline's face.

"Sorry it's such a rush," she apologised for the third time.

"It's fine Roz, now keep still a second."

Rosaline stopped fidgeting and glanced in the mirror at her whitened face, thank God it's not real lead based foundation, she thought, as Marla used the powder puff to smooth off the makeup. "There," the costumier said, "Now you can fidget."

Rosaline tugged her corset and wriggled her shoulders so her bust looked neat. She clipped her monitor round her wrist and pressed the tiny gold button to begin recording. As much as she hated wearing these period clothes, Rosaline loved working as a research historian. Good old Gramps, she thought as she looked down at the gold bracelet that disguised the monitor and twisted the St Christopher at her throat to set the date and time for recall.

"Thanks," she said to Marla, "you needn't bother coming in later, I can disrobe myself when I get back."

"I don't mind," the costumier replied.

"It's Friday night, go out and have fun. I'll be all right."

"OK. Well have a good time and don't work too hard."

"I'll fetch you Shakespeare's autograph," Rosaline called over her shoulder as she dashed off towards the Quantum room with three minutes to spare.

The End

Acknowledgments

A big thank you to Jan Greenough for her exceptional suggestions and edits. Thank you to Marissa De Luna, Tim Arnot, and especially Mark A. Trickett for their help and advice on preparing the book for publishing. Thanks to Gabrielle Aquilina for all the read-throughs and her lovely review. Thanks to all at Abigindon Writers for their helpful criticism and encouragements. And thank you to my good friends Gaynor, Simon, Gianna and all my other friends (you know who you are) for all their support. And most of all thanks to my parents for their continual belief in me and my writing.

Made in the USA
Charleston, SC
14 October 2016